D1355222

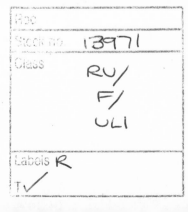

Daniel Stein, Interpreter

DANIEL STEIN, INTERPRETER

A NOVEL IN DOCUMENTS

LUDMILA ULITSKAYA

Translated from the Russian by Arch Tait

OVERLOOK DUCKWORTH
New York • London

This edition first published in hardcover in the United States and Great Britain in 2011 by Overlook Duckworth, Peter Mayer Publishers, Inc.

NEW YORK:
Overlook
141 Wooster Street
New York, NY 10012
www.overlookpress.com
For bulk and special sales, please contact sales@overlookny.com

LONDON:
Duckworth
90-93 Cowcross Street
London EC1M 6BF
www.ducknet.co.uk
info@duckworth-publishers.co.uk

First published in Russia in 2006 by Eksmo

Library of Congress Cataloguing-in-Publication Data

Ulitskaia, Liudmila.
[Daniel' Shtain, perevodchik. English]
Daniel Stein, interpreter : a novel in documents / Ludmila Ulitskaya ; translated from the Russian by Arch Tait.
p. cm.
1. Jews, Polish—Fiction. 2. Jews—Conversion to Christianity—Fiction. 3. World War, 1939-1945—Occupied territories—Fiction. I. Tait, A. L. II. Title.
PG3489.2.L58D3613 2011   891.73'5—dc22   2011002955

A catalogue record for this book is available from the British Library

Design and typeformatting by Bernard Schleifer
Printed in the United States
10 9 8 7 6 5 4 3 2 1
ISBN 978-1-59020-320-0 US
ISBN 978-0-71564-163-7 UK

FOREWORD

This world in which we have such difficulty living is filled with misunderstanding at every level. Within the family, parents and children often fail completely to hear each other. Between individuals teachers do not understand their pupils, neighbors do not understand their neighbors, cat lovers do not understand dog lovers. At the level of society the rich, as ever, do not understand the poor, the poor do not understand the penniless, and the police do not understand the homeless. To this we must add relations between states, ethnicities, and religions. The totality of this mutual misunderstanding and rejection breeds mistrust, fear, and aggression.

This book is devoted to a man who tried all his life to break down the wall of misunderstanding. The real-life hero, Brother Daniel, Oswald Rufeisen in the world, and Daniel Stein, the hero of this novel, are not the same person. Most of the novel's characters are fictitious, at least in part. It is they who tell us about Brother Daniel Stein, and through them the personality is revealed of someone who throughout his life, consciously and consistently, worked to promote understanding and reconciliation.

For all that, the story of the fictional character coincides almost entirely with the biography of the man. The historical setting has been retained but those peopling it have been changed. While many documents used in the book are authentic, many are fictitious, and the intention has been to allow the truth of literature to transcend the truth of mundane reality.

Brother Daniel was a Jew born in Poland who received a German education. When Poland was occupied he worked as a translator and interpreter in the Gestapo, and after Belorussia was liberated by the Red Army he served in the NKVD. In between he was a partisan in the forests of Belorussia. Sentenced on three occasions to be shot, he outwitted death many times. While working as an interpreter in the Gestapo he organized the escape of three hundred Jews from the ghetto, and after the war was awarded a medal by Russia.

He survived through a fortunate concatenation of circumstances, but was personally convinced that he had been saved by God's help. He was nobody's secret agent, and found his true vocation when he became a Christian—a Catholic monk and a priest.

Books, articles, and dissertations have been written about him. His wartime biography could provide the screenplay for a cliff-hanger of an action movie. Yet the second half of his life, after he emigrated in 1959 to a Carmelite monastery in Israel, although relatively quieter and more settled, saw him bearing a different kind of witness that is far less easily defined.

Through his love and compassion he built bridges between people afflicted by mutual incomprehension and loneliness. Polish Catholics turned to him for support and spiritual and practical assistance, as did Russian Jews and Orthodox Christians, Arabs, and people who would have been hard pressed to identify their national and religious affiliations even to themselves. He had a gift for understanding and empathizing.

His main mission in life he considered to be the creation of a Catholic community modeled on the Church of St. James, that first Christian church in Jerusalem before the great schism occurred between Judaism and Christianity. In the members of a single community, united in their worship of the One God, back at that remote moment in time, Brother Daniel saw his ideal for the relationship between man and God, and for relations between people. He was convinced that good acts matter more than dogma, and that a righteous life counts for more than any number of doctrines, declarations, or papal bulls.

In the eyes of conservative Jews he was not a real Jew, and in the eyes of the Roman Catholic Church he was a questionable priest. The State of Israel did not want to recognize him as a citizen, and he is buried in the Arab cemetery in Haifa. He was loved not only by his friends but by his enemies: an SS major helped him escape from arrest, and partisans who condemned him to death later gave him a medal. His views irritated the ecclesiastical hierarchy, but Pope John Paul II gave his blessing to Brother Daniel's ministry.

The community he created lasted several decades, but in effect dispersed after the death of its priest. What he left behind is the figure of an idealist—the world still smiles knowingly at this amazing type of human being—and what lingers is the memory of someone who radiated a climate of love, joy, and sympathy.

By the fact of his existence Daniel demonstrated that contemporary Christianity, for all its historical and moral ills, is still alive, and that beneath the crust of corruption and hypocrisy, beneath the formulas and adjudications now bereft of meaning, the spirit of Love, Compassion, and Mercy lives on. Brother Daniel professed a Christianity of the poor that retained the link with its Source, the same Christianity professed by St. Francis of Assisi and St. Seraphim of Sarov.

Oswald Rufeisen, like his literary alter ego Daniel Stein, was a builder of bridges between people from different streets and neighborhoods, races and religions. With his whole life he showed that understanding is possible.

I would like to thank everybody who takes the trouble to consider the great life of this humble man.

—LUDMILA ULITSKAYA

CONTENTS

PART THREE

Daniel Stein, Interpreter

I thank my God, I speak with tongues more then ye all:
Yet in the church I had rather speak five words with my
understanding, that by my voice I might teach others also,
than ten thousand words in an unknown tongue.

1 Corinthians, 14: 18–19

PART ONE

1. December 1985, Boston

EWA MANUKYAN

I always feel cold. Even in summer at the beach with the sun blazing down there is a coldness in my spine. I guess it's because I was born in winter in a forest and spent the first months of my life in a sleeve of my mother's winter coat. I was not expected to live, so if life is a gift for anyone, it truly is for me. I'm just not entirely sure it is a present I really wanted.

Some people's memory of themselves switches on very early. Mine starts with the Catholic orphanage when I was two. I always really wanted to find out what happened to me and my parents during the years I don't remember at all. I learned a few things from my elder brother, Witek, but he was too little then and the memories he passed down to me don't really fill in the picture. When he was in the hospital he filled up half a school exercise book and told me everything he could remember. We didn't know at that time that our mother was still alive. He died of sepsis when he was sixteen, before she came back from the labor camps.

My identity documents give my place of birth as Emsk, but in fact that is only where I was conceived. My mother fled from the Emsk ghetto in August 1942 when she was six months pregnant, and took with her my six-year-old brother, Witek. I was actually born about one hundred kilometers from Emsk in impenetrable forest, in a secret colony of Jews who had escaped the ghetto and hid there right until Belorussia was liberated in August 1944. It was a partisan unit, although in reality it was just three hundred Jews trying to survive in an area occupied by the Germans. I imagine the men were more concerned to use their weapons to protect this dug-out town of women, old people, and the few children who survived than to fight Germans.

Many years later my mother told me my father stayed in the ghetto and died there. A few days after my mother's escape, all the people still there were shot. She told me that he refused to leave. He believed an attempt to escape would only anger the Germans and bring forward the showdown, so my pregnant mother took Witek and left without him. Of the eight hundred people in the ghetto only three hundred decided to escape.

The Germans had herded Jews from Emsk and the surrounding villages into the ghetto. My mother was not a local woman, but she was there for a reason. She was a fanatical Communist and had been sent from Lwów as an agent. She had given birth to Witek in a Lwów prison in 1936. The father was a party comrade. My own father was someone she met in the ghetto. I have never in my life met a woman less suited to motherhood than my mother. I am quite sure my brother and I were born solely because of a lack of prophylactics and abortion facilities. When I was young I hated her, then for many years I viewed her with alienated amazement. To this day I can scarcely bear to be with her. Thank God I see her very rarely.

Any time I ask her about the past, she bristles and starts yelling at me. To her I have always been an apolitical bourgeoise. She is absolutely right about that, but I have had a baby myself and I know for a fact that when a child comes into the world, a woman's life, to a greater or lesser extent, is subordinated to that fact. Not in her case, though. She is a maniacal Communist Party member.

A month ago I made the acquaintance of Esther Gantman. She is a charming, transparent old lady, very white and with a blue-rinsed head of gray hair. She is a friend of Karin. They worked together for some charity and Karin had been telling me about her for a long time, but I took no interest. Shortly before Christmas, Karin arranged a party for her fiftieth birthday, and I immediately noticed Esther. She just somehow stood out among all these people I half-knew. The party was far more heartfelt and sincere than is usual in America. There were a lot of Poles, a few Russians, and a couple of Yugoslavs. The Slavic presence made itself pleasantly felt at this American celebration and you heard snatches of Polish conversation.

I speak Russian and Polish fluently, but I have a Polish accent when I speak English. Esther noticed that when we exchanged a few words. "You're from Poland?" she asked. I always have trouble with that question. It is difficult to give a quick reply, and you can hardly embark on a long explanation that my mother was born in Warsaw but I was born in Belorussia, don't know who my father was, spent my childhood in Russia, and went to Poland only in 1954, went back to Russia to study, moved from there to the GDR, and then on to America.

This time, however, I said something I never normally say. "I was born in Emsk. More precisely, in Czarna Puszcza." The old lady gasped and then asked, "When were you born?" I told her, "In 1942". I never try to conceal my age because I know I look young. People never guess I am forty-three. She gave me a little hug and the blue rinse wobbled as her old head trembled. "My God! My God! So you did survive! That madwoman gave birth to you in a dugout and my husband delivered you. And then within a month, I suppose, she took you children and went off who knows where. Everybody urged her to stay but she wouldn't listen. Everybody was sure she would be caught on the road or in the first village you came to. Glory be—you survived!"

We went out to the hallway and just couldn't be separated. When we took our coats off the hangers it was so funny. They were both the same, heavy fox fur, which is almost improper in America. I found out later that Esther suffered from the cold, too.

We drove to her house. She lives in the center of Boston, on Commonwealth Avenue, a marvelous district just ten minutes away from me. As we were driving, I was at the wheel with Esther sitting next to me, I had such a strange feeling. All my life I have longed for somebody older and wiser, someone who could guide me and whom I could obey and joyfully do what they told me to. I always felt the lack of that. In the orphanage, of course, the discipline was strict but it was quite a different matter. All through my life I have played the role of the senior person. My mother, my husbands, my friends—none of them were ever really grown up. There was just something about this old lady that made me want to agree in advance with everything she said.

We went into her house and she turned on the lights. The bookcases started in the hallway and went all the way back into the depths of the apartment. She saw me looking at them. "This is my late husband's library. He could read five languages and there are masses of books about art. I need to find a good home to leave all this to."

I remember Karin had told me that Esther was a widow with no children, quite rich but very lonely. Almost all her family were killed during the war.

Here is what Esther told me. She first saw my mother in the ghetto in Emsk, when people who lived in the surrounding countryside started being forced to move in there. Before that only Jews from the town lived there. They had apparently moved voluntarily, because shortly before they went to the ghetto there had been a terrible slaughter of Jews in the town. They had been assembled in the town square between the Catholic and Orthodox churches and the local people set about killing them. They killed fifteen hundred Jews, and those who were not killed took refuge in the ghetto.

It was not a ghetto in the customary sense of one or more districts where Jews had lived since the Middle Ages. In Emsk, people abandoned their houses in town and moved into a half-ruined castle that had belonged to a prince of some description. They put barbed wire around it and posted guards. At first it wasn't altogether clear who was keeping whom away from whom. The police were the local Belorussian police because the Germans considered that sort of work beneath them. Relations with the Belorussians were, needless to say, based on bribery. They were paid for everything and could even be bribed to supply guns.

"Your mother was not local," Esther said. "She was quite pretty but very abrupt. She had a small son. I've remembered her surname. Kowacz, wasn't it?"

I winced. I hate that name. I remember very well that my mother had a different surname. This was an assumed Party name used in one of the forged identity documents she lived under for half her life. One of the reasons I got married was to free myself of that false name. Everybody was terribly shocked. Fancy a Jewish woman from Poland marrying a German! Of course, Erich was a Communist, too, from the GDR. Otherwise he would not have been in Russia studying in the first place. That was where we met.

I gazed at Esther like a child mesmerized by a chocolate. She would have been the perfect mother, aunt, or grandmother, calm and gentle, elegant in a European way with her silk blouse and Italian shoes, but without ostentation or that naive American chic. She even called me "my dear child." Without any prompting, she told me the ghetto had a robust internal organization, its own administration and its own special figure of authority, Rabbi Shirman, a renowned and learned man who people said was very righteous. Esther and her husband were themselves Polish Jews, both medically qualified, and had moved to those parts a few years before the war. Isaak was a surgeon and Esther a dentist. She had graduated from dental school in Frankfurt. They were not freethinkers, just ordinary Jews who would light the Sabbath candles but might just as easily go out on the Sabbath to a concert in the next town. The local Jews considered them outsiders but went to them for dental treatment. When Germany annexed Poland, Isaak immediately told his wife it was the end of everything and they needed to get out and go wherever they could—he even thought of Palestine. But while they were thinking what was the best and practical thing to do, they found themselves under German occupation, in the ghetto.

We were sitting in the drawing room of a fine apartment, furnished in the European style, old-fashioned but, to my mind, in very good taste. Its owners' cultural level was plainly higher than mine, which is something I always sense because I don't often encounter it. It was the home of wealthy people, with engravings rather than posters. The furniture was not a suite but had clearly been assembled piece by piece, and on a kind of low cupboard there was a big, wonderful Mexican ceramic, the tree of life perhaps.

Esther was sitting in a deep armchair with her feet tucked under her in a girlish way. She had kicked off her shoes, navy blue, snakeskin. Details like that always make an impression on me. My mother has good reason to consider me bourgeoise. The home, the orphanage are something that that chill in my back doesn't let me forget. My mother regarded appalling penury as normal. She must have felt quite at home in Stalin's prison camps, but when I escaped my poverty as an orphan, I could have kissed every cup, every towel, and stocking. In the first year of our life together in Berlin, in Prenzlauer Berg, Erich took a second job so I could buy things: clothes, crockery, and all the rest. He knew it was my way of getting over the past. The frenzy gradually subsided, but still, even here in America, my favorite pastime is shopping at sale time, going around garage sales and flea markets. Grisha, my present husband, takes it in stride. He is from Russia himself and grew up among people who hungered after everything. My son Alex was born in America, but he loves buying things, too. We are real consumerists, and Esther seems to understand all that.

"We thought conditions in the ghetto were dreadful, because at that time we had yet to see worse. We knew nothing then about the concentration camps, or the scale of the mass murder being perpetrated all through Europe." She was smiling as she talked about all this, but there was something particular in her expression: detachment, sadness, and something indefinable. Wisdom, I guess. Yes, we were talking in Polish. That is always a treat for me.

"How long were you in the ghetto?" I asked her. "Less than a year, from the autumn of 1941. We left it on eleventh of August 1942. Then there were two more years in Czarna Puszcza, in the partisan unit. We lived in dugouts right through until liberation. A family partisan camp. By the end, out of three hundred there were one hundred twenty still alive. There were six children with us. Two more were born in the forest, you and a little boy, but he died. In spite of everything, we managed to keep all those who left the ghetto alive until the end of the war."

"Why did my mother leave Czarna Puszcza?" I asked, knowing the answer my mother had given, but knowing also that she is a habitual liar. No, it is not that she is a liar, just that I don't believe a word she says. That is why it was important for me to hear what Esther had to say. Esther wasn't crazy.

"We tried to talk her out of it. I remember it well. Isaak was indignant that she was putting her children's lives at risk by leaving our refuge. She did not even reply. The only person she had anything to do with in the ghetto was Naum Bauch, an electrician."

That is how I discovered my father's name. Mother never told me. If she had been a normal woman I would have been Eva Bauch. That was an interesting piece of information. "Do tell me about him," I begged Esther.

"I didn't know him well. I think he hadn't qualified as an engineer." She sat motionless, her back straight, every inch the aristocrat, and without a trace of the usual Jewish gesticulation.

"Isaak told me once, before the war, he asked Bauch to come to the hospital to repair some piece of equipment. He enjoyed a privileged position in the ghetto, as did Isaak, by the way. Some of the Jews had jobs outside, they had permits. Isaak saw patients at the hospital, and Bauch had work in the town, too.

"Your mother and Naum lived together in the ghetto. They had a little cell of a room in the left wing. The castle was half-ruined and we set about repairing it when we were forced in there. In the beginning we were even able to buy building materials. The Judenrat was in charge. Everything ended dreadfully. The fact of the matter was that the Judenrat was constantly buying off the Belorussian police. There was some complete louse, I don't remember his name, a local police chief. He promised that the 'operations'—you know what I mean, yes?—would not affect those of us in the ghetto as long as we kept bribing him. At this time all the Jews in the nearby villages were being exterminated, as we were well aware. The Judenrat was buying time, but that wretch couldn't have done anything for us even if he had wanted to. He was just making money. By then nobody really had any money left. Women gave up their engagement rings, the last of their jewelry. I gave up mine. I didn't know all the details at the time, and now they don't matter.

"Some people really believed they could buy survival, and that is why, when the escape was suggested, a kind of community assembly was called and there was a split. Half were in favor of breaking out and half against.

Those against were sure that after an escape attempt there would be terrible persecution of those who remained. Actually, things had moved on beyond mere persecution, you understand. Among those organizing the breakout were totally committed, real fighters. They wanted a showdown. They were receiving help from the town and there was contact with the partisans, although we didn't know it at the time. In reality everything was being organized by a single Jew, a young chap, Dieter his name was. He was working as a translator in the Gestapo. Somehow he succeeded in concealing the fact that he was Jewish. He was arrested later, but he, too, managed to escape.

"On one occasion, when the war was already nearly over, he visited our camp in Czarna Puszcza. He was fighting in a Russian partisan brigade and was sent to us with a cow. The partisans had either bought it or helped themselves to it, and they asked one of our lads who was a butcher to make sausages for them. Dieter came with this cow, our people recognized him and were delighted. Somebody produced hooch, he sat down on a tree stump and started talking about Christ. People started exchanging glances. You couldn't imagine anything sillier at that moment than talking about Christ. I think he had gone slightly mad. Believe it or not, by this time he had been baptized and was showing icons of some sort to us. It was hard to believe this was the person who had organized the breakout. In early 1945, after the liberation, we traveled with him on the first train into Poland. Somebody told me later that he became a Catholic priest after the war.

"Back then, though, on the night before the breakout, the disagreement in the ghetto was so violent that a fight broke out. Rabbi Shirman, who was already well past eighty, pacified them all. He was suffering from prostate cancer. Isaak operated on him in the castle. Well, it wasn't much of an operation. He just inserted a catheter. The rabbi stood up on a chair and everybody fell silent. He said that he would stay, he had no intention of leaving. Those who had not the strength to leave should stay, but those who did have the strength should escape. Isaak said we would leave and we did. Your mother also left, taking her son, but Naum stayed behind. Nobody knew she was pregnant, only Isaak, because she had come to him a short time before and asked for an abortion. He refused because the pregnancy was so far advanced." Esther shook her civilized head. "And you can see he was right—such a lovely girl was born, and survived."

Esther looked very wearied, and it was late. We agreed to meet again and I left.

I have a strange feeling. I have always wanted to know about that time, and about my father, but now I am suddenly afraid. I want equally strongly to know and not to know, because for so long I dragged my past around and it is only in the last few years, with Grisha, that it has fallen away from me. Ewa, that little girl from the Polish children's home in Zagorsk and the teenager from a Soviet orphanage, seem no longer to be me, just stills from a film I saw long ago. Now I have an opportunity of finding out how everything actually happened. I still cannot imagine what could make a young woman, a mother with two children, hand them over to a children's home. It still seems to me there must be something there that I do not know.

2. *January 1986, Boston*
ESTHER GANTMAN

I had supposed that by my age no new people would come into my life. In the first place, all the vacancies in my heart had already been used up by people who were dead. In the second place, here in America there are many worthy people but their experience of life is extremely limited, and that makes them rather flat and cardboard creatures. I also suspect that old age forms a kind of shell and your own emotional reactions atrophy. Isaak's death also revealed how dependent on him I was, and am. I do not suffer from loneliness, but I notice it envelops me like a fog. Ewa has suddenly materialized in the midst of these rather melancholy feelings. I sense something fateful in her appearing. Here is a young woman who could have been my daughter. It would have been good to discuss this with Isaak. He was always able to say something insightful and even unexpected despite our complete agreement about everything. What would he have said about this girl? The very fact of our meeting is extraordinary. Even more amazing is that we got around to talking about Czarna Puszcza. Her mother, that Kowacz woman, was a complete monster. Isaak thought she was a Soviet spy. He always said the Jews are a driven people. He put Jewish zealots, especially the Hassids with their silk hats, ridiculous caftans, and patched and darned stockings, in the same psychological category as the Jewish commissars, ardent Communists and members of the Cheka secret police.

The second time we met, Ewa said something similar about her mother, only in a different way. It is amazing that she saw this despite having no intellectual sophistication or even a decent education. She is evidently very strong-willed, and honest by nature. She wants to tell the truth to herself and about herself. She questions me avidly. One time she stayed until two in the morning and, as I later discovered, her husband suspected she was having an affair or something of that sort. This is the third time she has been married. Her latest husband is an émigré from Russia, ten years younger than her and, she says, a successful mathematician.

In our conversations we always come around to that area that Isaak found so important and germane. He was forever joking that there wasn't a Talmudist in the world who had thought at such length about the Lord God as he, a nonbelieving materialist.

She is young enough to be our daughter. Indeed, we were together in the forest at that time but she was born not to us but to other parents. Isaak used to say that in the twentieth century for Jews to have no children had become as much a gift from heaven as having many was in historical times. He never wanted children, perhaps because we weren't able to have any. When I was young I shed many tears over the insubstantiality of our marriage, and he comforted me by saying nature had made us elite. We had been freed from the slavery of giving birth to children. It was as if he foresaw the kind of future that awaited us.

When we came out of the ghetto and found ourselves in Czarna Puszcza he asked me, "Esther, would you wish that we had three children right now?" I honestly had to say no. We left Europe after the Nuremberg trials. Isaak was included as an expert witness as a doctor, a captive of the ghetto, and a partisan. After the trials we had an opportunity to emigrate to Palestine, a year before the creation of Israel.

Ewa asks so many questions that I have decided to reread the notes Isaak made in those years. Actually, he was writing a book, but in fits and starts, and he kept putting it off "till later." He died in his sleep at seventy-nine years of age, before he was old. He was robust and energetic. He never retired and the book remained unwritten.

Ewa is asking me about her father, Bauch. "Perhaps there is something about my father in your husband's papers? What if I have brothers or sisters? You understand, Esther, I'm a child from the orphanage. All my life I have dreamed of having a family!"

Isaak's papers are in perfect order, the notes sorted by year. I am a little afraid of opening them. Ewa said she would be happy to help me sort the papers—he wrote his notes after the war in Polish but switched to English in the late 1950s. I declined. It would be impossible to put his notes into somebody else's hands. As it happens, all the events relating to the 1940s were described many years afterwards. Not even in Israel, but after we came to America, after 1956, when he was invited here to work.

One other thing surprised me in what Ewa has told me. When she was three months old she and her brother were put in a children's home. Their mother was busy organizing the Gwardia Ludowa, fighting the Germans, and then being imprisoned in Stalin's labor camps. She was released in 1954 when Ewa was eleven or twelve. Her brother, Witek, did not live to see his mother's return. By that time Ewa was already a little Roman Catholic.

She is very pretty. Outwardly she belongs to the Sephardic type, with heavy black hair and a plain face, nothing overdone. Eastern eyes, not languid but fiery, like Isaak's.

3. 1959–83, Boston
FROM ISAAK GANTMAN'S NOTES

I have been interested all my life in the topic of personal freedom. It always seemed to me to be the supreme blessing. Perhaps in the course of a long life I have managed to take a few of steps in the direction of freedom, but one thing I most certainly have been unable to overcome or to free myself from is my national origins. I have not managed to stop being a Jew. Being Jewish is something intrusive and final, like the accursed hump of a hunchback, and it is also a beautiful gift. It dictates one's logic and way of thinking, fetters and enfolds us. It is as irrevocable as gender. Jewishness restricts your freedom. I always wanted to move beyond its confines, and did, and wandered footloose down whatever roads I chose to follow for 10, 20, 30 years, but at a certain moment realized I had got nowhere.

Jewishness is unquestionably broader than Judaism. The twentieth century has known a whole pleiad of scholarly Jewish atheists, but they were taken to the gas chambers along with their religious brothers. Accordingly, for the outside world blood was the conclusive argument. No matter how Jews attempt to define themselves, they are effectively defined by outsiders. A Jew is somebody non-Jews consider Jewish. That is why christianized Jews were given no quarter. They, too, were to be exterminated. My involvement in the Nuremberg trials was more onerous than living in the ghetto or being a partisan. The reels of film I had to watch, taken by Germans in the concentration camps and by the Allies after liberation, shattered my European outlook. I lost the wish to be Middle European and we emigrated to Palestine in order to be Jews, but I was insufficiently driven to bring that off.

The 1948 war left no time for reflecting, but when it was, temporarily, over I found myself plunged into depression by all the bullet and shrapnel wounds, the amputations and post-burn plastic surgery. What had become of gastric resection, removal of gallstones, the banal appendectomy, and removal of intestinal obstruction, the peaceful illnesses of peaceful times? I took up heart surgery.

Palestine was in paroxysms, the Zionist state became a religious symbol, Jews became Israelis and, in one sense, the Arabs became Jews. I was nauseated to see nationalism in any of its guises being adopted as an ideal.

What is the main constituent of the Jewish sense of identity? A purposeful intellectualism directed inward at itself. An agnostic and atheist, when I came to Israel I embraced what I had fled from when I rejected my family traditions in early youth. Back then my refusal brought about a break with my family. My father never forgave me, cursing me and my medicine, and then the whole family perished in the gas chambers.

He would be very pleased to know that in my mature years I decided to study what for two millennia Jewish boys have been studying from the age of five. The Torah. What had bored me as a child and been rejected I now found extremely interesting.

Almost as soon as I arrived in Palestine I started going to Professor Neuhaus's Jewish history seminars at Jerusalem University. I found them engrossing. Neuhaus was a brilliant scholar and viewed Jewish history not as a fragment of world history but as a model of the entire historical process of the world. Although that approach was alien to me, his lecturing provided much food for thought.

I discovered that the intellectual nimbleness of his students was of no less importance to the professor than the subject he was teaching. He was interested in their ability to pose, turn inside out, or even nullify the question itself. That was when I realized that the core of the Jewish sense of identity was seeing the burnishing of one's brain as the meaning of life, constantly working to develop one's thinking. This is what ultimately gave us the Marxes, Freuds, and Einsteins. Freed from the religious subsoil, their brains functioned even more intensely and brilliantly.

We really can regard contemporary (by which I mean Christian) history as a logical (Neuhaus suggests metaphysical) extension of the ideas of Judaism in the European world. It is extremely interesting to see the ideas of Christian and Jewish sages converging at this point, and there is no doubt that a surgeon needs a sharply honed brain no less than skilful hands.

It was at this point, partly because of my studies over these two years, that I took the major career decision to specialize in thoracic surgery, which had interested me since before the war. I should mention that the heart intrigued me not only from a medical point of view. I saw a mystery in what Leonardo da Vinci called this "miraculous tool created by the Supreme Artist," a completely unfathomable mystery, like the origins of the world and of life. It truly is difficult to imagine how this organ of modest dimensions, formed from fairly resilient muscular tissue that is nevertheless delicate and vulnerable flesh, copes with its demanding task. In the course of many years it pumps millions of liters of blood, imbuing it with the energy essential to support life in all the minute cells of the human body. For me that paradox contained the metaphysical essence of the heart's activity. It indicated that the heart was not a pump, or not just a mechanical pump, but that it functioned in accordance with something higher than purely mechanical laws. This vague surmise seemed to be confirmed by a golden proportion I saw clearly in the way cardiac structures related to the rules underlying how a heart functions. For me cardiac surgery was largely an attempt to understand and explain that mystery. Observing a diseased heart yielded invaluable information for understanding how infringing upon these divine proportions leads to impairment of cardiac activity and ultimately to death. I concluded that surgical intervention in the structure and functioning of the heart should aim to restore this proportion, to re-create the "divine curvature" so characteristic of healthy cardiac structures. This curvature is found in all of nature's creations without exception, from the whorls of sea shells and ancient fossilized molluscs to the spiral construction of the galaxies. You see it in the work of architects and artists, in the curving of old Italian squares, and the composition of famous paintings. Admittedly, Leonardo also said, "The more you talk about it (the heart), the more you will confuse your listener."

We found our feet in Israel immediately. I became head of the department of cardiac surgery at an excellent clinic and Esther set up in private practice as a dentist. Business was good. We bought a house in the marvelous village of Ein Karem, which had been abandoned by its Arab inhabitants in 1948. The view of the Judaean hills was a great joy.

One time a young Arab was brought in with a knife wound near his heart. We managed to save him. A doctor loves hopeless patients he has dragged back from the next world no less than they love him. The boy and I became friends. He told me his family had fled from Ein Karem, abandoning their home and an old orchard immediately after the War of Independence began. I did not tell him I lived there. I couldn't, and what would have been the point?

Esther and I climbed up one day to the Convent of the Sisters of Zion in Ein Karem. The hills of Judaea lay before us like a herd of sleeping camels. The 90-year-old prioress was still alive in those days. She remembered the convent's founder, Father Marie-Alphonse Ratisbonne, a christianized Jew from France. She came over to us and invited us to take supper with her. It was a modest affair with vegetables from the convent's garden. She asked which house we were living in and she said she remembered its old owners. Many other people too. She had no recollection of the young man who had ended up on my operating table, but remembered his grandfather well. He had helped to establish the convent's vegetable garden. By this time we had remodeled the old house. It was the first house we had had in our lives and we loved it greatly. We went back home that evening and Esther wept. My wife is not usually given to tears.

When I was young I wanted to be not a Jew but a European, and later I wanted, on the contrary, to be not a European but a Jew. At that moment I suddenly wanted to be neither, and so, after living 10 years in Israel, when I received an offer from America, I made an effort to break, if not with being a Jew then with Jewish soil, and moved to Boston. In 1956 open heart surgery was just beginning. I was tremendously interested in it, and had a few ideas.

What I really like about America is the concentration of freedom per square meter, but even here, in this old house built in the English colonial style, in the freest country in the world, we are living on land that used to belong to Wampanoags or Pequots.

Of course, there has long been nowhere on earth a Jew can feel completely at home.

Many years passed and I realized that I was just as far from personal freedom as I had been as a youth. Now, like a man possessed, I worked not only at my day job as a surgeon but also undertook experiments, constantly violating one of the seven commandments of Noah, addressed not only to Jews but to the whole of mankind: to not be cruel to animals. My poor primates. It was not their fault their circulatory system so resembles that of humans. Perhaps it is this ability to be possessed by an idea that is the defining characteristic of Jewishness. Our intensity. I am reminded of an extraordinary youth called Dieter Stein who organized the escape from the Emsk ghetto. First he went to work for the Gestapo on idealistic grounds, to save people from the jaws of hell. Then he became a Christian in order once again to save people from the jaws of hell. The last time I met him we were on a badly damaged train taking us to Kraków. It was night and we were standing at the end of the carriage. He told me he was going there to become a monk. I couldn't help asking him, "To save people?"

He looked no more than seventeen years old and was emaciated, a stunted Jewish teenager. How on earth could the Germans have thought he was Polish? His smile was childlike. "Almost, *Panie doktorze*. You saved me so that I might serve the Lord."

I remembered then having vouched for him to the Russian partisans. Memory expels everything it finds too difficult to cope with. How could I live if I had to remember all the evidence I was obliged to view during the Nuremberg trials?

4. January 1946, Wrocław
LETTER FROM EFRAIM CWYK TO AVIGDOR STEIN

Dear Avigdor,

Did you know I managed to find Dieter back in August last year? He is alive, but stuck in a monastery! When I heard he had become a monk I could not believe it. We were in Akiva together, we were Zionists, we were going to go to Israel, and suddenly this! A monk! After the war there are not that many of us still around. He is one of the lucky few, and all just to become a monk? When someone said he was in Kraków I went straight there. I was sure, and I still haven't changed my mind completely, he must have been tricked. To tell the truth, I took a pistol along just in case. I captured a good Walther a while back.

Twenty kilometers on from Kraków I found this Carmelite monastery.

They did not want to let me in. Some old geezer was the gatekeeper and he was having none of it. I waved the pistol at him and he let me in. I went straight to the abbot. There was another old fart there in a sort of reception place. I took the pistol out again and the abbot soon turned up. Old, gray, hefty geezer. Come in, *Panie*. Invited me into his study.

I sat down, put the pistol on the table, and said, "You are to let my friend, Dieter Stein, go free." He says, "Certainly. Only put your gun away and wait here for 10 minutes."

Sure enough, 10 minutes later in comes Dieter, not wearing one of those cowls, just a workman's overalls and with his hands dirty. We embraced and kissed. I said, "I am here to take you back. Let's go." He smiled and said,

"No, Efraim, I have decided to stay here." "Have you gone stark, staring mad?" I asked.

I could see the Abbot sitting at his big table smiling. I suddenly felt so angry, like he was laughing at me! How come he was so sure I could not take Dieter away? "What are you grinning at?" I yelled. "You have lured a good man here and you sit there grinning? You know all about tricking people! What is he to you? Are you running out of Jews?" He replied, "We are not detaining anybody here, young man. It is not we who are using force but you who have come with a pistol. If your friend wants to go with you, he is free to do so."

Dieter just stood there grinning like an idiot. No, really, like a complete fool. I shouted at him, "Come on, get your things together right now and come with me!" He shook his head. That is when I realized they must have drugged him, or put a spell on him. "Let's go!" I said. "Nobody is holding you here! This is no place for a Jew!"

At that, Avigdor, I saw them exchanging glances, that abbot and Dieter, as if it was me who was the lunatic. What can I say? I stayed there three days. Dieter is nuts, of course, but not in the usual sense. Something has gone wrong in his head. He behaved perfectly normal, he was not eating grass, but he has got some real God mania. He was such an ordinary regular guy, a good companion, really clever. No one had a bad word to say about him. Always ready to help, friends, enemies, and the main thing is—he survived! Then this!

Three days later we parted. Dieter told me he had decided to dedicate the rest of his life to serving the Lord, but why their Lord? It is not as if we do not have a God of our own. Anyway, I did not manage to make him see you can serve the Lord anywhere, not only in a Catholic monastery. We are 23, both of us. We could be doctors or teachers, there is no end of ways you can serve.

All in all, Avigdor, I am sorry for the lad. Come and see us. Perhaps he will listen to you. Bring him some photographs of Palestine or whatever. Perhaps you will be able to talk sense to him. For God's sake, if he loves the Jewish people so much why is he ditching them for strangers?

For now I have settled in Wrocław. How things will develop I have no idea, but for the time being I have given up the idea of moving to Palestine. I want to build the new Poland. There is so much destruction and poverty. We have to fight that and get the country back on its feet.

My best wishes to you and your wife.

Yours,

Efraim Cwyk

5. 1959, Naples. Port of Mergellina

Letter from Daniel Stein to Władysław Klech

. . . no staff, only a bag. I stayed for eight days in the monastery hostelry. At four in the morning I got up with everybody else for prayers, then went with the brothers to the refectory. After breakfast the cellarer allocated me my tasks and I performed them to the best of my ability. I lived that way for a week. Everybody was eagerly anticipating a visit from the bishop, and so was I. I had been promised money for the voyage to Haifa. I had no money at all. One morning the cellarer told me I should make a visit to Pompeii. I went to the local bus station and set off. The beauty along the way was almost more than I could bear: the Bay of Naples, Capri, everything dazzling. Our poor Poland, endowed with neither a warm sea nor sunshine! There is such a wealth of plant life and fish here. At the fish market you feel such joy and admiration at the beauty of the fish and all the creatures of the deep. Some are fairly terrifying, but mostly they are just a bit weird.

In Pompeii I encountered my first problem. They wouldn't let me into the excavations of the city and the museum was closed because the staff were on strike. Well, I thought, what a marvelous country Italy is. I would like to see the staff try to go on strike in Kraków at Wawel! Anyway, I didn't get in. I went for a walk, looked at the surroundings of the ruined city, admired Vesuvius, a mountain with such a delicate outline, not the least bit intimidating. You would never suspect it of the wickedness it demonstrated 2,000 years ago. I had just enough money for my return journey and a pizza bianca—that is, a piece of bread. As I walked through the modern city I saw a church, recently built, nothing special in terms of architecture. The noonday heat is really intense, so I thought I would go inside and rest in the coolness. It was the Church of Santa Maria del Rosario.

Oh, Władek, a tale unfolded which seemed to have been devised specially for me. Inside the church I found a collection of ex-votos testifying to the gratitude of people who had been granted a miracle when they prayed to the Mother of God. Usually, of course, these are depictions in silver of arms, legs, ears—whichever part of the body was healed. There were no arms or legs here, but drawings by the untutored hands of children and their parents illustrating the miracles. A child was shown being rescued from a fire. There were three pictures, one by the child, one by its father, and another by the fireman. A soldier in the First World War made a vow to marry an orphan if he returned alive, and his whole story was depicted. Here he was in the war praying in the midst of flames, here he was returning home and the prioress of a convent was bringing a girl out to him. The girl fell ill and was expected to die. The ex-soldier prayed to the Mother of God for her to be cured, and then the three of them are drawn by their five-year-old son. A driver who had been saved after an accident in the mountains had brought his driver's license as a gift to the Mother of God, and somebody else had presented their medals from the war. So much sweetness and thanksgiving.

But that was not the end of it. A nun came out and told me this celebrated place existed because of the efforts of a lawyer called Bartolo Longo. He was a poor man but educated and had managed the affairs of a rich Neapolitan widow. Bartolo had a vision in which the Mother of God commanded him to build a church here. He told her he was poor, and the Virgin asked him whether he had one lira. He had. Then she said this would be a church of the poor, and he should collect one lira at a time for it. From the rich or the poor made no difference. He was to take only one lira from each. He started collecting but there was not enough. Then the widow for whom he worked added money to make up the shortfall. Soon they were married and founded the orphanage here from which the grateful soldier had received his bride. They went on to establish trade schools and great forces of grace became focused here. Many were healed of illnesses and had favors bestowed on them. Now Bartolo Longo has been declared a "Servant of the Lord," which is the first stage toward being recognized as Blessed.

When I left the church there was a peal of thunder and a tremendous storm began. The thunder and lightning had such mighty power and were coming from the direction of Vesuvius, which made me wonder if the volcano was reminding us of its ancient self.

I returned to Naples, and the next morning the bishop came and gave me money for my journey. I went to the port and bought a ticket. The boat will sail for Haifa three hours from now. So here I am sitting and writing you this letter. Do you remember trying to restrain me, telling me one should stay where one has been placed? Perhaps you are right, but I am confident that my place is actually in Israel, and the proof is that from the first minute of this journey everything has gone in my favor. You can always sense whether you are moving contrary to Providence or in accord with your calling. God be with you, Władek. My respects to Father Kazimierz. I will write when I arrive.

Daniel

6. 1959, Naples

FROM DANIEL STEIN TO AVIGDOR STEIN

TELEGRAM

MEET 12 JULY HAIFA PORT STOP DANIEL

7. Tourist brochure

"VISIT HAIFA"

Haifa extends over the slopes of the biblical Mount Carmel and its foothills. Compared to other settlements in Israel, Haifa is a young city, having been founded in the Roman era. In the 11th century, Haifa flourished briefly during the Crusades, but by the end of the 19th century it was a modest Arab village. At one time Haifa was a focus for illegal immigration, and the majority of Jewish repatriates in the early 20th century entered Palestine through its seaport.

Mount Carmel is the jewel in Haifa's landscape. It is a mountain range some 25 km in length. The highest point is 546 m above sea level. The local soil is very fertile, and in ancient times its slopes were covered with vineyards and orchards.

In the distant past the local pagan population held Mount Carmel to be the abode of Baal, and traces of pagan rituals have been found at its summit. Here too the Phoenicians worshipped the local deity Hadad. The Roman emperor Vespasian made a sacrifice to Jupiter on the mountain, and an altar and temple of Zeus of Carmel was situated here.

Carmel is venerated by believers of the three monotheistic religions. The mountain is believed to be where the prophet Elijah spent his life. Several caves are pointed out to which the prophet withdrew. It was also from here that, according to legend, Elijah ascended to heaven.

Carmel is a place of ancient monasteries. The first monasteries are believed to have been founded here in pre-Christian times by the forerunners of Christian hermits, the Jewish Nazarenes.

With the triumph of Christianity a network of monasteries sprang up. The Crusaders discovered Byzantine monasteries here in 1150, and they had existed long before that.

Today the largest and most famous monastery is the Roman Catholic monastery of the Order of Discalced (or Barefoot) Carmelites. There has been a monastery of this Order on the mountain since the 13th century. It has been destroyed and rebuilt many times. In its present form the monastery has existed since the first half of the 19th century. It stands on the south-west face of Mount Carmel at a height of 230 m above sea level.

Not far from the monastery is a lighthouse. Above its entrance is a statue of the Madonna. The whole complex of buildings is called Stella Maris, a guiding star for sailors.

Descending the mountain from the Gan Ha'em metro station we arrive at one of the main sights of Haifa, the Baha'i Temple, situated in the Persian Gardens. This temple is the global center of the Baha'i religion. The founder and prophet of Baha'ism, El Bab (Mirza Ali Mohammed Shirazi) was pronounced a heretic and executed by the Iranian authorities in 1850. The prophet's remains are laid to rest in the Baha'i Temple. At the present time the faith has several hundred thousand adherents globally.

Baha'is believe their religion has assimilated all that is best from Judaism, Christianity, and Islam. The essence of the doctrine is expressed in the words, "The Earth is but one country and mankind its citizens." Some of the fundamental commandments of Baha'i are of interest: unity of God, unity of religion, unity of humankind, independent investigation of truth, harmony of religion and science, elimination of all forms of prejudice, dogmas, and superstitions.

In terms of its industrial importance Haifa is the second city of Israel, after Tel Aviv.

Haifa is Israel's main port. Construction of the port began in 1929 and was completed in 1933. There is a major shipbuilding works. Furthermore, with the expansion of the railway network during the British Mandate, Haifa became the central hub of Palestine's railways.

The country's only underground funicular train line operates in Haifa. It was opened in 1959 and has just six stations, from the foot of Mount Carmel to the terminus at Gan Ha'em ("The Garden of the Mother") on the mountainside at Carmel Center. Adjacent to the station is a pleasant park in which Haifa Zoo and the Museum of Prehistory are situated.

The city has the oldest polytechnical institute in the country, known as the Technion and founded in 1912.

Haifa has history and art museums. The Haifa Museum of Art has sections on ancient art, ethnography, and modern art. You can also visit the

Music Museum, the Clandestine Immigration and Naval Museum, and the Marine Museum.

The archaeological excavations of Tel Shikmona (Hill of Sycamores) are located on Cape Carmel. Remains of buildings and structures have been found which date from the time of King Solomon until the Seleucid Period (second century BCE).

They can be reached by the Nos. 43, 44, and 47 municipal bus services.

For sightseeing in Haifa you can book a tour with experienced guides who are fluent in many languages.

8. 1996, Galilee, Moshav Nof a-Galil

FROM A CONVERSATION BETWEEN EWA MANUKYAN AND AVIGDOR STEIN (*Audio recording transcribed by Ewa after a visit to the family of Avigdor and Milka Stein.*)

CASSETTE 1

AVIGDOR. By all means turn on your tape recorder, but I'm not going to be saying anything all that special.

EWA. I have a bad memory and I'm afraid of forgetting something important. When I talked to Daniel in Emsk I wrote everything down in a notebook when I got back to the hotel so as not to lose a single word.

AVIGDOR. Well, it was probably worth writing down what my brother said, but me? By the way, when he came here from Belorussia he told me about you, the little girl they put in the sleeve of a fur coat. So, what do you want me to tell you?

EWA. Everything. Where you were born, what your family was like, what life was like before the war . . . And why he was as he was.

AVIGDOR. Have you really come all the way from America to ask me about our family? Of course I will tell you. But why he was as he was, that I cannot tell you. I have wondered about it a lot myself. He was somehow different from other people even as a child. I used to think he was so special because he always said yes. If people asked him for something, or wanted something from him, he was always willing to say yes. Later, when we met again here, I saw that he was capable of saying no sometimes. So that was not it. I will tell you truthfully, to this day I don't know. He was one of a kind in our family. As for our family, it was completely ordinary. We lived in South Poland, an area which passed from one set of hands to another and had belonged to Austria-Hungary, Poland, and been part of the Principality of Galicia. My brother and I were born in a poverty-stricken village with a Polish-Jewish population.

Our Father, Elias Stein, was a soldierly kind of Jew the like of which you could find only in the Austro-Hungarian empire. Although he considered himself Jewish, attended the synagogue and associated with his co-religionists, he approved of secular education, which he had never received, spoke German fluently, and understood culture to mean German culture. He was a soldier and proud of it. He served in the Austro-Hungarian army for eight years and worked his way up from the ranks to finish as a junior officer, considering his period of military service the best years of his life. He kept his non-commissioned officer's uniform like a relic in the wardrobe, and brought it with him on the second of September 1939, the day we all found ourselves among the crowd of refugees trying to escape the German invasion.

Our parents married in 1914, before the outbreak of the First World War, during a break in my father's military service. They were distantly related. Such family marriages, arranged through a matchmaker, were commonplace in the Jewish community. My mother was an educated young woman who had managed to attend a school for future officials.

It was a late marriage. Now, looking back so far in time, it seems to me that they loved each other, but they had very different temperaments. My mother was two years older than my father, already an old maid of thirty. It was usual at that time and in that region for maidens to be given in marriage when they were no older than sixteen. My mother had a dowry. She had inherited an inn from an aunt, so even before marrying she had her own business. Admittedly it brought in a tiny income in return for a lot of hard work. My mother barely scraped a living from it, but for the whole of her life she clung to a comical belief that she was a woman of substance. Most of the people around were even poorer. When she married, my mother expected that her husband would run the inn. She had yet to discover what a highly impractical husband she had chosen.

My father did not enjoy being an innkeeper. He liked the company of clever, educated people, and here the only company was drunken Polish peasants. He did not have to sell vodka for long, though, because the First World War began and he went off to fight. My mother went back to trading and my father went off to the cannons. We have a photograph of him from that time, a gallant soldier with a moustache, in a smart uniform. He looks out proudly.

By 1918 everything had changed. The war had been lost and our village ceded to Poland. It was as if everybody had been deported from cultured, German-speaking Austria to backward, penniless Poland. Our father retained his German orientation right to the end of his life. He always preferred to switch from speaking Polish to speaking German, while at home, Yiddish, the main language of Polish Jews, was hardly spoken at all.

My elder brother was born in 1922. He was a late child but not the last, because two years later I was born. We were given traditional Jewish names, Daniel and Avigdor, but we have noble Aryan names, Dieter and Wilfried, in official documents. Those are the names we used as children, the names we were called at school. My brother reverted to his ancient name when he was ordained a monk, and I did when I came to Palestine.

Our family had a very hard life. My mother was in a constant rush to deal with the housekeeping and the inn. My father bought a shop because, as I have said, he did not care for the inn. This turned out to be the first of a succession of commercial disasters. All his enterprises failed, but for the first years at least my mother probably harbored illusions about her husband's business skills. Later it became obvious that the only thing he was good at was running up debts.

In those years we worshipped our father and spent a lot of time with him. He had a romantic military past and was forever telling us tales about life in the army. Being a soldier was one of the best roles he got to play in his life. It was the Austrian army he fought in, but he considered the German military machine the acme of perfection. When we were little he would give us rapturous talks about Bismarck and Clausewitz. He did not live to see the ignominious collapse of German militarism, because that ideal mechanism ground him to dust along with six million of his co-religionists. I don't think he was ever disabused of his faith that Germanic culture was the finest in the world. He read Goethe and adored Mozart.

Now, when I myself am long past the age at which my parents died in the concentration camps, I have a much better understanding of their edgy, touching relationship. My father was what Sholom Aleichem described as "a man of air." His head was swarming with hundreds of ideas, not one of which was brought to fruition. He built castles in the air which collapsed one after the other, and every time this reduced him to a nervous wreck.

My mother had a strong personality and there were constant conflicts between my parents. My father would demand that she should bail him out by borrowing money from neighbors who were better off or from her sisters.

They did sometimes help him to extricate himself from difficult situations. My parents often quarrelled, but for all that they were a devoted couple. Tempestuous disputes were followed by reconciliation. I think my mother felt sorry for my father.

We have never discovered how their lives ended. In the death camps, though. That much is certain.

EWA. When did you last see them?

AVIGDOR. On three September 1939. We parted on a road thronged with refugees, and all of us had a presentiment that we would never see each other again. Dieter was seventeen and I was fifteen. We were to be parted, too, for almost twenty years. I worshipped my elder brother. There was never a hint of rivalry between us, perhaps because he always treated me as his junior, playing with me, caring for me, looking out for me. Although there is a couple of years' difference in our ages, we were sent to school at the same time. It wasn't much of a school, Polish, for peasants' children. There was a single classroom for children of all ages and the level was decidedly modest, but at least you were taught to read and write. We had no religious education. There was no longer a heder in the village. There were no more than a score of Jewish families in the entire district. There were not many children, but the Jewish cemetery and the synagogue had survived. I know even that has all gone now.

EWA. Have you been back?

AVIGDOR. What is there for me there? Not even any graves. Childhood is childhood, the river, the forest, games. After the First World War there was an economic crisis and life was very hard for the adults.

EWA. What do you remember of those times?

AVIGDOR. It was a time of migrations. Everybody, Poles and Jews alike, was migrating to the towns. The villages were left empty. A great emigration of Jews began. The more pragmatic went to America. Others, enthused by Zionism, went to Palestine. It all hardly touched our family. Mother held on to the inn as if it were our ancestral stately home.

She had two major priorities: to hold on to her asset, the inn, and to get us educated. The more so because it was obvious very early on that Dieter was extremely able. As children we were similar, like twins really, but my brother was far more talented than I. I never resented that, not least because I had my own modest practical skills. I was much better than him at working with wood and metal. You can see that even here in Israel. Although I never went to college, I am always put in charge of the agricultural machinery. To this day whenever anything breaks down, people come running to me, even though I'm an old pensioner now. I know all about everything here because I've been in this moshav from the day it was founded.

EWA. Is a moshav the same thing as a kibbutz?

AVIGDOR. A moshav is a cooperative of owners of plots of land, while a kibbutz has complete socialism, with everything communally owned as it was on the Soviet collective farms. Don't interrupt! Now I've forgotten what I was saying . . . Yes, about Dieter, although nobody here has used his German name for a long time. Everyone just knows him as Daniel. Anyway, when he turned seven he was sent to live with an aunt in the nearest town so that he could attend a good Jewish school.

The school was exceptional. There was nothing like it in East Poland. It was a thoroughly up-to-date Austro-Hungarian teaching institution, secular not religious, and with the instruction conducted in German. It was really considered Jewish only because it was funded by Jews and most of the teachers were Jewish.

In those times it mattered very much what language the instruction was conducted in. German education was more valued than Polish, let alone the Yiddish or classical Hebrew used for teaching in Jewish schools. In spite of his flair for languages, Daniel did not know Yiddish well. Evidently destiny had a hand in that. He spoke without the least hint of a Jewish accent. In foreign languages his accent was unmistakably Polish. He mastered Hebrew quickly and spoke it fluently. He could read books I could never hope to read, whose titles I could barely pronounce, and yet he spoke it with a Polish accent. You may not believe it, but my Hebrew accent is better than his was.

My brother completed his primary schooling in four years. He came home only in summer, not very often in winter. There was no railway then, he couldn't walk the forty versts, over forty kilometers, on foot, and as for horses, either my father would be away on business or he would have lent them to some business partner. At the time, my father was trying to deal in timber I think. That didn't work out either. It was a great treat when my brother came home in the summer. He had so much to tell me. I sometimes think those talks we had went some way to remedy the deficiencies of my education. He had a knack of talking about complicated matters in a very straightforward and comprehensible way.

He had another stroke of luck when he gained admission to the Jozef Pilsudski State Academy. It was considered the best in the town and they accepted Jewish children. Teaching was in Polish, and they only separated Catholics and Jews for the religious lessons.

MILKA. Perhaps you'd like to pause now and I can serve lunch. I have it all ready.

AVIGDOR. Yes, good. Can I help?

MILKA. No need, just move to other seats so I can lay the table.

CASSETTE 2

EWA. Oh, Jewish food! Broth with kneidlach! Scrag end of neck!

MILKA. Why, do Jews eat this kind of food in America?

EWA. Only certain families. I have an older friend who cooks it. I really don't enjoy cooking.

AVIGDOR. What, you don't cook at all?

EWA. Almost never. My husband is Armenian and he has always liked to cook. Even today when we have guests he cooks lots of Armenian dishes himself.

AVIGDOR. Well, Armenian food is quite different. That's like Arab cooking.

MILKA. Eat up! Eat up!

EWA. No, really it isn't. They do have some Turkish dishes but the cuisine is far more refined. Very appetizing. But this Jewish food has the smell of home. It must be genetic memory. I was brought up in orphanages and nobody made broth for me when I was little.

AVIGDOR. Now, where did we get to?

EWA. You were telling me about the Pilsudski Academy, but I would like to know also about this society, Akiva, which you were a member of.

AVIGDOR. Ewa, all in good time. In that school he also learnt—you should find it interesting, because later on this ability proved very useful to Daniel—let me tell you . . . Jews were of course a minority in the school, but my brother was lucky to be studying in the same class as our cousin. The attitude toward Jews in the classroom was perfectly normal. I may be wrong, but I have always thought that anti-Semitism is in inverse proportion to a person's cultural and intellectual level. There were children from the most cultured Polish families of the town in my brother's group. At all events, neither he nor his cousin ever had to fight to defend their personal dignity. Daniel never did fight. It was not in his nature. Actually, I didn't notice much anti-Semitism even though I was attending a professional school, a kind of vocational college, where the children were from a humbler background.

I think the first time Daniel encountered anti-Semitism was when he was prevented from joining a Boy Scout group. He was very upset. To this day, I do not know whether it was a general rule of their Scouting organization or just the Scout leader who did not want a Jewish boy in his troop, but Daniel was turned down. It was a blow to him. He really had many Polish friends, although perhaps not particularly close friends.

However, one Polish friend who was the son of a cavalry officer, did him a very big favor without realizing it. This is the story I wanted to tell you. I've forgotten his name, but this lad's father was a colonel in the Polish army and ran a riding school. Twice a week Daniel and his classmates would go there to learn horse riding. This was a highly unusual activity for a Jew, but Daniel greatly enjoyed it and trained in this aristocratic sport for several years. He became a good horseman, and only a few years later that skill may have been what saved his life.

In the summer before his final year, Daniel came home for the holidays. That year we became particularly close. We no longer felt the age difference at all because we had new shared interests, and a new topic in family conversations was Palestine. We joined a Zionist youth organization called Akiva and attended meetings almost every evening. It was quite like the Scouts, with sports, hiking, nights spent out in the open, and training in endurance and loyalty. The big difference was that Akiva was a Jewish organization, political and educational. We were taught Hebrew, Jewish history and traditions. The Zionism in Akiva was not religious. They were not interested in Judaism. We were introduced to the Jewish tradition, a way of life and principles of moral conduct underpinned philosophically by altruism, pacifism, tolerance and contempt for acquisitiveness. These were straightforward but very attractive teachings and they became our philosophy of life. There was no chauvinism or anti-Communism in Akiva. Zionism had a strong socialist tendency which can be felt in Israel to this day. It was behind my decision to join a moshav. I liked the idea of a Jew who becomes the master of his land and lives by the fruit of his labors. I have been living here since I moved to Israel back in 1941. Nothing will induce young people to come here now. My children rejected any idea of staying here to live. As soon as they grew up, they moved away. The youngest, our son Alon, left home when he was sixteen.

Akiva became a home away from home for us. My brother and I would go off in the morning and come back in the evening with a new feeling of being part of a group united by shared values. Young people of our age who were religiously inclined probably experienced this sense of union with others during religious services, but we did not have that. At the traditional age of thirteen we observed the bar mitzvah rites—I do hope you know what those are, the celebration of coming of age—but it did not not make a great impression on me or my brother. It was just something that was done. Our mother wanted us to remain within the tradition.

The Akiva activities expanded our cultural horizons. Our parents' ideas about life struck us as provincial. They were concerned only about their daily bread, and it seemed to us that our teachers were bearers of higher values.

My brother and I longed to emigrate to Palestine, a prospect our parents viewed without enthusiasm. They felt too old for such feats of heroism as cultivating new lands. We could see for ourselves that they were too old for that kind of radical change, and had no wish to leave them without support in their old age. In any case, we had no money. At that time the British authorities were allowing Jewish immigration within an annual quota, but required a financial surety from those entering their mandated territory. Young people under eighteen years of age were not charged for the certificate, so the door was open for me and my brother.

In 1938 we had the idea that one of us should go, the other staying behind to look after our parents. One of the alternatives we discussed was for Daniel to go and study at Jerusalem University. Given how successful he was proving, it was not a bad idea, but that, too, required a financial outlay. Although the certificate would be free, the fare to Palestine was expensive and there were also tuition fees to be paid.

My brother in any case had a full year of study ahead of him, and he was already seventeen. At this point my mother's sisters decided to collect the necessary money to support their nephew. The hat was passed round the family. He worked exceptionally hard to pass his exams as an external student and gained his school leaving certificate a year earlier than his classmates.

One life ended and another began, but it was not the life everyone was looking forward to. On first of September 1939 Germany began its occupation of Poland.

MILKA. Can you not talk and eat at the same time?

AVIGDOR. I have already finished!

MILKA. You may have, but Ewa's plate is still full!

EWA. Tell me how you met up again. How many years was it since you had seen each other?

AVIGDOR. Eighteen years, from 1941 until 1959. How we met? I was waiting for him in the port from early morning. I deliberately went on my own. Milka was about to have Noami, and Shulamita was very little. Ruth wanted to come but I told her to look after her mother. She was the oldest, eight years old, but I wanted our first meeting to be just the two of us. To tell the truth, I did not trust myself not to cry. We had been writing to each other such a long time, since 1946, and had said a great deal in those letters. My brother had not even known then that our parents had died in 1943. There was a lot I found puzzling. Why had he not started looking for them the moment he got back to Poland? I don't understand. He had decided of course that they could not have survived, and that if they had they would only try to talk him out of his Catholicism, which he had already decided on, so he didn't even try to trace them. It seemed an odd logic. He only started looking for me one year later. A friend of ours had found out where he was and tried to rescue him, without success. But after that? I simply had no wish to return to Poland, and he could not just come to Israel as a visitor. Being a monk is worse than being in the army. Soldiers do at least get leave or have a fixed term of service, but there was no end for Daniel. He was running all over the place with that Cross of his . . . I don't even want to remember it. I'll show you the cemetery later. That is a whole other story.

Anyway, there I was waiting for the steamer. There were not that many other people. Even then Jews were arriving by aeroplane, only a few came by sea. The steamer arrived from Naples. I had noticed among those waiting one person wearing a soutane and immediately guessed that my brother was being met. Finally they lowered the gangway and people started disembarking. Tourists, of course. Still I could not see him, and then my brother appeared, in a soutane, wearing a cross. I was not expecting anything different—I had known for thirteen years that he was a monk—but I still couldn't believe my eyes.

Daniel did not notice me immediately. He was looking in the crowd for whoever was meeting him, and already that person was heading his way. I ran toward my brother, wanting to get to him first. He went over to that person who had come to meet him, they exchanged a few words, and I saw Daniel turn to me. "I will stay tonight with you, and go to the monastery in the morning," he said.

We hugged. Oh, my blood! Still that same familiar smell of the man I knew. He had a little beard. I had never seen him like that. He was nineteen when we parted, and here he was a grown man. I thought, too, that he had grown very handsome. What are you laughing at, Ewa? Of course, I wept. I thought it was just as well I had not brought my wife. You fool, I thought. What a fool I am! Who cares if he is a priest? Who cares if he is the Devil incarnate? Why am I holding on to him so? All that really matters is that we're both alive!

We got into the car and drove off. He read all the road signs and kept gasping. We came to the fork in the road where one arrow points to Akko and another to Megiddo and he said, "My God, where am I? Thirty-five kilometers to Armageddon. Do you see that?" I replied, "Dieter, I see it very well. Milka's friend lives there, we go to visit her."

He just laughed. "Megiddo! That doesn't mean anything in any language in the world except Hebrew!" he said. "Let's go there!" At that point I started recovering my wits and protested. "No," I said. "The whole family is at home waiting for you. Milka has not been out of the kitchen for two days." He was suddenly very still and asked, "Do you know what you just said? You said the family is waiting for me. I never thought I could have a family." I said, "Well, who else are we to you? You don't have any other one. That's what you chose."

He laughed, and said, "Okay, okay. Let's go and take a look at this family then." So I didn't drive him off anywhere else, we drove straight home. At that time, Ewa, we didn't live in the house we are sitting in now. On this same plot of land we had a little house without any amenities. It is still here, but only as an outbuilding now, directly behind this house. All our children grew up in it. In the 1950s our cooperative was not doing very well. It was really only from the early 1960s that everything took off. We had one of the best cooperatives in the whole of Israel.

Daniel and I got home and Milka and the children rushed out. Our little girl gave him a bouquet. What kind of flowers can you find in July? They are all long since withered. Shloma, our neighbor, had gone eighteen kilometers that morning to a flower farm and brought tulips, our flower. Do you think King David was singing his Song in the Bible about some other flowers? My girls crowded round him and I could see everything was fine. Of course he had that Cross hanging on him, which was odd, but I could put up with that. In Akiva we were taught to be tolerant of other faiths. I have been living so many years here with Arabs, and they are Christians, too. Did you know more of the Arabs here are Christians than Muslims? It is only lately relations have become tense. Before that we had many Arab workmen. One boy, Ali, lived with our family. He was older than our children. Of course, he has gone now . . .

So, Ewa, he came into the house and greeted us with "Shalom." He came to the table and gave the blessing in Hebrew. He did not cross himself, nothing like that. All I could think about was trying not to cry, but when Milka brought the soup terrine through from the kitchen, Daniel himself started crying. Then I did, too. If my elder brother was crying, so could I. I saw he had not changed at all. In the years that followed I can truly say he did not change a bit.

I am an atheist, Ewa. I have never been bothered about religion, or about God for that matter. All this talk about whether there is a God or there isn't. Some have proof that God exists, others that he doesn't, but to my mind, six million Jews buried in the earth is conclusive proof that there is no God. Well, fine, let's just say it is a personal matter what anybody thinks about God, but if my brother needed God so much, what made him choose the Christian one? How many Gods are there anyway, one, two, four? If you're going to choose one, wouldn't you expect a Jew to choose the Jewish God? To be perfectly frank, when you think back on all that happened then, what difference was there between God and the Devil? What a man my brother was! He was a saint. Incidentally, he wore that vestment for a while but then took it off and looked like anybody else. He loved wearing my castoffs. He didn't like new clothes and if you gave him something new he was always passing it on to another person. Look, this is our last photograph of him, taken a year before he died. My oldest daughter was here and she took it. No, that's me, and that's him. We look similar, of course, but there is a difference, a *very* big difference. Sit down, please. Milka will bring in the strudel now.

EWA. How did your children get on with such a strange uncle?

AVIGDOR. They adored him. He played with them. One moment he was a horse, the next an elephant or a dog. We had four children. You know how it is yourself, you're too busy, other things to think about. We didn't play with them all that much, and when Daniel came it was a real treat. If there was anything big in their lives they would go to him. Milka was sometimes a little offended.

MILKA. Stuff and nonsense. I was never offended. When we had that trouble with Alon I was even grateful to him.

EWA. What trouble was that?

AVIGDOR. Milka, bring those letters. I want to show them to Ewa. Alon was our youngest. He always had a strong personality. When he was sixteen he decided to move out and go and live with his sister. We only just managed to persuade him to come home. Then he went off to study somewhere, which means we almost never see him. It's been four years since we last saw him. We don't know where he is or what he's doing, only that he's abroad and that he's alive. And we know that if he gets killed our Ministry will inform us. Here, you'll have to read them right now. I can't let you take them away.

9. 1981, Haifa
LETTER FROM DANIEL TO ALON

Dear Alon,

Happy Birthday! You are 16 and have performed your first adult act by leaving home and going to stay with your sister. Sooner or later everybody leaves their parents, but you have done it in an unusual way, not because you have got married and decided to start a family, or because you have gone away to study or work. You have left because your parents do not understand you and because you are dissatisfied with the way they see things in general. What kind of position have you put your sister in? She loves you, of course, she is giving you a place to stay, but she is in a awkward situation in respect of your parents. It looks as though she is egging you on.

You know, you are right. It is not easy to live in a family where there is no understanding, but the fact of the matter, my dear Alon, is that this is a two-way process. They do not understand you, but you do not understand them. In our world there are altogether major problems of misunderstanding. By and large, nobody understands anybody else. I would go so far as to say that very often a person does not understand himself. Can you say, for instance, why you told your mother she was only capable of understanding the chickens on the farm? Can you say why you told your father that he had a mechanical understanding of life limited to the structure of carburetors and gearboxes? How very foolish it was to say such things. Yes, Milka understands her chickens. Yes, Milka knows what they need. When there was a plague of parasites and all the chickens in the district died, hers survived! For centuries people believed that only witchcraft could protect animals in that way, but your mother's straightforward understanding saved 5,000 chickens! Milka's kind of understanding is a rare gift.

And what about carburetors and gearboxes? These are complex mechanisms and your father has a profound understanding of them. He has invented numerous little mechanisms, all those crazy devices he attaches to his tractors! If he was a businessman and knew how to sell them he would be rich by now! He has a very astute technical mind and you seem to think that is of no importance. This is precisely the way human understanding connects with the world of plants and animals, and even with the universe. It is understanding of the highest, not the lowest, order!

To be frank, you have hit me where it hurts. I have spent my life wondering why there is such a lack of understanding in the world, at every level! The old do not understand the young, the young do not understand the old, neighbors do not understand each other, teachers their pupils, superiors their subordinates. States do not understand their populations, or peoples their rulers. There is no understanding between classes. It was only Karl Marx who came up with the idea that some classes are bound to hate others. The reality is that they do not understand them. That is true of people who speak the same language, but what if they speak different languages? How is one people to understand another? So instead, they hate each other because of their lack of understanding. I won't give examples, I'm sick and tired of it.

Man does not understand nature. (Your mother is a rare exception—she understands her chickens!) He does not understand the language in which nature is telling him as clearly as can be that he is harming the Earth, hurting it, and before you know it he will have destroyed it completely. Most important, man does not understand God, does not understand what He is trying to instil in him through texts which are familiar to everybody, through miracles and revelations and the natural disasters which periodically befall humanity.

I do not know why this is so. Perhaps it is because modern man considers it less important to understand than to conquer, to dominate, to consume. By tradition the confusion of languages came about when people tried to build a tower up to heaven, manifestly failing to understand how wrong, unattainable, and senseless the task was which they had set for themselves.

Now, where did I begin? Happy Birthday! Let's meet up. I have a small present for you. Call the church and Hilda will tell you where and when to find me. Or tell me where to meet you. Your Dodo,

Daniel

1983, Haifa
LETTER FROM DANIEL TO ALON

Dear Alon,

Two years ago you and I had a long talk about lack of understanding. On that occasion a family conflict was readily resolved and soon forgotten. This time I ask you to try to see your parents' viewpoint, especially the viewpoint of your mother, and to understand why they cannot bring themselves to support you in your choice and be glad that you succeeded in gaining admission to such a special college. All three of us, your parents and I, at your age found ourselves in the thick of a thoroughly vile war. As you know, I ended up interpreting for the Gestapo, your mother was a courier in the Warsaw ghetto, and for eight months your father made his way through many countries convulsed by war to Palestine. I want to say to you that war, like prison and severe illness, is a great misfortune. People suffer, lose those dear to them, lose arms and legs, and much else besides. Most important, nobody becomes a better human being as a result of war. Do not listen to those who claim that war steels a man, that war changes people for the better. I believe only that war fails to make very good people worse, but more generally war and prison make people lose their humanity. I say this so that you should understand why none of us are delighted to learn that you are entering this special college which is not just for soldiers but for extra special soldiers, intelligence agents, saboteurs, I don't know what to call them. In my younger years I came into contact with many soldiers, German, Russian, Polish, all sorts, and in all these years the only thing that gladdened me was that I was an interpreter. I was at least enabling people to reach agreement between themselves and I was not shooting at anybody.

Your parents hoped you would choose a peaceful profession, as an engineer or a computer programmer, as indeed you did yourself. I understand them, but I understand you too. You want to defend this country. Israel is like Holland with its dykes which constantly hold back the sea which wants to overrun the Netherlands, the low countries. Every Dutch person, even the children, is ready to block a hole in the dyke with their finger. Israel is in the same situation, except that in place of the sea there is the immense Arab world which wants to inundate our small country.

You expected your parents to be very pleased by your success, but instead they are upset because they love you very much and fear for your life. As for me, Alon, I will do my job and pray for you.

Best wishes,

Your Dodo,

Daniel

1983, Negev

POSTCARD FROM ALON TO DANIEL

(With a view of the Negev Desert.)

Dear Dodo,

I have no objection to your prayers, but don't insist on them. Since many others have claims, you can put me last on the list.

Yours,

Alon

1983, Haifa
Postcard from Daniel to Alon
(With a view of the Golan Heights.)

Dear Alon,
I have put you last, after the cat.
Dodo Daniel

10. November 1990, Freiburg
From a talk by Brother Daniel Stein to schoolchildren

I was born in south Poland. Until I was seventeen, I had never traveled more than forty kilometers from home, but my first real expedition, imposed upon me and lasting for many years, began when I was seventeen, on the day German troops attacked Poland. I will tell you about that journey, which for me had much the same impact as the forty years the Jewish people spent wandering in the wilderness. I left Poland in early September 1939 as a boy and returned in 1945 as a grown man. During the war, without traveling any great distance, I found myself at one time in west Ukraine, which before that had been east Poland and later became part of the USSR; in Lithuania, both independent and occupied by the Russians and then by the Germans; and later in Belorussia, which used to be part of Poland, and also found itself under the Germans.

The shtetl in south Poland where I was born was neither a town nor even a village. Its inhabitants were Poles and Jews, and panic broke out the day after the War began.

It was only one hundred kilometers to the frontier with Czechoslovakia, and the German army was rapidly approaching from that direction. A great mass of people emigrated northwards. My family hastily gathered our belongings and loaded them on to a cart. We had no horses so I and my brother took the harness, and my father pushed from behind. My parents were elderly and, as my mother was ill, we put her on the cart as well. Our progress was laughable. After a few kilometers we were caught up by relatives and moved only the bare essentials onto their wagon, which was harnessed with horses. We clambered on.

I have this picture before my eyes of a road jammed with carts and crowds of people on foot. Everybody was in very low spirits. We were fleeing from the Germans but did not know where we were fleeing to. Just to the north and the east. My father was particularly depressed. He would have preferred to stay, having served in the Austrian army during the First World War. He had two medals wrapped in a handkerchief in the inside pocket of his jacket. He had brought his uniform, lovingly kept in the wardrobe for twenty years, but had to leave it behind with all the other things abandoned in the cart. He was silent and brooding, as he always was when he had to defer to my mother's decisions. It was she who had insisted we should flee. Her plan was to reach Kraków and go east from there. My father did not like the idea and would have preferred to remain under the Germans.

What I most remember about that week was the constant worry about the horses. It was difficult even to get water for them. The wells along the road had run dry, and people were queueing to water their horses at any streams we encountered along the way.

There was nowhere to buy hay and my heart was filled with pity at the sight of our suffering nags. They were peasants' horses which bore no resemblance to the sturdy, well-groomed stallions provided for our exercises at the cavalry regiment's riding school. When we reached Kraków, I unharnessed them and bade them farewell. We left them in the street not far from the station in the hope that they would find kind owners.

Getting on a train was very difficult. We spent two days at the station before we managed to pile into a goods wagon. It was the last train to leave Kraków because a few hours later the railway station was bombed. A day later an attempt was made to bomb our train. The train escaped damage but the tracks were destroyed and we had to proceed on foot. I don't think we had come more than two hundred kilometers. The local population were almost nowhere to be seen. Villages had been abandoned, and many destroyed.

A huge crowd of refugees—it was amazing that so many people had managed to fit on to a single train—straggled along the pitted country road. After a few hours we learned that the town of B. which we were heading for had already been taken by the Germans. We had failed to outdistance the invading army. My father kept muttering, "I said this would happen, I said this would happen."

We decided to skirt the town. There were no Germans in the villages— they were consolidating themselves only in major centers. We turned off the road and set up camp in woodland. My brother and I were experienced campers. In Akiva we had been trained to take over new lands and we put up a small lean-to and somewhere to rest for my parents, made a campfire and started cooking kasha with what remained of the grain.

Our parents slept a little while the meal was cooking, and when they woke, we heard them talking quietly between themselves. My father was saying, "Of course, of course, you are right."

Mother took four silver spoons out of her bag, a wedding present from our aunt, polished them with a handkerchief and gave us each one. We sat on the ground and ate kasha from a sooty cooking pot with silver spoons. It was our last family meal together. When we had eaten, Mother said it was time for us to part—they were too old to go on with us. "We will only be a hindrance to you on the journey. We have decided to go back home," she said. "The Germans will do us no harm. I served in the Austrian army, they will take that into account. Don't worry about us," my father said. "And you try to make your way to Palestine. That would be best, because here you will surely be forced to work as laborers or they will think up something even worse," my mother said. There were already rumors that the Germans were capturing local young people and using them as human shields for their tanks during attacks.

Our parents stood side by side, so old and small, and with such dignity. There were no tears, no lamentations. "Only promise me that you will not under any circumstances be parted from each other," my mother added. Then she carefully washed the four spoons in what was left of the water, added two more from her bag, polished them with her handkerchief and admired them. My mother loved those spoons. They gave her a sense of her own worth. "Take them, even in the worst of times someone will give you a loaf of bread for a silver spoon."

My father solemnly took out his wallet. He, just like my mother, liked solid possessions he could ill afford. He gave us some money. I think it was all they had left. Then he took off his watch and put it on my wrist.

I wondered afterward why we had been so docile in obeying them. We were already grown boys. I was seventeen, my brother fifteen, and we loved them very much. I suppose the habit of obedience was very strong and it never occurred to us that we could disobey or act differently.

On eleventh of September 1939 we said good-bye to our parents. When they went back down the road in the direction we had just come from, I lay on the grass and wept for a long time. Then I and my brother gathered up our few possessions, I put on the one rucksack we had between the two of us, my brother slung a knapsack over his shoulder, and we walked away, leaving the sun behind us.

For several days we stumbled along the roads, sleeping at night in the forest. We had no food at all and skirted round villages because we were afraid of everybody. In the end we realized we would need to get work as farm laborers. A Ukrainian peasant family took us on, and we were set to digging potatoes. We worked in the fields for a week, not for money but in return for food and shelter, although when we left the farmer's wife gave us something to eat on the road and we again headed east. We had no plan at all, and knew only that we had to get away from the Germans.

The next day we encountered soldiers. They were Russian. We found we had escaped from the German occupied zone. It was completely unexpected. We knew nothing then about politics, and I can't say it makes much sense to me even now. We knew there had been a non-aggression pact between Germany and the USSR, but not about the secret clauses which provided for a partitioning of Eastern Europe. Latvia, Estonia, and East Poland (that is, west Ukraine and west Belorussia) and Bessarabia were ceded to Russia, and west Poland and Lithuania to Germany. Under this agreement Lwów became part of Russia. We did not know Poland had surrendered, or that under the agreement between Stalin and Hitler Russia had reannexed some of the territories it had been granted after the partitioning of Poland in 1795.

We walked all the way to Lwów and were amazed, never having seen such a great city before, with fine houses and broad streets. There was trading going on in the market square and we had a great stroke of luck there when we met our friend Aaron Stamm who was also a member of Akiva. Stamm was older than us, and he, too, was dreaming of getting to Palestine. We found many members of Akiva had come together here and were hoping to make their way to one of the neutral countries, from which it would be possible to emigrate. At that time Lithuania was still a neutral state, and we decided to head for Vilnius. It all took time. The Zionist leaders had first to organize transit points all the way to Palestine, and that was very difficult with a major war going on in Europe. They were looking for safe, roundabout routes. This group of young people were stuck in Lwów.

My brother and I immediately started looking for work, and from time to time managed to earn a little money. My brother was better at this than I was. He would get a job in a hotel, or a bakery. Mother was right about the silver spoons, one of which I exchanged for a rustic loaf of bread.

The situation in Lwów was very difficult and struck us as at the time as completely nightmarish. There were so many refugees from Poland, mainly Jews. Looking back later, after all our misfortunes in the war, we no longer thought it had been all that bad: nobody arrested us in the streets, or sent us to prison, or shot us.

We got by somehow, five of us renting a shack in the suburbs, in Janow, not far from the Jewish cemetery. In the evenings we came together, dreaming of the future and singing songs. We were very young and had neither the experience nor the imagination to foresee what was in store for us.

Winter came early. By November everything was deep in snow and the members of Akiva split into groups to cross the frontier, which at that time was between Russia and Lithuania. Initially the frontier was not closely guarded, but the situation changed and the frontier guards became vicious. Our groups were intercepted and several of my friends were arrested and sent to Siberia.

I was the leader of one group. We tried to get over the border near the town of Lida and took the train there. We were met by a local guide who promised to take us across at night. We made our way through a trackless forest, sinking knee deep into the snow and feeling terribly cold. We did not have proper, warm clothing. Then, when we were totally exhausted and thought we had already crossed the frontier, we were arrested, spent the night in the local jail, and were released in the morning after handing over all our money. The same guide met us again, and this time led us over the frontier along a well-trodden path without any further difficulty. We heard later that this was a trick he had devised to enable his friends in the local police to make a little money. He was not all that dishonest, because he could have simply abandoned us. The remaining family spoons were handed to the policemen. On the whole, we could consider ourselves lucky.

My brother was lucky, too. He crossed the border with a different group. They were stopped by the Lithuanians but allowed to pass when they showed their Polish documents. My brother said they lived in Vilnius and the illiterate guards didn't argue.

We were very pleased to have reached Lithuania and imagined that with a little more effort we would make it to Palestine. We were happy to have gotten away from Russian-occupied Lwów to Vilnius, which was Lithuanian only in a geographical sense. More than half the population were Jews and Poles.

11. August 1986, Paris
LETTER FROM PAWEŁ KOCIŃSKI TO EWA MANUKYAN

Dear Ewa,

I am perplexed by your refusal to read my book. At first I was offended, but then I understood you are one of those people who prefer not to know about the past in order to maintain their equilibrium in the present. It is an attitude I have met before, but if we conspire to erase the past from our memories and shield our children's minds from the horrors of those years, we will be failing in our duty to the future. The experience of the Holocaust should be assimilated, if only in memory of those who died. Mass ideologies cut people loose from their moral bearings. In my youth I professed one such ideology and later, in a territory occupied by the Fascists, I was the victim of another.

In those years I was fighting with the partisans in the Carpathians and your mother was fighting in Belorussia. I did not then know that an ideology which places itself above morality inevitably degenerates into criminality.

After the war I compiled the history of a country which never appeared on the map of Europe, a country without defined borders—Yiddishland, the country of people who spoke Yiddish. I gathered materials on the history of Jewish resistance in the territories comprising Yiddishland—Poland, Belorussia, Ukraine, Lithuania, and Latvia. I published it in a succession of historical journals, and wrote my dissertation, since I was living in postwar Poland, on the history of the workers' movement. The present book is not a scholarly monograph, however, but my reminiscences of those years and the testimony of people I knew personally.

We, the last remaining old timers of this charred continent, may not be on first name terms but at least we know each others' names. I have been a friend of your mother's from the earliest years of my life. We were children living in the same building on Krochmalna Street, which became known to the whole world thanks to the orphanage Janusz Korczak built there. Believe me, the name of your mother will be prominent when the history of this time is written.

I cannot demand that you should read the whole book, but I have made you a photocopy of some pages which I obtained from the archives with great difficulty. They tell of events which occurred shortly before you were born. I remember you complained that your mother wouldn't tell you anything.

You are unforgiving toward Rita, but you do not know what she went through. I think you should.

Yours affectionately,

Paweł

1956, Lwów

PHOTOCOPIES FROM THE NKVD ARCHIVE

(Central Card Index, No. 4984)

All prisoners sentenced under political articles who are members of Polish socialist parties and organizations are to be released. List of 19 persons attached.

Acting Prison Governor, NKVD Captain A.M. Rakitin

Signature

Date: 5 October 1939

AUTOBIOGRAPHY

I, Rita Kowacz (Dwojre Brin), was born on 2 September 1908 to a poor Jewish family in Warsaw. In 1925 I entered Mucha-Skoczewski College to train as a teacher. Regrettably, numerous arrests and periods of imprisonment have kept me from completing my studies.

In 1925 while studying at the college I enlisted in the ranks of the Grins revolutionary youth organization.

In 1926 I joined the Polish Young Communist League and organized a study circle at a hospital in Warsaw.

In 1927 I became secretary of the district committee in Wola, a suburb of Warsaw. Co-opted to the position of Secretary of the youth cell, I attended meetings of the Communist Party of Poland. During the period of disagreements between the "Bolsheviks" and "Mensheviks" I sided with the Mensheviks.

In March 1928 I was detained and arrested during a demonstration by a workers' group at the Pocisk Factory and sentenced to 2 years' imprisonment. I served the sentence in the Serbia Prison in Warsaw and the Łomża municipal prison.

In March 1930 I was released. I joined the regional committee of the Polish YCL and became secretary of the anti-war section.

In October 1930 I moved to Łódź and set up a study circle in the hospital finance department. In Łódź I was secretary of the district committee and a member of the provincial committee.

In January 1930 I was again arrested and given a three-year prison sentence, which I served in Sieradz Prison. There I was secretary of the prison Communist organization. Upon my release in 1934 I became a Party worker, first as secretary of the Częstochowa committee and subsequently of the Łódź committee.

In November 1934 I was arrested, but released two months later.

In January 1935 I joined the Communist Party of West Ukraine. I became secretary of the Young Communist League of Lwów and district (Drohobycz, Stanisław, Stryj).

In September 1936 I was again arrested, and sentenced to 10 years' imprisonment. In November 1936 I gave birth to my son Witold in the Brygidki Prison.

In April 1937 I and my son were transferred to the Fordon Prison near Warsaw. In both prisons I was leader of the Communist organization.

In January 1939 I was again transferred to the Brigitki Prison in Lwów, from which I was released after the arrival of the Soviet Army.

Rita Kowacz

APPLICATION
TO THE MUNICIPAL PARTY ORGANIZATION OF LWÓW
FROM RITA KOWACZ

Pursuant to the liberation of East Poland and the transfer of these territories to the USSR, anticipating that inhabitants automatically acquire Soviet citizenship, I, Rita Kowacz, a member of the Polish Young Communist League since 1926, apply for admission to the ranks of the All-Union Communist Party (Bolsheviks).

Signature

Date: 5 October 1939

A list of individuals is attached who are prepared to vouch for the truth of my statement and, as senior Party comrades, to recommend me for membership of the All-Union Communist Party (Bolsheviks):

1. Antek Wózek ("Pigsticker")
2. Antek Elster
3. Marian Maszkowski
4. Julia Rustiger
5. Paweł Kociński

12. 1986, Boston
FROM THE DIARY OF EWA MANUKYAN

Talking to Esther about my childhood, I have unexpectedly made some discoveries about myself. Esther is a remarkable person. She almost never comments or asks questions, but just her presence is so supportive, so intelligent that I seem to become more intelligent and sophisticated myself.

With Grisha it is just the opposite: intellectually he is so far superior to me that with him I am struck dumb and am terribly afraid of saying something silly. In the bedroom, however, I am completely in charge because I really am the cleverer one in bed. The thing I have discovered from talking to Esther is that my memories are far deeper than I thought and I am re-assessing them. Reminiscences, then, are not a constant. They are unstable and changeful. That is amazing!

Now, let's think less about the instability of memories and more about the facts. I don't really have all that much to go on. We know from official documents that my brother and I were taken to an orphanage by Sister Elżbieta. Almost nobody now remembers a Polish Communist writer called Wanda Wasilewska, a favorite of Stalin, but it was she who organized this orphanage for the children of people Stalin himself had murdered. Without her, there would have been nothing. Officially the refuge was under the patronage of the International Red Cross but secretly of the Polish Catholic Church. How we came to be with Elżbieta I have no idea. I know only that my brother and I were taken there not by our mother but by another woman and that the year was 1943. I was not even three months old at the time and Witek was six. Nor do I know how we were brought across the border. It must either have been done officially with documents from the Red Cross, or illegally. For two Jewish children the latter seems improbable, although for centuries village people in those regions have been crossing the border using secret tracks through the forest and swamps.

The Polish orphanage was in Zagorsk. Why this small town, a little Russian Vatican which had previously been known as the Troitse-Sergiev Monastery, was chosen for the home I do not know and now there is nobody left to ask. Perhaps there are still some old nuns living out their last years in Poland who looked after us then. After the war, in 1946 or so, the orphanage was moved to Warsaw, where I think it exists to this day. I was destined to return to it in the 1950s, when my mother brought me to Warsaw.

My first childhood memories are of huge church cupolas, the whistling of locomotives, white bread, cocoa, some kind of sweet paste, and American presidents. The Red Cross provided for us and the nuns had not learned how to steal. I was the youngest, the girls played with me and carried me around in their arms. The main thing was I had a brother, the first love of my life. He was so handsome. It is a pity not a single photograph of him has survived. Until I met Esther he was the only person I regarded as my senior. He died in 1953 when he was 16.

The orphanage went back to Poland in 1947 but Witek and I and a few other children were left in a children's home in the USSR. Nobody claimed us. My mother was still in the labor camps and there were no relatives who might have come to take care of us. It was such good fortune that Witek and I stayed together, that we were not separated. We stayed in Zagorsk. Witek always spoke to me in Polish, in a whisper. It was our secret language. It was funny that, later on when I was back in Poland, for a long time I spoke in a whisper. My brother always told me that we would go back to Poland. I loved nobody in the world as much as I loved him, and he loved me more than anyone else. Those last years, when I was already at school, he would take me to the girls' school which was in one district and then go on to the boys' school which was in another. I remember the details of my first day. We were issued brown uniform frocks and white aprons, and he held my hand. The other girls were there with their mothers and grandmothers, but I had my brother and felt very superior. I was so proud!

Apart from our secret language, Witek shared another secret with me, by which time we were in the Soviet children's home. He said we were Jews. He qualified this by adding that he believed in the Catholic God. I do not know whether he was baptized, but Witek told me I ought to pray and that the Mother of God was our patron. She looked after orphans. I did pray to her, but had not the slightest interest in her Son. I suppose my brother got all this from the nuns. When Witek died, I prayed for him to be resurrected but nothing happened. After that, relations between me and the Madonna went downhill and I stopped praying. Then I had a dream of her. It was nothing special. She stroked my hair and we were reconciled.

All these years my mother knew nothing about us. She did not know Witek was alive, she did not know he had died. She fought as a partisan, then she fought in the army, and then she was sent away to Stalin's labor camps. She was released only in 1954, a year after the death of Stalin, and after the death of Witek.

My reunion with my mother took place in a hospital. I had caught scarlet fever and been sent to a hospital in Moscow. She came into the ward. She was ugly! Badly dressed, wizened. It never occurred to me that the thing she most feared at that moment was that she might burst into tears. Instead, though, I burst into tears—of disappointment. My mother sorted out our documents and we went to Poland. It was dreadful, the most terrible thing in my life. She did not take to me, and I simply hated her. I knew nothing about how or why she had left us. She was a stranger to me, and looked like just another clapped-out Russian housewife or coarse-grained kindergarten minder. I had pictured my mother as a blonde woman in a silk dress, with broad shoulders and fair curls tumbling down from a pretty haircomb.

Esther, don't let this worry you. I am not insane. I have done the psychoanalysis. It's just that the child I was needed a mother, a normal mother, not one who talked constantly about politics and Communism. She worshipped Stalin and still believed, after all those years in his labor camps, that his death was a terrible blow for all progressive mankind. That's the actual expression she used, "progressive mankind"!

In Warsaw I met up with progressive mankind—a handful of comrades who had survived from the Communist underground. The most likeable was Paweł Kociński. We've stayed on good terms to this day. He's sweet and I feel close to him. He, too, fought in the war in a Jewish partisan unit in the Carpathians. Of its 300 members, only two survived. When Gomulka started driving Jews out of Poland in 1968, he resigned from the Party.

Neither the camps nor the prisons had any impact on my mother's beliefs, even though she was imprisoned, first in Poland and later in Russia, for over 10 years. She expounded her ideas to me endlessly, but my organism is astonishingly resistant to everything she says. I simply don't hear what she is saying.

I lived with her in Warsaw for a year but she couldn't cope with me. I behaved abominably. I was 13, a frightful age. Then she put me in that same orphanage which had previously been in Zagorsk and had now moved to Warsaw. That year was something special. I went to church with the other girls. We were surrounded by nuns who were quiet and strict and quelled by their mere appearance what was not even disobedience but mere murmurs of self-will. I battled my mother but submitted meekly and readily to the nuns. Soon I went to the church and got myself christened. It was what I wanted. Nobody pushed me into it. I probably did it partly to spite my mother.

I went to all the services and prayed on my knees for hours at a time. There was a great deal of persecution of Catholics then and the urge to resist the sheer nastiness of the world was very strong in me. It was probably the same spirit which made a Communist of her that brought me to the Church. I did not make friends among my classmates. I was a Yid, and to crown it all a zealous Catholic, two things any normal mind considered incompatible. I spent a great deal of time at the cathedral. It was no ordinary Catholic church but a truly enormous cathedral. It had a cathedra and everybody was busy during those months preparing for the installation of a new bishop. In the cathedral crypt were rows of tombs of bishops, priests, and monks—a succession of dates and names going back to the 15th century.

I prayed at every coffin, ardently, lapsing into a deep trance. The life aboveground completely passed me by. I didn't even want to go outside. What did I pray for? That's a good question. I would say now, for life to change, but then, at the age of 13 or 14, I prayed for nothing of the world that surrounded me to be there, for everything to be other. Without knowing it, I was probably on the brink of insanity. Perhaps the coffins protected me.

The nuns saw my fervor and I was given an important role in the approaching celebration. I would carry the cushion with the *korona cierniowa*, the Crown of Thorns. It was a day I will never forget. The church was thronged with people, thousands of candles were burning, the monks carried censers from which a heavenly aroma wafted. It is a fragrance which invariably takes me back to my short-lived and desperate faith. I was on my knees holding the Crown of Christ in my outstretched hands. My arms became numb and as cold as ice. With my knees I could feel the knots in the linen carpet covering the stone floor. It hurt. Then I ceased to feel the pain, ceased to feel my legs. I rose up with the Crown and floated toward the altar. I brought the Crown to the bishop decked in gold and heard the singing of angels. I was far away from everybody but at one with all of them. A monk gently took me by the hand, the Crown lay on the altar. I do not know what happened to me, but I think I had found faith.

I lost my faith again in a single day, when I was not allowed to take my first Communion because I did not have a white dress. When my mother came to the orphanage to visit, I implored her to buy me that wretched dress but she refused point blank. The priest would not allow me to take communion in an ordinary dress. The nuns loved me and, of course, they would have found me a dress, but I was ashamed to ask. That is because, as a person, I am much too proud.

All the other girls were deemed worthy of communion, and I was not. I walked out and left God and my faith behind in the church.

I lived in the orphanage for a year before my mother took me back. She tried one last time to make me into a family. She was going through a difficult time herself. The year 1956 saw the beginning of de-Stalinization. She fell out with all her friends, and only kindhearted Paweł Kociński came to visit her occasionally. Every time it ended with her shrieking and throwing him out. That year was the first time I felt sorry for her. She was as lonely and immovable as a rock.

I, however, was making my first friends. Actually, not friends. It was a romance with a guitarist, a real jazz musician. Those years were very difficult in Poland, but I remember 1958 as a year of great happiness. I had just turned 16. If anybody had brought me up, it was the Catholics. A conflict now arose: I had to choose between the Virgin Mary and the guitarist. Without a moment's hesitation I chose in favor of him. Our romance was tempestuous and brief and followed by several more lovers. My mother said nothing. In my last year at school I decided that I absolutely must emigrate. There was only one way I could go, to Russia. My mother helped me for the first and only time in her life, using her contacts. I was sent to Moscow to study at the Academy of Agriculture. It was called the Timiryazevka. Nobody asked me what I wanted to study. There was a place for me there, and that is where I went.

I lived in a hostel for foreign students, who were mainly from the people's democracies. I married Erich in my second year and never went back to Poland. My mother stayed there until 1968, when there were major disturbances throughout Europe, which spread to Poland. When the unrest was crushed, arrests began in Poland, dismissals. There was a movement in their Party against revisionists and Zionists. Gomulka expelled Jews, of whom there were still quite a lot in the Party, and all of them, as I recollect, pro-Soviet. My mother was expelled despite what she considered to be her great services to the cause. She fought to the last, writing appeals of some sort, and then she had a stroke.

She emigrated to Israel, a country for which at that time she had a deep loathing. She has lived in Haifa for 18 years now, in an old people's home. She is considered a war hero and a victim of Stalin's repressions, gets a pension and lives very decently. I visit her once a year. She is a wrinkled old woman with a limp, but her eyes burn with the old fire. I grit my teeth and spend three days with her. I don't hate her now, but have not yet worked out how to love her. It is a pity, of course it is.

She never asks after her grandson. Once, when Alex was six, the same age as Witek when she gave us away to strangers, I took him there thinking she might melt a bit. She started telling him about what she did in the war. He asked her to show him her rifle but when she said she had handed her gun in when the war ended he lost interest in her. He's a wonderful boy, very caring, and kind to animals.

In 1968, Paweł Kociński emigrated, too, but to Paris. He works at the Sorbonne in some institute for studying Jews. He left the Party, but my mother did not want to. She had to be expelled. Even in Israel she had the idea of sending a petition to be readmitted. She is mad.

I met Paweł some five years ago in Paris. He writes research papers on contemporary history and complains that his son has become a Trotskyite. How about that?

13. January 1986, Haifa
LETTER FROM RITA KOWACZ TO PAWEŁ KOCIŃSKI

Dear Paweł,

In spite of everything I do want to let you know I've moved. My room number is now 507 not 201. Everything else is still the same, I'm in the same almshouse just in case you feel a sudden urge to write although what is there for us to write to each other about? When you were in Israel in 1971 you didn't even bother to let me know let alone come to take a look at me although of course there's not much to look at. I am lame, I've only got one eye and I am cantankerous as my daughter keeps reminding me, that's what she says, why are you so cantankerous?

Last week one of the girls in the canteen here told me I was cantankerous too, she got fired on the spot but I've been thinking about it and decided I really am, it's true and I ought to face up to it. Of course a lot of irritation has built up in me but Paweł tell me, you have witnessed my life, we have been friends for as long as I can remember, has life been fair to me? You are the only person who remembers my mother and how she gave all her love to my brother and could not stand me, you witnessed that and the whole street knew it. I was a pretty girl and my first man who I loved passionately betrayed me and left me for my one-time friend Helenka who hated me even before that happened and how sickening it was to be left for her, my enemy. Don't you remember? The betrayals came one after another. When I was put in prison for the first time in 1928 do you think I don't know who put us all in there? After the war when I was working in the special department they showed me documents. Szwarcman betrayed everyone, he was a plant, but he wrote about me separately and blamed everything on me. I took part in a demonstration and he made it seem like I was the main Communist, probably I really was. Now, when so many years have passed and so many of our people have died ask yourself who has stayed true. Only the ones who died and me. I won't say anything about you, you left the Party, you betrayed it, you changed. You sit there in the Sorbonne writing about how wrong Communist ideas are instead of talking about the errors of the leaders at that time. I have stayed the same and nothing will change me, in my eyes you are just as much a traitor as all the others but you are the only one who can understand me, even my daughter understands nothing. You wouldn't believe it, sometimes she says the same words to me that my mother used. Ewa never saw her but she too accuses me of "egotism" and "inflexibility," word for word. What did I want for myself? I never had anything, I never needed anything, I lived my whole life only ever having one pair of shoes at a time. When I couldn't wear them anymore I bought new ones. I had one dress and two pairs of knickers and I am accused of "egotism"! When we were living in Warsaw Ewa told me I was a dreadful mother and no other woman in the world would have behaved like I did when I sent them to the orphanage she meant. It broke my heart in pieces but I did it for their future, so they would live in a just society. I sent my children away to keep them safe because I knew if they stayed with me they would be killed.

For a long time I knew nothing about them at all, it was only when the war was over I heard they were alive and first I couldn't go to get them then because I was working in a special NKVD department on secret work and later I was back in prison. I was betrayed again. I have been unlucky, always surrounded by traitors, you betrayed me too. My greatest misfortune was when you left me for Helenka, after that I never gave my heart to anybody. You were a double traitor because you left Helenka too and how many others you abandoned I have no idea. In that sense each and every man is a traitor, but by then that no longer bothered me, I kept love and physiology completely separate. Men do not deserve love, although admittedly neither do women. I gave my love not to men but to the cause. The Party too is not without sin, I understand now that the Party too made mistakes, but either it will recognize and correct its mistakes or it will cease to be the Party to which I gave my heart, my love, and my life. I will never regret saying "Yes."

I find Ewa just ridiculous. She lives the life of an empty-headed butterfly, fluttering from one man to the next. Every time she is happy, then unhappy, and she does not get bored by it all, if she gets depressed she just goes on holiday or changes her apartment, or buys another suitcase full of fancy clothes. When she comes to visit me she never wears the same dress twice. She brings two suitcases to last her three days!

If I try to say anything about it she starts yelling at me, I gave up trying to talk to her long ago, everything is my fault, even Witek's death! For heaven's sake, I was in a prison camp at the time, what could I do for Witek? And what could I do for either of them while I was tramping the front with my rifle, a tin of stew and a box of matches?

What could I do for them when I was sitting in a snowdrift for three days at a time waiting to derail a troop train? What does she know with her two suitcases of frocks? She comes to Israel and do you think she stays with her mother? No, she's off to the Sea of Galilee or visiting some convent, she needs to go and see the Virgin Mary when her own mother is stuck on her own for months at a time!

I'm sure you think I don't know how to get on with people and that's why I haven't any friends. Well what you need to understand is that this home I am living in is the best in Israel, and you also need to know that all the people here are bourgeois, rich people, bankers—the very people I have hated all my life, it is because of Jews like them that there is anti-Semitism! The whole world hates them and quite right too all these fine ladies and gentlemen! There are practically no normal people here, in the entire home there are only a few rooms paid for by the state and allocated to normal people, a few people who fought in the war or were wounded in the wars here, and heroes of the resistance. But why is Israel paying all this for me? It is Poland that owes me! I gave Poland all my strength, that is the country I fought for, the country whose future I lived for, and it threw me out, it betrayed me.

Anyway, Paweł, you get the idea. I want to see you. It does not matter all that much but I shall be 78 this year, and you and I played in the same courtyard and have known each other from the day we were born. I shall creak on a bit longer, but only a bit, so come and see me if you want to say good-bye.

I'm entitled to stay at a sanatorium once a year, a mud-bath spa on the Dead Sea, so if you do decide to come don't make it December because I shall be there. Of course, they only let us go there in the low season because we're getting it free. Or perhaps you will come in December and I will get you a room in the sanatorium. I will pay for it of course and we will be able to talk about old times there, so you would only have to pay your fare. Of course the sights in the center are not very cheerful, a lot of people in wheelchairs, me included incidentally. In spring, when it's the high season, needless to say it's only fat cats from all over the world who get treated there—and the veterans the heroes and all the old trash are not allowed anywhere near or they would spoil the look of the place. Our whole life has passed, Paweł, and the world is not a bit better than it was. You understand me.

Write before you come because Ewa is planning to come and I don't want both things to happen at the same time. Look after yourself.

Rita

14. June 1986, Paris
LETTER FROM PAWEŁ KOCIŃSKI TO EWA MANUKYAN

Dear Ewa,

I have just returned from Israel, after going there to visit Rita. I am very ashamed not to have done so before but only after receiving a desperate letter. Knowing her personality, I can imagine what it cost her to write like that.

First of all, let me reassure you that nothing bad is happening with your mother. She is growing old like the rest of us, and remains just as peremptory and unyielding, just as loyal and idiotically honorable. I have never come across anyone so willing to take the shirt off their back and give it to the first person they meet. It is not easy to have her as a mother or even, under anything like normal circumstances, as a friend. In appalling circumstances, though, in the face of death, you couldn't find a better person. She dragged a wounded companion on her back for two days. He was dying and begged her to shoot him, but she hauled him back to base, where he died an hour later. Who else is capable of that kind of heroism?

Ewa, you are a disgrace! Find the time to visit the old lady. Of course, she is made of iron, but try to find the time to stroke the hair of that diabolical old lump of metal.

Do not go on getting even with her. She is what she is, a real Jewish battleaxe, a Jewess with tight little fists she swings at the first sign of injustice. She is as intolerant and unbending as our forebears and she will go to the stake for her ideals. Anybody reluctant to be burned at the stake she despises.

Me, for example. I unwisely boasted I had received an award for my book about the partisan struggle in "Yiddishland," and for my pains had a whole bucket of shit upended over me for selling our sacred past for filthy lucre. It has been translated into English and German and you are wrong to refuse to read it. There are a few words in it about your mother, too. I will send you the book anyway and the time may come when you find it of interest. Which language would you prefer it in, English or German? It is never going to be published in Polish.

As always, Israel made a great impression on me. I had not been to Haifa before and was very taken by it. More so than by Tel Aviv, which I find a dull city with little history. Haifa has almost as many strata as Jerusalem.

Rita has moved to a new room and has an amazing view from the balcony of the whole of Haifa Bay. You can see the River Kishon. There is a fairly dire industrial zone there with cooling towers and warehouses but from above, you don't see the warehouses. I went there for its historical interest. As you are a young woman who, in Jewish terms, is wholly uneducated, you don't know "Mame-loshn," that is, Yiddish. Most likely you have never even dipped into the Bible, whereas I in my youth attended a heder and gained the rudiments of a Jewish education. So I will tell you that it was precisely here, near the source of the Kishon, that something extraordinary happened in the ninth century BCE, during the reign of King Ahab and Queen Jezebel, who encouraged the cult of Baal and Asherah. The prophet Elijah, a furious defender of the faith of the One God, organized a kind of competition in which he invited the priests of Baal to bring down fire from heaven to burn the sacrifices they laid on their altar. They called upon their gods at great length but to no avail. Elijah then laid a sacrificial animal on the altar of the One God, poured water three times over the altar, the sacrifice, and the firewood. He then prayed and fire immediately came down from heaven. Our side won. Elijah ordered that all the priests, 400 prophets of Baal and 450 prophets of Asherah, should be put to the sword immediately. That was done there and then. The people returned to the Lord, and Jezebel's corpse was thrown to the dogs.

That is how our forebears understood justice.

Then I went up Mount Carmel. It was getting dark by the time we reached the gate of the Stella Maris Carmelite monastery. Just as I got out of the car (I was being driven by a very sweet person, a doctor from Russia who works in an old people's home), a beat up motor arrived and out climbed a short man wearing a misshapen sweater and a battered straw hat. He was a monk from the monastery and, with a joyous smile, he told us all the sights which could be seen from this viewpoint by day. We thanked him and went on our way, and when we were back on the road, the doctor told me this monk was Brother Daniel Stein and very famous in Israel. It was only the next morning, when I was already waiting at the airport for my flight to Paris, that I put two and two together and realized that was the Dieter Stein I had written about in my history of the partisans. He was the one who led the people, including your pregnant mother, out of the Emsk ghetto! You keep asking who your father was. Well, that man did more for your life than your father. If not for him you would never have been born, because if he had not organized the escape, everybody would have been killed.

My slow wits had made me miss the opportunity of shaking a real Jewish hero by the hand. When you go to visit your mother, try to seek him out. As a Catholic there will be plenty for you to talk about.

Mirka sends greetings and invites you to visit us in Paris. We have moved to a new apartment and now live very pleasantly in the vicinity of the Mouffetard Market, a 15-minute walk from the Jardin du Luxembourg.

There will be a room waiting for you, but warn us if you are coming because we often have various people staying.

My very best wishes to you, dear Ewa.

Yours,

Paweł

15. April 1986, Santorini

LETTER FROM EWA MANUKYAN TO ESTHER GANTMAN

Dear Esther,

Our plans have been disrupted somewhat because when we flew to Athens, Grisha bumped into a friend of his in the hotel. Syoma is another mathematician and ex-Muscovite and urged us to change our itinerary and sail to Santorini instead of Crete. I was not keen at first, because I at least know something about Crete and had never before heard of Santorini, but then Alex surprised me. He was wildly enthusiastic and said he had read about it being a remnant of doomed Atlantis, so, after wandering around Athens for two days, we got on a boat and seven hours later were in Santorini. I can't say Athens made any great impression on me. I found it rather disappointing. The ancient history is completely removed from modern life, with odd fragments of the ancient world here and there. There were a couple of pillars immediately in front of our hotel windows but the whole neighborhood was covered with dreadful five-story developments exactly like the one my friend Zoya lives in near the Timiryazev Academy of Agriculture in Moscow. The people, too, seemed to have nothing in common with Homer's Greeks. An Eastern people, more like Turks than Europeans. It contrasted with Israel, where you have a sense of continuity with the past, and that the old ways of life have not been lost and even the people, their noses, eyes, and voices, remain the same.

That was my initial impression, but when we got to the Santorini islands, they simply took my breath away. The main island is shaped like a narrow sickle with a large bay in the middle, the remains of a volcano crater. It is said not to be completely extinct and to have minor eruptions from time to time, once in 100 years perhaps. We sailed up to sheer cliffs some 400 meters high, on top of which the city of Thira, a lot of little white houses, is perched. That same sheer rock face goes down an enormous depth. Just imagine, this is the inside face of a volcano which erupted 3,500 years ago. The island is a fusion of remnants of the volcano and of the island itself. We have been here three days already and it still quite takes my breath away. It is an enchanting tiny island. We rented a car and drove right round it on our first day.

Yet again I have to admire Grisha. He is knowledgeable about absolutely everything. He explains the geological strata to me and shows me the way they are layered. He spent half a day working something out on paper, complaining at not having brought his computer, and said that it was right that a tidal wave could have have reached Crete and destroyed the Palace of Knossos. I can't say I saw the need for him to calculate that when it's in all the guidebooks. You know, I have always loved traveling and now I'm certain that there is no better occupation. It is such a pity you weren't able to join us. You absolutely must visit Santorini.

You know I prefer an outing to the shops to hiking in mountains and forests, but there is something special about this place. For the first time I have had the feeling of seeing for myself the greatness of the Creator. It's not something you are aware of in everyday life, but here it's as if your eyes have been opened. I have not felt it even in Israel where, of course, all the discoveries are about history, which you begin to see as a river whose banks change constantly but which flows imperturbably on. Here, however, nature is so powerful that it rules out any possibility of there being no God. I am not putting that well but I know you will understand what I mean. The hand of the Lord is here and can't be overlooked. It is the hand of a Creator who has no interest in petty squabbles about what people ought to believe. It is such a pity your husband won't be able to see this now.

I'm also delighted by my boys, Grisha and Alex. They have climbed every rock. I tend to sit on the balcony and look out, or on the beach. The sand here is volcanic, almost black, but then on another beach it is red or white. It's magical. My boys have bought lots of books and are learning Greek! Alex says he wants to learn Ancient Greek as well.

Meanwhile, Grisha and I are enjoying something like a honeymoon and all these things taken together are making me happier than I have ever been in my life. I have bought lots of books and postcards, too, and Alex is snapping away with a new camera so you will shortly receive a full report. I lie in the hot midday sunshine when all sane people have gone indoors, but it has taken three days for me to lose that perpetual coldness in my back.

My very best wishes. I'm so sad you didn't come with us. I am sure that if you were here it would be even better.

Yours,

Ewa

PS. When I think that instead of taking this magical trip I ought really to be sitting with my mother in Haifa and listening to her cursing, I feel a little ashamed, but, I have to admit, not regretful.

16. 1960, Akko

FROM JULIEN SOMMIER'S DIARY

Someone phoned yesterday evening to ask if I could teach him Arabic as a matter of urgency. I thought wanting to learn Arabic in a hurry was really funny. He was keen to start straight away but I asked him to wait at least until today.

Quite early this morning, an hour before our appointment, there was a knock at the door and I opened it to a monk in the brown cassock of a Carmelite. He was quite short, with big hazel-brown eyes, and he had a smile as bright as the sunshine. Introducing himself as Brother Daniel, he immediately started thanking me for being so splendid in agreeing to teach him.

I had not yet had my breakfast coffee and suggested we might put the lesson on hold a little longer and first have some coffee. Yes, yes, of course! We were talking in Hebrew and he told me he had come to Israel from Poland about a year ago to minister to a small group of Catholics here. The community didn't have a building of its own but an Arab church had agreed to let them use it for services at certain times.

"They are such lovely people, these Arabs, and I felt that, living in Haifa where there are so many Arab Christians, it was somehow not right not to speak their language. I have been learning languages in a rush all my life, by ear or from a textbook, but Arabic really does need at least an introductory six or eight lessons," he said cheerfully.

I stared at him in amazement. Was he naive, overconfident, or just plain stupid? When I started learning Arabic, I had my nose in my books for over two years before I began understanding the spoken language, and he thought six or eight lessons would do the trick. I let it pass.

At first I thought he was quite garrulous, but then I realized he had a mild form of the Jerusalem syndrome. This is a state of agitation which affects believers of all faiths when they first come to Israel. In 1947 I myself felt I was walking on coals. My feet were on fire. I can imagine how much more acute that feeling must be for a Jew if I, a Frenchman, had that sense of agitation for several months.

I gave him a double lesson. He picked up the pronunciation quite quickly and gave the impression of being linguistically very gifted. As he was leaving he told me that he has no money at the moment to pay for the lessons, but will be sure to settle up with me at the first opportunity. He is the most original private pupil of the few I have had over the years. Oh, and he saw my index cards on the table and asked what they were for. I told him I was compiling a Hebrew-Arabic dictionary and was particularly interested in the Palestinian dialect. He opened his arms and rushed to kiss me. He really is quite small, barely as high as my shoulder. Very expansive and very observant. As he was leaving he asked if I was a monk.

"I teach French in an Arab Catholic school for girls," I told him, and did not mention that I am also a member of the Community of Little Brothers.

"Oh, you teach French!" he exclaimed in delight. "That's simply splendid! We can work a bit on my French as well!"

Is it really so obvious I am a monk? I would never have believed it.

17. 1963, *Haifa*
LETTER FROM DANIEL STEIN TO WŁADYSŁAW KLECH

Dear Władek,

Let me try to explain what is going on. The picture I had in my mind of the country I so loved from afar bore absolutely no relation to reality. I have found here nothing of what I expected, but what I have seen has greatly exceeded my expectations. I came to Israel as a Jew and a Christian. Israel has welcomed me as a war hero, but does not accept me as a Jew. My Christianity is the touchstone for my people. All the years I have been here, I have been reluctant to write to you about the long saga of my lawsuit, but everything has finally come to a conclusion and I will summarize what it was all about.

My difficulties with the immigration service began the moment I arrived at the port of Haifa. I considered that I had the right to come to Israel under the Law of Return, which was framed to enable Jews to come and settle in Israel no matter where they had been living before the state was created. For this purpose a Jew was defined as anyone born of a Jewish mother who considered himself a Jew. The young official when he saw my soutane and cross furrowed his brow and concluded I was a Christian. I confirmed this dreadful surmise and compounded his misery by informing him that by profession I was a Catholic priest and by nationality a Jew. A whole conclave of customs and immigration sages assembled who, after much disputation, put a line through the box for ethnicity.

This was the beginning of an epic which developed into a seemingly endless three-year lawsuit and reached its culmination a month ago. I lost. It was a ridiculous waste of time. I asked permission from my superiors at Stella Maris, they asked their superiors, and I was allowed to appeal to the Supreme Court of Israel. I then had to raise money for the legal fees. Everybody tried to talk me out of it but, as you know, I am stubborn. The other side proved even more stubborn. They have not granted me citizenship as a Jew but have promised it by naturalization. I will shortly become an Israeli citizen but will have no right to call myself a Jew in Israel. If I go to Poland or Germany everybody accepts that I am a Jew. Not the State of Israel. My certificate reads, "Nationality not established." I did pretty much come out on top in my struggles against the Gestapo and the NKVD, but suffered ignominious defeat at the hands of Israel's bureaucrats.

You are bound to wonder why I made such a fuss about this. Władek, I was thinking about the Jewish Christians who will come to this country after me. You cannot imagine what a hullabaloo there has been around this lawsuit. Judges and rabbis have fallen out over it, which was not at all my intention.

I would like Jewish Christians, and there are not a few of them in the world, to be able to return to Israel and restore the Church of St. James, the Jerusalem community whose origins lie in the Last Supper of the Master and his disciples, which all Christians venerate. So far I'm not succeeding too well. We have, nevertheless, a small group of Catholics, mainly Poles, which includes several baptized Jews. We meet in an Arab church, where our brothers allow us to celebrate Mass on Sunday evenings after their own service.

I'm very grateful for the magazines and have to admit that you are my only source of news about the Church. Our monastery lives outside of time and recent Catholic publications are rarely available. Instead the library is full of the kind of literature I am not very keen on, although sometimes it can be interesting. You do not write about the state of the Pater's health. Has he had his operation?

Brotherly greetings,

Daniel

18. 1959–83, Boston

FROM ISAAK GANTMAN'S NOTES

I have come across an Israeli newspaper with an item which took me back in memory to events which occurred 20 years ago. In the spring of 1945 Esther and I emigrated on the very first train out of Belorussia to Poland. A young Jew was traveling with us, Dieter Stein, who had played a crucial part in saving some of those in the Emsk ghetto. In other words, it was he who had saved our lives. We knew nothing about him at first beyond the fact that Stein had helped us in some way, been arrested and sentenced by the Germans to be shot, but had escaped. We were told there were "Wanted" posters with his portrait in the towns. A considerable reward was offered for his capture.

We met him later when he turned up in Durov's brigade. They very nearly shot him, too, but fortunately I had just been brought to the brigade to operate on a wounded partisan. Because I was there and able to vouch for him I managed to save the life of the man who had saved mine.

All the details of our train conversation two years later have quite gone from my mind. He gave the impression of being a somewhat exalted young man. He was talking about entering a Catholic monastery, but in those years to be unbalanced was the norm. Genuinely normal people were the first to die. Survivors were the few individuals endowed with exceptional tough-mindedness and a certain insensitivity. Highly strung people were ill-equipped to get through the ordeal. If I had been a psychiatrist I would have written a research paper about psychological adaptation in the extreme conditions of a partisan camp. Actually, that would have comprised only one section of a major study about prisons and camps. It is a book which should be written and no doubt someday will be, but not by me. I hope others will write it.

The mental adaptations I observed in this young man served a noble purpose, and no doubt originated in a refusal to accept the kind of actions he had observed. This rejection motivated him to withdraw to a monastery. It was an escapist impulse.

Over the following years I lost track of Dieter Stein and, although I maintained contact with one or two people, it was sporadic. Most of the "partisan" Jews who survived ended up in Israel or, less frequently, in America, but they were all "am haaretz." very simple country people, and I'm not so sentimental as to want to meet them more frequently than once in ten years.

To come back to the monk, Dieter Stein. Even after I moved to America, I always read the Israeli newspapers, and in 1960 or so discovered they were full of photographs of him. He had evidently gone to live in Israel, entered the Stella Maris Monastery on Mount Carmel, and promptly started a lawsuit against the State of Israel, demanding that he should be granted Israeli citizenship under the Law of Return.

The newspaper commentaries accompanying this news were fairly surprising and I could feel that the issue had brought hidden tensions to the surface. Stein was an unusual instance of a war hero who had achieved something extraordinary, but who had also to explain having served in the Gestapo, which in itself is considered a crime. To cap it all, Stein was a Roman Catholic priest, a Christian.

Living in Israel, I had been fully aware of the extent to which the country's unity and identity were defined by shared opposition to the surrounding Arab world. A theme, which could be heard in the articles and which people usually prefer not to articulate, is that the very existence of Israel is predicated on permanent resistance to Arab hostility. In addition, Jews profoundly believe that the Catastrophe which befell them ripened in the bowels of Christian civilization and was perpetrated by Christians. The Nazi state separated itself from the Church, and many Christians not only did not approve of the murder of Jews but indeed saved their lives. Nevertheless, there is no escaping the fact that for 2,000 years official Christianity, although supposedly guided by precepts of Christian love, harbored an undying hatred of the Jews. Accordingly, Stein's adoption of Christianity was regarded by many Jews as renegacy and betrayal of his national religion.

Stein, for his part, was claiming his right to Israeli citizenship under the Law of Return which grants it to anybody who considers himself a Jew and was born of a Jewish mother. Stein was turned down without being given any reason and then appealed to the Supreme Court.

The legal issue was that he was granted citizenship not under the Law of Return but through naturalization. He was demanding recognition of his Jewishness, and entry of the word "Jew" in the box on the form for "Ethnicity," in full accordance with Jewish law or Halacha.

All this prompts one to reflect that secular and religious laws should be more clearly separated, and that there is a disjunction between theocratic ideals and the democratic arrangements of the modern state.

We left Israel before the Stein lawsuit began and I simply lost sight of him. The lawsuit went on for several years and yesterday I read in an Israeli newspaper that Stein had finally lost. That seems to me the height of idiocy. Here is one Catholic who actually wants to be a Jew, so why stop him?

It would be interesting to know whether the situation is analogous on the Christian side, and whether Stein is persona grata with the Catholics.

19. *February 1964, Jerusalem*
LETTER FROM HILDA ENGEL TO FATHER DANIEL STEIN

Dear Father Daniel,

You probably don't remember me. My name is Hilda Engel. We met in a kibbutz in the Jezreel Valley where I was working and learning Hebrew. You brought a group and stayed overnight in the kibbutz hotel. I cooked for your group. People usually remember me because I am taller than anybody else. I should say immediately that I am writing because I want to work with you. I have thought a great deal about what you said after supper when we were all together in the dining room. It was just what I was looking for.

I did not write at once because I knew that without appropriate training I would not be much use to you. I took a parish workers' course in Munich for priests' assistants and Church social workers and came back to Israel. At present I am working at the Catholic Mission in Jerusalem, but I'm little better than a filing clerk and that is not what I had in mind in wanting so eagerly to return to Israel.

I know a lot about you, of course, while you know nothing about me, and since we shall be working together in the future, I want to tell you all about myself now. That is very important.

My family comes from the Eastern territories. To this day the estate of my great-grandfather is falling apart near Schwedt, not far from the border with Poland. He was a rich, eminent man with a political career. During the Third Reich my grandfather was a general and a member of the Nazi Party. He was a military specialist, a scholar even. At all events, I know he was involved in the German missile programme. I bear my father's surname and for a long time did not even know the surname of my grandfather. My mother never told me anything. My father died on the Eastern front in 1944 and after the war my mother emigrated to West Germany, married my stepfather, and I have three stepbrothers. I am on good terms with one of them but the other two are complete strangers to me, as is my stepfather. I know nothing about his past. He is a salesman and not very interesting. I spent the whole of my childhood not asking questions. In my family nobody ever talks about anything. They were afraid of questions, afraid of answers. We were most comfortable with silence. On Sundays we were taken to church, but even there we didn't talk to anyone. In the early 1950s my stepfather bought a big house in a small town on the banks of Lake Starnberg near Munich. A lot of people living there did not want to talk about their past. When I was 14, I came upon *The Diary of Anne Frank*. I had known before then about the extermination of the Jews. I had half heard certain things but my heart had been unmoved. That book broke my heart. I could tell it was best not to ask my mother about it, and that is when I began to read.

Later I did nevertheless ask her what our family did to save Jews. My mother said her life had been so hard during the war she had had no time to worry about Jews, and anyway, at that time she had known nothing about the concentration camps or gas chambers. I went to the town library and found a great many books and films there. More than that, I discovered there had been a vast extermination camp, Dachau, not far from Munich. What most shocked me was that people lived there, slept, ate, laughed—and it wasn't a problem for them!

My mother's cousin came from Schwedt to pay us a visit and I heard from her that my grandfather had committed suicide one week before Germany surrendered. She also told me my grandfather's name. If he had not shot himself, he would probably have been hanged as a war criminal. It was then I realized I wanted to dedicate my life to helping the Jews. Of course, the historical guilt of the Germans is immense, and as a German I share it. I want to work now for the State of Israel.

I am a Catholic, was a member of a Catholic children's group, and when

I applied for the Church training course, I was immediately given a reference. Now I have completed it, finished my fieldwork with problem children, and have been working in a hospice for three months. I don't have
much experience but am willing to learn. I also have some knowledge of
bookkeeping and speak Hebrew reasonably well. I thought it best not to try
to write to you in Hebrew because I did not want you to receive a letter
with mistakes, and it is in any case much easier for me to express my
thoughts in German.

I am 20 years old, in good health, and can work both with children and
elderly people. I am not well educated and at one time thought of going to
university, but that no longer seems to me to be necessary.

I look forward to hearing from you and can come to Haifa immediately
to start work with you.

Yours sincerely,
Hilda Engel

March 1964, Haifa

LETTER FROM DANIEL STEIN TO HILDA ENGEL

Dear Hilda,

You wrote to me in German but I am replying in Hebrew, which will
be good practice for you. You wrote me a very good letter which I fully
understood. I would be glad to work with you but we have only a small
congregation and no money for paying a salary, so how could you afford to
live here? I myself live in a monastery, but you would need to rent a flat.
So I think it best, when you are free at the Mission, for you to come any
time to Haifa for a service, to meet our congregation and spend time with
them. During the service we usually spend a few hours together, have a
simple meal, sometimes read the Gospel together, and then talk about
a variety of things. Give me a call when you intend to come and I will meet
you at the bus station because otherwise you won't be able to find us. It's
not a simple matter.

The Lord be with you.
Brother Daniel.
I prefer that form of address, is that okay?

May 1964, Jerusalem
FROM HILDA ENGEL TO DANIEL STEIN

Dear Brother Daniel,
My mother always said that my stubbornness would break down walls. I wrote to our board in Munich, then rang them up two or three times, and now they have promised to try to transfer my post of pastoral assistant from Jerusalem to Haifa. I mentioned that I have learnt Hebrew, but I don't know Arabic and that makes it difficult for me to communicate with the local Catholics who are all Arabs. They promised to reply promptly, but need a letter from you to say that you really do need me at your church. The address to write to is below, and then in a month's time I will be in Haifa. Hurray!
Hilda
Oh, by the way, I rang my mother and told her that now I would be working as an assistant to the priest in a Jewish church and she said I was mad. She thinks I have decided to work in a synagogue! I did not try to explain. Let her go on thinking that.

June 1964, Haifa
FROM BROTHER DANIEL TO HILDA ENGEL

My dear child,
You forgot half your belongings: a sweater, one shoe (were you wearing the other or did you bring a spare pair?), your Hebrew textbook, and a very badly written detective novel in English. Having piled them all together, I decided that being a pastoral assistant is your true vocation.
With love,
Brother D.

20. November 1990, Freiburg
FROM A TALK BY BROTHER DANIEL STEIN TO SCHOOLCHILDREN

We know that today many Christians do not conduct services together because they split in the past over theological disagreements. The Church, which at one time was united, divided into three main churches: Catholic, Orthodox, and Protestant. There are, however, many other smaller churches, some with only a few hundred members, which nevertheless have no liturgical relations with other Christians. They do not pray together or conduct services jointly. Among Christians such splits, or schisms, have sometimes been very violent, even leading to religious wars.

The Jews also experienced a schism of this kind in the late eighteenth century. Two tendencies arose at that time, the Hassidim and the traditionalists, or Mitnagdim. They did not recognize each other, although they never got round to waging war on each other either. The Jews living in Poland belonged in the main to the Hassidic tendency, while Wilno, as Vilnius was called at that time, remained a traditionalist city. The Hassidim were mystics who would lapse into prayerful ecstasy. They set great store by study of the Kabbalah and expected the Messiah to come soon. This latter belief makes the Hassidim resemble a number of Christian sects.

For the past two centuries Vilnius was the capital of Jews of the traditionalist tendency. To this day the differences between these trends are of interest only to practicing Jews. The Nazis took no interest whatsoever in such subtleties, and set themselves the task of exterminating all Jews, Hassidim, Mitnagdim, and nonbelievers alike. It was ethnic genocide.

When we young Jews from the Polish periphery reached Vilnius in December 1939, we found not only a great city in a European state but also the capital city of western Jewry. It was often referred to then as the "Lithuanian Jerusalem," and Jews made up almost half the population.

At the time of our arrival, Vilnius had been ceded under the terms of the Molotov-Ribbentrop Pact to Lithuania, and the Lithuanians promptly started expelling Poles. There was a brief period of Lithuanian independence. We believed our dream of reaching Palestine was about to come true. Little did we realize we had fallen into a trap which would shortly snap shut. In June 1940, Lithuania was occupied by the Red Army and within a month and a half had become part of the Soviet Union. In June 1941, Vilnius was taken over by Wehrmacht troops. There was no way we could have foreseen such a turn of events.

We really liked Vilnius. We climbed Mount Gediminas, strolled through the Jewish quarters, and walked along the embankments. The city had a smell of its own, with a suggestion of smoke from wood-burning stoves. There was almost no coal and it was thanks to that we were able to find work. The first winter we earned our living by chopping firewood and taking it around the apartments and to the upper stories of the houses in Vilnius.

A number of Jewish organizations were still functioning in the town, including Zionist ones, and we immediately got in touch with them. You needed a special certificate to be allowed to emigrate to Palestine. They were issued free of charge if you were under the age of eighteen, so for my brother, who was sixteen, the chances of emigrating were quite reasonable. As I was already eighteen, mine were very low.

We had to keep body and soul together somehow while we waited for a certificate, and organized a kibbutz, a commune where everybody works together and nobody has a personal income, like a monastery. We moved to a fairly spacious house where each group had its own room. The only girl among us did the housework and all the rest of us went out to work. The work was sometimes very hard. At first I worked together with all the others as a wood-cutter, and then I was invited to become an apprentice cobbler. The cobbler was very poor, with lots of children, and I spent almost the whole day with him. After work I stayed behind with the children and helped them with their home-work. I learned how to be a shoemaker and to this day mend my own sandals.

We managed to get in touch with our parents through the Red Cross and wrote to them. After we parted they had gone back home but immedi-ately been resettled to another part of Poland. The Red Cross forwarded the letters. Our parents were last seen alive by our cousins. For a time they all lived together in a small Jewish shtetl, but after that there was no more news. We do not know exactly in which of the death camps they were killed.

In the last letter from our mother to reach us, she begged us under no circumstances to separate, but separate we did. My brother obtained the certificate to emigrate to Palestine and made his way there by a very danger-ous route, via Moscow and Istanbul. That was in January 1941 and it was a very sad parting. We did not know if we would ever meet again.

After my brother's departure there were dramatic developments. On twenty-second of June 1941 the Russo-German war began. An hour after war was declared the bombing began, and three days later the Russians sur-rendered the city.

By then we had left and gone some sixty kilometers before finding we were in German-occupied territory.

We returned to Vilnius and heard distressing facts. On the day the Red Army abandoned Vilnius, Lithuanian gangs spontaneously organized them-selves and began murdering Jews, even before the city was taken by the Ger-mans. Later, large numbers of Lithuanians joined German execution units.

Anti-Jewish laws came into force: confiscation of property, prohibition of appearing in public places, prohibition of walking on the pavement. Finally, it was made compulsory to wear the Star of David as a distinguishing mark. Arrests began.

At that time I was so naive that I could not believe the Germans had a policy of systematically exterminating Jews. I had been brought up to respect German culture and argued with my friends, trying to persuade them that individual acts of violence and abuse were just a result of the general disorder. I simply could not believe it. Everything that was going on seemed an absurd mistake. I kept saying, "That's impossible! Don't believe the slanders! The Germans will soon restore order!" We had yet to see the reality of German order!

They began rounding up Jews in the streets of the city and people disappeared. There were rumors of shootings. I completely refused to believe what I was seeing.

All the Zionist organizations still in the city were disbanded. We could forget Palestine. I decided to find my parents through the Red Cross and make my way to join them. On the way to the Red Cross center I was caught in one of the hunts for Jews and arrested.

From that first detention on thirteenth of July 1941 until the end of the war I faced death every day. There were many occasions when it might have seemed that I should have died, and yet every time I was miraculously saved. If a person can get used to miracles, I got used to them during the war. In July 1941 the miracles in my life were only beginning.

What do people mean when they talk of a miracle? Something nobody has ever seen before, which has never happened before? Something beyond the limits of our experience, which is contrary to common sense, which is so improbable or happens so rarely that there are no living eyewitnesses of such an event? If it suddenly snowed in Vilnius in the middle of July, would that be a miracle?

On the basis of my own experience I can say that the defining characteristic of a miracle is that it is performed by God. Does that mean miracles do not happen to nonbelievers? No. The way a nonbeliever thinks means that he will explain a miracle by natural causes, the theory of probability, or as an exception to the rule. For a believing person a miracle is intervention by God in the natural course of events, and the mind of a believer rejoices and is filled with gratitude when a miracle occurs.

I have never been an atheist. I began consciously praying when I was eight, and I asked God to send me someone who would teach me the truth. I imagined this teacher would be handsome, educated, and have a long moustache, rather like the president of Poland at the time. I never did meet such a teacher with a moustache, but for a long time the One whom I met and whom I call my Teacher talked to me precisely in the language of miracles. Before learning to understand this language, you had first to learn its alphabet. I started thinking about that after the first roundup when I and my friend were seized in the street.

The group of Jews who had been arrested were taken from the police station to chop firewood for a German bakery. For the first time in my life I saw two German soldiers beat a young man almost to death for chopping logs badly. My friend and I were barely able to drag him to the courtyard of the Lukiszki Prison, to which we were marched after a long day's work. The courtyard was crammed with Jews, all men. They took all our possessions and documents and questioned us. When they asked what my training was I wondered whether to say I was a woodcutter or a cobbler but decided on the spur of the moment that I was a better cobbler than a woodcutter and answered accordingly. At that moment a miracle occurred. The officer shouted, "Hey, give Stein his belongings and documents back!"

I was taken to the stairs and a few others were brought, all of them cobblers. Cobblers, as we later discovered, were needed by the Gestapo because they had confiscated a large warehouse of leather from Jewish traders. The local German authorities decided to put it to good use, not sending it to Germany but using it to make boots for themselves. Of the one thousand people detained in that swoop, only twelve were cobblers. I was told later that all the others were shot, but I refused to believe it.

There was so much leather that the work lasted a long time. For the first six weeks they did not let us leave the prison, but then they gave us a pass with a Gestapo stamp and sent us home. We had to return each day to the prison workshop to make boots.

One day when I was going back home, a peasant offered me a lift on his cart. I did not realize at the time that my meeting this man, his name was Bolesław Rokicki, was itself another miracle. We know how many people have killing on their conscience, but he was one of those who saved lives. I understood very little at that time.

Bolesław lived on a farmstead two kilometers from Ponary. He told me some thirty thousand Jews had already been buried in the antitank ditches dug by the Red Army before it retreated. Mass shooting was going on around the clock. Again I refused to believe it.

Bolesław offered to let me move to his small farm, which he thought would be the safest place for me.

"You don't look like a Jew, you speak Polish like a Pole. You don't have 'Jew' written all over you. You can just say you're Polish."

I declined. I had a German pass with a stamp saying I was working as a cobbler for the Gestapo and thought that was sufficient protection.

A few days later, on my way back from work, I was again rounded up. The street was blocked and all the Jews in the crowd were forced into an inner courtyard, a dead end built of stone and with only one entrance through heavy metal gates. The roundup was being conducted by Lithuanian security guards in Nazi uniform and they were exceptionally brutal. They were unarmed but had heavy wooden truncheons and they made good use of them. I went to a Lithuanian officer, handed him my ID, and told him who I worked for. He tore up my precious pass and slapped me in the face.

All the Jews were herded into the courtyard and the gate was locked. The houses around the courtyard were empty, their inhabitants having already been expelled. Some people tried to hide in empty apartments, others went down to the cellars. I decided to hide, too, and found a cellar. Many houses in Vilnius had compartments in their cellars for storing vegetables. In the darkness I found a door but it was locked. I prized the planks apart and squeezed in. Instead of vegetables the little room was piled with old furniture. I hid there.

A few hours later trucks arrived. I heard orders shouted in German, and then Germans with torches appeared and started searching.

It was like a game of hide and seek, except that you would only lose once. Light fell on me through the cracks in the planks.

I heard a voice say, "The door here's padlocked. There's nobody else. Let's go," and the torch beam disappeared.

"Look though, there's a gap in the planks," someone replied.

I had never before prayed so hard to God.

"Are you joking? A child couldn't squeeze through that."

They left. I sat for an hour and then another in total silence. I had to get out somehow. My German document issued by the Gestapo had been torn up by that Lithuanian officer and all I had now was my school ID card issued in 1939. It gave no indication of nationality, only the name Dieter Stein, an ordinary German name. I tore the yellow star off my sleeve and decided my Jewish self would be left behind in the cellar. The person emerging would be a German and would behave like a German. No, a Pole. My father was German and my mother Polish, that would be best. And they had both died.

I went up and out to the courtyard where dawn was already breaking. I pressed against the walls of the houses like a cat and crept to the gate. It was locked and mounted so close to the stonework there was no way I could squeeze through the crack. The stones were laid close together and you would need a tool to prize them out. I had that tool: a small cobbler's claw hammer! Everybody had been searched as we came into the courtyard but the hammer in my boot had been overlooked. "It's a miracle," I thought, "another miracle."

It took fifteen minutes for me to chip out two small stones. There was only a small space but it was big enough for me. Even now, as you can see, I'm not a big person, and in those days I did not weigh even fifty kilograms. I squeezed through the gap and found myself out in the street.

It was early morning. A completely drunk German soldier came staggering around the corner surrounded by small boys who were taunting him. I asked him in German where he was going and he held out a piece of paper with the address of his hotel. I sent the boys packing and hauled him there. He was muttering something barely audible, but from his rambling I gathered that he had been involved that night in a massacre of Jews.

I must behave like a German, no, a Pole I thought, and said nothing.

"One and a half thousand, can you believe it, one and a half thousand." He stopped and began retching. "I don't like them, but why should I have to do this? I'm a linotype operator, a linotype operator. The Jews are nothing to do with me."

He did not look like he had enjoyed shooting people.

I got him to the hotel at last. It would never have occurred to anyone that a drunken German soldier was being helped back home by a Jew. That same evening I sought out Bolesław's farm. He was very welcoming. Two Russian prisoners-of-war who had escaped from their prison camp were already in hiding there, and a Jewish woman with a child.

That night, lying in the boxroom after a good meal, wearing clean clothes and, most importantly, feeling safe, I was filled with gratitude to God who had gone to such pains to rescue me from these traps.

I fell asleep rapidly, but was wakened a few hours later by bursts of gunfire coming from the direction of Ponary. I now no longer had any doubt what was going on there. Much of what I was to encounter is unacceptable to any normal human mind, and what was being enacted just a few kilometers away was even more unbelievable than any miracle. I had personal experience of miracles as expressions of a benign supernatural will, but what I now experienced was an agonizing sense that the supreme laws of life were being violated and a supernatural evil was being perpetrated which ran counter to the fundamental order of the world.

I lived on Bolesław's farm for several months, working in the fields with other hired workers, but in mid-October the Germans issued a law imposing the death penalty on anyone who hid Jews.

I did not want to endanger Bolesław and decided to leave. An opportunity soon arose when the local vet, who had come to deliver a calf, suggested I should move to Belorussia. His brother lived in a place so remote that no Germans had even been seen there.

The day came for me to take to the road. I was very frightened and thought as I walked along that I would not survive unless I could conquer my fear. My fear would betray me. It was a fear of being a Jew, of looking like a Jew. I decided I must stop being a Jew and become the same as the Poles and Belorussians. My outward appearance was fairly neutral, and in any case, I had no way of changing it. The only thing I could change was my behavior. I must behave like everybody else.

The road was full of German cars. From time to time men would hail them, and sometimes they would get a lift. Women were afraid of hailing anybody and preferred to walk. I overcame my fear and hailed a German truck, which stopped. Two days later I reached the remote Belorussian village which was my destination.

Except that the Germans had not overlooked it. The week before I got there all the Jews had been shot. The largest building in the village housed the school, which had had to make room now for a police station. In one place there was a store for clothing which had been taken off people while they were still alive, or removed from them after they were killed.

Most of the police were Belorussians. There were fewer Poles because around one and a half million of them were deported from the eastern regions to Russia in 1940 and early 1941.

I went to the police station the next day to obtain a permit to live in the village and was seen by the police secretary who was a Pole. My cover story about my parents aroused no suspicions. My school card was my only identification document and could not be faulted. It gave no indication of ethnicity and Polish really was my first language. I now received documents confirming that my father was German and my mother Polish which conferred the right to become a Volksdeutscher, an ethnic German, a privilege of which I did not avail myself. Knowing German was to prove sufficient.

Thus I became legal. At first I earned my keep by shoemaking and was paid not in cash but in food. Later I was invited to become the school cleaner and given a small room next to the one occupied by the chief of police. My duties included cleaning, cutting firewood, and keeping the stoves alight. Soon, teaching German to the pupils was added to my duties.

When the cold weather arrived, I had no warm clothing and the police secretary, who was in charge of the store, invited me to choose some new clothing. I had a dreadful feeling when he opened the door and I saw the piles of clothing which belonged to Jews the Germans had killed. I was frightened even to touch them. What should I do? I prayed and mentally thanked my murdered kinsmen. I took a worn sheepskin coat and several other items. There was no telling how long I myself might be fated to wear these clothes.

When German authorities came, I was summoned to translate for them. This was worrying, because I knew very well I should keep as far away from Germans as possible. On one occasion the district police chief, Ivan Semyonovich, arrived at the police station. The Belorussian Auxiliary Police of the German Gendarmerie in the Occupied Territories was a Belorussian organization subordinate to the Germans, and its chief had a bad reputation as a brutal drunk. He was accompanied by some German high-up and I was asked to translate. That evening Semyonovich summoned me and invited me to work for him as his personal translator and German teacher.

I had no wish to work for the police and had just one night to come to a decision. The very thought of a Jew collaborating with the police was appalling, but even then it occurred to me that if I did work for Semyonovich, I would probably be able to save the lives of at least some of those the police were hunting, to do something at least for people in need of help. The Belorussians were a very poor and downtrodden people fearful of anyone in authority, and were impressed even by such a paltry post as interpreter in the Belorussian police. The job would give me influence.

I agreed to work for Semyonovich and, oddly enough, felt a sense of relief that I could now be useful to the local people and those in need of help. Many simply did not understand what was required of them, which led to their being punished. That opportunity of mediating gave me back a sense of self-respect, and it was only by doing something for other people that I could salve my conscience and retain my integrity. From the instant I started my new job I understood that the least slip could be fatal.

I began acting as an interpreter between the German gendarmerie, the

Belorussian police, and the local populace. I shed the last trace of my Jewish legacy, the clothing from the police store, and now wore a black police uniform with a gray collar and cuffs, breeches, boots, and a black peaked cap which did not, however, sport a skull and crossbones. I was even issued a pistol. SS units wore a black uniform and ours differed only in having a gray collar and cuffs.

I thus became in effect a German policeman with the rank of Unteroffizier. I entered military service with the rank my father had risen to when he retired. Nobody could have foreseen such a quirk of fate. It was December 1941, I was nineteen, I was alive, and that was a miracle.

21. June 1965, Haifa

BULLETIN BOARD IN THE VESTIBULE OF THE ARAB CATHOLIC CHURCH OF THE DORMITION OF THE MOST HOLY VIRGIN MARY IN HAIFA *(Notices in Hebrew and Polish.)*

Dear parishioners,
On 15 June at 7 pm there will be a reception for representatives of the American organization Jews for Jesus.
Hilda

Dear parishioners,
A family outing is being organized to Tabgha on the Feast of Peter and Paul. Meet outside the church at 7 am.
Hilda

Dear parishioners,
Our newly organized old people's home needs a heater, a camp bed, and several large saucepans.
Hilda

Dear parishioners,
Study and reading of Holy Scripture are canceled because Brother Daniel is away. Instead Professor Chaim Artman of the University of Jerusalem will visit us and talk about Biblical archaeology. Very interesting.
Hilda

Children's bunk bed available. If anybody needs it, please see Hilda.

Children's hour—drawing.
Hilda

22. 1964, Haifa
LETTER FROM DANIEL STEIN TO WŁADYSŁAW KLECH

Dear Brother,
Apologies for the delay in replying to your letter and for not thanking you for sending the magazines. Thank you very much, although unfortunately I have not read them yet. The trouble is that I have found myself in the thick of quite different problems, far removed from issues of theory and theology. We have long known, of course, that theological controversies are invariably a reflection of the circumstances of the Church and of the people who comprise it. The people around me can hardly even be characterized as a congregation in the traditional sense, and confront me with entirely different issues. Working in Poland, I was dealing with Polish Catholics who had been brought up in a certain tradition within the framework of their national culture. What I observe here is nothing like that. While recognizing the catholicity of the Church, we sometimes forget that in practical terms we are always dealing with ethnic religion. The Christian ambience which has evolved in Israel is highly diverse. There is a multiplicity of Churches, all with their own traditions and outlooks: even Catholicism is present here in a wide variety of forms. Besides my brother Carmelites, I find myself talking to an assortment of Maronites, Melchites, and many other Christian organizations, many of them monastic "Little Brothers of Jesus" and "Little Sisters of Jesus." each branch with its special characteristics and insight. There are pro-Palestine and pro-Israel 'little brothers and sisters,' and these have their own particular areas of contention. One such Jerusalem Brotherhood was even closed recently because it proved too difficult to live among the Arabs without sharing their hatred of Jews. I make no mention of the various Orthodox churches which are also unable to agree among themselves. The Church of the Moscow Patriarchate is at loggerheads with the Russian Orthodox Church Abroad, and so on ad infinitum. I won't even attempt to take in the whole picture.
As a parish priest I constantly encounter problems within my own small

community. Polish women and their children, Hungarians, Romanians, individual people who were unable to live their lives in their homeland but who remain loyal to the traditions of their homeland find the process of cultural assimilation in their adopted country very trying. Jewish Catholics, no matter which part of the world they live in, do not generally feel at ease there, but mine are especially uneasy.

Here, in Israel, in this Babel of nationalities, I have seen for myself that in practice a priest works not with individuals in a vacuum but with representatives of a particular people, each of which evidently has its own, national path to Christ. The result is that in the minds of that people there appears an Italian Christ, a Polish Christ, a Greek Christ, a Russian Christ.

My mission here in this land, among the people to which I belong, is to seek the Jewish Christ. There is no need to labor the point that He, in whose name St. Paul declared earthly nationality, social distinctions, and even gender to count for nothing, was, as a matter of historical fact, a Jew.

I have made the acquaintance of a young Ethiopian bishop. He said something important: "Africans cannot accept European Christianity. The Church lives within its own nationality, and you cannot impose the Roman interpretation on everybody. King David danced before the throne, and the African is ready to dance. We are more ancient than the Roman Church. We want to be as we are. I studied in Rome, and prayed for many years in Roman churches, but my black-skinned parishioners have not had that experience. Why must I demand that they renounce their nature? Why must I insist that they become the Roman Church? The Church should not be so centralized. Universalism is in delegated freedom!"

In this I agree with him. The Ethiopian Church formed before the split into Eastern and Western Christianity. Why should it concern itself with the problems which arose after that?

I can share that point of view, not as an Ethiopian but as a Jew. In Poland that would never have occurred to me. You know, in Belorussia, among the Germans, I wanted to seem to be a German, in Poland I was almost a Pole, but here in Israel it is as plain as can be that I am a Jew.

Something else: while I was showing Mount Carmel to two seminarists from Rome, we wandered into a Druse settlement and, higher up the hill, came upon a derelict church. Two monks once lived in a hovel adjacent to it but there is nobody there now. It isn't obvious whom to ask for permission. I got my parishioners together and we set to tidying it up, clearing away all the rubbish and litter. We placed 12 stones for an altar. Of course, a great deal of money would be needed before it would be fit for holding services, but in the meantime I have written to the local authorities asking for permission to restore the church.

By the way, I have been granted Israeli citizenship, but not at all as I would have wished. I have been naturalized on the grounds of having been resident here, but they have not registered me as a Jew. I think I may have told you about this already. After I lost my lawsuit the law was amended, so that now a Jew is defined as somebody born of a Jewish mother, who considers himself a Jew, and has not converted to another religion. I have only succeeded in making matters worse than they were. Now on entering Israel an immigrant has to declare which faith he professes, and Jewish Christians can be refused citizenship.

The entry in my identification document reads, "Nationality not established"!

Dear Władek, there is a great deal of work to do here, so much that I sometimes have no time to think. Why has the Lord arranged my life this way? When I was young I hid from the Germans for a whole year and a half with nuns in a ruined monastery, not daring to poke my nose outside. I had more time for reflection than I had thoughts to fill it. Now I constantly feel a lack of that "empty" time. There is no time for reading either, but in that respect I have a request. If you should come across the works of the English biblical scholar Harold H. Rowley, not *The Relevance of Apocalyptic* but his old book about the faith of Israel, please send it. I found a mention of it, but without a bibliographical reference.

It has long been understood that Pilate's question, "What is truth?" was mere rhetoric, but the question "What is faith?" is not rhetoric but essential for living. There are too many people in the world who believe in rules, candles, sculptures, and other bits of this and that. They believe in interesting people and peculiar ideas. Perhaps it is just as foolish to seek there for meaning as for truth, but I would like faith, which is the personal secret of each one of us, to be stripped of the husk and the clutter, down to the wholesome, indivisible grain. It is one thing to believe, and another to know, but most important of all is to know what you believe.

Your Brother in Christ,

Daniel.

23. *January 1964*

On 4 December 1963 Pope Paul VI announced his intention of making a pilgrimage to the Holy Land.

He made no mention of the State of Israel, but instead used the word "Palestine," which of itself shows Paul VI's attitude to the Jewish people and their state.

In Jerusalem the Pope's decision has caused consternation. The customary prior consent when a head of state visits has not been sought. Press reaction has been hostile to a perceived slight. Doctor Herzl Rosenblum writes in a lead in *Yedioth Ahronoth*, "It is astounding that no attempt was made to inform us, that our ambassador to Rome learned of the decision of the Holy See from the newspapers, while members of the government heard about it on the radio."

The Italian Information Agency has declared on behalf of the Vatican that the visit is of a purely religious nature and in no way implies recognition of the State of Israel.

The Vatican has announced that on 4 January 1964, Paul VI's plane will land at Rabat-Ammon Airport in Jordan. From the Jordanian capital "His Holiness" will proceed in his limousine to the Old Town (Jerusalem) where he will spend the night in the Vatican Mission. The following day Paul VI will cross the border to Israel. He will visit Galilee and Nazareth, proceed to the Jewish part of Jerusalem, ascend Mount Zion, and then return to the Old Town through the Mandelbaum Gate.

On the third day of his visit the Pope will visit Beit Lechem and will then return to Rabat-Ammon, from where he will fly back to the Vatican.

A desolate stretch of road between Jenin and Meggido has been chosen as the venue where the head of the Catholic Church and the leaders of the State of Israel will meet. It is an ordinary place on the map which testifies eloquently to the state of war in which our country finds itself.

Maariv wrote that Paul VI's choice of Meggido for the meeting had hidden implications. "Is there really nobody out there conversant with the Book of Revelation? It is explicitly stated there that at the End of Days a battle will take place at Meggido between Good and Evil (the forces of the Antichrist). Are we really going to meet the Pope there and, moreover, with a full government turnout? In recent weeks the Vatican has repeatedly declared that it does not recognize the existence of the State of Israel.

This is the spot Paul VI has chosen to meet the leaders of the Jewish state, on a ruined road nobody has traveled along since 1948."

A ministerial commission recommended raising no objection to the Pontiff's wishes and organizing a ceremony at Meggido. It was decided that President Zalman Shazar, Chief Rabbi Yitzhak Nissim, and several ministers would go to Meggido. This was given a chilly reception by the Israeli public.

Dr. Zerach Warhaftig, a member of the commission, expressed the view that since the visit was of a purely religious nature, neither the president nor the members of the government should be in any hurry to pay their respects to "His Holiness." That could perfectly well be taken care of by officials from the Ministry of Religions.

In the midst of the preparations for this exceedingly important event the Chief Rabbi of Israel, Rav Yitzhak Nissim, announced that he would not be going to Meggido. There was an almighty scandal. Everybody promptly forgot about controversy over the president's attendance. The Chief Rabbi refuses to go along with the government's decision and nobody can change his mind. Rav Yitzhak's refusal has become a hot topic for the world's mass media. The Pope's pilgrimage was been pushed off the front pages and now all the talk is about a standoff between the head of the Catholic Church and the rabbi, which is, of course, being presented as a confrontation between Catholicism and the Jewish world.

Rafael Pines, Special correspondent

REPORT ON THE VISIT OF POPE PAUL VI TO ISRAEL

Pope Paul VI spent just 11 hours on the territory of Israel, from 09.40 on 5 January 1964 until 20.50 on the same day. The Pontiff entered Israel via the Jenin-Meggido Highway and left through the Mandelbaum Gate in Jerusalem.

The previous day he flew from Rome to Rabat-Ammon, from where he traveled to Jerusalem. The Jordanians exploited the Pope's visit for a barrage of furious anti-Semitic propaganda. In the Old Town crowds of people turned out to meet the Pope and the police had difficulty in controlling the pressure. The Pontiff almost got crushed. His reception in Israel was fairly cool. In Nazareth 30,000 people gathered in the streets of the city, but little excitement was evident in Jerusalem.

The formal meeting in Meggido was attended by the President of Israel, Zalman Shazar; Prime Minister Levi Eshkol; his deputy Abba Eban; the Minister for Religious Affairs, Zerach Warhaftig; the Chairman of the Knesset, Kadish Luz; and the Minister of Police, Bechor-Shalom Shitrit. Golda Meir broke her leg the day before, so was unable to see the Pontiff, whom she "adores." Anybody expecting the Pope to mention the State of Israel was sadly mistaken. Although government representatives tirelessly repeated that the visit was of a purely religious nature, they emphasized that Paul VI's visit was of great significance for the state. Eleven hours after arriving, the Pope gave a farewell speech in which he first thanked the "authorities" and said he would never forget his visit to the Holy Places. He also noted that "the Church loves all," but then, like a bolt from the blue, the Pope referred to Pius XII. "My predecessor, the great Pius XII, did everything he could during the last war to succor the persecuted irrespective of their origins. Today we hear voices which accuse this holy man of sins. We declare that these accusations could not be more unjust. His memory is sacred for us." (Who was Pius XII? It was in large measure with the connivance of this "holy" man that 6 million Jews died. He did not raise a finger to try to save them. He had only to say a single word! How many lives could have been saved!) Even Catholics were outraged by Paul VI's claims. The very mention of the anti-Semitic pope's name in Jerusalem was, at best, tactless. From on board the aircraft the Pontiff sent telegrams expressing gratitude to all who had received him. He addressed King Hussein of Jordan with his full title, added his thanks to "our beloved people of Jordan." The pilgrim did not give Israel the same treatment. His telegram began, "To President Shazar, Tel Aviv." Not Jerusalem. God forbid.

From our own correspondent, Ariel Givat

24. July 1964, Haifa
LETTER TO THE PRIOR OF THE LEBANESE PROVINCE OF THE ORDER OF BAREFOOT BROTHERS OF THE MOST HOLY VIRGIN MARY OF MOUNT CARMEL

Your Grace,

I have to inform you that last month I received distressing information regarding the reaction of one of the brothers of our house to the meeting of the Pontiff with a group of political leaders in Meggido. I refer to Brother Daniel Stein who transferred to our monastery from Poland in 1959. There was a great need at that time for a Polish-speaking priest to conduct services and pastoral work among the Polish-speaking population of Haifa. Brother Daniel copes successfully with his duties and all comments from the parishioners are extremely positive, which is more than could be said of his predecessor.

After receiving an appeal from one of our brothers, I summoned Brother Daniel Stein for an exhortatory talk. He informed me of his viewpoint on certain issues of Church policy, which can be summarized as follows:

1. Brother D. believes that a Jewish Christian community should be re-established in the land of Israel.(!)

2. Brother D. believes that the contemporary Catholic Church, having broken with the Jewish tradition, has been severed from its roots and is in a diseased state.

3. Brother D. believes that this "disease" can be healed only by "de-Latinizing" the Church and inculturating Christianity into local cultures.

I drew his attention to the ecclesiastical discipline to which he is obliged to adhere in his service, about which he agreed with me only in part and stated that conducting services in Hebrew, something he is attempting to effect, does not contradict any church directives.

Not feeling sufficiently competent to reach any decision in this matter, I consider it my duty to convey to you the gist of our talk. I attach with this letter the primary document on the basis of which the present talk was conducted.

With profound respect
Brother N. Sarimente
Abbot of the Stella Maris Monastery

June 1964

Reverend Father,

I consider it a duty of my monastic obedience to tell you about impermissible things being said by our fellow monk, Brother Daniel Stein, which he has been indulging in for a long time in respect of the position of the Holy See.

In the past D. Stein has made statements saying he disagrees with the Church's policy in the Middle East. He has declared that the Vatican not recognizing the State of Israel is a mistake and a continuation of the Church's policy of anti-Semitism. He has allowed himself to make a number of specific statements condemning the position of Pope Pius XII during the years of

Nazism and blaming him for not opposing, the extermination of the Jews during the war. He has also expressed himself to the effect that the Vatican is engaging in political intrigue in favor of the Arabs because it is afraid of the Arab world. Brother Daniel is a Jew and has pro-Israel views and I think that is because of his origins and that partly explains his position.

However, his comments on the most important event of recent times of the visit of His Holiness to the Middle East and His Holiness's historic meeting with Israeli state leaders on the Jenin-Meggido highway amount to condemning the Church's position, which I find very upsetting and which I cannot but bring to your attention. His views appear not altogether to correspond with the opinions accepted within our Order.

Brother Elijah

August 1964
LETTER TO THE GENERAL OF THE ORDER OF CARMELITES FROM THE PRIOR OF THE LEBANESE PROVINCE OF THE ORDER OF BAREFOOT BROTHERS OF THE MOST HOLY VIRGIN MARY OF MOUNT CARMEL

Your Eminence, dear Brother General!

I am forwarding to you a number of documents relating to the presence and activities in the Stella Maris Monastery of the priest Daniel Stein. May you perhaps consider it expedient to forward these documents to the competent departments of the Roman Curia?

I had a talk with Father Stein and invited him to put in writing his views regarding the conducting of services in Hebrew. I do not presume to reach a decision without your recommendations.

Prior of the Lebanese Province of the Order of Barefoot Brothers of the Most Holy Virgin Mary of Mount Carmel

25. 1996, Galilee, Moshav Nof a-Galil
FROM A TAPE-RECORDED CONVERSATION BETWEEN EWA MANUKYAN AND AVIGDOR STEIN

CASSETTE 3

AVIGDOR. Well, Ewa, what can I tell you about Daniel's life in the monastery? In the first place, I have never been there. You went there, you know better than I do how everything stands in that place.

EWA. I didn't see much. They wouldn't let me through the door. They don't allow women in. They only once admitted Golda Meir. Nobody wanted to talk to me. They said the abbot wasn't in, and his secretary, a Greek, didn't speak English. He just waved his arms at me as if to say, "No, no!"

AVIGDOR. If you remind me, I will show you a letter I received from one of our friends in Akiva shortly after the war. I have kept it. It speaks about the beginning of his monastic life, back in Poland. Why did you not ask him about it?

EWA. At the time, he was asking me the questions. Anyway, we were talking about other matters.

AVIGDOR. That's quite right, he did not like talking about himself. He was like a partisan: if he didn't feel it was necessary to say something, he didn't give anything away. Five years must have passed before I realized how difficult he was finding life in the monastery. A great deal depended on the abbot, you see. If the abbot was a tolerant, broad-minded person, sensible relations were possible, but abbots change. Every three years, I think it is. They changed many times during the years he lived at Stella Maris. Just short of forty years Daniel lived in that place.

One abbot, as I recall, positively hated him. I do not know what the other monks there do or how they live, but they all live in the monastery and hardly ever go outside. None of them can speak Hebrew. If one of the monks fell ill and had to go to hospital, Daniel always went along as the interpreter. Without him they could do nothing that involved the world outside. And then there was the car. You see, soon after he arrived he bought a motor scooter, a Vespa, and started haring all over the country. Then he bought a car. That was after he had started earning money as a tour guide.

First he had a completely beat up Mazda, then a little antediluvian Ford. You can imagine how I viewed all this from the wings. There were perhaps twelve or fifteen monks living there. Daniel would get up at four in the morning to pray. What the rest of them do I don't know, I suppose they work in the orchard. There is a marvelous orchard there and a small vineyard. Daniel never worked in the orchard. He would leave after morning prayers. From the very beginning he became a kind of social worker. He was a priest only in name! You see, the truth of the matter is that he should have been a doctor or a teacher. He would have made a very good doctor. He was probably a good monk. Absolutely everything he did, he did honestly and conscientiously, but the local monks were a different kettle of fish. For them he was an outsider, in the first place because he was Jewish. There was one monk living there who would not even speak to him. He spent his whole life in the same monastery and to the day he died he never talked to Daniel. Daniel would laugh about it. He would take him to visit the doctor and the monk would say nothing and look away. It was a difficult situation for him. But you know what he was like. He never complained, only gently laughed at himself.

And what about his parish? What kind of parishioners did he have? They were adrift, people displaced from their homes, mostly Catholic women who had married Jews. Some were ill, some were crazy, with children who were completely disorientated. Please don't think I don't know how difficult it is for a non-Jew to live in Israel. It is extremely difficult. Before Daniel came, the priest was an Irishman and the parishioners just wanted to get rid of him because he was a real anti-Semite. All these local Catholic women were linked to Jews by ties of kinship. One of Daniel's parishioners had saved her husband's life. He had lived in a cellar for a year and a half and every night she brought him food, took away his chamber pot, all this under the nose of the Germans. And that priest told this extraordinarily brave woman, "You have just spawned a lot of Jewish brats!" In the end, the Irishman was transferred to a Greek island where nobody knew anything about Jews and everyone was happy. Daniel, though, was sent to Haifa, to the Catholics here. During his first years, he conducted the service in Polish, but then to the Poles were gradually added Hungarians, Russians, Romanians. He had all sorts, speaking all sorts of languages. All the new arrivals were learning Hebrew, finding out how to travel around, how much to pay for bread. Gradually their common language for communicating became Hebrew, and after a few years Daniel began conducting the service in Hebrew. Almost all his parishioners were penniless, incapable of real work, all having babies and living on social welfare.

I came to Israel in 1941 and within three days I had a job. In the same place as I am now. At first, of course, I was just an assistant technician, but the thought of social welfare never entered my head! All those parishioners of his, though, were helpless and hopeless. My brother became a social worker. He filled out forms for them. He got them into schools, and their children too.

Then there were the tourist groups. At first there were Church delegations, Italian Catholics, German. He took them everywhere. Then it was non-Catholic groups which came, just plain tourists, and they wanted him to show them the Holy places. He knew Israel better than I do. I haven't traveled around the country much. Where would I find the time? I had my work, my children, but he knew every bush here, every byway. Especially in Galilee. He made money that way. Part of it he gave to the monastery and part he spent on his parishioners. My elder daughter always said, "Our uncle is a real manager. He can organize anything." He set up a school for newly arrived children, and a children's home, and an almshouse. He bought a community center for the parish.

EWA. Why didn't he leave the monastery?

AVIGDOR. I think because he was a soldier! He was like a soldier doing his duty. There was a strict discipline there. He always went back to stay overnight in the monastery. In the morning he would leave, but he was always back before midnight. I don't know what use the monastery was to him. I told him long ago he should come and stay with us, especially later after the children had left. We already had this house, a big house. There were just Milka and I here. He could at least have enjoyed a bowl of homemade soup! But he wouldn't hear of it.

People wrote denunciations against him. I had one sad little paper here for a long time which Daniel brought. He was summoned one time by the abbot and given a notice to attend the Office of the Prime Minister. Daniel came and showed it to us, wondering what it was all about. This was after his court case. All that fuss in the press seemed to have died down. I looked at the paper and the address there was not the Prime Minister's Office at all but the Israel Security Agency, Shin Bet. Something along the lines of your CIA. I told him not to go. He sat there, said nothing, scratching behind his ear. He did that when he was thinking.

"No," he said. "I shall go. I've been dealing with these services the whole of my life. I worked in the police, and I was in the partisans. By the way, I have two medals, one with Lenin on it and one with Stalin. I even worked for the NKVD for a couple of months before I ran away."

I was amazed. He had never told me about the NKVD before. He told me that when the Russians entered Belorussia, they first awarded him a medal but then he was summoned to the NKVD. One officer interrogated him while another took notes and a third just sat there listening. When and where was he born, who were his father and mother, his grandfather and grandmother, who had he sat next to at school, who was his neighbor to the right, to the left. He gave them the answers and then they repeated the questions for a second time, then for a third: when, where, mother, father. Then they said, "Help us and we will help you." "I told them, 'I don't need your

help, but what can I do for you?'" "Help us to make sense of the secretariat
where you worked in Emsk. Everything is in German. We need to trawl
through it and find their agents."

Daniel wanted only to get away from the lot of them. He had already
decided to become a monk but knew they wouldn't just release him, so he
agreed to translate everything they needed, all those Gestapo documents.
They took him to Emsk, to the very house he had escaped from, back to that
very table, except that now he was working under a Russian captain instead
of a German, and now there were two lieutenants, one Russian, one Belorussian. They provided him with a uniform and gave him the right to eat
in the same canteen he had sat in with the Belorussian police. The work was
exactly the same only everything he had previously translated from Belorussian into German he now translated into Russian. He had not the slightest
doubt that as soon as it had all been translated, they would arrest him. A couple of months passed until a day came when the captain was called to Minsk
and the Russian lieutenant went with him, leaving the Belorussian in charge.

My brother was a highly intelligent man. He thought carefully and went
to the lieutenant to ask for leave. He told him, "I have done all the work as
agreed. I have family in Grodno and want to visit them. Give me a few days'
leave." The Belorussian lieutenant felt very competitive toward Daniel. He
was afraid Daniel might get his job because of his knowledge of foreign languages, so he thought it over and said, "I don't have the necessary authority
to grant you leave, but if you go to visit your relatives I can personally know
nothing about it." He didn't say straight out, "You can go absent without
leave," but that was more or less what he implied. At that, Daniel escaped,
for the last time as far as I know, from the secret services.

Now he was being called in by his own, Israeli, secret service. What
should he do? I told him not to go. I said, "You have a perfect right not to,
and moreover you are a monk. You shouldn't go. That's it." Daniel finished
scratching his ear and said, "No, I shall go. This is my country. I am a citizen
here," so he went.

He came back three days later. I asked him how he had got on and he
laughed. "In the first place," he said, "All these captains are as alike as peas
in a pod. They asked exactly the same questions: when and where were you
born, who were your father and mother, your grandfather and grandmother,
who did you go to school with, who was on the right, who was on the left? I
told him and he asked all the same questions again. And for a third time. It
seems they all go to the same academy!"

He told it so amusingly, Ewa, although there didn't seem much to laugh about. Then he was asked whether he wanted to help his country. Daniel said he was always glad to help his country. The captain got excited and asked him to pass on information about his parishioners. He said that there were bound to be one or two agents sent by Russia among them.

EWA. What are you saying, Avigdor! I can't believe it!

AVIGDOR. What is so impossible, Ewa? All sorts of things go on! You think there were no agents? There were dozens. Here from Russia, there from us. All over the place. Everybody knows how many British intelligence services there were here. After all, this is the Middle East. Do you think that, living here in a village, I don't know anything about politics? I know no less than Daniel, even though he read all the foreign newspapers.

Anyway, what happened then was that he refused. He told the captain, "I have a professional duty and a professional duty of secrecy. If I detect a threat to the state, I will think what to do about it, but so far I haven't encountered that situation."

Then the captain said, "Perhaps we can do something to help you? We respect you, know about what you did in the war, and your medals. Perhaps you have some problems we can help you to resolve?" "Yes," Daniel said, "I have left my car in a paid parking place. It will cost three lirot. Perhaps you could reimburse me."

That is how the story ended.

EWA. What year was that?

AVIGDOR. I don't remember exactly. I remember he said lirot, so it must have been before 1980.

26. *August 1965, Haifa*
LETTER FROM DANIEL STEIN TO WŁADYSŁAW KLECH

Dear Brother,

Thank you for the books. I have just received the parcel. Unfortunately, at the moment I have no time at all for reading, or even to reply properly to your letter. I therefore promise to write a long letter with "explanations." You were right in intuiting that a certain internal process began shortly after I arrived in Israel and a great many of my old views were shaken. This is a country of incredibly intense living, social, political, and spiritual—a word I don't care for because I don't accept the distinction between life on a higher and lower, a spiritual and a material plane. I would formulate the question which so agitated me after my arrival in Israel as: what was the faith of our Master? The issue is not what he preached, but what precisely he believed in. That is what is of supreme interest to me. I can't promise to write to you with my thoughts on this matter in the immediate future, but will not fail to do so eventually.

I send you my best wishes on this festival of the Transfiguration. I served Mass on the top of Mount Tabor yesterday. There are two temples there, one Catholic and one Orthodox, and and they have railings fencing them off from each other. We found a place on the mountain slope slightly below the summit. I believe it was the very spot where the apostles fell to the ground blinded by their vision. Then we prayed. There were two Anglican women and several Orthodox in addition to my regular parishioners. It was a great joy.

I even dreamed about that rusty railing separating those two churches. It is dividing Peter from Paul, and in such a place! I couldn't stop thinking about it and, since pondering matters at great length is not my style because I am quite impulsive, I have already written a petition to the Latin Patriarch seeking permission to create here in Haifa a Christian union of all the denominations for communal prayer. I am also turning over in my mind the possibility of a common liturgy. If we work toward that, we could see it during our lifetime. I am not mad. I am well aware how many obstacles there are on that path, but if God wills it, it will come to pass.

With brotherly love,
Your Daniel

1 March 2006, Moscow
LETTER FROM LUDMILA ULITSKAYA TO ELENA KOSTIOUKOVITCH

Dear Lyalya,
I have something unexpected to tell you. Back in November, in Vollezele, with a telephone which had been cut off, a computer which didn't work, and a landlady who spoke only Flemish, in a room with a meditation mat of Indonesian tapa, I realized that what I want most of all is to write about Daniel. Not a gripping mythological theme, not *Imago*, which is already partly written. None of that, only about Daniel. However, I have completely rejected the documentary approach, although like a conscientious slave I have studied all the documents, books and papers, publications and remi-

niscences of hundreds of people until I know them by heart. I have started writing a novel, or whatever it will be called, about a person in those circumstances, with those problems today. With the whole of his life he raised a heap of unresolved, highly inconvenient issues which nobody talks about: the value of a life turned into mush beneath one's feet; the freedom which few people want; God for whom there is ever less room in our life; efforts to extricate Him from archaic words, all the ecclesiastical garbage, and life which has closed in on itself. Have I packaged that temptingly?

From the day I met Daniel I have been circling around this and you know how many times I have attempted to make contact with it. Well, I am making another attempt, only this time I shall try to free myself from the pressure of documents, of the names of real people who might be offended or harmed, and to retain only what has "non-private" significance. I am changing names, inserting my own fictional or semi-fictional characters, changing the setting and time of events, being disciplined, trying not to be capricious. In other words, I'm interested only in complete truthfulness of utterance, although as always I retain the right to fall flat on my face. That is perhaps the greatest luxury an author can afford in this age of market relations.

Be that as it may, I am sending you the first part of what I have written so far. I don't believe I can cope without your support, friendship, and professionalism. I have told you a lot about this before, but you will meet completely unfamiliar characters I have just invented, so that they are still soft and warm like new-laid eggs. Did you know that inside the hen an eggshell is far softer than after it emerges from the cloaca? Birds, my dear, do not have a backside but a cloaca. That is one of the remnants of my biological education.

How are the children and your Andrey? My Andrey has flown to Zürich in the wake of his works. The children are fine and not giving me too much trouble. The big news is that I will have a second grandchild by the summer.

Love,

L.

PART TWO

1. September 1965, Haifa
LETTER FROM HILDA ENGEL TO HER MOTHER

Dear Mother,

Happy birthday! Unfortunately I wasn't able to phone you because Daniel and I were in Jerusalem for a few days, going around to see officials at the Ministry of Religions and the Latin Patriarchate. We even had to see a Russian archimandrite. It is all in connection with an amazing plan. I don't know whether it will work out, but I very much hope that it does. I will tell you all about it in detail later. But first, about you.

From your last letter I know your most recent analyses have been normal. Thank God! It is dreadful that you were so ill, but even from that something good has come. We have never before been so close. During the month I spent with you I came to understand you far better, and I feel you understand me better, too. Is it always necessary to pay such a high price before we can understand each other?

You asked me to explain in more detail what I am doing here, but that is quite difficult. I am rushing about a lot, but by no means all of it makes sense. Brother Daniel—the more I know about him the more I want to tell you—is always laughing and teasing me. He says I spin my arms like a windmill but what spills out of me is not flour but handkerchiefs, purses, and ballpoint pens.

Last week I did lose my purse again, but it had only 15 lirot in it. Fortunately I had taken 300 to a needy family that morning and transferred 800 for a young woman's studies. Last month we received a donation from Germany and were able to pay the electricity bill. We pay for the electricity in the Arab church. They have their service in the morning and don't need to put the lights on, but ours is in the evening and we can't do without light. Since they allowed us to hold our services in their church the cost of electricity has gone up fourfold.

Now, about our plan. Some time ago we went on a trip to Mount Carmel. Daniel took a group of 10 or so of our young parishioners and of course I went too. It was a wonderful place, an ancient Druze village. You have probably not heard about the Druze. They really are a unique people, quite unlike anybody else. Daniel said that they were originally Muslims, but venerate a saint called al-Hakim whom Muslims do not recognize but who in many respects resembles Jesus. Just like the Christians they live in expectation of the Second Coming but keep their faith profoundly secret. They venerate the Torah, the new Testament, and the Quran, and also have some secret books of their own. They even have a special principle, I've forgotten what it's called, which requires them to conceal their true views and adapt externally to the morals and religion of those around them. As always, Daniel talks about them very interestingly. We did not go into their village but climbed on up the mountain.

Wherever you excavate in these parts you can be sure there was already something there in olden times. Not far from that village Daniel showed us an old church. It was in ruins but had not yet completely collapsed. We thought how marvelous it would be to rebuild it for ourselves. After all, we are a community with nowhere to live. We could reconstruct it. Admittedly, there is no water supply and no electricity. The nearest spring is in the Druze village and the electricity lines end there too. We could just about get by without electricity, but not without water.

Daniel said he would try talking to the village elder and see whether they would give us permission to tap into their water supply. If our venture succeeds it will be brilliant. We could leave Haifa and live here autonomously, and it would be a pleasant 5 kilometer walk for Daniel to the monastery. To drive there you would have to make an almost 30-kilometer detour.

Daniel said getting water from the Druze would be far more straightforward than getting permission from the Church hierarchy. Anyway, we went to petition them. He will speak to the Druze elder in a few days' time. I wanted to go with him but he said it would be better for him to go alone and tell me all about it afterwards.

As I am writing I realize I have forgotten to tell you something important. Daniel says that with my entirely respectable Hebrew I could go to study at university. He promised to find the money for it. There is a preparatory department called Mehina which has a distance-learning course. You go to lectures for a few days each month, and the rest of the time study on your own. After the first year they transfer you to the first year of the Judaic Studies course. I would really like that.

That's all. I must go to bed now because I have to get up at five tomorrow.
Lots of love to you and all the family,
Your Hilda

Before I had time to post this, Daniel came back from the Druze very
pleased.

The main thing is, they will allow us to divert some of their water. What he
had to tell me about them was also very interesting. Their village is quite large
with modern houses and everything is extremely clean. An old man, evidently a
saddler, was sitting in a courtyard under an awning sewing something with a large
needle. Daniel told the first person he met he would like to talk to the elder and
that person immediately took him to his home for something to eat. Their village
elder is a teacher and just at that moment he was teaching at the school. While
they were talking, a young man was making coffee. There was a minor commotion at the back of the house and, as Daniel discovered afterwards, they were
slaughtering a lamb for plov. They drank the coffee and the house owner, Salim,
took Daniel around the village. The first place he was shown was the cemetery.

Twelve people from this village had died in the fighting. One was a colonel,
and there were several officers and private soldiers. Salim was very proud of the
cemetery and showed it as if to say, "We are a warrior people." It was strange,
because outwardly they seemed very peaceful people, peasants. They had fine
orchards and vineyards. They walked on and Daniel asked him why there was no
mosque or anything of the kind. They don't have mosques but they have a *khal-
wah*, a house for prayer meetings. Muslims do not consider them to be believers
because they have, apart from the Quran and the Bible, some other sacred books
of their own which they keep secret from everybody else. They also have a very
strange, special doctrine, called *Taqiyya*. It is a secret teaching, only for Druze.
Their elder is initiated into this secret and conveys it orally only to those who are
worthy. Their main principle in life, though, is that they live at peace with the
religion of the country in which they are dwelling. They have no homeland apart
from their doctrine. Daniel even said sadly, "There, Hilda, that is how it should
be for Christians, too, that is what was intended, only it didn't work out. Now
we can see that the Druze have managed it. They accept the external, changing
laws of the world but live in accordance with their own inner, immutable laws."

They believe God has been incarnated in the world seven times: in
Adam, Noah, Abraham, Moses, Jesus, Mohammed, and their sacred fatimid
Sheikh al-Hakim. They preached their doctrine until the 11th century, but
then there occurred the "Closing of the Gate," and since then you cannot

become a Druze. They call themselves *muwahiddun*. You can only be born a Druze. It is truly a closed religion. You can leave it but you cannot enter it. There is no proselytizing. The gate is closed.

Then the *uqqal* arrived, their elder and teacher. He was very old and courteous, and they sat and ate plov.

They don't drink wine, only water and juice. At the end, when Daniel said he wanted to restore the church on the mountain but there was no water there, the elder said there was water. In the old days there was a spring. It had dried up but could be found again. He also said that if the spring did not run again, they would donate their own water. The land there is not Druze. It is Arab, but the Arab village which was there until 1948 has all gone. The ruins are very old. It was the Crusaders who built the first Christian church there. The uqqal said the Druze came from Egypt and the village was already in existence at that time. They had seen the church being built. Daniel has doubts about that but says it is quite likely they did come from Egypt, only much later than the Jews. I found the way he spoke amusing, as if he had been there and seen it all himself.

"Build," the Druze elder said. "We are the enemies of nobody, neither Jews nor Christians nor Muslims, but we are citizens of this country and we will defend it."

That's the kind of people they are, Mother. The elder's name is Kerim. In a few days' time Daniel will introduce me to the Druze builder who is going to help us restore the church. Like the Arabs, they are good builders. I am to be in charge of the building work! Can you imagine it? I have to prepare the project, draw up the estimates, find the money, and hire the workers. Please tell that to my stepfather and let me know how he reacts!

Love,

Hilda

2. 1961, Kfar Tavor
LETTER FROM GRAŻYNA TO WIKTORIA

Dear Wiktoria,

I was so pleased to get your letter! My dear schoolfriend. We shared a desk for four years. The happiest memories of my childhood are associated with you. Do you remember the play we put on in primary school? And running away from home and getting lost? And my little brother was in love with you. I was sure your family had been lost in Russia. What a joy that you survived and have returned. I am so glad you have sought me out, so glad you have obtained an apartment after so many years of privation. How I would love to see you! I can only imagine what you must have been through when you were exiled to Russia. Was that at the end of 1944 or already in 1945? We lived in Kielce until the end of 1951.

It is more than 10 years since we emigrated to Israel. It sometimes seems a very long time ago and our old life seems like the distant past. In all those years I have only been back to Poland once, when Mother died. You can imagine what that journey was like, just sorrows and regrets. Mother never did forgive me for marrying Metek. It still upsets me deeply. I sometimes dream that I and my brother are staying with our grandmother in Zakopane. I remember going to Kraków once on a school trip, but I try not to remember Kielce. It is just too painful.

Of course I passed Metek your invitation to come and stay, but he said, "Never, Grażyna. I will never go back there. Go on your own if you want to."

His attitude to Poland is complicated. Culturally he is a Pole. He knows Polish poetry by heart and he worships Chopin, but he cannot forgive the Poles for the pogrom in Kielce. He says the 6 million Jews who died during the war were a cosmic catastrophe, something caused by a misalignment of the planets, but those 42 Jews who were killed after the war, in July 1946 in Kielce, are a stain on the conscience of the Poles. Did you hear about the murders or did it not reach you in Russia?

They say the pogrom was organized by the KGB, Polish or Soviet makes no difference. The police and the army were implicated. What difference does it make? The murders were committed by Poles, all just as in the Middle Ages. Once again a rumor was spread that a Christian child had been abducted—blood, matzah, the "Jewish Easter."

It happened after nearly all the Jews of Kielce had died in the death camps and only a couple of hundred who had survived returned after the war. They were rehoused on Planty Street. There, in a large apartment block, the upper floors were occupied by Jewish Communists, Chekists, and everybody who welcomed the new authorities. Downstairs were ordinary people and it was on them that the pogrom was unleashed. Metek was not in the town. He was in Warsaw for two days for an audition. I think he had been invited to join an orchestra.

The pogrom began with people breaking into the lower stories of the house. First they looked for the abducted child, and then for gold. What gold? Everybody was penniless. They found nothing and started murdering.

Metek's entire family died in the camps, only his younger sister Riwka survived. When he returned from Warsaw she too was dead. The victims lay in a shed near the station and he was called to identify her.

She was buried and Metek said to me, "Grażyna, I can't stay here. Let's go to Palestine." I agreed, Wiktoria. He is my husband, Andrzej had already been born, and I did not want my son to grow up in fear.

For five years Metek tried to get permission to emigrate. We could not understand why everybody was being allowed out except him, but then Metek guessed it was because he was from Kielce and had been in that shed. The authorities were trying to conceal the truth about the postwar pogroms and Metek was a witness. There were pogroms in Kraków and Rzeszów, too, and Metek later met Kraków Jews who had not been allowed out either. In 1951 permission was finally granted and we emigrated.

I can't say I find life easy in Israel, but in Poland my heart was shredded by sympathy for my husband. The only thing that justifies the move is that the children are very happy here.

Metek has a difficult personality and has been through so much that his constant depression is readily understandable. I can say to you, dear Wiktoria, that we are a good married couple and bring meaning to each other's lives. We love our children very much, of course. Metek is particularly attached to our daughter and I, I suppose, am closer to our son, but the two of us are like a single entity. It is only thanks to our love that we have managed to survive, both in the war and now. Life here is very, very difficult.

Sweet Wiktoria, send me your photograph. I am sending you ours so that we will recognize each other if God grants that we should meet. One day, perhaps?

I'm so glad you have reappeared in my life. I hope that this time we will not lose each other again.

Love,
Your Grażyna

March 1965, Kfar Tavor
LETTER FROM GRAŻYNA TO WIKTORIA

Hi, Wiktoria!
I've been back home for two weeks now and just can't collect my wits. Before the trip I still thought I might be able to change my life and go back to Poland, but I see now that's impossible.

After Metek's death, when I realized that now I could leave Israel, all that held me back was Hanna. Metek adored her. He was never so close to Andrzej. Andrzej was alienated, and now we will never know why he was so chilly toward his father. Andrzej was my favorite, while Hanna was and remains to this day her Daddy's girl. She has been miserable the whole year since he died. She is at a difficult age and is such a mixture of brashness and vulnerability. How could I leave her alone?

Now that Andrzej has been killed they won't take her into the army. There is a rule that if only one child is left it is not called up. She dreams every night of joining the army, and goads me by saying she will join the paratroops. She is musical like Metek, has a good figure like I had when I was young, and she is pretty. I don't know where she gets that from. Metek and I were never very good looking. After Andrzej was killed and Metek died I would have gone straight back to Poland, but Hanna adores Israel. All the young people here adore their country. She will never emigrate. Anyway, what is Poland to her? And what sort of a Catholic is she? I so wanted to keep her in our faith. All through her childhood I took her to church, and she came willingly. Later, though, she dropped it like a brick. She told me she wanted Giur, that is, to become a Jew. As the daughter of a Christian woman she was not considered a Jew under the laws here. She had to convert to Judaism.

"I have no interest in God at all. I just want to be like everybody else." That is what she tells me. She is a Jewish girl, an Israeli, and her dream is to get into the army as soon as possible and get a rifle in her hands. She used to come with me to see a Catholic priest here. He is from Poland, too. From the very outset he said a person should make a conscious choice, especially here in Israel. The fact that you baptized her means nothing until she has grown up. He told me to take her to church while she was little, but warned that in our difficult situation you have to have the patience to let someone make their own mind up. I can see now he was right. She doesn't go to church anymore. She has clearly left all that behind. She would never come back to Poland with me and now I have nobody other than her. She is 17. I used to think that when she grew up and married I would go back and live out my last years in my homeland, but when I saw Poland again after so many years, I realized that life would not be good for me there either.

Why have things turned out like this? There seems to be no place on earth where I can feel at home. I am very unhappy in Israel, but I was unhappy in Poland, too. Here so much gets me down: the noise, the over-expansiveness of everybody. The neighbors yell, people on the bus yell, my employer yells in the workshop. I hear Arab music incessantly and just want to turn off the sound. The sun is too bright here and I would like to turn it down a bit, too. I find the heat exhausting, and our house is unbearable in the summer. The heat makes me feel like my blood has congealed. Looking out the window I can see Mount Tabor, the place where the Transfiguration of Jesus occurred, but I would prefer to live in one of the new apartments in Kielce. The trouble is that now, having just come back from our dreary Kielce, I have to accept that I couldn't live there either. All I have left is two graves in the Holy Land.

I am very grateful to you, Wiktoria, for being so hospitable. You proved kinder than a sister to me, but that is not a basis on which to return to Poland. Everything there is so gray and colorless, and the people are just too dour.

It was a year yesterday since Metek died, two days before his 50th birthday. Andzrej was killed two days before he would have been 20. Yesterday our neighbors and Metek's colleagues from the College of Music came and brought food and vodka. They said such good things about him. To start with, Hanna laughed to the point of indecency, and then sobbed. She has really quite a hysterical personality. Andrzej was just the opposite. So calm and serene. I realized yesterday what a happy family we were four years ago. I can't bear it. I can't pray. I have a stone where my heart should be. Hanna at least cries, but I have no tears.

Wiktoria, my dear, all sorts of dark thoughts come into my mind. I long to fall asleep and never wake up. Waking is dreadful. I am fine while I'm asleep. There are no dreams, there is no me, and that's so good, when you leave yourself and your thoughts behind. When I first wake up I'm like a baby, everything has been washed and smoothed away, but then comes the blow. The two military men, a colonel and a sergeant, arrive and inform me of Andrzej's death and everything breaks inside me all over again. Within a minute the whole reel has been run through, right up to the funeral with the sealed coffin. There is such a gaping hole in my heart.

No less unexpectedly, the director of the College of Music came to see me at the workshop, and the elderly lady who taught piano, Elisheva Zak. Here in Israel there is an accepted way of notifying someone of a death. They rarely just telephone, they come to see you. Every morning I relive the death of my boy and my husband. I am 46, in good health. The way it was for Metek, his heart stopping and his life being over, is not how it is going to be for me. I have another 40 or even 50 years ahead of me, waking up like that every morning, then dragging myself to the workshop and the sewing machine to stitch curtains, curtains, and more curtains. I need those curtains. I get a generous pension for the loss of my son, but if I wasn't stitching I would hang myself. I wouldn't even notice. I would do it without hesitation, without having to decide or prepare. It's only too easy.

How bizarre and absurd life is. Thinking back, I can see now that my best years were the years of the occupation when I ran every night to the cellar of the bombed-out house next door along a secret path and through a narrow opening only I could jump through. And I really did have to jump because three treads were missing. I had to jump down into the darkness, into Metek's arms. We would light a little candle because Metek did not like to hold me in the dark. He wanted to see my beauty. Oh, Wiktoria, all around was death, killing and more killing, but we felt as if we were in paradise, a paradise which lasted one and a half years. One thing Metek didn't know, and I never told him, was that our neighbor Moczulski had been spying as I went in the night to Metek, and blackmailed me. What did I have? I had nothing except what women have under their skirts. He was old, and repulsive, and a villain, but he would call and I would go to him. He didn't need me often, he wasn't that virile. Afterwards I would just give myself a shake and go to Metek to cleanse myself of the vileness. Well, the Lord gave Moczulski his just desserts. He ended up in the labor camps in Russia after the war, somebody else denounced him, and gangsters in the camp cut his throat in 1947 or so.

Metek loved me and music, and of course he loved our children. That was his whole world, and I was at the center of it. It was because of me that he didn't pursue a musical career. He was offered a place in the Boston Symphony Orchestra in 1951 but I said there was no way I would go to America, so we went to Israel instead. That's fate for you! He always did what I wanted. He said, "You took out so many chamber pots of my shit that you deserve a statue of pure gold." Well, now I have my monument—two graves. Dearest Wiktoria, I really don't want to go on living.

I'm writing all this in such detail because I want you to understand, and not be angry or offended that I have decided finally not to return to Poland. Please give my best wishes to Irenka and Wiączek and all or friends when you see them. May God be with you.

Your friend Grażyna

3. April 1965, Haifa

LETTER FROM DANIEL STEIN TO WŁADYSŁAW KLECH

What inexpressible sorrow, my dear Brother. *Sic transit* everything on this earth. I am deeply despondent and dismayed. I usually don't have time for moods. A busy man can't afford to have them, but the last few days have been filled with dismay and grief. I have buried one of my parishioners who committed suicide. I had known her since my first days in Haifa, a quiet Polish woman, more a village than a town person, but very likeable; one of those early risers who are kindly and cheerful in the morning but by evening have wearied and closed up like a flower. I am a great connoisseur of women, uniquely so for a monk. I see you smile wryly, dear Władek. My vows have probably saved the world from a great Casanova, because I like women very much. It is indeed fortunate that I am unmarried as I would cause my wife great anxiety by ogling other women. I find almost all of them attractive, but Grażyna, of whom I am writing, was truly delightful. She looked like a vixen, with her russet coloring, her pointed chin, and sharp teeth like a little animal.

The war did dreadful things to people. Even if they survived physically, it crippled their souls. Some became cruel, some cowardly, some barricaded themselves behind a stone wall from God and the world. Grażyna and her husband went through a great deal. She hid him in a cellar for a year and a half, endured no end of terror, and gave birth to her elder child before the liberation. She suffered a terrible rupture with her family because of the baby, and then they got married. He was a brooding, artistic man, a not entirely successful violinist. Their firstborn, whom I knew very little because he was killed in the year I came here, died on the last day of his service as a conscript. His vehicle was blown up by a mine on the road he was traveling back to Jerusalem from where his unit was deployed. At that very moment Grażyna was preparing his welcome home party, but her son did not make it home. A few years later, Metek unexpectedly died of heart failure and she became totally withdrawn. I spoke to Grażyna several times during those years and her conversation was invariably polite but completely without substance. I could see only that the threads which bind a person to life had been greatly weakened.

I know even more about death than I do about women, and again it is through the war. There is nothing more vile and unnatural in this world than war. How it perverts not only life but even death. Death in war is bloody, full of animal fear, always violent, and what I was obliged to witness—mass murder, the execution of Jews and partisans—was fatally destructive also for those carrying out the atrocities. People know very little about those who did the killing, but I was intimately familiar with them. I lived under the same roof as one of them, a Belorussian called Semyonovich, and I saw him drinking himself to oblivion and the terrible way he suffered. His sufferings were not just physical or moral, but an inextricable combination of the two. They were the torments of hell.

When I became a priest in a Polish parish I saw another side of death with the old village women dying after the war. I would be called to administer the Viaticum and there were times when I clearly saw whose hands I was committing them to. They were met by the Powers of Heaven, and departed with happy faces. Not always, but several times I witnessed that and so I know how death should be in a world which has not been perverted.

But suicide, Władek, suicide! The soul itself repudiating its existence. Poor Grażyna! Extroverted people rarely resort to this act. They are able to find a way of projecting their suffering outward, sharing it with somebody, distancing themselves from it. She saved her husband's life but found herself incapable of living after he was gone. They went everywhere together. She never left the house without him. In the morning he would accompany her to the sewing business where she worked, and come in the evening to bring her home.

If he was teaching in the evening, she would wait at the workshop for an hour, for two hours, until he came to collect her. He always brought her to Mass, and waited patiently in the garden for the service to end. When I invited him to come in and join us at table after the service he would usually refuse, but sometimes he did come in. He would sit silently and never ate anything. He had an ascetic, very handsome Jewish face. They say he was a very good teacher, and small boys with tiny violins were brought from the surrounding towns to study with him.

Grażyna suffered silently for a year, then she arranged the wake, asked the local Jews to assemble the requisite minyan of ten Jewish men, and they read the Kaddish. A week later her daughter went off to the army, and the next day she took something and did not wake up.

I have not encountered suicide for many years now. In the partisan brigade and among the Jews in the ghetto it was not uncommon. People had been hounded into the darkest of corners and rejected the gift of life, preferring death to agonizing ordeals by hunger, fear, the torture and death of those they loved, and the dread of dying hideously at any moment. It was an attempt by desperate people to forestall what was coming. I remember being totally appalled when I heard of the suicide of Goebbels and his killing of his six children. He had no trust in God and believed that neither he nor his children were deserving of grace. He passed sentence and executed it himself.

But poor Grażyna! The one thing she needed was her husband's love and she knew of no other. Or had little knowledge of it. It never occurred to her how cruelly she was treating her daughter. Poor Hanna, first her brother, then her father, and now her mother. The army gave her three days' leave but she came back only for a few hours, to attend the funeral. She did not want to stay or go into the house. What a trauma that girl will live with now!

We buried Grażyna in the local Arab cemetery. It is a small Catholic cemetery belonging to our brothers on the outskirts of town. The Arabs allow me to conduct services in their church and I use the same altar as they do for Mass. We had a joint service on Holy Thursday, celebrating the Mass in Arabic and Hebrew, and on Friday she did not wake up.

It is difficult, dear Brother, for Christians to live in Israel, for many reasons. It is even more difficult for Arab Christians, who are mistrusted and hated by Jews, and even more by Arab Muslims. But how difficult it is to bury a Christian, especially one who is not a monk living in a monastery with its orchards, lands, and cemeteries; not an Arab either, who has settled here better than others; but somebody without roots, who is in Israel more or less at random, and who belongs neither to the clergy nor to officialdom.

There are so many tragedies here. Immigrants arrive with mixed families. They bring their aged mothers, who are often Catholic, or sometimes Orthodox. When these old people die, something unspeakable happens: there is nowhere to bury them. There are Jewish cemeteries where they bury only Jews; there are the cemeteries of Christian monasteries but these, too, refuse to bury outsiders because of lack of space. The unbelievable price of land means that a plot in a cemetery is beyond the means of poor people. Of course, those of us who come from Poland know only too well how many people the land can accommodate.

The Arab priest in charge of the church where we conduct our joint services occasionally allows me to bury someone in the cemetery there, and that is where we buried Grażyna. I ask you to pray for her, dear Brother Władek.

I have written you such an inchoate letter that it is only now as I reread it that I see how plaintive it is, not at all the letter of thanks I intended to write. I have indeed received three books from you and one of them has proved invaluable. I am grateful to you also for the total understanding that you express in your letter. I have to confess that in my difficult situation your support is extremely important to me.

Your Brother in Christ,

D.

4. *December 1965, Kraków*

FROM A LETTER FROM WŁADYSŁAW KLECH TO DANIEL STEIN

. . . Really, Daniel, you never cease to amaze me. Your letter is truly inchoate. I understand your grief, I feel sorry for the woman who died, but the Church long ago designated suicide a sin and you are indulging in emotions which can only devastate the soul and weaken faith.

All imaginable questions have long since been posed and answers received to them. It is our problem if we cannot read, and with our excessive cleverness find difficult and perplexing what our predecessors found as clear as God's day. Do you really think that all divisions and schisms are purely human? Is there not God's truth in them? Perhaps, to put it another way, what God has put asunder let no man seek to join?

No, I don't even want to hear about this trend in your thinking. If, as you suggest, we were to create a common liturgy for all Christians, what place are you to find for those Protestants who in their practice have totally rejected the Eucharist as we understand it? I do not know, I really do not know, dear Daniel. If anything of that sort is to come about, it will not be in our lifetime, and most likely only in the Kingdom of Heaven. It strikes me that life in Israel is well and truly addling your clear mind. You never used to come out with this sort of thing.

You have written to me more than once about how great the dissension is between Christians in the Holy Land, but what I would like to know is what relations are like with the Jews. If Christians cannot come to terms among themselves, how are they to talk to the Jews? To say nothing of the Muslims—another issue which is quite beyond resolution.

We have had very heavy frosts this year, and I had a beggar freeze to death beside the church. It is not you in warm countries who should be build-

ing shelters for the homeless but we here in the North. We ought to arrange
a transfer and send our beggars to you.

Your Brother in the Lord,

Wl.

5. *September 1966, Haifa*

FROM A LETTER FROM HILDA TO HER MOTHER

Don't be upset that I am not coming home this year, Mother. Ask yourself how could I go on holiday when I am responsible for all the building
work? You wouldn't believe how much we have managed to do over the past
year, despite the fact that we meet nothing but obstructiveness at every turn,
both from the Church authorities and the state. Our only help is from Germany. Also, one local Arab donated a truckload of stone to us. In Germany
it would cost an absolute fortune, but in Israel building materials are cheap.
In July a whole brigade of German students arrived. They worked on the
building site for two months, excavated the foundations for the church building, and began digging the foundations for the shelter. Nearly all the students
were from Frankfurt and they were really special. I never met anyone like
them in Germany. They have already tapped into the water from the Druze
village.

And what a beautiful church it is! We have restored the walls and hung
the doors. We have a roof! The only thing we don't have is windows. Daniel
says we don't need to insert window frames, and if we just make shutters to
keep bad weather out that will be enough. It's not a large space, he says. In
the summer it will be cooler without windows, and in the winter we will heat
it with our breath. Although the building is not yet complete, we are
already holding services in it. We have an altar and a porch where we can sit
in the shade. We found a blocked spring and restored it, not without help
from our Druze neighbors. So now we are called the Church of Elijah by
the Spring. Doesn't that sound good?

I was all for moving right now, but Daniel says he won't let me live here
on my own. While the students were staying we had a kind of open-air camp-
site. We didn't even put up a tent because it would have been very stuffy
inside it. We cooked on an open hearth and ate once a day, in the evening.
In the morning we just ate a very little—pancakes with honey and coffee.

Can you imagine it? I am keeping all the accounts, paying the roofers we
had to hire. We put on a tiled roof. It was expensive but we got help.

Brother Daniel spent very little time here so I took nearly all the decisions on my own. Even in the summer he has a lot of work, but the main crowds of tourists come in the autumn for the Jewish festivals. He conducts tours all over Israel. I was able to go along with him this summer, although not very far. Only to Zichron Yaakov. Do you remember the Rose of Sharon mentioned in the Bible? It originated in the Sharon Valley. There had been no cultivation there for 1,000 years. There were swamps everywhere, but then at the end of the 19th century, 10 Jewish families came from Bessarabia. They wanted to turn the region into orchards again but were getting nowhere until Baron Rothschild gave them money and sent experts. Then they made real progress and drained all the swamps. They started making the land workable again. Daniel showed us those vineyards and orchards. You can see the luxuriant plantations from Rothschild's grave, because he directed in his will that he should be buried here. What a fortunate man—how wisely he used his money! Swamps were turned into orchards and now fruit from those orchards is sent all over the world. There is a genetic laboratory there where they perform miracles. The most interesting thing, though, is that Daniel knows all this. He pointed out different cultivars to us and told us about the flowers. He knows exactly which plants have been here since biblical times and which are later introductions. In Zichron Yaakov there is even a small botanical garden with plants mentioned in the Bible. The only tree missing is the Cedar of Lebanon. For some reason it won't grow by itself. Now in order to grow a cedar they have to go to great lengths. Every tree has to be specially tended. Each one has a special passport, and yet in olden times there were forests of cedars and oaks here.

Can you imagine, there is a science of biblical palaeo-botany! Its scholars have recreated a picture of what grew here 2,000 to 3,000 years ago. As we were looking around the garden, the botanist himself came, Musa, a local Arab. He showed us a plant which didn't look anything special but which is like the bush out of which God spoke to Moses. The plant has a very high content of volatile oils and even, he said, if you carefully light a match, the oil will burn and there will be flames around the bush, but the bush itself will not be consumed. The burning bush!

Musa is from an old Arab family and was educated in England. They have a lot of land here and they used to own the plot where there is now a prison for Palestinians who are fighting the Jews in all sorts of illegal ways. It is called Damun Prison, but we did not go there because we were short of time. I did manage to see another amazing place, though, along with the rest of the group, out toward Shechem. It was there that Joseph's brothers were grazing cattle. At first he couldn't find them, and when he did they threw him into a dry well because they were angry about his interpretation of a dream. Daniel showed us just such a dry well, possibly the very one. Some 20 kilometers away there is another, and it was probably from one of these, within an area of about 20 kilometers, that he was dragged and sold to passing merchants. Not far away, a caravan route passed along a dried-up riverbed—a "wadi." So the whole story described first in the Bible and later by Thomas Mann quite literally took place here. The merchants bought Joseph as a slave. He cost far less than you would pay nowadays for a sheep, and they took him to Egypt. Such is the story, and in some places you can still see the caravan route. Right beside that dry well we came across two Arab boys grazing goats.

Musa said goats are the worst pests in the country: they ate all of Ancient Greece and Palestine. I listened to him with my ears flapping and realized that what I want most of all in the world is to go and study at Jerusalem University. Daniel says that it is perfectly possible. He had thought about it himself, but it would be difficult for him to do without me. You can't imagine how pleased I was to hear that. Now I am quickly finishing off this letter and will give it to a German girl who is going back to Germany and will drop it in a mailbox in Munich. I hope your health is all right and that you won't be cross with me for not coming back this holiday.

If everything gets organized as Daniel intends, I shall start studying at the University in January. I have absolutely no idea how I will get on, but I am very keen.

Best wishes to everybody at home,

Your Hilda

6. September 1966, Haifa

A NOTE HILDA FOUND THAT EVENING IN HER BAG

Hilda,

If you wouldn't mind my coming to your building site, please call me on 05-12-47 and just say you have no objection.

Musa

7. 1996, *Haifa*
FROM A CONVERSATION BETWEEN HILDA AND EWA MANUKYAN

No, it doesn't surprise me at all that three days talking to Daniel caused your life to change direction. After all, I myself only survived thanks to him. For many years he tended me like a goat. The story began thirty years back and came to an end long ago. I sometimes feel it was not my life at all but something out of a cheap novel.

In autumn 1966 I found a note in my bag from Musa, I phoned him and he came. I knew his family was very rich and I hoped this meant he wanted to make a donation toward the building work.

I was twenty, and for my age I was exceptionally silly in feminine terms. When a man looked at me I was afraid there was something wrong with my appearance, a stain on my blouse perhaps, or a torn stocking. I always had a very low opinion of myself, and my stepbrothers called me a plank.

As a child I was very self-conscious about being so tall. I wanted to be short and chubby and have a well-filled brassière, but there was absolutely nothing for me to put a brassière on. I was only fit to be trained up for some kind of sport, skiing or racing, something where you need long legs. Unfortunately, I hated races and my lack of competitiveness was instantly detected by every coach whose path I crossed. The sport was my stepfather's idea. He was a great sports fan, but anything he suggested I automatically disliked. In those years my mother did not take much interest in me because my younger brother, Axel, was sickly and she was constantly fussing over him. Too much height and too little love was how I diagnosed myself many years later.

After I had moved to Israel my mother had an operation for cancer and our relations got better. It's probably no exaggeration to say they only really began after she became ill. I know much more about her now than I did when I was young and have come to understand her better. Although I only go back to Munich to visit her every two or three years, we correspond constantly and are very close. She has come out here several times in spite of her ill-health. When I was young, though, we were distant and I was a very lonely girl.

When I met Daniel, I stopped being unhappy, because he spread happiness around himself. From the moment I saw him, I knew I wanted to be by his side. He was a father figure for me, of course, and well aware of it. For many people he was a substitute father, or elder brother, a replacement for a child which had died, or even a husband. Half the women parishioners were secretly in love with him. Some made no secret of it. One crazy woman pursued him with her love for a good eight years until he managed to find her a husband.

But I want to tell you about Musa. He came to the building site and I was pleased, expecting a donation, but he brought marvelous Arab sweets. A few days later he came again and helped the workers to drive piles into the ground. The students had left by then. For a month there was no sign of him but then he arrived with a small digger. By evening they had finished digging out the foundations for the staff premises and he paid for the work. I hardly spoke to him. We exchanged only a few words at supper before he left. I thought he was very handsome and admired his hands. Europeans don't have hands like his. All Arabs, both women and men, have perfectly shaped hands and they are extraordinarily refined. It's probably because their bodies are so enveloped in clothing and this is the only part of a woman she doesn't have to keep under a covering, so her hands try to stand in for everything else. Men's faces are not particularly visible either. There is all that vegetation, the keffiyeh covering their heads, so that only their nose sticks out, like Arafat's. Arabs do not show their bodies. I was working there in shorts and a sleeveless T-shirt, and Musa did not look my way because it "hurt his eyes," as he told me later. He was consumed by passion and I was completely unaware of it. He was in despair because he thought I did not consider him a man. He was almost right, except that it was myself I did not consider a woman.

One time he said he had planned an orchard which he would plant when the building work was complete, and told me what kind of trees would grow there. He had a sheet of paper in front of him and drew on it with a blue felt tip pen. He left the paper when he went away, and I put it in a folder.

We met for almost a year and I liked him very much, the way you delight in something beautiful: an antique bronze, a picture, or the binding of an old book. He was all gold and brown like the shell of a nut in the forest, but his body was not hard, it was soft and firm, and he could weep for love. These things I learned later. I'm sure I would never have known anything if I had not been bitten by a snake in the springtime. We were sitting under the awning next to our almost completed building and drinking tea he had made. It was the place where we always spent the hottest hours of the day, when it was impossible to work. The ground was flat and well trodden there, so why nobody noticed that a snake had glided in is puzzling. I took a cup of tea

from Musa and settled down comfortably, leaning on my left hand. I felt a
slight prick in my forearm and fleetingly glimpsed a length of dark cord out
of the corner of my eye. Before I knew what had happened, Musa had already
wound a towel into a tourniquet and bound my arm tightly above the bite.

"A viper. It was a viper," he said. I knew that in the spring Israeli vipers
are very active. Musa fell upon my arm and seemed to bite me hard. He spat
out. The snake bite was so small I couldn't even see it. He took me in his
arms and carried me down to the car.

"I can walk! I'm fine!" I shouted, but he said I needed to move as little
as possible until they injected the serum. He laid me down on the back seat
and drove me to hospital. My arm was very sore where he had bitten it.

At the hospital I was immediately given an injection and told to lie down
for an hour. There was reddening around the wound and bruising caused by
Musa's teeth. The doctor said that if there was no reaction after an hour,
Musa must have succeeded in sucking all the poison out. It was very rare to
manage that so speedily.

I was laid on a couch and Musa waited for me out in the corridor. Then
he came in and said he had almost died of worry. He started crying but I
didn't, because I realized he loved me, and that was even more of a surprise
than the snakebite.

After that everything happened very quickly. We had after all been getting ready for this for a whole year. Well, perhaps not exactly, but all year I
had been bathing in his lovelorn gaze, and I even got rid of my pimples. In
the past I sometimes got small pimples on my chin and forehead, but now my
skin looked as if I had been grooming and pampering it in a beauty salon. I
rented a little flat in the Middle Town from Arabs. There was one room the
size of a large divan and a small kitchen. Musa lived in the Upper Town, in
a large house with an orchard. The day came when he did not return home.

No, it is not at all what you are thinking. He knew nothing about me,
but intuited everything. He was an emotional genius. He approached me so
cautiously, as if I were a spirit or a mirage. I was a wild animal with its femininity completely suppressed. I suspect I am one of those women who find
it easy to live out their lives as a virgin. Very gradually I learned to respond
to him. It took almost a year before my body could do that, but during that
year it was as if a different, quite separate creature was growing inside me.

Then there came the Six-Day War. Everybody was euphoric. East
Jerusalem was occupied, part of the Judaean Desert, Sinai, Samaria, the
Golan Heights. It seemed as if the only two people with misgivings were

Daniel and Musa. Daniel said this was a hostage to fortune and that seizing territory did not resolve the issue but complicated it. Musa, who as an Arab was not taken into the army, said the consequences were unforeseeable.

I remember them talking one morning and Daniel said the Six-Day War was like a chapter in the Bible. Victory had come at the wave of a hand. "And defeat with a wave of the other hand?" Musa asked quickly. I was suddenly afraid.

Outwardly, little changed. I worked from morning till night. We were organizing a kind of crèche at the church. Most of our women were unable to take jobs. There were few crèches, and it was difficult and expensive to transport children. We did have a group for working mothers, and one or two of them would take turns to look after the children. Usually there was a lactating mother. I remember one, Veronica, fed half the children in the community with her breasts. This was the time when we finished building the Church of Elijah by the Spring. The Druze had found the spring for us, but it was such a trickle that it could have provided only enough water for the birds to drink.

We became a real community, even slightly communistic. There were always people with nowhere to go living in the church shelter. Sometimes they were completely random people who were homeless, and a number of drug addicts attached themselves to us. One managed to cure himself of drug taking, pulled himself up, and even finished his studies. Daniel and I bought food and there were charitable aid packages. We boiled, fed, washed dishes, and prayed. He conducted the liturgy, a large part of which was in Hebrew. Musa often came to help. Sometimes he invited me to go on an outing, showing me beautiful places. Whenever he did, I would ask Daniel whether I could take the time off. He would be cross and say, "Why are you asking me? You are a responsible adult. You know Musa is married. If you cannot go, it's better for you not to."

Of course I knew that Musa was married, but I also knew he had been married when he was still just a boy of seventeen. His wife was older. She was related to him on his mother's side and there were some family considerations which obliged him to marry her. Of course, nobody asked his opinion. By now he had three children.

Twenty-one years passed from the day he slipped that note into my bag until the day he died. Twenty-one years of suffering, happiness, breaking up, reconciliation, ceaseless pangs of conscience, shame, and a union as heavenly as anyone could imagine.

At the very beginning I went, confused, to talk to Daniel and for a long time couldn't say anything. Then I said just one word, "Sin." He was silent, then took the clasp from my hair. It fell about me. He stroked my head and said, "What beautiful hair you have, and your forehead, your eyes and nose . . . You were created to be loved. The sin is with the other person. It is he who took the vow, but I can understand him, too, Hilda. In love, women are almost always the victims. Women suffer more from love, but perhaps, too, they gain more. There is no escaping life. It takes what is its due. Do not be hard on yourself. Endure. Try to protect yourself." I hardly understood what he was saying. It was astonishing the way people would come to him with banal problems, but he never gave them banal answers.

Musa and I tried to split up many times but we just couldn't do it. Like two drops of mercury we were constantly coalescing. Such was the chemistry of our love, or passion. I remember one other time when I had split up with Musa, I went to Daniel with my mind made up. I would go to a nunnery! I thought that behind the walls of a convent I would be able to hide from illicit love.

Daniel produced beautiful Italian sweets, chocolate-covered cherries somebody had brought him, and he put on the kettle. He infused tea very well, with great concentration, sometimes in the Chinese, sometimes in the Russian manner. He rinsed the teapot with boiling water and covered it with a towel. Later he poured it into the teacups. We were up there on the mountain at the Church of Elijah late one evening. I was waiting to know what he would say, because my desire to go into a nunnery was immense, almost as great as my love.

"My child, it seems to me you want to go to a nunnery to run away from love. That is not a correct decision. You should enter a nunnery because you love God, not because of your love for a man. You should not deceive yourself. It would only make matters worse. When you recover from your love, we will talk about this again." I kept on and on, "I want to go to a nunnery! I want to go to a nunnery!" At that he got really angry. I don't think I had ever seen him so angry.

"What do you want to bring to God? Your amorous sufferings? Is that what you want to bring him? What will you do there? Perhaps you are a great prayerful saint? Perhaps with your prayers you will preserve the world like the thirty-six Jewish righteous men? Or can you meditate? Perhaps you are St. Francis de Sales or St. Teresa of Ávila? Perhaps you want that samovar gold halo to gleam above your head which they paint on Eastern icons? Don't talk rubbish! We have so much to do. Work here!"

I still could not hear what he was telling me. I was even inwardly rather indignant. I suppose I had been half-expecting him to praise me and bless me, to be touched by my resoluteness, but he was angry. His hand flew up and a cup fell from the table and smashed.

"If you cannot change anything, endure. This can't go on forever. One of the three people always gives in. You should give in, you should remove yourself, but if you can't, then wait. Do not try to bind yourself with vows. Monasticism is a hard path which few can bear. I, for one, cannot bear it. It is so hard for me to be a monk. Throughout my life I have been in anguish, without children, without a family, without a woman. But my life was given back to me so many times that it no longer belonged to me and I brought it as an offering, because it really no longer belonged to me. Understand, I do not regret having taken the monastic vows. I affirmed them and with God's help I shall live as a monk to the end of my days, but I would never, never do you hear, bless anyone on their way to this path. If you want to serve God, serve Him in the world. There are plenty of people here who need your service."

Once more Musa and I found ourselves on the crest of some wave of love and ran away to Cyprus. We lived there for four months. He wanted us to get married. I was so troubled and longed to die just to get all this over with. That was when Daniel told me, "It is time to stop, otherwise somebody will die." I wanted it to be me. I even prayed that it should happen of its own accord. I did not consider suicide, it was too simple a solution and I knew that for Daniel that would be a terrible blow. He felt responsible for me.

At the height of all this passion a telegram arrived in Cyprus from Musa's father to tell him that David, his middle son, had been knocked down by a car. He was fifteen then. We got on the ferry and returned to Haifa. The boy underwent a four-hour operation but did not regain consciousness. He was in a coma. Daniel and I prayed in the church for two days without a break.

I vowed at that time that there would never again be anything between me and Musa, and at that same hour he, quite independently, made the same vow. There was no collusion. We both recognized that we had to give this up. The boy recovered.

From that time, Musa and I saw each other only occasionally in church. We stood side by side and prayed together but said not a word to each other.

In 1987, when the first Intifada began, the Muslims murdered Musa's entire family. His uncle owned a small restaurant by the bus station. It was a busy spot and all sorts of people would come together there because they liked his courtesy and conscientiousness. They were celebrating the birthday of Musa's father. The whole family had gathered in the restaurant when Muslims burst in and killed everyone. They were terrorists. They wanted to use the café as a meeting place but the uncle had turned them down. Then they ordered him to sell them the café. They said they would pay money but the uncle had to get out. He refused, so they took their revenge. Four men, two women, and three children were murdered. Musa's son David was in England at that time and had been unable to get back for his grandfather's birthday. A great deal was written about the tragedy at the time.

But you know, Ewa, nobody said a word about what was the most important aspect of this atrocity. The situation of Arab Christians in Israel is far worse than that of the Jews themselves. The Jews live on an island in a sea of Arab hostility, but the Arab Christians are under suspicion from both sides. Daniel saw that better than anyone here. He had an extraordinary sense of humor. He once told me that a lack of magnanimity on the part of an elderly woman called Sarah and her unreasonable jealousy led to a family conflict which assumed the proportions of a global catastrophe. If she had had a big enough heart to love Ishmael, the elder brother would not have become the sworn enemy of the younger Isaac. I talked to Musa a lot about that. I have kept only three letters from him, one of which is devoted to his experience of what he called "being an Arab." He didn't study only botany at university. He was well versed also in philosophy and psychology but abandoned them in order to dedicate himself to what gave him most joy, plants. He came from a good family. His ancestors planted orchards for all the rulers of the East, and the Persian Gardens of the Baha'i Temple in Haifa were designed by his grandfather.

In the last years of his life, Daniel used to call me "daughter." How about you, Ewa?

8. December 1966, Haifa

RECORDING OF A TALK BY BROTHER DANIEL AT THE CHURCH OF ELIJAH BY THE SPRING

Eldar has made a marvelous table at which a multitude of people can sit. Our thanks to you, Eldar. Put the plates in the bowl, we can wash them later, but don't put the glasses away. Somebody is bound to want to drink. Yes. It is far better now, the table is excellent. Hilda will make us tea and Musa will make coffee. He does that better than anyone else. And a cup for me, okay?

Last week I was guiding pilgrims in Jerusalem and happened on a cemetery near the Old Town where they are conducting archaeological excavations. We were shown some very interesting burials of the second century
where Jews and Christians were buried together, all members of one family.
It was a time of coexistence for Jewish Christianity and Judaism, when everybody prayed together in the synagogues and there was no conflict between
them. Of course, Jews who were the disciples and followers of Christ did not
yet call themselves Christians. Of course, early Christianity was intimately
connected with the Jewish milieu of that time, if only because that was the
milieu from which Jesus himself came. Jesus's mother was the Jewess
Miriam. He spoke the Ancient Hebrew and Aramaic tongues. When he was
eight days old, the rite of circumcision was performed upon him. Jesus, as we
know from the texts of the New Testament, observed the Sabbath and
attended the Temple. As modern specialists in Jewish letters of that time
have shown, he expressed his teachings in the same language and used the
same examples as the rabbis of that time.

In the first century, many participants and witnesses of events were still
alive, the closest relatives of Jesus were alive, as was Miriam herself. After the
death and resurrection of the Master, the Apostles Peter, James, and John
chose James as their bishop, the brother of Jesus, and he led the Jerusalem
community. For the Apostles the resurrection of Jesus was the eschatological
event which had been foretold by the prophets of Israel. That is why Christ's
disciples called on all Jews to acknowledge that they were the true Israel,
the community of the New Testament. Here, however, they came up against
the stubborn, unrelenting hostility of official Judaism. The apostles then
formed a special group which existed within Judaism, alongside other Jewish
sects, but remained true to the provisions of the Law and the divine service
of the Temple.

In the year forty-nine, the Council of Jerusalem legitimated the practice
that Gentiles who had converted to Christianity, "Gentile Christians," need
observe only the commandments given to Noah, which were seven in number. They were not obliged to undergo the ritual of circumcision or the other
provisions of Judaic law. The Apostle Paul considered that Jewish Christians
themselves were not obliged to adhere to the ancient rules, for example, they
need not observe the prohibition on eating with Gentiles, or at the same
table as Christians who had not been circumcised. Many Jewish Christians
objected to his ruling.

This was the reason behind a dispute which arose at Antioch in that same year of AD forty-nine. In the view of St. Paul, circumcision, observing the Sabbath, and attending divine service in the Temple were no longer required even of Jews, and Christianity was set free from the Judaic religio-political milieu to go out and embrace other peoples. Do you remember St. Peter's vision on the roof of the house of Simon the Tanner in Jaffa? From the heavens a sheet was lowered containing animals considered unclean by the Jews, and this spectacle was accompanied by a loud voice crying, "What God hath cleansed, that call not thou common!"

This was the moment when a parting of the ways began. The Church in Jerusalem did not break with Judaism, but the teaching of St. Paul led toward a schism which occurred after his death.

Hilda, my dear, the kettle is on the edge of the hob and likely to tip over. It's full of boiling water and there is nobody among us who could instantly heal you.

The schism deepened when the Romans destroyed the Temple in Jerusalem in AD seventy, and after the defeat of the bar Kokhba uprising in AD one hundred forty or so, the split became final. Before that Jewish Christians lived in Pella and other trans-Jordanian towns, but now Palestine became hellenized, and Jewish Christians began to leave the Middle East. After the second century AD, Jewish Christianity had died out in the East— in Palestine, Arabia, Jordan, Syria, and Mesopotamia. The last remaining Jewish Christian communities were swallowed up five centuries later by Islam. In modern Christianity we find only occasional "archaeological" remains in the liturgy of the Ethiopian and Chaldean Churches.

Thank you, Musa, your coffee is without compare.

A lot of books have been written on this subject and I won't trouble you with more detail. The most remarkable thing is that the earliest Jewish Christian literary works are very little different from the midrashim, a particular genre of interpretations of text which the rabbis of that time compiled. The Judaic tradition is still there to be seen in the works of such church writers as Barnabas, Justin, Clement of Alexandria, and Irenaeus.

The period of coexistence of Jewish and Greek Christianity ended in the fourth century when the non-Jewish Christian Church became powerful. It assumed a Graeco-Roman form and became the religion of an empire. There is no place in the contemporary Church for the Jewish Church. Christianity as it exists in modern times is Greek Christianity and it repudiated the Jewish influences. The Jewish tradition with its emphasis on strict monotheism is more evident in Islam, which is a kind of interpretation of the Jewish Christian religion. It is the Jewish Christian Church which provides opportunities for a future three-way dialogue between Judaism, Islam, and Christianity.

The Church needs to restore its initial pluralism. Among the world's many Christian churches, which speak different languages, there should be a place for the Jewish Christian Church. We should go back to the point at which the old division occurred and see what can be put right. Historical Christianity has committed numerous errors. They cannot now be corrected, of course, but understanding what they were and what caused them is something we can do. This new understanding could yield good fruit—reconciliation and love. Christianity is deprived of its universality because of the absence of the Jews. The loss of the Jews is a wound in Christianity which has never healed. The Greek Byzantine component largely distorted the essence of primal Christianity. I would like to return to the source, together with you.

9. *December 1966*
MEMORANDUM TO THE JERUSALEM PATRIARCHATE

To Monsignor Mattan Avat
From Brother Elijah
On 11 December 1966, Brother Daniel Stein gave a talk to his community in the recently restored Church of St. Elijah by the Spring. I am placing at your disposal a tape recording of what he said.
Brother Elijah

10. *June 1967, Haifa*
FROM A LETTER FROM HILDA TO HER MOTHER

. . . Daniel had a fever, but I know he can't bear staying in bed when he is ill. I bought him a lot of medicine and climbed up to the Stella Maris because transportation is unreliable as a consequence of this war. I thought that rather than wait an hour and a half for the bus, it would be better to walk. It would still only take an hour and a half. Would you believe it, when I climbed the mountain, got to the gatekeeper, and handed him the basket of medicine for Daniel, I was told he had gone off early in the morning and wouldn't be back until evening. I returned to Haifa and had almost reached the town when I saw Daniel whizzing along the road perched on a Vespa motor scooter, his soutane billowing in the wind, with a skinny Hassid being bounced up and down on the pillion. With one hand he was holding on to his broad-brimmed black hat and with the other to Daniel. It was unbelievably funny and the whole street was in stitches. Next day the war came to an end and I cannot describe the scenes here.

There was such joy, such jubilation. They immediately called it the Six-Day War. And then, in the midst of the general rejoicing, Daniel arrived looking out of sorts, sat down, and said, "Happy victory day! This war will figure in every military textbook from now until the end of time. The Arabs will never forgive us for humiliating them like this." Musa, who had also dropped by, disagreed. "Daniel," he said, "I know the Arabs better. They will find a way of interpreting their defeat as a great victory. They will not allow the rest of the world to laugh at them."

Daniel nodded. He really likes Musa. They understand each other at some deep level. He said, "Of course, Musa. Only someone with inner freedom can laugh at himself, and allow others to laugh at him."

I remembered the side-splitting spectacle of the Hassid on the back of his scooter and said, "Very true. The day before yesterday all of Haifa was laughing at you when you gave that Hassid a lift!" "What, did you see it?" Daniel asked in alarm.

"Of course," I said, "and it wasn't just me. The whole town was laughing itself silly!"

He seemed a bit disconcerted, and started giving explanations. "He was late for Kaddish, you see, and there wasn't a bus or taxi to be had. I saw the rush he was in and stopped and offered him a lift. He got on. It was nothing special. I took him where he needed to go, he said 'Thank you,' and that was that. What's so funny about it?"

Musa clutched his stomach laughing. Daniel was still puzzled. "I was going in that direction anyway!"

"It was because you are both Jews, but Jews will never be going in the same direction as Arabs. I'm telling you that as an Arab. We Arab Christians have no escape, both because of your victories and because of your defeats."

We had a coffee and before leaving, Daniel said, "Hilda, don't go telling everyone I gave a lift to a Hassid."

"Daniel, I promise not to say a word to a soul, but the whole of Haifa saw it!"

"Well, perhaps it wasn't me but some other priest."

There isn't another priest like him.

11. 1967, Jerusalem

HILDA'S NOTES FROM A PREEXAMINATION TUTORIAL WITH
PROFESSOR NEUHAUS

NOTE IN MARGIN: Discuss with Daniel!

1. The Second Temple Period ends in Year 70. The Temple was destroyed and Temple sacrifices ceased. The Period of Synagogal Worship began. Jews are believed to have come to the Temple while it existed three times a year, for Sukkot, Pesach, and Shavuot.

NOTE IN MARGIN: The latter correspond to the Christian Easter and Whitsun. Need to ask about Sukkot.

It is difficult to believe that peasants from Galilee undertook such pilgrimages three times a year. In those times the journey one way took a week and the festivals lasted a further week. Could a peasant leave his farm for three weeks? In the synoptic gospels, Christ is said to have visited Jerusalem for a festival only once during his boyhood.

A more convincing hypothesis is that every Judaean undertook such a pilgrimage once in several years. Shmuel Safrai, a modern scholar, considers that in the early first century, even before the destruction of the Second Temple, there existed synagogues, assemblies of Jews to read the Torah and pray together on the Sabbath. It was at such assemblies that Christ healed the sick.

Although Jewish researchers do not usually use Christian sources, it is interesting in this case to see what the New Testament says. There are numerous references to synagogues in the text of the New Testament. Possibly these were the private houses of rich people who made room available to their neighbors and fellow villagers for communal prayers and the reading of scripture.

I believe the ruins of the synagogue at Capernaum, a Christian holy place still extant, are wrongly dated, but we shall leave that on the conscience of modern archaeologists and the tourist business. It does however suggest that synagogue services were taking place before the Temple was destroyed.

Not all researchers share this point of view. Adherents of a more conservative school consider the synagogal era to have begun only several years after the destruction of the Temple. I incline to the viewpoint of Shmuel Safrai.

I remind you that a relentless struggle to ban all worship outside the Temple began centuries before this time! This gives grounds to surmise that even before the destruction of the Temple, clandestine activity was preparing the way for a new phase in the history of Judaism—post-Temple, synagogal —which took shape in all its diversity during the period of the Exile.

Why were synagogues being created so early? Was it a historical presentiment? An unshakeable faith in prophecies of the destruction of the Temple? Farsightedness on the part of religious leaders of the time who foresaw the catastrophe? There is something for you to reflect on.

How was the Temple viewed by different strata of the population? The charismatic and ecstatic Qumranites shunned the Temple as a sink of corruption. Intellectuals found the Temple's ideology too inflexible. Pharisees stressed study of the Torah and not services at the Temple. As a result the Temple was the province of priests and the simple people. The former, as always and everywhere, had power and wealth, the latter can be blamed for nothing because of their ignorance.

In the first century of the new era, in a crucial period of transition which was to shape the destiny of the world, the Jews were not yet clearly differentiated from Christians. They were still together in liturgical communion and joint creativity. They were still Jewish Christians venerating the same Torah, the same Psalter, and with the same prayers of thanksgiving and supplication to the Lord. The texts of the Gospels had not even been compiled yet. The new shoot of the olive tree had yet to be severed from the trunk by the sword of St. Paul.

2. A further topic for consideration: at this time the status of the Temple was undermined. The Qumran community had begun creating prayers not associated with the Temple. These texts have now been found.

Around Year 50 of the first century, Philo of Alexandria died, the same Philo who had gone at the head of a delegation of Alexandrian Jews to Rome to petition the Emperor Caligula against erecting statues of the Emperor in the synagogues of Alexandria and the Temple in Jerusalem. His description of his less-than-successful journey has survived. Thanks to the Christians, many of Philo's works have come down to us in their Greek original. He is an astoundingly bold and talented popularizer of the Torah. From an orthodox viewpoint he is infected with Platonism, Stoicism, and other newly fashionable Greek influences, but it is thanks to his treatise *On the Contemplative Life* that we know about the existence of the sect of the Theraputae.

NOTE IN MARGIN: Need to look this up!

Philo writes, "If you have not brought your sins to the altar of your heart, it is of no avail for you to go to the Temple. And if you have come to the Temple and are thinking in your mind of some other place, then that is where you are." Philo readily transfers the material to the spiritual plane. "We do not eat pork because it is a figure of ingratitude as the pig knows not its masters," he writes. Following the Prophets he spoke of "circumcision of the heart". He was a contemporary of Jesus and in some matters a fellow-thinker. Under Philo of Alexandria several families in the community did not circumcise their sons, and he chided them mildly: "One should observe tradition in order not to lead others astray." How agreeable that is! But it would be well for me to stop here. I have a personal weakness for Philo of Alexandria.

Note in the margin: Must get this Philo out of the library!

Let us return to the religious service. The church service hours of the Christians derive from the Jewish times. In the Torah the Lord God prescribed that Jews should perform a morning and evening sacrifice. Before Solomon built the First Temple, sacrifices were made on altars in the open air. At the time of the Babylonian Captivity, Jews began praying in meetings in set locations. The service came to be a reading of the Torah at particular hours, of psalms and hymns. The blood sacrifice began to be replaced by the "sacrifice of praise." This kind of religious service, devised during the Babylonian Captivity, served as a prototype for the later liturgy in Christian churches. Here is an excellent subject for independent research: comparison of the historical development of liturgical texts! It is impossible to imagine Christianity without the Torah. The New Testament was born of the Torah.

After that Jews and Christians cease their communal praying and move to separate locations. Gradually texts of a new kind appear among the Christians which are directed against Judaism and Jews. This is a huge area for research. Let us return to this issue when we come to the liturgy.

3. The liturgy. This is a particularly sensitive topic. There is a parallel between the Jewish Passover Seder and the Christian Mass. (A very interesting exercise is to compare the text of the Haggadah of Pesach and the Mass.) The Christian liturgy is linked very closely indeed to the Jewish Passover Seder. I am just touching here on various issues, reminding you of some basic matters, commonplaces, if you like. At the same time, however, I urge you to examine everything critically and creatively.

I urge you to test and question everything. Knowledge obtained without personal effort and concentration is dead knowledge. Only what has passed through your own consciousness will be of value to you.

And so, textological analysis of the Jewish Passover Seder and the contemporary liturgy of both the Western and Eastern Churches indicates a structural link between them, with the exploitation in both services of exactly the same prayers. Look closely at your notes on this topic. I am not going to repeat myself here.

A separate topic, which is constantly researched by both Jewish and Christian authors is the anti-Semitic character of certain Christian texts, particularly of those relating to Holy Week, that is, the days immediately preceding Easter.

The Second Vatican Council of 1962–65 repudiated most of these texts, and in particular those written by the Fathers of the Church, for example, St. John Chrysostomos.

The Eastern Churches view these excisions negatively, and in many Orthodox churches the texts are read to this day.

This is a sensitive topic which undermines several major authorities both of Christian and Jewish theology. In the works of Maimonides, known in Jewish sources as Moshe ben Maimon or Rambam, a Jewish teacher and commentator of the 12th century, we come across virulent attacks on Christians which are just as baseless as the anti-Jewish utterances of some of the Fathers of the Church. Thus was the gulf between the Jewish and Christian worlds deepened. It is immense but does not seem to me to be insuperable. Working with this material requires knowledge, honesty, openness, and boldness. As another Father of the Church, St. Gregory the Great, said, "If truth may cause a scandal, it is better to allow that scandal than to deny the truth."

My dear students! The final thing I want to say to you today is that it is practically impossible to pass this course. In it religious history and the history of the human race are intertwined. Here is the tragedy of Jewry and the tragedy of Europe. In this place the heart of history beats. There will accordingly be no examination. There will be a discussion. With each of you we shall talk about what has seemed of most significance in my course. If you like, prepare notes for this in writing. That is particularly prudent for students who come from afar. You can carry out a comparative analysis of documents. Arad, as an Ethiopian Jew, might take the texts of the Ethiopian Christians— I have some which are very interesting—and compare them with Jewish texts of the same period. Now we shall say good-bye for a week, and then I will expect you in accordance with the timetable.

NOTE AT THE END: There is an anecdote to the effect that in one of these "discussions" Neuhaus asked a girl student how many canonical Gospels there were. She did not know and he did not ask any more questions. He let her pass. When asked why, he replied that there was only one question she couldn't answer.

12. 1967, Haifa

LETTER FROM DANIEL STEIN TO WŁADYSŁAW KLECH

Dear Brother W.,

As you see, I took a long time getting into harness, but then ran very well, and indeed so fast that I have broken my leg. It was set in plaster and I was immediately discharged from hospital, but now it seems it was wrongly set and I have had to have an operation. Accordingly, I am now in the hospital for several days and it has turned out to be the most perfect sanatorium. This frozen moment in the race is totally relaxing, and in addition, my leg hurts, so I have no guilty sense of neglecting my duties. At last I can write to you a thorough letter about my present mood. Immediately before I left Kraków for Israel, the abbot of our monastery told me Israel is an even thornier field of operations for a Catholic priest than postwar Poland, and that Christian missionary activity is impossible among the Jews in Israel. In fact, it is prohibited by law.

He was right. The Jews did not need me. Religious Jews were certain I had come here for the sole purpose of converting Jews to Christianity. The Catholics living here certainly did need me. I do not know how many Catholics there are from Poland. More than 1,000, I imagine, and there are numerous children from mixed marriages whose problems are even more intractable than those of Polish Catholic women. In fact it is not only Poles who are here. There is every living thing, two by two: Catholics from Czechoslovakia and Romania, from France, Lithuania, and Latvia. Almost half my parishioners know no Polish, but everyone who comes here studies Hebrew.

Thus it has come about that my idealistic dream has dovetailed with stern necessity, since Hebrew is the only common language among my parishioners. The paradox is that the Church which speaks the language of the Savior is a Church not of Jews but of displaced persons, outcasts, people the state judges to be of low value or significance. That is Christian linguistics for you: in earlier times a liturgy derived entirely from Judaism passed from Hebrew to Greek to Coptic, and later to Latin and the Slavonic languages. Today, Poles, Czechs, and the French come to me to pray in Hebrew.

Actually, the Jews are fewest of all in the community. In all the years I have been living here I have baptized just three. I baptized them wonderfully, in the River Jordan. They were the husbands of Catholic wives and I hoped they would stay in Israel, but they have all emigrated. They are not the only ones. I know other Jewish Christians who are leaving Israel, and several families of Arab Catholics have gone to live in France and America. I do not know how hospitably they will be received there, but I do understand why they have left.

The baptized Christians in far-off times left Israel and went out into the world, leaving behind only the unbaptized apostles. The Savior baptized nobody, and that is fairly intriguing. Indeed, the relationship between the two great figures of John the Baptist and Jesus is highly intriguing. Not counting the meeting of their pregnant mothers, when the babe leaped in the womb, the only time they met, at least the only meeting described, was at the River Jordan. All their lives they lived on the same scrap of land, a tiny country, but did not meet, and that despite the fact that they were related and without doubt there were shared family events, weddings, and funerals. Not to meet in these circumstances could only have been intentional. They did not want to meet! What secret is behind this? A remarkable person I talked to, a professor of Judaic Studies, David Neuhaus, gave me a glimpse into it. He studies Jewish religious trends of the Second Temple period. For him the two most important figures are "the historical John the Baptist" and "the historical Jesus." Neuhaus uses sources little known to Christian researchers. I admit I am overcome with emotion when I come into contact with Jewish documents of those years. Here, sealed behind seven seals, lies the answer to what, for me, is the most important question of all: what did our Master believe? Did he believe in the Father, the Son, and the Holy Ghost? In the Trinity?

Neuhaus analyses the difference between the views of Jesus and John the Baptist, and that lies in their understanding of redemption. John was sure that the world would shortly end and lived in expectation of the Last Judgment, like the Qumran sages before him and St. John the Divine after him in the Book of Revelation. In Neuhaus's opinion, this longing for speedy judgement and the desire to chastise the ungodly without delay were alien to Jesus. Jesus did not follow John the Baptist despite the high renown and authority of the latter. We may surmise that he was repelled by John the Baptist's eschatological aspirations and passionate focus on the end of the world. The Master's subsequent preaching is wholly devoted to life, its value and meaning. A living God for living people.

Historical Christianity subsequently sought to visit judgment on the world, and judgment on the Jews, in the name of Jesus, without delay! That is, divine justice was replaced by human justice meted out in the name of the Church.

David Neuhaus studies Jesus in the context of Jewish history. You can only obtain an answer to the question of what our Master believed through that approach, proceeding from the Jewish context.

Professor Neuhaus invited me to his home, which I considered a great honor. He has a fine house in an old district of Jerusalem which emigrants from Germany began to build many years ago. It is occupied now by rich people, a lot of university professors, famous doctors and lawyers. It is reminiscent of a comfortable suburb in a South European city. When I went in there was a large hallway, a mirror, a table. Everything very respectable and bourgeois, and in the most prominent place was the statue of a rather fine pig. I immediately asked why he accorded such honor to a despised animal and he explained that he was born in Bohemia. When the Germans occupied Czechoslovakia, they initially gave Jews permission to emigrate. "I applied to emigrate to Palestine, but when I went to obtain the permit, the German officer dealing with the paperwork demanded that I should shout out three times, 'I am a filthy Jewish pig!' This beast stands there in commemoration of that event."

I've just seen through the window that the consultant in charge of the department I am in has arrived. I shall go and try to persuade him to discharge me. If he does, I shall go about my business and finish this letter at the first opportunity.

D.

13. November 1990, Freiburg

FROM A TALK BY BROTHER DANIEL STEIN TO SCHOOLCHILDREN

The chief of the Belorussian district police, Ivan Semyonovich, took me from the village to the town of Emsk and moved me into his house. He wanted me constantly on call. Semyonovich lived with his young Polish wife, Beata. She surprised me by being completely different from the uncomplicated and primitive Semyonovich. She was very pretty. Educated and aristocratic, even. I later discovered that she was indeed from a very good family. Her father was the headmaster of the Walewicz Grammar School and his elder brother was the local priest.

Ivan had been in love with Beata for many years, but she always refused him and had only married him recently, when he became the chief of police. It was her way of trying to protect her family from persecution. The Polish settlers were more educated than the local Belorussians but they were few in number because most of the Polish intelligentsia had been sent to Siberia when the Russians arrived.

The Nazis did not persecute only Jews. They regarded gypsies, negroes, and Slavs as racially inferior, but the hierarchy was such that Jews were first in line for extermination. I claimed to be a Pole.

The local Poles were well disposed toward me. They had heard I was half-German, half-Polish, and when I registered in Emsk, I registered as a Pole even though I could have put myself down as German. My choice was entirely deliberate. The only document left from my previous life was my school identification booklet which gave no indication of my nationality but indicated the town in which I was studying. The Germans could easily have made enquiries and then I would have been exposed. To the Poles, however, my choice demonstrated unambiguously that I was a Polish patriot. Beata's family were also patriotic.

I soon got to know them all better. Her father and her sisters, Halina and Marysia, were very pleasant. There was such a warm, homely atmosphere that you were reluctant to leave. Occasionally their priestly uncle would come to the house, but when I met him there I was always tense because I had no idea how a Catholic should behave in the presence of a priest. Luckily he was a well-intentioned man and did not expect any special treatment.

The sisters were roughly my age, Halina a year older and Marysia a year younger. They were the only people I could talk to and relax a little from the constant tension I lived under. I went to see them almost every day and would stay until evening. I played cards with the sisters and we kept ourselves entertained. I told them funny stories, since amusing things did occasionally happen even in the police station.

Socializing with Jews away from my work was out of the question. I would have attracted suspicion immediately, and the Jews themselves, as soon as they saw my black uniform, looked away and tried to become invisible.

Of course, I could never come too close to the Walewicz family. I was always acutely aware of the unbridgeable gulf separating me, a covert Jew, from these dear, likeable and well-educated Christians. I was in love with Marysia and knew she liked me, but I also knew I would never cross the boundary, would never develop a serious relationship because that would subject her to terrible risk. I do not know how my life might have turned out if I had met her in peacetime, in a country at peace. Alas, Marysia and her entire family were soon to die, and I was unable to save any of them.

My duties at work were quite varied. In the first place, I acted as interpreter between the German gendarmerie, the Belorussian police, and the local populace. In the second place, I had to investigate crimes and minor offences and collect testimony. I tried to steer clear of political cases involving investigation of the activities of the former Soviet administration, communists, and the partisans who appeared shortly after the occupation. In particular I wanted to avoid Jewish cases, but that was the most classified part of the work and they did not involve me in it.

At first I lived in Semyonovich's house, ate at his table, acted as his interpreter, and tried to teach him German, if with little success. In the morning I would saddle the horses and we would ride to the office. In the evening when he might have been able to study, Semyonovich usually got drunk.

He was pleased with my work. My predecessor had been a Pole whose German was poor and was also a drunk. Now Semyonovich lumbered me with all his correspondence and record-keeping and I had to compile the endless idiotic reports demanded by his German superiors. I coped and Semyonovich appreciated that.

Quite a long time later, Beata told me that she had immediately suspected I was Jewish, but had realized her mistake when she saw me on horseback. I sat in the saddle like a real cavalry officer, not like a rural Jew. I really was a good horseman. I loved horses and riding and had even won races on several occasions when I competed against my classmates at the riding school.

Beata thought well of me. I lived in her house, helped her in whatever way I could, and more than once had to help her calm Semyonovich down because, when he was drunk, he could be mean and violent. Every time he had been on a binge he was grateful to me. I could feel that. I would even say he respected me. On one occasion his respect put me in a very difficult situation. He knew, of course, that as a Pole I must be Catholic. Under the hierarchy Semyonovich had established, a Jew was beneath a Belorussian but a Pole was higher. As regards the Aryan race, Semyonovich never doubted its superiority. He was an ideal policeman, his heart untroubled by the anti-Jewish operations he was conducting. During these months, they were destroying Jewish farmsteads and small settlements of thirty to sixty souls, and the operations were at first carried out by the Belorussian police. I cannot imagine why Semyonovich suddenly took it into his head that those policemen who had been born Catholics should go to confession, but one fine day he entrusted me with the task of ensuring that Catholic policemen did so.

This was more than absurd. It was a kind of diabolical farce sending murderers to observe religious rituals, go to confession and take communion. I realized he expected me to do the same.

I went to the church accompanied by fifteen policemen. They all waited their turn to confess, and I was the last. I sat apprehensively in the pew, afraid of giving myself away because I had no idea how to behave during confession. It certainly never occurred to me that within a few years I would myself be hearing confession from my parishioners.

When all the policemen had gone, I went to the priest. I had several times dined with him in the Walewicz household, and asked whether he would be going to visit his brother today.

"No," he replied, "I shall see them in the middle of the week."

We said good-bye and I left. None of the policemen noticed my ploy.

I did not know then that Father Walewicz was sympathetic to Jews and even, as I later learned, helped them. To this day I do not know whether he guessed I was Jewish. Perhaps he did. I am still greatly saddened that I was unable to save him, although I did try.

One and a half months later, returning home late in the evening after work, I saw a column of trucks parked by the roadside. This time the Belorussian police had received no notification of any imminent anti-Jewish operation, which could mean only one thing: the trucks were intended for Poles. They had not advised the Belorussian police because, as everybody knew, Semyonovich was married to a Pole. I had not been told because I was believed to be a Polish patriot.

I ran to Walewicz and warned him about the trucks and my suspicions. I thought they should hide immediately, take to the forest or flee to some remote farmstead. I asked him to warn his brother and all his Polish friends, but Walewicz did not believe me. He hated Communism and Fascism equally, but believed that as a loyal citizen he could not be subjected to repressions. The entire family was taken away, Father Walewicz, an engineer, a doctor, and twenty other people. The Polish intelligentsia. They were shot that same night. They did not come for Beata.

Sweet Marysia, poor Halina. The list of those we pray for is infinitely long. There was only one Pole I managed to warn that evening that was saved. He left Emsk within the hour.

When Semyonovich brought me to Emsk, the local Jews had already been moved to the old castle. I learned of a tragedy which had been played out two weeks before my arrival. The Jews were ordered to gather in the town square and obediently came at the appointed time, bringing their children and old people, bundles of clothing and supplies for the journey. There, in the town square, between two churches, one Orthodox and one Catholic, a terrible massacre took place. A police unit together with the Sonderkommando shot more than fifteen hundred civilians. The Jews who survived, about eight hundred people, were transferred to the half-ruined castle, which was turned into a ghetto.

It was after this incident that a new chief, Major Adolf Reinhold, a professional policeman with thirty years of service, arrived in Emsk. He found the state of the administration highly unsatisfactory and introduced his own "civilized" measures to establish order. He turned the castle into a real ghetto, establishing tighter security and making this the responsibility primarily of the inhabitants of the ghetto themselves. The Belorussian police were also involved, under German supervision. Major Reinhold began by requisitioning a Catholic nunnery as a police station and moving the nuns to the building next door, which had belonged to a Jewish family killed in the pogrom.

Accompanying Semyonovich as his interpreter, I naturally came to the notice of Reinhold, and a few weeks later he said he wanted to draft me into his department. Semyonovich could hardly refuse and, needless to say, nobody asked me whether I wanted to work for the Gestapo. Semyonovich thought I would see it as a good career move. I looked back at my teaching in the village school nostalgically. Now I was to work for the Germans! There was no escape. I had no option and agreed, well aware that my situation was now even more precarious.

My duties with the Gestapo were little different from what they had been before. As their secretary, I answered the telephone, allocated the policemen's shifts, and kept the accounts. My duties included translating documents and working with the local population, and this I did conscientiously. I tried to translate matters relating to criminal cases with total accuracy. There were many of these—fights, thefts, murders,—but I was acutely aware that, working for the Gestapo, I had a share of responsibility for what was going on there. I was not directly involved in killing people but had a sense of complicity. I desperately needed to maintain an inner counterbalance to the things I was indirectly participating in. I felt an obligation to do things which would enable me later to look my parents and brother in the eye without shame. If I was not always successful in exploiting situations to help people, I believe I can say I never missed an opportunity to try.

Working in the police station was very unpleasant. I cannot tell whether the people chosen to work there were particularly brutal and stupid, or whether working there brought out the worst in them, but there were some real sadists, and others who were mentally retarded, in a clinical sense. Most of them came to a bad end and I try not to remember that. There is a lot in my memory I would prefer to forget but cannot.

Surprisingly enough, the person most deserving of respect there was Major Reinhold. Although a member of the Nazi Party, he was a perfectly decent individual and conscientious executive. Before the war, he had been a member of the Cologne police force. Having worked under him for a few months, I noticed that he tried to avoid involvement in the operations to exterminate the Jewish population. When he did have to be present, he tried to observe the outward norms of legality and to prevent gratuitous brutality.

Another striking and regrettable feature of the atmosphere of that time and place was the flood of statements landing on my table from local inhabitants. There were denunciations of neighbors, complaints, and accusations, almost always illiterate, often untruthful, and invariably shameful. I was constantly in a state of profound depression but had to conceal the fact at all costs from those I worked with. I suppose it was the first time I had come into such close contact with vile human behavior, ingratitude, and meanness. The only explanation I could find was that the local Belorussian people were dreadfully poor, uneducated, and downtrodden.

Happily, I did often manage to protect people whose neighbors had denounced them. I soon started conducting many of the investigations myself and was able to defend innocent people, deflect suspicion from those seen to have links with the partisans, and simply to facilitate justice. The only thing which gave me strength to get through the day was this constant search for ways of helping people.

The Walewiczes were dead, their property plundered. Several Belorussian families had seized their house and were now arguing about how to share it. Poor Beata, the only survivor, lay for days at a time with her face to the wall and did not want to see anybody. She was in the last month of pregnancy and Semyonovich was getting drunk and going on a rampage. I didn't see much of him because I spent whole days inside the police station. There was a vast amount of paperwork, bulletins, laws, public announcements. They had to be translated into Polish and Belorussian so the population could be informed of them.

The partisan movement was becoming ever more evident, and greatly worried the Germans. At first I had no direct link with the partisans, but each time I received information from local informers about partisan movements, I did everything I could to delay or stop operational intelligence from reaching my superiors. I was not a member of any organization or resistance group, but after a time managed to establish contact with the Jews in the ghetto.

This contact occurred right in the police station. Jews were not allowed to leave the ghetto except for those working in the town for the Germans. Every day two Jewish cleaning women came to the police station but I did not risk talking to them. Another Jew worked in the stables, but I did not feel he could be trusted. This groom fell ill and his replacement was Moshe Milshtein, a member of Akiva I had known in Vilnius. He did not recognize me at first, the black uniform acting like camouflage. Through Moshe a chain of couriers was organized which enabled me to pass on information about operations being prepared against Jews and partisans.

My first attempt to save a Jewish village from destruction failed. The courier passed a warning about the planned operation to the Judenrat but they demanded to be told the source of the information. The courier refused to compromise me. Everybody was afraid of provocations, but the Judenrat finally sent a warning to the village. Here the story was repeated and the villagers sent a girl to Emsk to check how reliable the information was. When she returned home two days later there was not a living soul left.

This village was the first I was sent to as an interpreter. In order to avoid what he called "brutish behavior," Major Reinhold required the unit to assemble all the Jews in one place and read out the order declaring them enemies of the Reich. As such, they were then shot. Avoiding personal participation in such operations, he instead sent his sergeant-major who, as ill-luck would have it, was a complete sadist.

I hoped that when we arrived we would find the place empty, but to my horror the villagers had not fled. They were all brought to one room, I read out the directive and the officer then wrote down the names of the adults. The children he merely counted. They were all taken to a shed. I hid behind it until the shooting was over. The memory is still as vivid for me as if it happened yesterday.

After operations of this kind there was usually a drunken binge. I sat at the table, translating the soldiers' jokes from Belorussian into German and greatly regretting that I had no taste for alcohol.

The Judenrat no longer questioned my information and sometimes people did manage to escape to the forest. It is a great puzzle of human psychology that these old Jews, who in their lives had experienced numerous pogroms and the massacre in the town square, obstinately refused to believe there was a plan to exterminate Jews systematically. They had their own survival plan. They had come to an understanding with one of the top local Belorussian officials that he would prevent destruction of the ghetto if they paid him an enormous sum of money. They did not have enough, the official agreed to staged payments, and had been paid a first instalment. Many of them knew perfectly well that this was the trick of a blackmailer, but went on hoping.

Fortunately, there were people in the ghetto who intended to resist and sell their lives dearly. These were mainly young Zionists who had been unable to emigrate to Palestine. They had almost no weapons and I was able to organize a supply. Often the transfer point I used was Semyonovich's house.

14. 1987, Redford, England
LETTER FROM BEATA SEMYONOVICH TO MARYSIA WALEWICZ

Dear Marysia,

A week has passed and it is only now that I have gathered up my strength to write and tell you that Ivan is dead. He died on 14 May after a year of terrible suffering. The kind of cancer he had did not respond to painkillers and only vodka partly relieved his agony.

His right leg was amputated a year ago, and that may have been a mistake because afterward that dreadful sarcoma spread like wildfire to his bones and he suffered beyond all measure. He did not want to go into the clinic because till the day he died he was afraid the Jews would kidnap him. For some reason he was convinced they would not take him out of our house while I was there, but would for sure if he went to the clinic. He had a whole file of news clippings about war criminals the Jews had abducted, even from Latin America, and put on trial. Even more than a trial, he feared the children would learn the truth about his past. He never got on well with them. The children attended his funeral but left the next day.

I wander through the house for days at a time. It is quite large, with a dining room and kitchen downstairs and four rooms upstairs. The most comfortable, west-facing one I have mentally reserved for you. I so much wish you would come to England and move into this house. Then we would be as happy as we were as children. Do nuns really not have to retire? You will be 63 soon and I am 68. We have another 10 years or so to live. We will go to Mass together the way we did as children, and I will make bigos stew with English cabbage, which is nothing like Polish cabbage, and draniki potato pancakes.

Ivan has left me a large legacy. His greed, from which I suffered all my life, has generated a very substantial sum which will be enough for you and me to live out our lives without cares or having to stint ourselves. I have nobody in the world closer to me than you are. You belong to the one time in my life which was really happy, before the war, in our beloved home with mother, father and Halina. I so loved all of you that I made the sacrifice of marrying Ivan, hoping that he would protect our family, but in the end I saved nobody and only ruined my own life.

After the funeral, I feel desolate. I have dark thoughts, old and new, and they do not leave me in peace for a moment. When I was young I hated my husband. After our family was killed and Henryk was born Ivan tried his best. He helped me to recover my wits and even stopped drinking for a time. The whole of that first year he almost never let Henryk out of his arms. If there was anything good in him it was his love for me and his sons. In truth it is I who wronged him, because I married without loving him in the slightest, and even hating him, while he loved me very much. When the German retreat began and we left with them, how many times I cravenly prayed to God to free me of him. No matter how great his crimes, he never treated me badly. It is I who wronged him. If anyone can judge him it is not I.

My dear Marysia, perhaps my destiny, too, would have worked out differently if we had found each other earlier, before the war ended. I might have had the strength to leave Ivan, but 10 years had passed before I discovered you had survived. It is a miracle that we managed to find each other. I was not looking for you because Ivan was told for a fact that all the Poles had been shot that night. Who could have guessed you had managed to escape?

My invitation for you to come and stay here is entirely serious. I am not extending it in a state of despair or at all frivolously. I can believe you might not want to move to England, but in that case we could settle down in some other part of Europe. We could buy a little house in a quiet village in the South of France or Spain, in the Pyrenees. It's very pretty there. I remember it from our dreadful journey through France and Spain. I cannot imagine living in modern Poland, but I would consider even that.

Neither of my daughters-in-law, the wives of Henryk and Teodor, would ever move to this house, and anyway, what would they find to do out here in the back of beyond? There isn't even a decent school. I shall be living here alone until I die. If you should decide to come we could live very happily together. I beg you not to reply immediately but to think it over carefully.

I'm enclosing some photographs, although they are a bit dated. Ivan took them when he was still well. That is our garden around the house. It is a bit overgrown now. I haven't done anything to it all year but will pull myself together and sort it out. In one photograph you can see our house from the front and in the second, taken from the balcony, you can see the garden. There were photographs of the rooms, too, but they came out very dark and I put them away somewhere and now can't find them.

All my love, my dear sister. Remember us in your prayers.

Beata

15. December 1987, Boston
FROM EWA MANUKYAN'S DIARY

For the first time I told Esther yesterday what has been worrying me so much lately, and felt a great sense of relief. I find she is the only person I can talk to about it, especially because there is really nothing to say, nothing specific. While I was choosing my words, trying to talk to her about these things which matter to me so much, I was also getting my thoughts together. Just having her there, silent, was very helpful. I noticed a long time ago that when you are with a clever, positive person, they seem to transmit those qualities to you, too. It works in reverse when I'm talking to Rita. I become aggressive and rather stupid and hate myself. This last time, though, talking to Esther, I finally managed to express my dreadful suspicions.

It really is a very long story. When I met Grisha, Alex was six and I was married to Ray, although our marriage was barely smouldering. Ray's career was just taking off. He started giving a lot of guest performances and I already knew various women had appeared in his life. He started getting paid a lot, but it was fly-by-night musician's earnings, no sooner received than spent. I could not give up work, and sat in my laboratory analysing soil and going crazy. And then there was Grisha! What a boy! He fell passionately in love with me. We met in the street, by chance. He saw me and followed me, and it was just what I needed!

At this point Esther raised her eyebrows slightly. She is not, of course, the kind of woman who makes the acquaintance of men in the street, but I told her everything exactly the way it happened. Grisha and I began seeing each other. He was ten years younger than me. Ray is older and always did have problems with sex. I have a suspicion that all the aggression and dynamism and temperament his admirers so love him for is used up in his music and not much is left over for himself. None of that matters now. The point is that Grisha appeared and I was bowled over. Relations with Ray even improved, because now I didn't give a damn about him.

My clever Esther looked at me in surprise, put her little hand on my arm, and said, "Ewa, what you are talking about I know only from literature. I have to confess, at the risk of losing your respect, that I am hardly an expert. All my life I had only one man, my husband, and I know very little about lovers. My relations with my husband were so full that I never wanted anything more. Go on, but do not rely on my being able to give you any sensible advice in these matters."

At this I realized I was taking too long to get to the point about what was really disturbing me. "Yes, yes, I have not come to ask for advice about my relations with Grisha. It is something quite different, and much more painful."

Alex was six when Ray and I divorced by mutual consent. He was not then as rich and famous as he is now, but the court was favorable to me and Alex and I were well provided for. Alex adored his father, and when Grisha and I married, he found it difficult to accept this new man. He kept pointing at objects, a chair, a plate, a cushion, and demanding that Grisha shouldn't touch anything because it belonged to his Daddy.

A psychologist advised a change of surroundings so we moved to a new apartment. Alex still would not accept Grisha and didn't want to go to bed in the evening without Daddy, even though Ray had never tucked him up in bed. In short, for two years Alex was very put out and made life difficult for Grisha and me. Then I was taken into hospital for almost a month, and during that time everything came right. I was no longer there and Alex evidently came to feel that he had Grisha, not only me, to protect him. By now Ray had moved to California and saw very little of his son. Alex was hurt and one time refused to meet his father when he did come to Boston. Ray forgot his birthday and Alex was very upset.

For the last three or four years, relations between Alex and Grisha have been excellent. Alex adores Grisha and Grisha spends a lot of time with him.

They have many shared interests. What more could I say to Esther? They get on so well without me that I'm jealous.

She did not understand what I was getting at, and I myself was expressing this nightmare suspicion for the first time. At the moment I said it out loud it was as if something broke inside me. I felt sure it was true. Of course, I don't know how intimate they are, what exactly is going on between them, but it is suddenly quite obvious to me that they are in love with each other.

Alex is fifteen. He gets on splendidly with his classmates, but has no interest whatsoever in girls. I do not know what to do. I am afraid of knowing for sure what at present is just a vague suspicion. I am at my wits' end trying to foresee various outcomes. What if my suspicions are suddenly confirmed? What should I do? Kill Grisha with my own hands? Have him thrown in prison? Separate from him immediately?

Of course, it is driving me crazy, and on top of the nightmare there is the jealousy, the dreadful sense of humiliation as a woman. I simply couldn't handle finding out that my husband and son are homosexuals. Anyway, I blurted all that out to her, and then I was shown what true wisdom is: a slightly detached attitude toward life, a long-term view.

Esther extracted from the depths of a cupboard a dark bottle with no label, which had already been started. She set down two large liqueur glasses and said, "Calvados was Isaak's favorite drink. It has been there since he died. One of his young colleagues from France brought him a very high proof bottle from a farm in Normandy. You see, it doesn't even have a label—it's homemade! Isaak never did finish it. He would drink only one glass at a time, in the evening."

She poured out a dark liquid which looked like brandy and we drank. It managed to be mild and searing at the same time. Then she said very carefully, "We lived through a dreadful war. All our relatives were killed. We saw villages after massacres. We saw piles of corpses gnawed at by animals, which had been hidden under the snow and thawed out after the winter, children who had been shot. I had forbidden myself to recall these things but now I have to say to you, your boy is alive and happy. If everything is as you say, that is a misfortune, for you but not for him. There are many misfortunes about which I know next to nothing. Of course, I see this as a big problem, but your boy is alive and enjoying life. I don't know anything about these relations. They puzzle and indeed perplex me, but it is all outside my experience, and outside your experience too. For now, leave things as they are. Wait. It is probably difficult now for you to be around Grisha. You need to think things through, but do not be in a hurry. If the situation is really as you think, then it did not start yesterday. Just remember that nobody has died."

How lucky I am to have Esther!

There was still half the bottle left and I drank it all. Esther put me in a taxi and I left my car at her house. When I got home Grisha and Alex were sitting in front of the television as good as gold, watching a film.

I went straight to bed but felt so chilled and feverish that only Grisha was able to warm me up, using a tried and trusted method.

16. *April 1988, Haifa*
LETTER FROM EWA MANUKYAN TO ESTHER GANTMAN

Dear Esther,

You remember what a rush and panic I left in. There really was no need. A week has passed since the stroke and the doctors tell me her condition has stabilized. Everything is rather sad, but at least it is better than a funeral. She has been transferred today out of intensive care into an ordinary ward. She is still festooned with tubes and flat on her back but the doctors say there is a "positive dynamic." They are very good. They operated on Mother to remove the haematoma in the brain and believe she can be rehabilitated to some extent. At all events, she can feel the right side of her body although she can't move either her hand or foot. She isn't talking but I have the impression that is just because she doesn't want to talk to me because I went to Santorini instead of going to see her. Yesterday while I was with her she said fairly distinctly to the nurse, "Bastard!" which made me think I could come back home now. She is well looked after here, much better than she would be in America unless she was in a private clinic. No, do not think that I am going to leave right now. I shall stay here some time yet, at least until she is moved back to that almshouse of hers.

I have nevertheless allowed myself one little treat and went to Jerusalem for a couple of days. I was there a few years back, just passing through, and it was so hot I hardly poked my nose outside the hotel. As if that wasn't enough, I decided last time to go and take a look at my roots. I went to the religious quarter and got mugged. Well, not mugged perhaps, just scratched, but it was tremendously interesting. The males were all wearing caftans and had their hair in payots, and the females were in wigs and hats. In America you sometimes meet this kind of thing, too, but here it all seemed much more real. The faces were attractive. I was incredibly curious because I can see that if fate had taken a different turn, these medieval beings might have been my own relatives, friends, and neighbors. While I was just staring at them everything was fine, but when I went into a shop to buy some water, two old ladies pounced on me. One pinched my criminally bare arms, and the other started pulling my hair. They were completely off the wall. I was barely able to fight them off and escape. At the edge of this kosher paradise I stopped by some school railings. It was time for their break and boys of every caliber, from scrawny five-year-olds to well-fed bullocks came primly into the courtyard and started walking around in pairs, occasionally forming groups, and gravely discussing weighty matters. I stood by the railings gaping and waited for them to start playing football or at least fight. It never happened. My first attempt at investigating my roots thus came to an entirely inglorious end. I didn't much care for the roots, and my arms were all scratched.

This time I decided to adopt a different approach to delving into the past and went to the Old Town to see the two main sights, the Temple of the Holy Sepulchre and the Room of the Last Supper. The Temple of the Holy Sepulchre I found less impressive than expected. There was a crowd and it was an ordinary tourist attraction just like anywhere else in the world. There were even Japanese groups. Where the sepulchre used to be, there is now a small chapel with a queue, and before entering, each tourist turns around and the next one photographs him or her. I just left. I found my way to the Room of the Last Supper using a guidebook. I have to confess, dear Esther, that I still have a few favorite themes from my Catholic childhood and the Last Supper is one of them.

I went inside and immediately felt that nothing of the sort had ever happened in this building. The Master and the twelve disciples had never assembled here, no bread had been broken, no wine had been drunk. They had clearly met in a different place which did not have Leonardo da Vinci windows. That room had been small and quite possibly had no windows at all. It would have been somewhere modest on the outskirts of town and not right on top of the Tomb of King David. In other words, I was having none of this Last Supper of theirs.

The next morning, though, I climbed up to the Garden of Gethsemane, and the olive trees growing there were entirely real and so old that they might well have been growing there all that time ago. The olives I really did find convincing, and stood there desperately wanting to break off a twig as a souvenir but could not bring myself to do it. Just then a little monk who looked completely penniless came out of a door, broke off a twig and gave it to me. I was so delighted. I climbed higher up the Mount of Olives, walked along the walls of the old Jewish cemetery and came to a chapel. It was a small modern building in the shape of a teardrop, the Dominus Flevit Church. The Lord wept. It was in this place that Christ lamented the coming destruction of Jerusalem. Since then Jerusalem has been destroyed and rebuilt so many times that now there is no knowing quite which destruction he was lamenting. Do we have to expect another or have there already been enough?

The view which opens before you is indescribable, but the place itself is compact and welcoming. The grass is vivid with tiny poppies and white daisy-like flowers. It reminded me of my favorite tapestry from Cluny, only without the unicorn or Virgin, but you feel they will be back any minute. It's because of that precious grass. The spring is so short here, and the fact that in a week's time everything will become parched and turn into whitish hay means that you are particularly aware of the blessedness of this place.

I did afterward go into the old Jewish cemetery, which takes up half the mountain. I was reluctant at first because I don't like cemeteries, but if I had to be dragged to the Père Lachaise Cemetery in Paris, it was ordained by heaven that I should go in here. It was a place of dust, stones and rubble. Near one rock an elderly Arab suddenly materialized and offered to show me around for $10. I declined saying that I was not an American tourist but a simple woman from Poland. Then he offered me a cup of coffee but this, too, seemed to be fraught with far-reaching implications and I again declined. Then he told me he had 50 camels and I expressed my admiration. I said, "Goodness, very well done! 50 camels is better than 50 cars." He was terribly pleased and we parted as friends. Tell me truthfully now, Esther, do you know anybody who has 50 camels? Then I took a taxi to the bus station and a few hours later I was in Haifa. I ran to the hospital and sat under the burning coals of her eyes. She is not speaking, but in any case I know everything she wants to say to me, down to the very last word.

In the depths of my heart worries about Alex and Grisha are constantly stirring, but I drive them away.

Love from

Your Ewa

17. *April 1988, Boston*

LETTER FROM ESTHER GANTMAN TO EWA MANUKYAN

. . . I just can't get through to you on the phone. I have a favor to ask. I'm not sure whether you can do it, but perhaps while you are in Israel you will be able to help me. The thing is, recently all my time has been taken up with sorting out Isaak's papers, of which there are a great many, and I unexpectedly happened upon a registered parcel he had not opened. It proved to contain a book sent after his death from an auction sale. Only now, two years later, I have opened the parcel and found an antique book of heavenly beauty. It seems to be a manuscript with wonderful illuminations. I took it to the Jewish Museum and they told me it was a rare edition of the Haggadah. They immediately offered to buy it, but for the time being I have no intention of selling the book.

What I really want is to restore a number of damaged pages. They told me at the museum it was best to have such books restored by Israeli craftsmen, but the one they employed died recently and they have yet to find a replacement. Perhaps you could ask your friends whether they can find such a person. If not, never mind. After all, the book has been lying there for such a long time that it can lie a bit longer just as it is.

Love from

Esther

18. *April 1988, Haifa*

LETTER FROM EWA MANUKYAN TO ESTHER GANTMAN

Sweet Esther,

I am staying here for another week. I have changed my departure date again and it is now 6 May. I have finally hired a car and driver. All the cars here have a mechanical gear change, which I'm not used to. I have been driving automatics for a long time and did not want to take a risk. The country is so small that if you get up early, by four in the afternoon you can have seen half of it. I have been back to the Dead Sea and the Sea of Galilee. I only didn't make it to Eilat. How I like the miniature nature of this land! Everything is within easy reach.

Yes! Your request! One of the best restorers is the neighbor of my

Jerusalem friends, Steve and Isabel. I had only to mention it to be invited to his house that very day. Here in Israel every person is a walking novel. They have such improbable histories, such biographies that even mine pales by comparison. When Steve told him I had been conceived in a ghetto, the restorer was overcome with such sympathy that he invited me on Friday evening to his home. As a result I found myself at a real Shabbat for the first time ever. You know all about it, of course, but it made a profound impression on me. I think I have told you that throughout my childhood I always longed to have a real family. There was the refuge, then the orphanage, then life with my mother who totally rejected family values, then life with Eric, which was nothing special, no love or friendship, just a lot of thrashing around in the sack. Then my unsuccessful attempt with Ray when Alex was born. It didn't even occur to him to cancel his tour! When Grisha came on the scene, I thought at last everything had fallen into place, but what I now foresee is the complete and utter collapse of my family dream!

And here, picture it, was the table with candles and a beautiful Russian woman, past her first youth, who I later discovered had converted to Judaism. She was so big, with large hands, and she moved like a great animal, perhaps a cow, but in a good sense. She slowly turned her head, slowly moved her eyes. She had a great bosom which hung over the table, and she had red hair which was already fading a little. The head of hair she must have had in the past you could tell from her two boys with their fiery ginger mops. Her two girls resembled their father, with fine noses, fine fingers, very miniature. I realized later that Leya is really not much taller than her husband, but Yosef is such a thin, fleshless person, he looks like an elderly angel. I think I mentioned that I brought my love of icons with me from Russia. I suddenly understood why Jews don't and couldn't have them. They themselves have such faces they have no need of icons.

Before supper Yosef took me to his workroom. He is very highly skilled. There were books of miniatures, and simple antique prayer books. He said the greater part of his work comes from America now. American Jews buy old Jewish books at auction, have them restored, and then present them to museums. It's a kind of *mitzvah*. Yosef is an ex-Muscovite. He graduated from some department of restoration and in Russia restored icons. He lived in a monastery for several years and was presumably Orthodox, but I didn't care to ask. Isn't that interesting? He was in prison for three years because icons he restored were smuggled to the West and somebody informed on him. He also met his wife through restoration.

She was an elder in an Orthodox Church and gave him work. He told me all this himself, then smiled and fell silent. I could see a story here fit for a novella. My friends told me afterward that the older boy was from her first marriage. We spoke Russian until we sat down at the table. Leya lit the candles with a prayer—in Hebrew. I was too shy to ask what kind of prayer it was, but even without translation it was clearly some kind of Grace. Anyway, why am I describing things to you which you already know very well?

Then the man of the house broke bread with a prayer and poured wine into a large wine glass. It was the Eucharist, there's no two ways about it. Then came all kinds of food: two challot under a napkin which Leya had baked herself, fish, some salads, a roast. There was an old Russian lady at the table, Praskovia Ivanovna, Leya's mother, in a headscarf! Before the meal, she crossed herself and with her wrinkled hand crossed her plate! Shabbat shalom, Christ is risen!

I was consumed with envy. For my whole life this is what I have been yearning for. Half the people with whom I have met on this visit, the doctors, these restorers, another neighbor of my friends who is an English nurse from the hospital, every one of them has an improbable history.

Rita is clearly feeling better. She met me with the words, "Ah, you're back . . ." as if I was 15 and had come back from a party in the small hours of the morning. Next week she is being taken back to the home. I will stay here for a few more days.

Love from

Ewa

19. 1988, Haifa

CASSETTE SENT BY RITA KOWACZ TO PAWEŁ KOCIŃSKI

Dear Paweł,

I am sending you this cassette in place of a letter. I can no longer write, my hands no longer do what I tell them. My legs neither. I am altogether lying much like a corpse with only my head working. It is the most dreadful torment which only God could have invented. Now I think He does exist, or more likely the Devil does. At all events, if the existence of the Devil can be regarded as proof of the existence of God, then I acknowledge that this pretty pair exists, although I don't see any fundamental difference between them. They are the enemies of man. But now for some reason I am alive instead of lying peacefully in the cemetery and not bothering anybody.

You can't imagine the fuss they made over me, and for some reason brought this old bag of bones back to life. Whatever I ask for they give me. They even bring me millet porridge, but I have one special request they won't fulfil and that is to let me die. I say that entirely calmly. I often found myself in situations where I was within a hair's breadth of death, but I wanted to live and fight and I always won. You may not believe it, but I always came out on top, even in the camp. In the end they rehabilitated me, which means I won. Now for me to come out on top means to die when I want to, and I do want to, but they are treating me. You understand, they keep on treating me. The most ridiculous thing about it is that they are even having a bit of success. They drag me to a chair, I slowly move my arms and legs, and that's called a "positive dynamic." All I want from this dynamic of theirs is to be able to drag myself to the window, upend myself over the balcony railings and hurtle down. There is a very pretty view and I am increasingly drawn to it.

Apart from you nobody will help me. You loved me when I was young and I loved you for as long as that itch was alive in me. You are my comrade, we come from the same nest, and that is why you are the only person who can and should come to help me. Come and help me. I have never asked anybody for anything. If I could do without someone else's help I would not ask, but I cannot even get off the bedpan by myself. If we were in the war I would ask you to shoot me but my request is more modest. Come and take me over to the balcony. Is that too much to ask?

Yours,

Rita

20. 1988, Haifa
LETTER FROM RITA KOWACZ TO PAWEŁ KOCIŃSKI

There Paweł I write like a chicken but at least I can write. My hands are just about moving but not my legs. I expected nothing better from you never there when you are needed. Well, fine. Don't think you and Ewa that I can't do anything without you. There are other people who will give me support. Pass my greetings to your wife Mirka and remind her that a heart attack is better than a stroke. As to your son I share your regret. What on earth has he done your Trotskyite? Do not forget that I spent eight years in Polish prisons and another five in Russian prisons. I don't suppose a French one is any worse. Three years is not a long sentence especially when he is still young. In today's Western prisons they serve coffee in the mornings change the bed-linen once a week and put a television in the cell so the prisoner does not get bored. That is more or less what I myself have now with all my medals only the television is in the corridor.

Rita

21. May 1988
FROM EWA MANUKYAN'S DIARY

How deep seated all this is in me! Not only do I regularly go to see Es-ther as if going to confession to receive absolution of my sins, I even have to write it down. The sad truth is that I cannot free my head of all the accusa-tions I have been storing up against my mother all through my life. I have long ceased to experience the fury and indignation she used to make me feel when I was young. I feel infinitely sorry for her. She lies there pale and dry, like a shrivelled wasp, and her eyes are like headlamps, full of energy. But, Lord have mercy on us, what kind of energy is it? Distilled, concentrated hatred. Hatred of evil! She hates evil with such passion and fury that evil can rest assured. People like her make evil immortal.

Looking at Rita, I have long found social injustice preferable to the strug-gle against it. When she was young, she had cosmic ambitions. They scaled down over time until now she seems to be fighting the injustice of fate toward herself. Before her stroke, she concentrated her fire on the director of the old people's home, fat, bald Yohanan Shamir. First she quarrelled with him, then she started writing denunciations of him until a commission of some description arrived. After that, I don't know all the details, he retired. On my visit this year, Yohanan visited her while I was there and she talked to him amicably enough. That was all before her latest stroke. She is already back to talking a little now but cannot get out of bed, of course. In fact, she can't even sit up on her own at present.

When she had the stroke I thought, with relief, that the poor woman would now finally die. Then I was ashamed of myself, and now I'm even more ashamed. Did I really want her to die? Now I don't want anything for her. I just keep thinking how odd it is that she is still able to torment me. Why, from morning till night, do I think, not even about her but about my attitude toward her? Of course, she thinks I am a bastard, and has told me as much on many occasions. Now, however, I have to agree with her because I cannot forgive or love or feel sorry enough for her.

Esther listened to all my ramblings and then said, "There is no advice I can give you. We are fated to feel this way. Those left behind always feel guilt toward those who have gone. It is a matter of time. A few decades from now your Alex will tell somebody close to him how guilty he feels about not having loved you enough. It's like some basic chemistry of human relations." Then she said very firmly, "Be at peace with yourself, Ewa. What you can and need to do you should do, but what is beyond your ability you should not attempt. Allow yourself that. Look at Rita. She cannot be different, and you let yourself be the person you are. You are a good girl." Her words left me feeling happy.

22. 1996, Galilee
LETTER FROM AVIGDOR STEIN TO EWA MANUKYAN

Dear Ewa,

A few days ago Noami brought me a letter Daniel sent her some 20 years ago when she was bedridden in a sanatorium for six months being treated for osseous tuberculosis. It is one of the few extant letters he wrote so I am sending you a copy.

You have no idea how many people come to ask me about my brother: journalists from various countries, an American professor, a writer from Russia.

Milka sends you her best wishes. If you decide to come to Israel, we will be glad to put you up.

Avigdor

1969, Haifa
COPY OF A LETTER FROM DANIEL TO NOAMI

My dear, good Noami,

Can you believe it? A certain very attractive individual, very fluffy with very green eyes, has drawn me into her life and is demanding that I should adopt her three children. Here is what has happened. We have no locks on the monastery cells. We don't really have anything for anyone to steal, and in any case, outsiders are never allowed into the monks' living quarters. My door does not close very tightly and no effort is needed to open it. Anyway, imagine, I came home late one evening and saw the door was ajar. I went in, washed without lighting a candle, sat on my chair, and started pondering. It is a habit I have had since I was young: before going to sleep I spend a little time thinking over what I have done during the day and about the people I have met or, indeed, not met. For example, you. I haven't seen you for more than a month, and very much miss your sweet little face. So, there I am sitting in the dark quietly thinking about one thing and another when I suddenly sense that I'm not alone. There is someone else and I am certain it is not an angel. How can I be so sure? Although I have never met an angel, I am just sure that if one did appear, I would be in no doubt about it. I don't think anyone would be likely to confuse the coming of an angel with the arrival of the gardener or our hegumen. Be that as it may, there was someone there. I stayed motionless and did not light a candle. It was a very strange feeling, with even a slight suggestion of menace.

Outside the moon was bright, so the darkness was not so much dark as rather gray. I cautiously looked from side to side and saw somebody lying on my bed, someone small and round. Very carefully, scarcely breathing, I went over to the bed and found there an enormous cat. She woke up, opened her eyes, and they shone with a terrible light. You know yourself how animals' eyes glow in the dark. I said hello and asked her to let me have my bed back, but she pretended not to understand. Then I stroked her a little and she immediately started purring loudly. I stroked her some more and found that she was not just a cat but an exceedingly fat cat, and one which was very quick on the uptake because she promptly moved over to make room for me. I tried to explain to her that I was a monk and there was no way I could share my bed with a lady, so would she mind moving to the chair. She refused. Then I had to put my sweater on the chair and her on the sweater. She did not resist, but as soon as I lay down, she got back on to the bed with me and delicately settled down on my feet. I gave in and fell asleep. When I woke in the morning she had gone, but that evening she again appeared and showed she was quite unusually clever. Can you imagine, I found her sleeping on the chair, and when I got into bed she again settled herself on my feet. To tell the truth, I found it rather pleasant.

For five days she would be there on the chair in my room every evening, and when I went to bed she moved over to join me. I never did get a good look at her, because when I awoke she had already gone. In any case, I'm always in a hurry in the mornings and had no time to go looking for her in the monastery or the orchard, which is fairly large.

Anyway, picture the evening when I came back and didn't find the cat on my chair. I wasn't sure whether I was feeling disappointment or jealousy. Where had she gone? To whom had she transferred her affections? I even wondered about it during the day. I was stung by her infidelity!

Imagine my astonishment when I came home the next day to find a whole feline family on my bed. So that's where she had disappeared to the night before! Hiding herself from people, in the dark and in secret, she had given birth to three kittens and brought them back to me. I was rather touched that the cat had considered she could trust me with her newborn kittens. To cut a long story short, she has been living for a month now on my blue sweater together with Alef, Betka, and Shin. As regards Shin, I have some doubts about him and think that he may yet turn out to be Shina.

Now I have to provide for an entire family. When I come back in the evenings, I bring a carton of milk for Ketzele (as I have called the cat) and some leftovers from dinner, if I have happened to dine that day. Oh, and I have omitted to mention one very important thing. In the light of day, my cat has proved a rare beauty. She is fairly dark gray in color and has an especially fluffy white patch of fur on her chest. One ear is white, which makes her look rather flirtatious. She is very fastidious and spends half the day washing and grooming herself and her kittens. If only I could train her to clean the room she would make an excellent cleaner. On top of that she is highly intelligent. She has somehow detected that keeping animals in the monastery is prohibited and behaves like a specter. To this day nobody has seen her, and I, too, pretend not to see her, so that when the hegumen asks me what this delightful creature is doing in my room, I will say I hadn't noticed her.

No, unfortunately I will not be able to say that because I am a monk and monks are not allowed to lie. That is really unfair, because everybody I know does just occasionally tell a little white lie, but I am not supposed to. No doubt that moment will sooner or later arrive, so I need to think about the fate of the entire family.

I am planning to negotiate with my brother over this but am not sure the negotiations will be successful. As you know, I constantly disagree with your father about all sorts of things. Here, though, I am counting on his kind heart, and for some reason I am sure of Milka's support.

The fate of the kittens is already almost decided. One will be taken by my assistant, Hilda, a second by her friend Musa, and a third perhaps by a sister from Tiberias.

My love to you, dear niece. Ketzele sends you her very best wishes and hopes you will get well soon.

Your Dodo,

Daniel

23. *November 1990, Freiburg*

FROM A TALK BY BROTHER DANIEL STEIN TO SCHOOLCHILDREN

A direct link with the ghetto was established through Moshe Milshtein. I soon started stealing firearms from the store in the police station attic. These were mainly captured Soviet weapons. Forwarding them to the ghetto was not easy, especially the rifles. Every item taken from the store I first hid in the garden, then tied it in the evening to my bicycle frame, wrapped it in rags, and cycled home by a roundabout route past the castle. Near a hole in the wall, young people were waiting to take the gun from me. I never once went into the ghetto. A number of those living there were already aware that they were marked for extermination and wanted weapons in order to defend themselves and their families. My view was that they needed to decide on a mass break-out. I knew that the partisans included local Communists, escaped Red Army soldiers, and Jews from the ghetto, but at first those still in the ghetto would not listen to me. Many had had bitter experiences in their dealings with non-Jewish fellow citizens, who had betrayed to the Germans both Jews and Red Army soldiers who had escaped the encirclement. In any case, the people in the ghetto were far from certain that the partisans would welcome them with open arms.

In the end they no longer had any choice. In late July 1942, I was present when Major Reinhold was talking on the telephone. His concluding sentence was, "*Jawohl.* Operation Iodine will take place on thirteen of August!" I knew immediately what was meant. The major said to me, "Dieter, you are the only witness of this conversation. If anything leaks out, you will bear full responsibility!"

I replied, "*Jawohl!*"

I had very warm relations with Reinhold. He was old enough to be my father. He had sons in Germany and there was something paternal in his attitude toward me. Like me, his oldest son was called Dieter. Believe me, I got on very well with Reinhold, better than with his subordinates. I knew he respected my honesty, so by doing my duty as a human being I would be betraying this man personally, as well as signing my own death warrant.

When I entered service in the police I had to swear an oath of allegiance to the Führer. Later, as a Russian partisan, I swore allegiance to Stalin, but these oaths were invalid because they were sworn under duress. Breaking them was the price I paid to save not only my own life but the lives of other people.

Among the situations I was fated to experience, some were tragic, some painful, and some very frightening. I can talk about them now, although I do so reluctantly. Nevertheless, I believe I should share these experiences with you because there is no knowing in advance what kind of situations a person may face in their life.

I reported the planned operation to the couriers that same evening. They were determined to defend themselves with the weapons I had given them but I managed to persuade them that that was pointless. They had far too few firearms and would all be killed. It was considerably more important that at least some of them should be saved. That mattered more than shooting back for ten minutes at the Belorussians and Germans who would be coming to destroy the ghetto. I managed to persuade my contacts they should attempt to escape, but the ghetto's affairs were managed by the Judenrat, and it was for the Judenrat to take the decision.

Was I afraid? I don't remember. I adapted to the circumstances and they dictated my actions. I had an awareness of bearing responsibility for many people, and accepting responsibility is more important than carrying out orders. I thank God for endowing me with that ability.

The date of the breakout had to be agreed upon and the night of ninth of August was chosen. The Judenrat was not in favor of the plan and granted permission only for those in the resistance group to escape. The old gentlemen were still hoping that the Belorussian official they had bribed would save everybody.

The day before the escape, I fed my chief a false report that that night a group of partisans would be passing through a village located to the south. This was in the opposite direction to the vast and almost impenetrable forest into which the ghetto dwellers intended to flee. All the police and gendarmes went off to catch the partisans, leaving behind only four men at the police station. The ghetto was not being patrolled. Along with the other policemen, I sat all night in a futile ambush waiting for the promised partisans.

We returned early in the morning. At eight o'clock I was already at the police station when the agitated Burgomeister came to tell my chief three hundred Jews had escaped from the ghetto. As always, I translated. Major Reinhold asked why that had happened and the Burgomeister told him Jews were being shot in one place after another and those in the ghetto had decided their turn had come. The previous day peasants had come wanting to buy their furniture, and the people in the ghetto had taken fright. The chief ordered sentries to be posted to secure those who were still there.

When I heard only three hundred people had escaped, my heart sank. Why had they not all broken out? I had hoped to save the whole ghetto! It was only many years later that I learned the details of the tragedy which occurred the following night. To this day it is a source of great pain.

I was arrested the next day, betrayed by one of the Jews in the ghetto. It was someone I knew. He was an electrical fitter, Naum Bauch, and came several times to the police station to repair electrical wiring. He came to see Major Reinhold the morning after the escape and talked to him in his office for a long time. Reinhold did not invite me in. Up till then not a single conversation had taken place without my involvement and I realized I must be the topic of their conversation. I could have fled while they were talking, but where to? I could not go to the partisans because as far as they were concerned I was collaborating with the police.

After midday he finally ordered me to be summoned and said he suspected me of treachery. I made no reply. Then he asked, "Is it true that you revealed the date the ghetto was to be destroyed?"

"Yes, Herr Major, it is true." It was the only reply I could give to his direct question.

He was astonished. "Why do you admit it? I would have been far more likely to believe you than this Jew. Why did you do it? I trusted you so completely!" That reproach hurt me. I replied that I did it out of compassion, because these people had done nothing bad. They were no Communists, just ordinary workers, artisans, and simple people. I could not do anything else.

Reinhold said, "You know I have not personally shot a single Jew, but somebody has to do it. An order is an order." It was true. He had never taken part in the executions. He understood what an injustice was being perpetrated against defenseless people, but his human decency had a limit beyond which his duty as a soldier took over and could silence his conscience.

He then asked me about the weapons, and he himself listed the quantity and type of weapons transferred to the ghetto. I realized they had already checked the store. I admitted everything. Then he said he had no option but to arrest me. I was disarmed and imprisoned in the basement.

The next day he summoned me again. Major Reinhold told me that he had not slept all night and could not understand what secret motives were behind my behavior. "I imagine you have acted as a Polish nationalist, in order to take revenge for the extermination of the Polish intelligentsia," he said.

At this I thought it would be easier for him if I told the truth. "Herr Major, I will tell you the truth on condition that you give me the opportunity of committing suicide. I am a Jew!"

He clutched his head. "So the police were right after all. Now I understand. What a tragedy!"

I repeat this word for word, because it is impossible to forget something of that kind. You see the kinds of situations Germans sometimes got themselves into. They did not know how they should behave or what they should do.

"Write me a detailed confession," he ordered. No punch in the face, no harsh words. Our relations remained as they had been before, like between a father and son. There is no other way of describing it. I wrote the confession and said, "Herr Major, one time I looked death in the face and managed to escape. I ended up here through chance. I was brought here, could not refuse, and in my situation had no option. I think you understand me."

He called the sergeant-major and said, "Make sure he doesn't do anything foolish." I asked him to give me an opportunity to shoot myself before the Gestapo started liquidating the other Jews. Now I could only wait and was completely calm.

During the day and evening everybody usually ate together and that day I still ate with the gendarmes. In the evening my chief again summoned me and I reminded him, "Herr Major, you promised that you would give me an opportunity to shoot myself." He said, "Dieter, you are a levelheaded and brave young man. You managed to avoid death once before. Perhaps you will succeed on this occasion too."

I had not been expecting that. It was the amazing reaction of an honest man in an impossible situation. I held out my hand to him and said, "Thank you, Herr Major." He hesitated, but then shook my hand, turned, and left. I never saw him again. I was told much later he had been severely injured by partisans and died of his wounds. At that time he gave me courage and the will to live.

The gendarmes did not treat me like a criminal. Even after reading my confession and discovering that I was a Jew, they took me from the locked room where I was detained to the communal table. The way my escape was arranged was that I said I wanted to write a letter to my family, and they took me to my old workplace. I wrote a letter in the office and said I wanted to ask the boy who did the cleaning to take it to the post office. I knew he had already left. I went out unhindered into the corridor and ran from the building toward the fields. Three policemen were standing talking in the courtyard. They were from a different station, not from Emsk, but I knew them. They paid no attention to me.

When I had run quite a long way, I was pursued by some forty people on horseback and bicycles. I lay down in a freshly harvested field and hid among sheaves which had been piled up in a stack. Somebody ran past. They knew I was hiding somewhere and started combing the field in broad rows. As they were passing barely five meters away from me, the sheaves collapsed and the stack leaned over.

To this day I cannot imagine how they failed to notice me. I prayed fervently. Everything inside me was screaming. There have been two moments like that in my life, the first time in Vilnius when I hid in the cellar, and again now. They did not notice the movement of the sheaves and ran on. I heard one of them shouting, "It looks as if he's got away!"

I lay there and waited for darkness to fall before coming out. I wandered to a shed, went in, and fell asleep. Later, at around five o'clock in the morning, I heard protracted shooting. It was Operation Iodine. They were shooting the people who had remained in the ghetto. It was the most dreadful night of my life. I wept. I was destroyed. Where was God? Where in all this was God? Why had he hidden me from my pursuers but not had mercy on those five hundred children, old people, and invalids? Where was divine justice? I wanted to get up and go back there to be with them, only I had not the strength.

24. 1967, Haifa
FROM HILDA'S DIARY

Today is my 25th birthday. How awful! It seems no time at all since I was 16, and wailing because I had won the girls' skiing competition and Toni Leer told me it was unfair because I ought to be competing with the boys. He said I needed to be checked to see whether I was really a man or a woman. I beat him up. Musa came early this morning and brought me a present, a staggering gold bracelet in the form of a serpent with sapphire eyes.

I prefer silver, as Musa knows, but he said he couldn't give me silver when I am gold myself. He wanted us to go to Netanya for a whole day but I was busy all morning. I had promised Kasia to take her to find a job and then to collect a parcel for Daniel from the post office and go to the library. Musa waited four hours for me and then we did go to Netanya.

Today he absolutely had to go back home and I was a bit hurt that he had to leave immediately when I so much wanted to stay with him a bit longer. We had only three hours at the hotel and I cried when we had to part. He tried to explain that he does not belong to himself as much as Western people do. He is dependent on his family. His uncle had arranged to meet him today and he could not refuse or postpone it. He was very upset, too. We have been meeting for almost three years but I never know the next time we will see each other. We meet very rarely, apart from in church. It's dreadful. Musa told me I look more like a boy than a 25-year-old woman, and I remembered thumping Toni Leer for saying just the same thing. How funny.

25. May 1969, Haifa
LETTER FROM MUSA TO HILDA

Dear Hili,

I couldn't sleep last night after what you said yesterday about how difficult it is to be a German in the modern world. Daniel will tell you how difficult it is to be a Jew, and I can tell you what it's like being an Arab. Especially if you're a Christian by faith and an Israeli by citizenship.

It's fine being German. Germans live in shame and penitence. It's not too bad being a Jew. The whole world hates them, but everybody knows they are the chosen people. They amaze the world with their Israel, built among rocks and ruins, their tenacious brains and many talents which put all other peoples in the shade. There are any number of Jews in prominent positions all over the world: scholars, musicians, writers, lawyers, and bankers. This annoys the majority.

But what's it like being an Arab? There are 1,000 times more of us than there are Jews but who does the world know? Nasreddin Tusi? Avicenna? Imagine belonging to a people which always feels slighted and is always right. Islam gives the Arabs confidence and a sense of superiority. Arab Muslims are underestimated by the outside world and praise themselves. An Arab Christian is an unfortunate creature: the Jews barely notice the difference between an Arab Muslim and an Arab Christian. For them, both are their historical sworn enemies, except that a Muslim is a more reliable enemy.

The Jews do not trust us, even though we have chosen Israel and become its citizens in the hope that it will be our shared home. We are not trusted by the Muslims either. For them we are worse enemies than the Jews.

I would emigrate to Europe or America, but being an Arab I am bound by extremely strong family and tribal ties. My family does not see me as a separate unit. I live subject to all my relatives: the elder because it is my duty to respect them, and the younger because it is my duty to support them. It is almost impossible to escape from this. I would divorce Miriam if only I could, and you and I would immigrate to Cyprus, get married there, and live in any country where trees and flowers grow and people need parks and orchards. For that, though, I would need to stop being an Arab, which is impossible. You will remain a German, lamenting the aberration and brutality of your forebears, Daniel will remain a Jew with his crazy idea of making all people the children of God, and I will remain an Arab, longing for liberation from the oppressive Arab tradition of not belonging to myself but always to someone above me, be that my father, God, or Allah.

Dear Hili, when I am with you, just your presence is enough to free me from these burdensome thoughts and the hopelessness of our situation. Only when I am with you do I feel happy, and believe me there are very few Arab men in the world who could bring themselves to say such words to a woman. I love you, and I love the freedom which stands behind you, although both of us suffer from knowing it is not for us, that we are stealing it, although I do not know from whom. I am, nevertheless, profoundly convinced that God is on our side.

Do not leave me.

Musa

26. 1969, Haifa
FROM HILDA'S DIARY

Daniel brought me a branch of flowering almond yesterday. I can't believe he cut it. I looked at him in astonishment and he said, "Hilda, we have been together for five years." Daniel is right, it is precisely five years since I came to Haifa. The flowers are somehow only half real, as if made of mist or vapor, and they smell of something nice which is not in them. Perhaps the germ of the almonds which will come later? No, almonds have a much more definite and edible smell. This smell is not at all culinary.

Daniel celebrated the Mass. I was the only person there. He is disappointed that almost none of our residents are much bothered about the church but, as he says, "We are not feeding them with an ulterior motive. Who knows, perhaps they will come and pray with us sometime."

Actually, that is not really fair. On Saturdays and Sundays quite a lot of people come together here. In the evening, after Daniel had gone, I decided to write down how many of us there are. Here's the list: Daniel, me, Vera, Kasia and her children, Irena and her children, Olaf, Shimon, Yosef and his family, the sisters Susanna and Cecile, Bożena, Chris, Aidin and his family, Musia and Tata, Henryk and Louisa, Elena, Isidor. Those are the ones we can rely on. Then there are another twenty or so people who come from time to time, for festivals, but who do nevertheless participate in the life of the community. There are perhaps thirty or so who drop in occasionally, like Musa. We can add those in the shelter who, whether they like it or not, belong to the community by the fact of staying there. Eight of them are permanent and perhaps another ten are transient. Beggars, tramps, and drug addicts: we call them "residents." They are ours, too. A rough total is around sixty people.

We have also lost people. Samuel and Lydia emigrated to America. Miriam died, poor Anton was killed, and Edmund and his family went back to Europe. Aaron and Vita and their children and a few other people have left us for the synagogue.

Daniel is very upset when he loses a person, but also always repeats that, "Every person should seek their own way to God. The path is personal, otherwise we would not be a community of volunteers in the Lord but an army led by generals."

We have most difficulty with the transients. Daniel insists nobody should be sent away, so we sometimes get homeless people coming here. In Israel there are fewer of them than in Europe, but they are drawn to us like a magnet. Since the night shelter was built we always have a few people settling there for several days, or even for up to a month. Daniel said they should pay by bringing a bucket of water up from the spring. It has wonderful drinking water but the stream is very weak. The water we get from the Druze does not taste so good.

Now my German experience is proving unexpectedly useful. There are certain rules for treating homeless people which really do help us to find a common language. We currently have a pair of junkies, a very pleasant girl and a young man from Hungary, and they smoke some kind of trash. They are spaced-out, slowed down, and good humored. The girl, Lora, is Jewish, a hippie, and covered in flowers.

She is a real musician and plays the flute marvelously. I told her how good she is and she laughed and said that she is really a violinist but doesn't have a violin anymore. She has such a vivid personality that her young man, a gypsy called Giga, rather pales in comparison. They have been living here for two months already. I have heard that Lora plays in the street near the market. She sometimes even brings money for the church funds, and Giga washes the dishes very conscientiously.

Last week a terrible drunkard wandered in. He was really ill, made everything filthy, and I spent two days cleaning up after him. Then I persuaded him to go to the hospital and drove him there. I went to visit two days later only to find he had run away. We can't afford a cleaner or a cook and do everything with our own hands. It's lucky Daniel earns money with his guided tours, and we get donations from abroad.

Daniel works very hard. Now that he has his own corner in the church he often stays until late. He is translating the New Testament and other texts from Greek into Hebrew. Actually, there have long been translations but Daniel considers them to be full of inaccuracies and even downright mistakes. I once asked him how many languages he knows. He said he knows three well, Polish, German, and Hebrew, and thinks he speaks others very badly. That is simply not the case. He conducts tour groups in Italian, Spanish, Greek, French, English, and Romanian, and I have heard him speak with Czechs, Bulgarians, and Arabs in their languages. That he has conducted services in Latin all his life goes without saying. It seems to me he has the gift of speaking in tongues which once descended on the apostles. He does have textbooks of various languages on his bookshelf, so some things God has given him but others he has learnt himself! Where did he find the time to learn all these languages? I asked him one time and he said, "Do you remember the Pentecost?" and laughed.

Of course, I well remember this extract from the Acts of the Apostles, when "tongues like as of fire" came down upon the apostles and they began speaking with other tongues and every man out of every nation under heaven heard them speaking in his own language. Daniel seems to be endowed with that tongue of fire.

Although, one time when we were expecting Romanians, I bought him a Romanian textbook. He had it on his table for two weeks and used to take it away with him in the evenings. "It's very beneficial to put a textbook under your pillow," he told me. "You wake up in the morning and all the lessons have been learned."

Looking at him, I recognize that language is not that important. All that really matters is what the language is expressing. I feel there is something of a contradiction here. If it doesn't matter which language you conduct the service in, why make so much effort to translate everything into Hebrew? I am forever making new copies of the liturgy with variant translations because he believes every word has to be comprehensible. I do occasionally notice contradictions in his views. He will sometimes says one thing and sometimes another. I can't always keep up with him.

27. 1959–83, Boston
FROM ISAAK GANTMAN'S NOTES

The problem of national consciousness here, in America, is to some extent subsumed by the problem of self-identification. Although close in meaning, these are different things. National consciousness, at least among the Jews, has both internal and external constraints. Declaring themselves the People of the Book, Jews have programmed themselves to master, assimilate, and implement the Torah. It is an ideology. It establishes the chosen nature of the Jews, their exclusiveness and preeminence over all other peoples, but also their isolation in the Christian and any other communities. Needless to say, there have always been individual representatives of the Jewish people who have demurred from the overall fixed programme and not fitted into the mainstream of the national life.

The hermetization of Jewish society led naturally to the legend of "the Secret of the Jews," which developed over many centuries into the notion of the "global Jewish conspiracy" against everybody else. The last exposure of such a plot, already within living memory, was the Doctors' Plot in Russia shortly before the death of Stalin. In our secular age the blow fell not on the traditional Jewish community but on professionals, the majority of whom, if I understand correctly, were not religiously inclined. They were no more than the remnant who had survived the Catastrophe. It is probably the same "remnant" spoken of by the Prophet Isaiah. It is not the first time in history that this kind of destruction of the majority of the people has occurred. The

Babylonian Captivity, of course, reduced them to slavery but did not take lives. The same occurred in Russia during the Stalin period.

European Jewry as it had existed for the last three centuries has been destroyed. I do not think it is capable of regeneration. A few hundred Hassids who have removed themselves from Belorussia to New York with their charismatic Lubavitch tzadik and several hundred yeshiva students led by Orthodox Mitnagdim rabbis are unlikely to prove viable in the modern world. The children of Orthodox Jews who wore tallit prayer shawls are taking Hollywood by storm, and also the Arabs in Palestine. I may be mistaken, but it seems to me that after the Catastrophe, the Jews have lost the rigorous skeleton which supported them. As an atheist, I encountered, both during the war and in the postwar years, many Jews who had suffered a crisis of faith. Our people turned into a collective Job sitting in ashes, having lost their children, their health, their property, and the very meaning of their existence. They had also lost to a large extent the treasure they most prized, their faith itself.

My wife's unfortunate niece, Tsilya, at the age of six stood in a village street, in a crowd, a Polish peasant woman holding her by the hand as all the local Jews were locked in a shed which was going to be set on fire. The little girl prayed to God to save her mother but they set light to the shed and 80 people, including her mother and sisters, burned to death. Tsilya was hidden by kind Catholics, survived the war, and emigrated to Israel. She was from a very religious family but since then has never once been inside a synagogue. "If He exists," she says, "He has wronged me and I will not forgive Him; and if He does not exist what is the point of talking about Him?"

That is logic. I do not suppose Job was placated by the new children he was given in place of his earlier ones. And those innocent children killed by a collapsing roof purely because of a questionable wager between the Creator and some monster known as the enemy of the human race, is he supposed to have forgotten them? The book of Job is very poetical but lacks logic. As was demonstrated to us by that delightful and intelligent man, Professor Neuhaus in Jerusalem, the reading of Jewish texts is a great art which I have scarcely approached—only enough to understand what it is that Jewish thought ponders.

I have found that to be a cosmogony of the most abstruse nature, entirely divorced from reality, a grand Glass Bead Game. Over the course of the 2,000 years during which boys from the age of five have studied at this school of logic, Jewish brains have been trained to a very serviceable level. All those Jewish mathematicians and physicists, Nobel prizewinners and unsung inventors are byproducts, people who renounced the royal road of the Kabbalah, which considered the same problems as all the other esoteric sciences of other times and peoples. It was, however, the Kabbalah which became suspected of being a kind of intellectual terrorism extending over half a millennium. It is pointless to seek to disprove this craven idea: all intellectual activity can be seen as terrorism against established canons, whether in science, culture, or sociology.

Ultimately, any attempt to establish identity, to provide a rigorous definition of one's personality, is based on a particular hierarchy of responses taking in gender, nationality, citizenship, educational level, professional affiliation, political affiliation, and the like.

My own identity derives from my profession. I am a doctor, and this is the foundation of my life and activities, as it was even in the ghetto and the partisan unit. In all contexts I remained a doctor. The most unsettling time of my life was after the war when I was required over a period of many months to provide a medical assessment of evidence at the Nuremberg Trials. With the threat of physical annihilation no longer present, I lost my inner bearings, my equilibrium, and the ground shifted beneath my feet. It was not living in the ghetto or our uncertain existence in the forests, but the sum of the knowledge about what happened to the Jews from 1939 until 1945 which changed my outlook. My self-identification as a doctor became irrelevant. As far as the Nazis' Nuremberg laws were concerned I, as a Jew, was subject to the 1935 "Law for the Preservation of German Blood and Honor." The law forced me, an atheist who had consciously repudiated Judaism, to resume my national identity. I readily rose to the challenge and the outcome was my illegal immigration to Palestine.

For almost ten years I lived in Israel. I was there when the United Nations declaration creating it was signed, and I hope the Jewish state will continue to exist far into the future. I have never shared the ideals of Zionism and have always believed that the modern world should be organized not along lines of religion or nationality but on a straightforward basis of territorial citizenship. The state should be organized by citizens living within the borders of a particular territory and that is what its legislation should ensure. Few people agree with me, not even Esther. I had no hesitation in accepting the Boston offer. From a professional point of view, I could find no better place to work anywhere in the world. Having lived several years in the United States, I have concluded that it is the US which most closely adheres to the principle, which I believe optimal, of organizing the state on a basis of territorial citizenship. In other respects, it is the same cesspit you find anywhere else in the world.

Any thorough religious upbringing promotes rejection of those who think otherwise. It is only through general cultural integration, with religion removed to the sphere of private life, that a society can develop in which all its citizens enjoy equal rights.

This was the guiding principle of the Roman Empire, and Joseph II, Emperor of Austria-Hungary in the 18th century, tried to apply the same principle in 1782 with his *Toleranzpatent*, the "Decree on Tolerance." This proclaimed the principle of the equality of all the state's citizens before the law. It is an extremely interesting collection of documents and undoubtedly reflects the influence on the Emperor of Joseph von Sonnenfels. The decree offered Jews the prospect of assimilating without being subjected to compulsory baptism, and opened the way for development of a secular state which integrated all its citizens. Von Sonnenfels himself was a baptized Jew, and his ideas about the structure of the state were not supported by the majority of Jews who viewed the new laws as merely impeding their traditional way of life. It was Joseph II who abolished the self-governing Kahal which allowed Jews to live in a state within the state. He allowed them to engage in trades and agriculture, accorded them freedom of movement, and gave them access to higher education institutions. He introduced conscription for Jews, giving them equality with other citizens in that onerous duty also, made German the medium for teaching in Jewish schools, and Germanized Jewish names and surnames. That is where such surnames arose as Einstein, Freud and Rothschild. Amusingly, I read somewhere that Hoffmann played a part in devising such extravagant German-sounding names as Rosenbaum and Mandelshtam. These laws, which so upset simple people, nevertheless created a community of educated people free from national narrowness who could participate in the overall activity of the state.

Right up to our own days there was an underlying difference between the descendants of the Western, "Austro-Hungarian," Jews and the Jews of Eastern Europe. The latter, until the end of the war, or more exactly until the Catastrophe, preserved an inward-looking way of life in the stetls. The exception were the Jews of Communist Russia, some of whom were carried away by the new ideology in the early years of the Revolution. For the most part, however, the Jews of Yiddishland—Lithuania, Latvia, and Poland—tended to look back to the old traditions. Even today there is no shortage of Jewish men wearing long-tailed early 19th-century lapserdaks, and women with wigs on their shaven heads.

My redoubtable teacher, Professor Neuhaus, calls modern Hassidism "a glorious victory of the letter over the spirit." In his criticism he went further, considering all the ultra-conservative trends of Christianity, both Western and Eastern, to be the cousins of Hassidism. National consciousness in our time draws strength not from the veneration of dogma but from recipes, the cut of your clothes, how you perform your ablutions, and also from the fallacious but ineradicable conviction that traditionalists possess the full measure of truth.

28. *May 1969, the Golan Heights*
LETTER FROM DANIEL STEIN TO WŁADYSŁAW KLECH

Dear Władek,

The bus bringing a tourist group to the Golan Heights has broken down. There is an oil leak which indicates lengthy repairs. We have already seen all the sights, I have told them all I have to say, and now we find there will be at least a three-hour delay before another bus can be sent for us.

The Germans from a Cologne evangelical group have gone off for a walk. I am sitting beneath a fig tree, my helper Hilda is asleep, her head covered with a cowboy hat she was given by a tourist from Texas.

It is not the first time I have brought tours here. There is an enormous graveyard of military equipment, Russian tanks, armored personnel carriers and trucks, antitank ditches which have caved in, and an enormous quantity of mines. It seems nearly everyone has been planting landmines for several decades, Turks, English, Syrians, and Jews. Several hundred Soviet tanks were destroyed here. You can only walk in areas which have been cleared of mines. The local sappers are goats and donkeys, which get blown up periodically. So do people sometimes, but there are few people here. It is a No Man's Land, a vast plateau and mountains of volcanic origin. In the crater of one extinct volcano there is a radar station. There are black and gray boulders, thorn bushes, and occasional clumps of trees. There is an almost biblical legend about the trees. An Israeli agent in Syria occupied a prominent post in the government. When Israel was created in 1948, the Syrians constructed a strong defensive line here with underground fortifications. The agent suggested to the Syrian government that they should plant trees by each of these so that soldiers could shelter in their shade from the heat. A bonus was that the soldiers would be invisible from the air. His proposal was considered sensible and trees were planted.

The Golan Heights are a strategic area from which you can fire on the whole of Northern Galilee, and Syrian missiles were sited here. During the Six-Day War the Israelis were able to destroy them from the air within ten minutes. The Jews knew that above each of the secret installations they would see a grove of trees. Over 20 years these had grown to maturity and pinpointed the targets. The agent, Eli Cohen, was arrested and publicly executed in a square in Damascus. The Jews did everything they could to ransom or exchange him, but Syria was adamant. Tourists tend to be far more interested in stories of this kind than in facts from biblical history.

The early Syrian Church was just as ascetic and forbidding as the volcanic plateau here. Perhaps the extraordinary diversity of the scenery in Palestine, so still in Galilee, so harsh in the deserts, so harmonious in Judaea, engendered the diversity of religious schools. Everything was born here.

All these lands conquered in the Six-Day War are to be given back, but you have the impression that nobody particularly wants them. They are not unpopulated. There are 1 million Palestinians in Gaza. Does Egypt really want them with all their problems? There are several hundred thousand Palestinians on the West Bank and these are a great burden on Hussein. The only point of this whole campaign has been to demonstrate military might and there will be a high price to pay in years to come. Such are the local problems as I see them. It is almost impossible to live here without getting caught up in the daily flow of events. Indeed, working as a priest in Poland, are you able to ignore the pressure from the Soviet Union? We know that in every age it has been raw politics which has determined the direction of the life of the Church.

The most important thing for me has been a gradual recognition of the oneness of life. In the past I had a great sense of hierarchy and ranked events and phenomena in terms of their relative significance. That sense is dwindling. "Significant" and "insignificant" prove equal. More precisely, what you are doing at a particular moment is significant, and then washing up the dishes after a lot of people have had dinner becomes entirely the equal of the liturgy you celebrate.

I will finish. My helper Hilda has woken up, seized the binoculars, and immediately spotted a local cliff hare, which actually looks more like a badger. Jewish hares don't look anything like Polish hares. Even without binoculars the very sight of them lifts your heart.

With brotherly love,

D.

29. May 1969, Haifa
LETTER FROM HILDA TO HER MOTHER

Dear Mother,

Yesterday Daniel and I went to the Golan Heights with a group of German tourists from Cologne. It was the first time I had been there and it was staggering—the ancient ruins, the scenery, and the signs of war. Absolutely everything there, even the ancient history, is evidence of warfare, destruction, and an endless barbaric militarism. Since ancient times everything that has been ruined here has not just collapsed from being old or becoming decrepit. It has been smashed and destroyed by enemies. It's probably the same everywhere in the world, but here you really notice it. That, though, is not what I am writing about. You know Daniel worked as an interpreter in the Gestapo during the war, and when he was arrested for helping the partisans he was saved by his superior officer who let him escape. They were on very good terms, and this Gestapo officer had children who were Daniel's age, and even a son born in the same year. Perhaps it was thinking about his son that made him treat what he thought was a Polish youth so well.

Can you believe it, in the German group there was a man, he was one of the oldest because most of them were young, and he turned out to be the son of that same major. As the sightseers ask their questions, Daniel always invites them to give their names, and the man said he was Dieter Reinhold. Then Daniel said, "The father of Dieter Reinhold saved my life during the war." They shook hands and embraced. Nobody knew what was going on, and this German knew nothing about the story. His father died on the Eastern front in 1944 and all he knew was that he had been a major and served in the Gestapo, so he was a war criminal. Such a silence descended. Nobody asked any more questions. They were all silent and only Daniel and Dieter Reinhold talked together quietly. I don't know what they said. Of course I was thinking about our own family, you, your father, and grandfather. It struck me that this simple division of people into Fascists and Jews, murderers and victims, evil and good is just too straightforward. These two men, I mean the major who was killed and Daniel, stood on the very borderline where things are not that simple.

Daniel told me that when he is remembering those who died, he always prays for that major. I found that meeting so moving that I can't tell you everything that is in my heart. I want to learn to pray like that, too, for everybody, but not in the abstract, really and truly.

Love from
Hilda

Oh, I forgot to write that there is an ancient monument here on the Golan Heights which looks like Stonehenge in England. It is the place where the legend of Gilgamesh was acted out! They are excavating it at present and Daniel knows the archaeologist in charge and has promised to show me over it some time. He says that there is evidence of the most ancient civilization in the world and even, perhaps, of the presence on Earth of people from other planets! Everything here is like that. No matter where you turn you just gasp in amazement.

30. *June 1969, Haifa*
SERMON OF BROTHER DANIEL AT PENTECOST

My dear friends, brothers and sisters!

Every festival is like a bottomless well. You look into it and see down into the depths of human history and the depths and antiquity of relations between man and his Creator. The Jewish Feast of Shavuot, or "Weeks," predates the Feast of Pentecost historically. It is entirely possible that the festival existed even in the pre-Christian, pagan world. Then, too, people brought the first fruits of their harvests in thanksgiving to the Lord. On this day Jews commemorate the giving of the Torah, the ten commandments. In the Christian world, Pentecost acquires an additional significance. The first fruits of the harvest are still brought, and that is a reminder of the ancient sacrifice of thanksgiving. But we also remember another event, the pouring out of the Holy Spirit of the Lord upon Christ's disciples. The disciples heard "a sound from heaven as of a rushing mighty wind" and they saw "cloven tongues as of fire, and it sat upon each of them. And they were all filled with the Holy Ghost, and began to speak with other tongues." The Acts of the Apostles go on to list the tongues which were heard from the lips of the disciples: the languages of the Parthians, Medes and Elamites, of dwellers in Mesopotamia, Judaea and Cappadocia, in Pontus and the province of Asia, Phrygia, Pamphylia, Egypt, in parts of Libya, and in Rome, Crete, and Arabia. In effect this was all the languages of the ecumene, the known inhabited earth. It was a prototype of the world in which you and I live now. Today Christ's disciples speak all the languages of the world, and you and I celebrate the Feast of Pentecost in the language of our Master.

There is one more thing I would like to say on this day: tongues of fire appeared above each of the disciples, but what happened to the tongues after that? Is there a vessel in man, a receptacle in which he can retain that fire? If we do not have that receptacle within us, the Divine Fire departs and returns to where it came from, but if we have that vessel within ourselves, it will stay.

Jesus in his human life was a vessel which fully received the Holy Spirit poured into it. The Son of Man became the Son of God.

Human nature combines with Divine nature following just this recipe. Each of us present here today is a vessel for receiving the Spirit of the Lord, the words of the Lord, Christ himself. That is all theology has to tell us. We are not going to be asked for our thoughts about the Divine nature, but we will be asked, "What did you do? Did you feed the hungry? Did you help those in trouble?" May the Lord be with us all.

31. November 1990, Freiburg

FROM A TALK BY BROTHER DANIEL STEIN TO SCHOOLCHILDREN

I lay there and waited for darkness to fall before coming out. I wandered to a shed, went in and fell asleep. Later, at around five o'clock in the morning, I heard protracted shooting. It was Operation Iodine. They were shooting the people who had remained in the ghetto. It was the most dreadful night of my life. I wept. I was destroyed. Where was God? Where in all this was God? Why had he hidden me from my pursuers but not had mercy on those five hundred children, old people, and invalids? Where was divine justice? I wanted to get up and go back there to be with them, only I had not the strength.

I later recollected blundering through the forests not far from the town for three days, but then I lost track of time. I desperately wanted not to be, just to cease to exist, but I never thought of committing suicide. I had a feeling of having been killed five hundred times already, of being lost between earth and heaven and, like a ghost, belonging neither among the living nor among the dead. At the same time, the instinct of self-preservation was alive in me and, like an animal, I started back at the slightest threat. I must have been close to madness. My soul was crying out, "Lord! How could you allow this?" There was no reply. He was not in my mind.

I was wearing a police uniform. It made me a target for everybody: the Germans who had announced my escape; the partisans hunting down stray Germans; and any local villager wanting to claim the reward for turning in a Jew and a criminal all in one.

For three days I ate nothing. I remember at one time drinking my fill from a brook. I did not sleep either. I stumbled deep into a place to hide, among bushes, fell asleep for a minute but immediately leapt up when I heard the rattle of machine gun fire. Again and again I had flashbacks to that moment when I realized the inhabitants of the Emsk ghetto were being executed. From time to time I heard real shooting. One evening I came out to the edge of a village which I had saved from the executioners but even there I could not count on refuge. I sat down on a fallen tree and no longer had the strength to go on. Anyway, where should I go? For the first time in three days I fell asleep.

The prioress of the displaced Convent of the Sisters of the Resurrection, Mother Aurelia, came to me. She was wearing a long black habit which had turned reddish-brown over the years and a winter jacket which was too small for her and was patched at the pocket. I could see all the details incredibly clearly, as if they were slightly magnified: her pale face covered with a fine down, her sagging cheeks, and her unwavering bright blue eyes. I began speaking but do not remember the words I spoke, although we were talking about something more important than my life, far more important and significant. I asked her to take me to someone. I think we were talking about the Walewicz sisters. At all events, I imagined that dead Marysia was also there, nearby, only no longer looking at all as she had. Her appearance was not altogether human. She was shining and radiating peace. Before I had finished speaking, I suddenly realized I had asked the prioress for death, and that this figure which looked like Marysia was not her at all but Death. The prioress nodded, agreeing, and I woke up. There was nobody beside me. I could not remember what exactly I had said, but after this vision I felt amazingly serene. For the first time since my escape, I had slept properly.

That same night I returned to Emsk. I knew where the sentries were posted, where I needed to take particular care, and went to the nunnery in the building next to the police station. I knocked and one of the nuns opened the door to me. I rushed in past her to the prioress. She knew I had helped the partisans because sometimes my information to them had been conveyed through her. By this time there were notices on every post in town that I was wanted, and everybody by now knew that I was a Jew.

I did not have to explain anything to her. I was hidden in the attic.

It was a Sunday. Every Sunday since Father Walewicz had been murdered, the nuns had walked to the nearest church, sixteen kilometers from Emsk. The prioress said to the sisters, "We shall ask our Lord for a sign as to what we should do about the young man."

The prioress and one other sister entered the church just as an excerpt was being read from the Gospel about the Good Samaritan. You may have forgotten that extract. It is a parable which Jesus taught his disciples. A certain Jew was traveling from Jerusalem to Jericho when he was attacked by bandits. They robbed him, beat him, and left him by the roadside. A passing Jewish priest saw him and walked by on the other side. In just the same way another Jew walked past. And then a foreigner, a man from Samaria, walked by and took pity on him. He bound up his wounds and took the unfortunate victim to an inn. There he left the sick man, paying the landlord to take care of him. Jesus then asks which of the three was the neighbor of the man who had fallen among thieves. The one who had shown him compassion. "Go, and do thou likewise."

It was these words that the nuns saw as a sign from God. They returned and told the others what had happened. It has to be said that of the four nuns, two were against allowing me to stay, but they accepted the sign.

I hid in the attic. This house had belonged to a Jew who had been shot, and his books had been put up there. The nuns had also stored the convent's library there. The first book I picked up was a Catholic magazine in which I read about the apparitions of the Virgin Mary at Lourdes. Before this I had read the Bible and knew about miracles, but none of it had seemed to have any bearing on my life. The miracles in Lourdes had occurred only a few decades previously and were being described by one of my contemporaries. I was amazed by the sense of their immediacy, especially after the incredible events I had experienced myself. After all, had not my salvation, in Vilnius and in the field when my pursuers passed within a few yards without noticing me, not also been a miracle of this kind?

I asked them to give me the New Testament, which I had never before held in my hands. In the Polish school where I had studied, I was excused from the Scripture classes. I read it for the first time and found the answer to the question most urgent for me at that time: where was God when those five hundred people from the ghetto in Emsk were being shot? Where was God in all these things which were happening to my people at that moment? What was one to make of Divine justice? Now it was revealed to me that

God was with the suffering. God can only be with the suffering and never with the killers. He was killed together with us. The God suffering together with the Jews was my God.

I saw that Jesus really was the Messiah, and that his death and resurrection were the answer to my questions. The events in the Gospel had happened in my ancient land, to Jesus the Jew, and the problems dealt with in the Gospel were so important to me precisely because they were Jewish problems, associated with the land for which I was so homesick. Here everything came together: the resurrection of Christ with the testimony of St. Paul, and the discovery that the Cross of Christ was not a punishment from God but the path to salvation and resurrection. I identified that with the cross which my people bears and with all I had seen and experienced. This understanding of suffering is also to be found in the Jewish religion. There are rabbis who think the same way, but at the time I did not know that.

I became reconciled to God through Christ, and it occurred to me that I should be baptized. For me this was an extraordinarily difficult decision. For Jews it means taking the path "down the stairwell which leads away." Anyone who accepts baptism no longer belongs to the community of the Jewish people. I wanted, nevertheless, to be baptized without delay.

The prioress considered that I needed first to be prepared, to learn more about Christianity. I protested, "Sister, we are in a war. Nobody knows whether we will be alive tomorrow. I believe that Jesus was the Son of God and the Messiah. I beg you to baptize me."

The prioress was perplexed and went to pray in the shed in order to reach a correct decision. At noon she came to me again and said that when she prayed she had suddenly sensed that I would become a Catholic priest. That really had not occurred to me! I forgot her words for several years, and recalled them only much later. That same evening I was baptized. One of the nuns christened me.

I left their house then, because I did not want it to seem that I had been baptized only in return for the refuge they had granted me.

For several days I wandered through the surrounding area, afraid that people I met along the way might recognize me. There were posters everywhere, detailing the reward for my capture. I could not go into the forests because the partisans would not take long to make up their minds about me. For them I was a German policeman.

I could see no alternative, and four days later I returned to the sisters.

They took me in and I spent the next fifteen months with them. Their windows looked out at what was now the police station.

32. 1972
From Hilda's diary

We left the car and went up the track. Daniel had a small sack with about 10 kilograms of flour. An Arab came toward us with a donkey with two panniers. We said hello and went on up to the village. A Syrian village still surviving in Israel after the war is a great rarity. Either they had not heard the news or hadn't taken it in. There was a wonderful, verdant valley between brooding hills through which a stream which, curiously, hadn't yet dried up was flowing. There were fig trees and olives. It was not particularly dirty but so poor they didn't even have the usual old car tyres strewn around the place. Daniel confidently climbed the hill above the village towards a remote spot where there was something halfway between a house and a dog kennel. A little courtyard had rocks piled up in it and there was a strange round stove which looked African.

Daniel shouted, "Rafail!" Out came a decrepit old grasshopper with a big bony head, wearing an Arab galabiyya smock and a Central Asian tubeteyka on his head which had faded until it was quite colorless. Daniel said, "This is my assistant." Rafail nodded and did not once glance at me. Daniel gave him the sack of flour and he took it, muttering what sounded like "Good" rather than "Thank you." "I have no tea or coffee," he said, as if apologizing. "That's okay, I wasn't expecting any," Daniel murmured.

Within ten minutes, a flock of Arab children of varying ages had come running. They squatted among the rocks and stared avidly. "Go away now. I'm busy today. I've got guests. Tomorrow morning," the grasshopper said, and the children moved away. They stood a little way off and listened to a language they couldn't understand.

"There's only one girl here speaks Hebrew. She lived in Haifa and learned it there. She's very proud of it. The others speak Arabic, but can't write. I am teaching them. There is no school in the village, and 13 kilometers is too far for them to walk." We drank some water from a jug. "Do they annoy you?" Daniel asked, pointing to the children. "I chase them away sometimes, and sometimes I just go away myself. I have a cave I can hide in in the mountains. Well, not a whole cave, I only rent half. The other half is occupied by bats," he said as if he'd made a good joke. I felt sick. I am scared of ordinary mice, and can't bear even to think about bats. We spent less than an hour in his courtyard and left.

On the way back, Daniel told me Rafail was born in Jerusalem, in the old Bukhara Jewish quarter which still exists. He was the fifteenth son in his family and ran away to the Jesuits. They brought him up in a Catholic school, he became a monk, and has only recently come to live in the Golan Heights. Before that he lived 15 years or so with the Bedouins.

"Was he trying to convert them?" I asked, but Daniel laughed. "He tried when he was young. Now he says that he just lives with them. He says he doesn't believe he can teach anybody anything."

"Is he as fatalistic as that?" I couldn't refrain from asking, although I always curse myself for asking too many questions. But Daniel laughed again and replied, "No, he's just very intelligent. He is really one of the most brilliant people I have ever met. It's just that all his teeth have fallen out, he goes around barefoot and in rags, and washes only when it rains and a lot of water gathers in his trough. That's why nobody wants to see how clever and educated he is. If you were to put a jacket on him and boots and make him give lectures, he would do it better than anyone. Better than many, anyway. I made a point of bringing you with me so you could take a look at him. He is a great rarity is Rafail."

I had a strange feeling. It's as if Christianity in Europe and here in the East are completely different things. With us everything is terribly decent, rational, and genteel, but here it has something extreme about it. A stone hovel with an earthen floor, ancient asceticism, a complete break with civilization. What do the two things have in common? Nothing. So why are they both called Christianity?

Is it only Christ? Which one? The Christ of the Crucifixion or the Christ of the Transfiguration? The Christ performing miracles or the Christ preaching sermons? Lord, help me to love everybody.

33. 1972, Dubravlag-Moscow
CORRESPONDENCE BETWEEN GERSHON SHIMES AND HIS MOTHER, ZINAIDA SHIMES

I got my latest instalment of mail on Wednesday, four postcards and two letters. The men in neighboring bunks are amazed and wonder who writes to me so much. Today is the Sabbath. We don't go to work on Saturdays. We managed to negotiate that. Instead we have a roster, but that is our choice so it's cool. I have had no time all week to finish writing my reply. I will hand the letter in tomorrow morning and may add a bit more. Yesterday morning we went to work early and saw an aircraft in the sky. It looked so beautiful, leaving a thin trail behind it. A long, long tail.

I have finished *Joseph and His Brothers*. Many, many thanks to Kirill for getting it and sending it. How amazing the book did not disappear on the way, which happens sometimes. It is both incredibly interesting and tedious but there is so much information about history and all sorts of thoughts. Personally I prefer Feuchtwanger as a writer, although as a child he was too keen on big moustaches.

It seems to me that Kirill exaggerates Thomas Mann's significance, but I love Kirill so much and I'm so grateful for everything that I am prepared to agree with him about anything. Let Thomas Mann be the greatest genius of all times and peoples, a coryphaeus of the sciences, and even the best basketball player in the Uruguay national team. Unfortunately the little book written for our grandmother in spidery lettering got lost in the post, but here I have met an old shoemaker from Grodno who speaks the language of the people to me.

The inmates are very interesting. There are Lithuanian and Ukrainian nationalists, all sorts of religious types. One young guy is a Baptist and refused to serve in the army on religious grounds. There is one amazing geezer serving out his time. He is a writer. There were a couple of them, really famous. I see him when I have free time, which isn't often, but it's like being at the university.

Thank Kostya and Masha. Their letters are fun. Ask them to tell me when the heir arrives. I am not losing hope we will live on the same street one day. I even dream of it sometimes, although in my dreams it looks more like Koktebel than anywhere else.

Svetlana's postcard is so funny. I liked the picture. It doesn't say who the artist is, but I think it must be Chagal. My wish to get a real education gets stronger and stronger. When everything finally comes to an end, I shall study, study, and study, as Lenin said we should.

Medvedev will probably be interested to know there is a library here with prewar magazines, not complete series just odd issues. I sometimes find very interesting articles in them. The older the magazine the more interesting it is likely to be.

Last month I fulfilled my work norm for the first time and for some reason felt very proud.

Dubravlag, Lagpunkt No. 11

1976, *Flight from Vienna to Lod Airport, Israel*
LETTER FROM GERSHON TO ZINAIDA SHIMES

Dear Mama,

You always said I had a hellish character. I thought so myself, but apparently it is not so. The proof is this letter I am writing to you directly from the plane. I thought it would be a long time before I wrote to you, and perhaps even . . . I was very disappointed with your choice but will try nevertheless to understand why you have decided to stay in that cesspit. The plane has been flying toward Eretz for two hours. I feel a greater happiness than I have ever felt before. No joy can compare with that of someone flying back to a home he has never seen. Our group consists of twelve people and we spent several days together in Vienna: a Jewish family from Riga, religious, with an old man in a skullcap leading them. They speak Yiddish among themselves! How on earth did they survive the war? Then there's another couple on the plane who are very famous, a China specialist and his wife who have been campaigning to emigrate for a long time. He gave an interview to an American radio station and there were protest meetings in support of him at Columbia University which caused a big stir. He also signed a letter to our defense just after we were arrested and there was hope we might be released without a trial, so it did us no good at all. I want to go over to him but he looks very important and I am just "'an ordinary Soviet prisoner."

Don't be sad, Mama. Concentrate on Svetlana. My dear sister will give you plenty to worry about and have lots of baby goyim whose noses you can wipe. I have nothing against Seryozha, but Svetlana always finds "nonstandard solutions." She should have married a nice Jewish boy and we could all have emigrated together but no, she had to marry a Cossack. I don't understand why she spent so many years trying to emigrate and then got stuck in such a banal manner "at the prompting of her heart"! That's it! The plane is coming in to land! Through the window I can see the Mediterranean and the coast of Israel.

1977, *Hebron*

FROM A LETTER FROM GERSHON TO ZINAIDA SHIMES

. . . can't compare it with any anything else. Of course, it is a mobile home not a real house but it is fair enough for the home of a Jew to be a tent, a tabernacle or a shelter. We live like the settlers of the early 20th century, except that where they had rifles we have machine guns. Ever since I landed at Ben Gurion Airport I have been feeling a little drunk. For now there are five of us men, four women, and a child. The man without a woman is, of course, me. Only it's not because I have a hellish personality, as you have always been telling me. It's just that I suggested to the girl I brought here that she should leave. At least now I know exactly the kind of woman I do not want by my side, but the kind I do need I have yet to find. In general I like Israeli women very much. The ones I met while I was in the ulpan learning Hebrew were very strong and independent. Admittedly it was mostly Russians there (they call Jews from Russia "Russians" here). Only the teachers were Israeli. I like the Russians here very much, too, but you meet such beauties among the local girls they take your breath away. What would you say if I married a Hebrew girl who couldn't speak a word of Russian? We work, we stand guard, and we sleep in turn. We have a tractor we bought with a bank loan. It is six kilometers to Hebron, but the road is not safe. It passes an Arab village. Something you will find interesting is that the Cave of Makhpelah where all the patriarchs, Abraham and the others, are buried is near here. It didn't make a great impression on me, but the others were in raptures. To tell the truth, I have no time left for raptures. There is a lot of work. I remember sewing mittens in the camp. What a nightmare! At that time I could not imagine that all those samizdat Jewish magazines, Hebrew language circles, and Jewish discussions in kitchens would lead to a real life like this. The people are mixed. Among the settlers there are religious and non-religious Jews, like us. The local rabbi from Hebron visited us recently. He is very famous, and right wing. Incidentally, it is very interesting. In Russia I was considered practically a Trotskyite in our circles, very far-left, but here I am considered to be on the right. In Israel there's no telling your left from your right!

I used to not have much time for the lads who wore skullcaps, but here they are splendid, sturdy boys and very jolly, especially the rabbis.

INSCRIPTION ON A PHOTOGRAPH: Our women prepare for the Sabbath. You can see part of the laid table.

1978, *Hebron*
FROM A LETTER FROM GERSHON TO ZINAIDA SHIMES

. . . came over to me. He looked a hundred years old, but his mind was completely clear. He asked whether my ancestors might have been from Nikolayevo. I said yes. Then he asked whether I might be a relative of David Shimes. I said yes, he was my grandfather. At this the old gentleman gave a little wail of delight. "Oy, weh! He was my best friend!" I said, "Don't be upset, but he got shot in the 1930s." "That," he said, "is really no surprise. All his brothers and sisters were shot and poisoned, too."

"Perhaps those were not his brothers and sisters, but somebody else's," I said. "My grandfather did not have any brothers or sisters because he was born in shame. His mother bore him out of wedlock, and in a good Jewish family that was a great scandal. My grandfather's mother, my great-grandmother, contracted tuberculosis because of a nervous disorder and was sent to Switzerland for treatment, where she died."

"Entirely so," said that frail old man. "The father of your great-grandmother was a grain merchant, and there has never been a poor grain merchant since the world began. It was he who sent Rakhil to the sanatorium, to escape the disgrace. But everybody in the town knew which revolutionary had given her the baby. Entirely so. David was brought up by two maiden aunts. We were in the same class at grammar school, and he was the only friend I had in the whole of my childhood. In 1918 my father brought me to Palestine and I have lived here ever since. It was only after the war that I read Stalin had managed to murder the father of my friend David even though he was in Mexico. Stalin murdered all of David's brothers and sisters who were born legitimately, too. I read a big book about it. It's all described there."

I was simply astounded, Mother. How come this old stranger knows more about our ancestors than we do ourselves? Or did you know but concealed it from your children? In short, when this old man mentioned Mexico, I realized who he was talking about.

Perhaps in his old age he is confusing everything, but if this is true, it is a complete kick in the back for me. Knowing how cautious you are, write back just one word, "ice-pick," and I will take that as full confirmation. To tell the truth I just can't believe it!

Ma! I remember now why I am writing to you. I have gotten married. My wife is an American Jewish girl. You will like her very much. Her name is Debbie, Deborah. When I have photographs I'll send them.

So long,
Gershon

1981, Hebron
FROM A LETTER FROM GERSHON TO ZINAIDA SHIMES

. . . Why are you so surprised? It is iron logic. In the early 20th century all nonbelieving Jews rushed to support the revolution because socialism was a very seductive idea and I understand my ancestor very well. He was an idealist. They were all idealists, only first they had no luck with socialism and then they did no better with internationalism. It all fell through. The next step was for new idealists to immigrate to build socialism in one country, Israel. That's what we have now. What is more, it was all non-religious lads again, because the believers had a religious idea: we already have our Holy Land. It was the non-religious men who came to the Holy Land to build socialism, and I am one of them! I do not like capitalism, I like socialism, only not the kind we had in the USSR.

You are surprised I am living on something like a collective farm, but it is my collective farm, a kibbutz, and I like it. I have an even bigger surprise for you. I did not write about it before, but now I don't think you will be surprised by anything I do. When Binyomin was born I was circumcised at the same time as him. I won't discuss the reasons I did that with you, but I am sure I did the right thing.

I am glad my wife supports me. So there, I have become a Jew at 30 years of age, together with my firstborn. Deborah will be having another baby soon, another boy I hope. She promised me to have as many babies as she has strength for, and she is a very strong and sturdy woman in every respect.

I have never referred again to your refusal to immigrate to Israel because of Svetlana's idiotic marriage, but now you write that relations between her and her husband are terrible and that they are practically at each other's throats. Perhaps we should look at that again. Let her divorce her Cossack, take her daughter, and I will send you all an invitation. Nowadays it is all much simpler than it was five years ago. I am quite sure that if my father were alive, he would have brought you here in 1976. You will always think I killed him with my samizdat and prison sentence and that his heart failure was my fault. Perhaps you are right, but do you really not understand that even if I had not been so determined to emigrate then, I would still have come into conflict with the regime over something else? Think about my suggestion. I am quite sure father would have sided with me.

INSCRIPTION ON A PHOTOGRAPH: This is a view from my window. To the left in the distance was the Oak of Mamre, but now there is not even a stump left and one can only point out where it used to stand.

INSCRIPTION ON A PHOTOGRAPH: This is Binyomin. He has puffy cheeks when he is lying down, but when you pick him up he is less of a piglet.

June 2006

LETTER FROM LUDMILA ULITSKAYA TO ELENA KOSTIOUKOVITCH

Dear Lyalya,

I am sending you a revised section of text, provisionally Part Two. The editing is insanely difficult. The whole vast amount of material crowds in on me, everybody wants to speak, and it's difficult to decide who to allow up to the surface, who should wait, and who I should just ask to keep quiet. Teresa Vilenskaya is particularly persistent. There have been many Saint Teresas, of Ávila, of Lisieux (who was called "of the Child Jesus," or "the Little Flower of Jesus"), and the contemporary Mother Teresa of Calcutta who died recently. That is just by the way. My Teresa is alive and well and awaiting the appearance of the Messiah.

Like the other major books, this one is grinding me down. I can't explain to myself or to you why I ever took it on, knowing in advance how impossible the task would be. Our minds are such that we reject the notion of insoluble problems. If there is a problem there must be a solution. It is only mathematicians who know the redeeming formula that "under the given conditions the problem is insoluble." Even if there is no solution, it would be good at least to be able to see the problem, to view it from the back, the front, the sides, from above and below. Ah, that is what it is like: it can't be solved. There are so many such things—original sin; salvation; redemption; why God, if he exists, created evil; and, if he does not exist, what meaning life can have. All questions for good children. While they are little, they ask the questions; and when they grow up, they find a handy answer in a tear-off calendar or a catechism.

I would very much like to know, but no logic provides the answers. Neither does Christianity, or Judaism, or Buddhism. "Reconcile yourselves, ladies and gentlemen, to the fact that many problems have no solution. There are things you just have to learn to live with, and put up with, and not resolve."

Now something splendid: my grandson Luka has been born. He weighs 3.2 kilograms and is 53 centimeters in height. The threatened snagging of the umbilical cord did not happen and everything went fine, without a Caesarean section. I saw him the day after he came into the world. What a remarkable distance there is in a single generation: you are still standing there, but now there is a new main character, who is concerned solely about physiological matters. You see the magnificence of the event which is the birth of a new infant. It is the formation of a new world, a new cosmic bubble which will reflect everything. He wrinkles his nose, wiggles his fingers, jerks his little feet, and does not yet give a thought to all the nonsense which so preoccupies us: the meaning of life, for example. For him his digestion is the meaning of life. I will send you a photo eventually, when I have learned how to download it from a telephone to a computer.

How are Marusya and Lyova? Have you stopped taking their temperatures? I suspect it was no coincidence that Marusya's thermometer broke. She wanted you to give up taking her temperature, decide it was always high, and stop taking her to school!

Love,

L.

PART THREE

ER 4 *(Translated from Lithuanian.)*

Mrs. Jonavičute,

sending you a remarkable book with Janis. It has been translated
lish by a Moscow translator who is very close to us in spirit. The
manuscript and although it has been offered to a Moscow pub-
use there is little likelihood that it will be printed, although some-
acles do happen. After all they published the magnificent Teilhard
in! As your journal is independently minded, perhaps you will be
rint at least some excerpts from the book, but translated into
n. We have people who can help with that and would produce a
ity translation quickly.

hanks in advance,

a Benda

ENT OF TECHNICAL CONSULTANT

4 (four) letters received for technical assessment were written by
rzysztofowna Benda.

first addressee is a Moscow translator, Valentina Ferdinandovna
andidate of Philological Sciences, lecturer at the distance learning
of Culture, reference material No. 0612/173P.

second addressee is Asta Keller, resident of Vilnius, housewife,
of a prisoners' support group, engaged in constantly sending postal
to camps. Reference to card index materials 2F-11.

hird addressee is Anna Gediminovna Jonavičute, editor of the prose
f the Lithuanian journal *Young Lithuania*. See catalogue 2F-11.

author referred to, Teilhard de Chardin, died in 1955. He was a Je-
est and a palaeontologist. He did not engage in anti-Soviet activity.

or Archive Research Assistant Lieutenant Kuzovlev

ON: Archive.

r Perevezentsev

ilnius

PEREVEZENTSEV TO LIEUTENANT-COLONEL CHERNYKH

RNAL MEMORANDUM

my duty to inform you that the activities of the underground
convent accommodated in three private apartments in Vilnius is en-

1. 1976, Vilnius

FILES FROM THE ARCHIVE OF THE DISTRICT KGB DEPARTMENT

FROM AN OPERATIONAL SURVEILLANCE FILE
DOC. NO. 117/934

STATEMENT

I wish to bring to your attention and request you to take measures in
respect of the fact that the woman living in Apartment 6, No. 8 Tilto Street,
Teresa Krzysztofowna Benda, is a furious Catholic and brings many people
to the apartment block. They assemble regularly like they are having a meeting, pretending to drink tea. While other more deserving people live in small
rooms with 12 square meters despite all they did in the war and have been
awarded personal pensions, Benda occupies 24 square meters and has a balcony. It is known that her father was a Pole and Polish nationalist and it is
unknown how he managed to avoid being punished. He died in 1945 after
liberation by the Soviet Army from tuberculosis.

What is more, for eight years she has been paying the rent and communal charges but living who knows where. Not that she has been subletting or
speculating with the accommodation. No. But we are fed up with it. I draw
to your attention that this disgrace is taking place.

SIGNATURES OF RESIDENTS: illegible
ACTION: Refer to Agent Guskov for investigation

REPORT FROM LIEUTENANT GUSKOV

I have to report that on 11/04 this year an investigation was conducted
on the basis of a statement from residents of No. 8 Tilto Street with illegible
signatures. The source of the statement was found to be Nikolai Vasilievich
Brykin, with whom the appropriate work was conducted. It was confirmed
that 4–8 people gather in Benda's room on Wednesdays and Sundays from

7–9 in the evening. There are invariably two men and the number of women varies. All are Lithuanian and conversation is conducted in the Lithuanian and Polish languages.

In the course of an operational investigation it was established that Teresa Krzysztofowna Benda is a covert nun who took her vows in 1975. Additional information may be obtained from No. 8 Section upon application to the deputy chief of the operational section.

It is believed that on Wednesdays and Sundays, Benda conducts a meeting of evangelical groups in her apartment.

In order to establish the identity of those attending, further operational activity is required.

Benda graduated from Leningrad State University and was directed to work at the Vilnius City Library in the capacity of bibliographer. She worked there from 20 August 1967 to 1 September 1969. A reference from the workplace is attached.

Prophylactic measures are not considered necessary.

Senior Lieutenant Guskov

ACTION: Archive

Major Perevezentsev

FROM SECTION PT-3 TO OPERATIONAL INVESTIGATION SECTION

Report

Section PT-3 encloses copies of 4 (four) letters from Teresa Krzysztofowna Benda to diverse addresses.

LETTER 1

Dear Valentina Ferdinandovna,

The purpose of my letter is to thank you. Your words that "The Gospel is not an icon, its purpose is not to be kissed but to be studied" are going round and round in my head. The fact that even just reading the Gospels in a different language gives additional depth of understanding I can well understand. I have read the Gospels in Polish, Russian, Church Slavonic, Lithuanian, German, and Latin and have always been aware that there were distinctions in the perception of the text. Truly, God speaks to people in different languages, and each language subtly corresponds to the character and characteristics of the people. The German translation of the Gospels is striking for its simplification, by comparison, say, with the Church Slavonic. I can only guess what rich nuances are contained in the Greek and Ancient

Hebrew texts. I am thinking of the text of the O

Everybody who was at our tea party was gr
brother S. sends you greetings. Tell me in advan
to come to Vilnius. We will try to organize a moc

Accept my sisterly love. May God protect yc
Teresa

LETTER 2

Dear Valentina Ferdinandovna,

I have been brought a remarkable present f
I need most of all. The profundity, the boldness,
tunately I do not know English and am unable to
translation, but the impression from the book is
an original. There is no strain, complete freed
Thank you so much for your hard work. The autl
and very topical.

I have been ill for almost two weeks, and sin
the convent all that time, I was allowed, while I v
ment. Here, too, I have devoted myself to readir

Next week L. is returning from the Vatican a
with great impatience to seeing him. Can you ima
who saw that person.

May God protect you,
Teresa

LETTER 3 *(Translated from Lithuanian)*

Dear Asta,

I am sending you some warm clothing to pa
isn't much money, unfortunately, but I will send
need to tell me yourself what to do about food pr
a food parcel is just sent to a particular address,
there are many restrictions.

Perhaps when you are in Vilnius you will coi
keeper to call me or leave a note, and I will write t
The best time is Sundays from 4 to 6.

May God protect you,
Teresa

tirely under control. Over the past year the number of so-called nuns has de-
creased: one of the sisters (Jadwiga Niemcewicz) has died, a second (Teresa
Benda) has left the convent and is again living at her registered address. On
Sundays a priest, Jurgis Mickevičius, visits an apartment at the address Apartment No. 1, 18 Dzuku Street, and celebrates Mass, and on the other days of
the week the nuns read the rosary. The majority of them are of pensionable
age and many have been released from prison. Prosecuting them for their
misdemeanors is not considered expedient. Operational surveillance of the
apartments has been discontinued. They remain under surveillance by local
personnel with district-level authorization.

Major Perevezentsev

PRIVATE LETTER FROM MAJOR PEREVEZENTSEV TO LIEUTENANT-
COLONEL CHERNYKH

Dear Vasiliy Petrovich,
I have written an internal memorandum to you as required, but wish to
add that the situation in Vilnius is such that we have neither the time nor the
resources to concern ourselves with half-crazy old women. Anti-Soviet na-
tionalistic feeling is very strong, and I am much more concerned about young
people. We are currently preparing two major samizdat cases. We could clean
out this nest of old women in a day, but I can see no point whatsoever in
doing so. The journalists will make a fuss and what will we gain? It is, of
course, for you to decide. We are subordinate to the Center, but I urge you,
under the old pals' act, not to burden us with religious oddballs. We have
more than enough to cope with already. Give my best wishes to Zinaida and
Olga. I think back to how good life was in Dresden!

Alexey Perevezentsev

2. *January 1978, Vilnius*
FROM A LETTER FROM TERESA BENDA TO VALENTINA
FERDINANDOVNA LINTSE

. . . the brazenness of this request, or perhaps its audacity. When I arrived
at the clinic on 13 February, L. was the color of old paper and looked to have
been drenched with water. You cannot imagine, even his lips, which were
always so firm and purposeful, had slackened and become as puffy as those of

a child. His arms were so swollen he could barely raise them. Every movement clearly cost him an effort. I left with the feeling that he might die at any minute. That night when all the sisters had retired and that special night-time tranquillity had descended which is so conducive to prayer, I got up and prayed fervently. The thought was vouchsafed me that I might depart in his place. In the morning I went to the prioress who is well disposed toward me. I told her that I felt a call to leave in place of L., and she gave me her blessing.

I went immediately to the Church of the Immaculate Conception on Žvėrynas and again began to pray. That golden moment duly arrived when I knew that I was being heard, and I called out in prayer, "Take me instead of him". I did not leave the church until late evening, entirely absorbed in a trance of prayer, and returned to the sisters late at night.

The following morning the prioress whispered to me, "L. underwent an emergency operation last night. He has had a kidney removed. He is at death's door." She smiled, as it seemed to me, a little sardonically.

Imagine, everybody had prepared themselves for L.'s death but he turned the corner. His recovery was exceptionally rapid.

Just three weeks later he was discharged from the clinic. The bishop would not allow him to return to Kaunas but himself accommodated L. At Easter he officiated. Throughout the service I was weeping tears of joy. My sacrifice had been accepted and I began to prepare myself.

Immediately after Easter I began to weaken. I lost ten kilograms or so. Alas, my joy and exultation were replaced by such terrible physical and spiritual weakness that I will not attempt to describe it. Last week I fainted twice. The sisters are very gentle and caring. Our life is complicated by inner relationships. By no means everything lies on the surface, but I always knew this was the price we pay for our closeness to the Source.

L. is back in Kaunas and I do not see him. That upsets me, because his compassion would be so precious to me. I ask your prayers, dear sister.

May the Lord bless you,
Teresa

3. May 1978, Vilnius

FROM A LETTER FROM TERESA TO VALENTINA FERDINANDOVNA

. . . indescribable fear. I fell asleep with difficulty and awoke five minutes later in a fit of panic. I kept returning in my mind to that moment when, in a state of exaltation incompatible with a sober spirit, I asked for this substitution. I was then in such a state of grace that my departure at that moment would have been blissful. Now however I was at the very bottom, and a heaviness was crushing me. I was in a dreadful state and my horror at the imminence of death, an all-enveloping animal fear, sickened me. Although I had eaten nothing, I was constantly vomiting a foamy acid which tasted horrible. It was the taste of fear. One further completely appalling thing began to happen to me. Against all the laws of nature, excrement, buckets full, began to gush from me. You could not imagine anything more vile. I felt at that time as if my whole physical self was being expelled from me in that stinking form, and that in a few days' time, I would have been consigned in my entirety to the sewers. There would be nobody left to flush away the last pile of filth. And then I cried out. This was not what I wanted! In sacrificing myself I had been expecting rewards, beauty, justice for heaven's sake, but I had received something quite different! But then, where had I gotten the idea from that a sacrificial victim would experience joy? There was only nausea and terror, and not a hint of bliss. As I knelt at a toilet brim full of excrement, I prayed. Not before the image of the Virgin, not before the Crucifix, but before an evil-smelling pile of shit I prayed, "Let me not die now. Let the worst thing imaginable happen, let me even be expelled from the convent, only let me not die now."

A week later I was able to walk again, and three months after that I was expelled. The prioress treated me as if I had deceived her. She had not expelled Sister Joanna, even though she is an incorrigible thief. The sisters shunned me like the plague, after looking after me and expressing so much sympathy.

For the first time in 20 years, my Easter has been not a resurrection but a dying. There is no joy. Like Lazarus, I am in my grave clothes although my life has not been taken. My isolation is complete, almost without relief. It is only your letters, sister, if I may call you that, which support me, and one of my old colleagues from the library who attended our meetings. He still comes to visit me and sometimes takes me outside for a walk.

I am so sad that you cannot come in the summer as you had planned. We could have gone to the Curonian Spit. My aunt still lives there and cells could be found for us in her house.

Remember me in your prayers,

Teresa

4. July 1978, Vilnius
LETTER FROM TERESA TO VALENTINA FERDINANDOVNA

Dear Valentina Ferdinandovna, dear sister,

As things have turned out, you are the only person left I can talk to about what is most important to me. I am only too aware that an admission of this kind may cause great embarrassment to the person to whom it is made, but knowing your immense spiritual reserves, I implore you to hear me out. The form of a letter is best suited to this because there are things about which it is even more difficult to speak than to write, but I know that you cannot fail to understand me. It is precisely because you have had that rare and ineffable experience you told me about when we last met, the experience of direct communion, the experience of hearing and seeing the invisible. The existence of the spiritual world was revealed to me when I was still barely a child, and that revelation distanced me from girls of my own age.

I told you I lost my father very early and have no memory of him. My mother died when I was nine and I was brought up by an aunt, a good woman but very dry. She was childless and no longer young. She married for the first time when she was around 40, and her marriage brought me many trials. Her husband had some admixture of oriental blood. Although his surname was Russian, his appearance was completely Tartar, and he had the cruelty of a Tartar. My aunt worshipped him. She was attached to him like a cat, and I have ever since been revolted by physical love. We lived in the same room, and their proceedings during the night made me feel literally sick. I prayed to the Mother of God to protect me from this, and then I started to hear music. It was the singing of the angels and it enveloped me like a cloak. I became peaceful and fell asleep, and my dream continued to the sound of that music. My aunt's marriage lasted four years. It was a carnal frenzy, and their shamelessness continued to be an ordeal for me although the music shielded me from much.

And then that dreadful Gennadiy was transferred away. He was a soldier, and he disappeared forever. At first my aunt tried to find where he had gone, but he had evidently given instructions that she should not be given his new address. Their marriage had never been formalized and, to tell the truth, I think he already had a wife who had refused to move to Vilnius with him and had gone to live somewhere else. But that is neither here nor there. My aunt went completely mad. She was in and out of psychiatric hospitals, and it was a great relief for me when I went away to St. Petersburg to study. I am ashamed to say I visited her rarely, and she met me with such hostility every time that I couldn't be sure whether I should go to see her at all. I remember from those difficult years the protection granted me by the Virgin and her angelic music. How often I have lamented that God did not give me the gift of memorizing that music and noting it down. Ever since, I have been certain that the great composers like Bach and Handel were only writing down sounds which reached them from heaven by the grace of God.

I almost starved during my student years in St Petersburg. But what do I mean, almost? I did starve. The girls with whom I shared a room in the hostel were just as poor as I was but, as if by design, all of us were pretty. In the second year one of us began engaging in what was little short of prostitution, then a second. The third, like myself, suffered from the situation, but one way or another our enterprising roommates brought back men, usually during the day, because it was more difficult to gain admission to the hostel in the evening. Sometimes, though, they brought men to stay the night, and then I seemed to find myself back in the times of my unhappy childhood, when the squeals and grunts of concupiscence kept me from sleep. Once again, only prayer and the music were my consolation. I graduated with distinction. I am an art historian by profession and was invited to stay on as a postgraduate student, but I was so weary of that hostel! Imagining another three years of living like that, I declined the offer. My aunt was almost constantly in the hospital and I was left on my own in a large room.

What a joy it was to be alone, not to hear other people you had no wish to hear. I started work at the library. By then I was already so accustomed to praying and had grown so firmly into the Catholic life that I resolved to enter a convent. Soon I was introduced to a prioress and became a novice. Needless to say the convent was clandestine. We lived in apartments but under a strict rule.

I had wonderful support. My prayers at that time were so full of grace that I heard not only the sounds of wonderful music but also sensed the presence of Him who is the Source of Light. Two years later I took full vows. The trying life of a convent I found easy and joyous. I was constantly anticipating these visitations and they even became the object of my prayers.

One time when I was at prayer, something happened to me. It was as if a hot and playful wind enveloped me, caressed all of me and wordlessly asked me to consent to surrender to it. I had experienced nothing similar previously, and despite an unusually strong desire to prolong these sensations, I refused. But the caressing continued and the hot air spiraled around me, penetrating my breasts and loins. Then, as if awakening, I cried out to the Lord, and immediately heard hissed cursing and a slight jolt.

These phenomena began to recur. I told the prioress about them. I fear she was not discreet and many heard about it from her. I began to gain the reputation of a madwoman. Remembering my aunt's illness, I realized that there might be a hereditary tendency to insanity and, eager to persuade myself that this was not the case, that is, that I really was being tempted by the Devil and was not merely ill, I learned to summon this demon. It gave me the feeling that it was not he who ruled me, but I him. The more so since I was always able to stop the temptation in time. Now I realize this was a dangerous game, but that did not immediately occur to me. At times the demon simply paralysed me so that I could not move my hand to protect myself with the sign of the Cross. I couldn't even say a prayer, my throat seemed to freeze. These nocturnal battles lasted for hours while the other sisters were sleeping peacefully.

The priest forbade me to have any contact, to inwardly consort with a being to which he gave the name of Satan. I was afraid to utter that word, but after it had been said by the priest, I could no longer deceive myself. The priest assured me that the Enemy can never cause us harm unless we ourselves consent to it.

The more Satan tormented me, the more the Lord consoled me. This lasted for several years, and then there occurred what I have already told you about. I took the vow relating to L. which I was unable to honor.

I would not burden you with this tale of my oppressive spiritual phenomena of years past if this temptation had not befallen me again. To my profound regret I no longer receive those prayerful joys, those quiet rapturous moments of the presence of God which were there in the past. The prayers I incessantly send heavenwards remain unanswered.

Your unfortunate

Teresa

5. *October 1978, Vilnius*

LETTER FROM TERESA TO VALENTINA FERDINANDOVNA

Dear Valentina Ferdinandovna,

Over the past month so many completely astounding things have happened that I really don't know where to begin.

After prolonged but unsuccessful attempts to meet the prioress she consented to see me. Our conversation was unpleasant in the extreme. She said she would not give refuge to one possessed and that I was leading the other sisters astray.

After this devastating encounter I went to my father confessor, who was even more firm with me. He said that I evidently had a different vocation, that a good Christian could work for the Lord in the world, too. I really do not understand why they are so intent on driving me away, and when I broached the matter with him he spoke terrible words to me. He said that my spiritual experiences testify to the fact that I am completely in the power of Satan, and in the Middle Ages people like me were burned at the stake for associating with him.

"But St. Anthony, too, had his temptations," I protested timidly. "If he had had you as his father confessor, would you have sent him to the stake?"

He smiled sarcastically and said, "That is the path the saints tread." What was he implying? My mind and heart cannot take it in.

Nevertheless, when I left him I had a strange sense of relief. Now I can rely on nothing except the love of the Almighty, and I have given myself to Him. Prayers to the Virgin, whom I always loved so much, have become completely impossible. Her immaculate nature does not allow me to address her. Only Mary Magdalene can now be my protectress. Does my absurd situation not make you smile? Having preserved my virginity for the Lord, I have been expelled for the most dreadful of perversions and feel profoundly guilty for these nocturnal manifestations to me of a power which I hate with all my heart.

The Catholic Church is expelling me, and into whose arms?

I have moved back to my old room, to my dreadful neighbors who hate me and dream only of getting their hands on my accommodation. I spend my days in prayer and in cruel temptations. As before, I go to the Church of the Immaculate Conception on Žvėrynas, but there, too, where before people treated me kindly and with openness, I'm met with disdain and suspicion.

6. December 1978, Vilnius

FROM A LETTER FROM TERESA TO VALENTINA FERDINANDOVNA

. . . now I am coming to the last part of my sad tale. My only friend, Efim, to whom fate guided me at the library, has greatly supported me all these past months. I do not know how I would have survived physically and financially if it had not been for his unstinting succor. He is a lonely man, and now he has made a very unexpected suggestion that I should enter into a fictitious marriage with him and emigrate to the State of Israel, to the Holy Land.

My mind is in such a state of confusion that I have forgotten to mention the most important thing—Efim is a Jew, although all his spiritual striving is directed toward Orthodoxy. For a long time he did not undergo the sacrament of baptism, and did so only two years ago after his mother died. She would have found it very painful. Since then he has entered ever more fully into the life of the Church.

He attends church services every day and even serves at the altar. He compiles surveys of current spiritual literature for the abbot here, writes papers, and makes translations from foreign languages if the abbot considers a book to be of interest. The abbot has great respect for Efim and loves talking to him. There seem to be very few people so educated and serious-minded within the clergy. In the end, Efim shared with him his intention of becoming a priest. To this the Father Superior said very emphatically that his nationality was a major obstacle on that path and he could hardly imagine a Jew in the role of parish priest. For a Russian flock, the abbot remarked, it would be too great an ordeal.

And this, dear Valentina Ferdinandovna, despite the fact that the abbot is one of the most liberal and enlightened priests! A long time ago, before the war, he went through the ordeal of the labor camps and survived only by a miracle.

There is an Orthodox bishop who lives, or rather, hides, in Vilnius. He, too, is an ex-prisoner, and at the abbot's request sometimes ordains young people as priests, secretly, of course. A bishop, as you know, has the right to ordain through the laying on of hands anybody he considers worthy, even without their having attended a seminary.

How absurd it is. Efim has a university degree in classics. He is proficient in Greek, Latin, and Hebrew. He is a Candidate of Philology and is so versed in theology that he could lecture at any seminary. The abbot himself told Efim that under different circumstances he could have been a professor at a theological academy! That is how highly the abbot respects him, but even so he refused to give his blessing to his ordination.

Efim has considered becoming a monk. He even traveled to the Pskovo-Pechorsky Monastery and stayed there last year for a month, but when he came back he told me he was not ready to take such a step.

At the same time Efim is thinking of emigrating to Israel. He has an uncle and several cousins there who managed to leave Lithuania before the Germans came. Efim's mother was saved during the war by a Lithuanian peasant woman.

So now, finding himself in an uncertain situation and seeing that I am in an equally uncertain situation, he is proposing that I should enter a fictitious marriage with him and try to make a new life in the Holy Land where there are convents and other houses for those who incline to the monastic life. Although rejected by the convent, I remain a nun. Nobody has released me from my vows and this proposal of Efim's is my only chance of starting a new life.

Dear Valentina Ferdinandovna, I value your advice above all others' because you have long been close to the Dominicans and lead the perplexing and dangerous life of a nun in the world. You are so active and do so much valuable work that it is by you that I would like to be advised. The main problem is deciding for myself to emigrate to the Holy Land, because neither our prioress, let alone the bishop, will give me their blessing to do so. Even if the difficult formalities of emigrating can be overcome, I am accustomed to monastic discipline and obedience and find it very difficult to undertake such a wilful action.

In order to merit your advice, I must tell you everything I myself know about the situation. Efim is a man of quite exceptional nobility of spirit. I even believe that in pondering the option of emigrating to Israel he is mindful of the opportunity it would give to repair my destiny. Of himself he says that it will be there, in the land of Jesus, that he should be able to overcome his indecision regarding his future path, whether as a priest, a monk, or simply as a lay person.

I have never before met a man so profoundly immersed in Orthodoxy, so splendidly informed on the texts of the liturgy, and so knowledgeable about theological subtleties. He has the inspiration of a Catholic and the conscientiousness of a Protestant. For him the library is truly his home and he is in the full sense of the word a man of the book. He has long been writing his own treatise on the history of the Eucharist from the earliest times up to our days.

My sweet Valentina Ferdinandovna, I feel guilty about pouring all these tormenting problems out on your poor head. Forgive me, but I know that without your advice I am incapable of reaching a decision.

May God keep you, dear sister.

Your Teresa

7. December 1978, Vilnius
LETTER FROM TERESA TO VALENTINA FERDINANDOVNA

Dear Valentina Ferdinandovna,

Events are developing so rapidly that I am writing to you even before receiving your reply to my last letter.

Yesterday Efim came and told me he had had a two-hour talk with the abbot. Efim informed him that, as he sees no prospect of being able to participate in the life of the Orthodox Church in Lithuania, he is inclined to emigrate to the Holy Land. Completely unexpectedly, the abbot then said he would be prepared to bless his ordination as a priest on condition that he emigrated. There is now only one obstacle to his becoming a priest: Efim is a bachelor and has no intention of marrying. In the Russian Orthodox Church there is a tradition, almost a law, that only married men are ordained into the priesthood. That is a complete reversal of the celibacy of Catholicism. Is this not a sign from above?

Efim and I knelt down to pray and prayed almost until dawn. Needless to say he has never thought that his companion could be any woman other than me, but each of us has had to make a sacrifice. I must change my faith and convert to Orthodoxy, he must take it upon himself to be responsible for me, and we have both undertaken to bear witness to God in a marriage of the spirit, a brother-and-sister relationship, a perpetual living of a shared life and shared service. What is that service to be? This decision we entrust to the Almighty.

I wept for the rest of the night. My tears and prayers delivered me from my usual nocturnal trials. I remembered those first tears of happiness after I had become a nun, when I would be wakened in the night not by fear and torment but by joy, by a prayer rising from the depths of my soul and rousing me from sleep. The sad thought occurs to me that I have lost that greatest of gifts. Next week I shall go to Father L. and hope very much that he will support me.

I ask your prayers, dear sister. May the Lord bless you.

Teresa

8. 1979, Vilnius
LETTER FROM TERESA TO VALENTINA FERDINANDOVNA

Since that day everything has rushed by like something out of a movie. After five days I was anointed with Holy oil and was accepted into the

Orthodox Church. Holy Communion came as a great surprise to me. It was one of the most powerful spiritual experiences I have ever had. I can tell only you and Efim that by comparison with the True Wine I drank of from the Orthodox chalice, the Catholic communion seemed rather feeble.

My vow, after changing my denomination, was purely a matter for my conscience, and on 19 May we were married. The application to register a civil marriage had been made earlier, and the day after we signed the register we applied to emigrate. Efim's cousin had found a speedy way of sending us both an invitation through the consulate here. To this I can add that the abbot has told Efim we will face no objection from the authorities because he has personal contacts in this area. He also said Efim might be called in for a discussion by a very important department and asked him not to refuse to collaborate because it is only by agreeing that he will be able to serve the Church. That, after all, is the one thing we are both longing for, and no price seems too high to pay.

We may leave very soon, but the two of us are sitting here in a state of paralysis when we should be packing books. Efim has a large library he could not think of leaving behind. There are a great many books in foreign languages, there are ancient volumes in Hebrew which were saved from being burned during the war, and before they can be exported we need to obtain various special permits and there are lots of other forms we have to obtain.

Whenever I hear someone say "Israel," my throat tightens. I cannot believe my own feet will walk the Via Dolorosa, and my own eyes will see Gethsemane, and Mount Tabor, and the Sea of Galilee.

I have one very important question. Can I write from abroad directly to your address or should I use other ways?

With love,

Your Teresa

9. 1984, Haifa
FROM "READERS' LETTERS," *HAIFA NEWS*

Dear Editor,

Several days ago I was walking down a street in the city of Haifa when I saw the following notice on a house in one of the streets in the city center:

"There will be a meeting of the Association of Jewish Christians at the Community Center on 2 October at 18.00 hours."

I don't give a tinker's curse about this society, but it does raise two issues: who is financing it, for one. And secondly, why is it being allowed to exist in Israel at all? We got by without this organization in the past. Why has it been set up now? The Christians have brought down so much war, persecution, and death on Jews from ancient times to the present that no Arabs even come close. What are we doing encouraging the existence of such organizations in Israel?

Shaul Slonimsky

REPLY FROM THE EDITOR

Dear Mr. Slonimsky,

Our newspaper could reply to your question itself. The traditions of our young state are in accordance with democratic principles, and the creation of an Association of Jewish Christians reflects the freedom of religion embraced by Israel. We have, however, invited a reply to the question from Father Daniel Stein, a war hero who has received many awards for fighting Fascism, a member of the Order of Carmelites, and director of the Association of Jewish Christians.

REPLY FROM FATHER DANIEL STEIN TO MR. S. SLONIMSKY

Dear Mr. Slonimsky,

I'm very sorry our notice so upset you. That was not part of our intention. The Association survives heaven knows how, but, at all events, at no cost to the taxpayer. There is too much enmity in the world we have inherited. After the experience of the last war in Europe, it seemed impossible that such a charge of hatred as was expended by the peoples during those years should accumulate ever again. Alas, we find that there has been no lessening of hatred. Nobody has forgotten anything; nobody wants to forgive anything. Forgiving really is a very difficult matter.

That Galilean rabbi the world knows as Jesus Christ preached forgiveness. He preached a lot of things, and to Jews most of them were familiar from the Torah. It was thanks to him that those commandments were made known to the rest of the non-Jewish world. We Jewish Christians respect our Master, who said nothing that would have been totally unknown to the world before his coming.

Christianity in history has indeed persecuted the Jews—we all know the history of the persecutions, pogroms, and religious wars—but in recent years a painful process of revising Church policy in respect of the Jews has been taking place within the Catholic Church. Specifically, in recent years the Church in the person of Pope John Paul II has acknowledged its historical guilt.

The land of Israel is a place of great holiness not only for the Jews who live here today. By Christians and Jewish Christians it is venerated no less than by Jews who profess Judaism, to say nothing of our brother Arabs who have settled this land, lived here for a thousand years, and whose ancestors' bones lie side by side with those of our own ancestors.

When our land withers and is rolled up like an old carpet, when dry bones arise, we will be judged not by the language we prayed in but by whether we found compassion and mercy in our hearts. That is all our organization has been set up to achieve. It has no other aim.

Daniel Stein, Priest of the Catholic Church

10. November 1990, Freiburg

FROM A TALK BY BROTHER DANIEL STEIN TO SCHOOLCHILDREN

Those fifteen months I spent with the sisters, in their secret convent which looked out at the police station, were very dangerous and difficult. More than once there were situations in which I, and accordingly the sisters too, came within a hair's breadth of death. There was, however, also a lot that was touching, and even comical. It is only now I can say that, after the passing of so many years. I remember the Germans came unexpectedly one time to search the convent. They came down the corridor toward the room I was in. The room had a washbasin and screen and all I could think to do was to rush behind the screen, hang a towel on it, and make a lot of noise at the washbasin. The Germans who had entered laughed and left without looking behind the screen. Another time, when the nuns were obliged to move to another house on the outskirts of town, I had to dress like a woman, shave myself closely, powder myself with flour, and hide my face behind a bouquet of dried flowers and a plaster statuette of the Virgin Mary. Together with three of the sisters, I walked in procession through half the town.

I shared their life. We ate, prayed, and worked together. They earned a livelihood by knitting, and I too acquired that feminine skill. On one occasion

I knitted a whole dress. I read a great deal, not only the Gospel but other Christian books. I suppose it was then that I became a Catholic and the idea that my life would be linked with the Catholic Church took root in me.

In late 1943, as a result of serious defeats on the front and the growth of the partisan movement, the Germans adopted harsher policies toward the local population. Arbitrary large-scale searches and arrests began, and I felt I could no longer put the sisters at risk. I decided to join the partisans. For several days I wandered aimlessly along the roads in remote areas where the Germans practically never ventured. I knew these woods were the partisans' domain and eventually I ran into four former Red Army soldiers. One was a man I had managed to save while working in the police and he recognized me immediately. He started thanking me and told his comrades I had saved his life. They were friendly toward me, but said I could not join their unit without a weapon. If I could get my hands on something, that would be a different matter. They gave me food and I went on my way.

In one village I came upon two Polish priests who were also hiding from the Germans. I told them about my circumstances and my conversion and expected that they would at least let me spend the night under their roof, but they didn't. In a small village nearby, however, I was given shelter by a Belorussian family.

I was standing at the window of their house in the morning when a cart trundled by. There were a number of men on it and I recognized one of them as Efraim Cwyk, an old friend from Akiva who had escaped at the time of the breakout from the ghetto. Fortunately, Efraim was one of those who knew I had organized the escape and supplied arms from the Gestapo arsenal. I had grown a moustache in order to disguise myself and he did not recognize me at first. He had been sure I was dead and we met like long-lost brothers. Efraim took me to a Russian partisan unit, and on the way I told him about the most important event in my life, my conversion. Needless to say, he neither understood nor sympathized and advised me to clear all this silliness out of my head. I can see now how foolishly I behaved.

During the night we made our way to a brigade under the command of a Colonel Durov. He had heard something about a commandant at the German police station who had helped partisans and saved the lives of Jews, but was far more interested in my links with the Fascists. He promptly ordered my arrest and conducted the interrogation personally. I was searched and my New Testament was taken away, along with a number of icons the nuns had given me.

I told Durov in detail about my life and work among the Germans. I told him how I had escaped and about my subsequent conversion to Christianity. He demanded to know where I had hidden in the fifteen months since escaping from the Gestapo, but I could not tell him I had been concealed by the nuns all that time. If it had become known in Emsk, they would unquestionably have been executed. Durov did not trust me, but neither did I altogether trust him, so I refused to give him his answer. How could I tell him about the nuns when I knew the Communists' attitude toward believers?

My refusal to reveal my hiding place struck Durov as very suspicious. The interrogation lasted almost two days without a break. I would be questioned by Durov personally and then by his assistant. He came to the conclusion that I had spent those months in a German spy school and had now been sent to the partisans to collect intelligence. I was sentenced to be shot. Efraim was beside himself, having brought me to this brigade and now not being believed. I was locked up in a shed, and kept there for several days. I still have no idea why they did not execute me immediately. It was one more miracle. I was completely calm and sat in the dark and prayed. I commended myself into the hands of the Lord, prepared to accept whatever He might send.

On the morning of the third day, help arrived. A doctor came to Durov's brigade, another escapee from the ghetto by the name of Isaak Gantman. He was the only doctor in the entire area who treated the partisans.

There was a wounded man in urgent need of an operation and Gantman had been called from Czarna Puszcza. He was an irreplaceable person with great authority. Efraim immediately told him about me and I was again subjected to interrogation, this time in the presence of both Durov and Gantman. At first the proceedings were in Russian, then I and the good doctor changed to Polish because he was not fluent in Russian.

I explained that I could not reveal where I had been hiding for fear of endangering the people who had helped me. Durov trusted Gantman, who was in any case the only doctor they had, and I trusted him, too. We agreed that I would tell him where I had hidden on condition that he would not divulge the secret to Durov or anybody else. Gantman persuaded Durov that the reason I could not say where I had stayed was entirely personal and offered himself as a guarantor of my innocence. The second guarantor was Efraim. Durov said that if I was tricking him, both guarantors would be shot along with me. He imagined I had been hidden by a lover. That was evidently something he could understand. My execution was put on hold.

Before the interrogation was over, two partisans from the Jewish unit, also from Emsk, arrived. They had been sent by the commanding officer of the Jewish unit to testify to my having saved the lives of Red Army soldiers and Jews while serving with the Germans. News spread surprisingly fast in the forest, considering how uninhabited it appeared.

In the end, our joint efforts persuaded Durov I was innocent. The report about my sentence had already been sent to General Platon, the head of the Russian partisan movement in Western Belorussia, and a new report was now sent in its wake requesting that the death sentence should be annulled as there were witnesses to my innocence. I was allowed to join the brigade.

I spent a total of ten months with the partisans, from December 1943 until the Red Army liberated Belorussia in August 1944. Looking back now after so many years, I can honestly say that being a partisan was worse than working in the gendarmerie. There I knew I had a mission to help people and save lives as best I could. Matters were considerably less straightforward in the forests with the partisans. Life in the brigade was brutish. When I joined, it consisted of Russians, Ukrainians, Belorussians, and a few Jews. There were already no Poles. Some had fled and the rest had been shot by the Russians, as I later heard.

A partisan was half-hero, half-outlaw. In order to survive we needed provisions, and these could be obtained only from the local peasants. They were robbed by the Germans and they were robbed by the partisans. The peasants never willingly surrendered anything and we were obliged to take it by force. Sometimes we took their last cow or horse, and it was not unknown for the stolen horse then to be exchanged for vodka. Vodka was more highly prized than bread. These people could not live without it.

When raids of this type were being conducted, I was usually one of the sentries guarding the village while the others went and seized everything they could find. My conscience was nevertheless not clear.

I took part in combat only once, a sabotage operation to blow up a bridge and derail a German train. I did my best to avoid bloodshed and tried to make myself useful in other ways, by guarding the camp and working in it. There was no shortage of work.

I found the situation of women in the unit deeply dispiriting. There were far fewer of them than men, and I saw the way they suffered. It was hard enough for them to be living in the forest in dugouts, with all the privations, and to this were added the sexual demands of the men which they could not escape. There was ceaseless rape. I felt very sorry for them, but had also to recognize that most of them when they yielded to violence were hoping for favors in return. I had old-fashioned views on relations between men and women and could not reconcile myself to what I constantly encountered. I was appalled by the thought that Marysia, too, if she had survived and been here, would have had to submit to these ways. This was probably when I began thinking of becoming a monk. I stopped viewing women as a man, and for me they were not sex objects but only suffering human beings. They sensed that and were always grateful to me.

At the end of the war the Russians started giving out medals. I was awarded one also and kept it for a long time. It had Stalin's profile on it. In August 1944 the Russians liberated Belorussia. We were all very glad to see the Red Army and most of those in the brigade merged with it. By this time, however, I had decided to enter a monastery and in order to do so needed to get to Poland. It was clear to me that east Poland would be retained by the Russians. Warsaw was still occupied by the Germans. When the people of Warsaw rose up against them, the Red Army stood aside for two months on the far bank of the Vistula and gave them no support.

While I was wondering how to get home and find my parents—although there was little likelihood of their having survived—the NKVD caught up with me and I was taken back to Emsk on a special mission. I had no desire whatever to work for the NKVD, but nobody asked me.

Emsk was almost empty. All the people I knew had left the city, and those who had collaborated with the Germans had vanished. Many houses had been burned down and the fortress was half ruined and empty. I was issued with a Soviet uniform and allocated a room in the very building the Gestapo had occupied. There I was to write reports on people who had collaborated with the Germans. To my relief, they were long gone. My reports were mainly about German operations against the Jews. I compiled a list of all the Jewish villages and hamlets which had been destroyed while I was working there. My bosses were far more interested in anti-Soviet sentiment among the local population, but I gave them no help with that.

A number of Jews who had survived returned to Emsk. They hailed me as a hero, but we could not find a common language. My Christianity had been baffling for those I had become close to in the partisan unit, and now I had to recognize that it was unacceptable to my old Jewish acquaintances. Indeed, to this day many Jews consider my choice a betrayal of Judaism. The person who tried most energetically to change my mind and turn me from Christianity was Efraim Cwyk who, along with Dr. Gantman, had once staked his life on my not being a traitor. Later, when I was already in a monastery, he came and tried to rescue me from the clutches of the Christians. The people closest to me at that time were my nuns. They supported me.

It did not take long for me to see that the NKVD would not just let me walk away. I sought a means of escape and the opportunity arose when the chief went off to the district center for a couple of days. His deputy saw me as a dangerous career rival and gave me permission to go to work for a secret service major in Baranowicze, a place whose only advantage over Emsk was that it was closer to the border with Poland. I reported to the major, he inspected my documents, saw that I was a Jew, and refused to have me. This was just what I had been hoping for. I asked permission to travel to Vilnius and he wrote me out a pass. My only joy in Vilnius was meeting up with Bolesław again. The Germans had not harmed him and everyone living on his farm had survived through to liberation. He greeted me warmly and again offered to let me stay with him.

Vilnius, like Emsk, was half ruined and empty. Many Polish townspeople had fled to Poland, those who had collaborated with the Germans had left with them, and six hundred thousand Lithuanian Jews had been shot. These postwar sights only strengthened my resolve. I went to the Carmelite monastery in Vilnius but the abbot refused to admit me.

In March 1945 I was on the first train taking Poles back to their homeland. So were Isaak Gantman and his wife. I told him that I was going there to enter a monastery. "You are turning away from life's great treasures," he told me, and I was unable to make him see that I had chosen the most precious treasure of all.

In Kraków I went to the abbot of the Carmelite monastery, who received me benignly and asked me to tell him my story. I spoke to him for almost three hours and he listened attentively without interrupting. When I had finished, he asked me the title of the article about Lourdes which had triggered my conversion. I told him the name of the magazine and the author. He had written it himself.

That year there were two candidates wishing to enter the monastery as novices, myself and a certain young actor from the local theater. There was only one vacancy. The abbot chose me, saying, "You are a Jew and it will be far more difficult for you to find your place in the Church." He proved right. The second applicant was one Karol Wojtyła, who certainly did find his place in the Church.

11. 1970

<small>FROM HILDA'S DIARY</small>

What happened last night is beyond my comprehension. It had to be when Daniel was away! Our community was attacked. It was a real pogrom, dreadful. Of course, it had been coming for a long time. I have been a complete idiot not to have been more concerned last month when Sister Lydia, who was praying at night in the church, was alarmed by intruders talking nearby. When she went out and asked what they wanted they immediately vanished. She could not see who they were in the darkness, but noticed there were three of them. She thought that one resembled that homeless Serb I took to the hospital.

I thought no more of it, and did not even mention it to Daniel. That was such a mistake! We were attacked last night. Our watchman, Yusuf, a distant relative of Musa's, is elderly and rather deaf and might seem better suited to be a resident in our old people's home than employed as a watchman. He is very keen, though, and has been working with us from the outset, almost three years already, in return for board and lodging. I buy him whatever he needs but that is almost nothing. He was asleep in the annex and woke only when the women in the main building began screaming. A fire had been started on the ground floor. Nurse Berta was on duty in the old people's home last night and she was also asleep on the second floor. After setting fire to the building, the intruders broke into the church, smashed and stamped on everything they could, and ran away. Yusuf put a ladder up to a second-floor window and all who were able to walk climbed down. Someone happened to be driving along the lower road and rushed to help when he saw the fire. He turned out to be an ex-soldier from the renowned Givati Brigade. The first thing he did was to get Rosina out. She has been bedridden for many years. Then he went back for poor Ans Broessels, who by then had severe burns. The soldier, his name is Aminadav, immediately took her to the hospital. He came back this morning and helped us clear everything up. I told him the story of Ans. She is Dutch. She saved a Jewish boy during the occupation and then emigrated to Israel along with him. The boy's parents were religious Jews and they died in a concentration camp. Ans considered it her duty to bring him up in the Jewish faith. Tragically, after they came to Israel the boy became a soldier and died in the Six-Day War. Shortly after that she went back to Holland but did not feel at home there and returned to Israel. That is the kind of person who lives in our old people's home.

An interesting detail Ans told us was that the deportation of Jews from Holland began the day after a Dutch bishop publicly expressed his disapproval of the Nazi policy. The bishop's letter in defense of the Jews was read out in the churches, and the German commissar immediately responded by deporting 30,000 Jews, mainly Jewish Catholics. Ans believes condemnation of Pius XII for failing to rally the Church in defense of the Jews is unjust. He knew only too well that outright condemnation of the Nazis would have likely only worsened the situation for the Jews, as it had in Holland. Well, that was her point of view.

Aminadav, who helped us so much, is very influential in Haifa and promised that the investigation will be conducted meticulously and the villains caught. He came back to examine the results of the pogrom by the light of day and concluded it must have been a gang of thugs but that most probably they had been hired. We discovered they had made off only with the money in the candle box, and had failed to find the rest of it in my table. Perhaps they just didn't have time. Fortunately, the fire did not get as far as my table. The refectory has been virtually destroyed. We have lost all the furniture, crockery, and food supplies. I spent the whole of today finding homes for the old ladies with parishioners. They are all lovely, and as a result two women even squabbled over which of them Rosina should stay with.

I went to see Ans at the hospital. The doctors say her condition is critical. They weren't going to let me see her, but did after much pleading. She looks in a bad state. I am not sure she recognized me. How I wish Daniel was back. I couldn't even phone him. He has gone to Sinai with a group of tourists.

On the other hand, what a pleasant surprise it was that the Druze came to see us and asked what kind of help we needed. They sent up eight young people who did more in a day than our parishioners could have managed in a month. I am hoping we will shortly have a group of students from Holland and Germany and everybody will join in and put things right again.

12. 1970, Haifa

LETTER FROM HILDA TO HER MOTHER

Dear Mother,

It is quite a long time since I last wrote because we suffered a great misfortune. Some criminals wrecked the church and one woman was so badly

burned in the fire that she has died. We are all very upset. Daniel is beside
himself. I have never seen him in such a state. Almost all the property we
have been collecting for the past three years was destroyed and the old people's home we built has been burned down. We worked for two weeks without a break but now we have to admit that it cannot be rebuilt here because
it is just too dangerous to keep helpless old people in such an insecure area.
We have 12 of them to look after and for the time being they have been
farmed out among the parishioners. I am trying to get them into state institutions but the problem is that they have no citizenship or documents and
accordingly have no entitlement to anything. The church has been almost
completely restored through the joint efforts of our Druze neighbors, the
parishioners, and, in part, the hired laborers, but the main problem was the
old people's home. Then, just when I was in complete despair, a miracle happened. German settlers have been living in a small town not far from Haifa
since the end of the nineteenth century. They are quite well off because they
own chemical factories, and when one of them, Paul Ecke, heard about the
fire, he sought Daniel out and offered to buy him a property in Haifa to use
as a home for the community.

I had been very depressed all this time until Daniel told me about Paul's
offer. He was so pleased, and comforted me and said that there is another
book, apart from the Bible and the New Testament, which it is important to
be able to read. That is the book of life of every individual, and it consists of
questions and answers. The answers rarely come before the questions, but
when a question is asked the right way, a reply is usually not long in coming.
The only thing is, it takes a certain knack to read the book. The question being
asked was, "What should we do now?" and the answer came in the form of
Paul, who offered to buy us a house. The main thing to recognize is that if
what you are doing attracts no outside support, your venture may be without
foundation. If it is firmly grounded, help comes. It is as simple as that.

Actually, of course, there is nothing simple about it. While we are
repairing the church, we have no time to do what we were always doing. We
have been neglecting our old people, our homeless people, and all our work
with children is impossible without premises. So for the time being we are
in a strange situation which goes right to the heart of the life of the community, our church services. As of now we have no place of worship.

Daniel says, "Hilda, the Temple in Jerusalem has been destroyed for
almost 2,000 years and there is no longer any worship there, but liturgical life
has evolved. Part of it has assumed a family form, another part takes place in

the synagogue, and Judaism has survived because that is what the Lord wanted. Never fear, Hilda. We do what we can on this earth, and judgments as to the value or otherwise of what we do will be taken upstairs without our involvement."

Meanwhile, Paul has found a house. It is not vast but has a wonderful garden and I will be able to live there and no longer have to rent. It is also in need of repair. The main thing is the really quite large garden in which we can build a new home for our old people. I've already thought all about it. It will have two stories, with small bedrooms upstairs (but each with a balcony), and all the amenities and a hall downstairs. Musa has a builder friend with several teams who will construct it.

I cannot say my life here is straightforward. It is far from that for many reasons, but what a joy it is to be here, in the place where I am right now. Do you remember I wanted to become an artist, to work in the theater, or something of the kind? I find it strange now even to remember that. Was it really me? Do you remember how you tried to steer me away from the arts and advised me to study something useful—accountancy, or a secretarial course? I have to thank you. You were right about everything, though I did move in a different direction.

How are my brothers? Axel wrote me a lovely letter. Did you know he has a girlfriend he is completely crazy about? Or am I giving away secrets? Please write.

Lots of love,

Hilda

13. 1972, Haifa

LETTER FROM HILDA TO HER MOTHER

Dear Mother,

I can see from your letters how orderly and unvarying your life is. One thing follows on from another like clockwork. Here in Israel, in our parish at least, extraordinary things happen all the time, some of them very amusing or instructive. Last Sunday a nun from somewhere in the Balkans, I didn't gather where exactly, wandered into our morning service. She was wearing a kind of floor-length brown habit and had a pectoral cross like a bishop. There was a cap on her head and a rucksack on her shoulders.

As we started, she took out a rosary and knelt with it, and stayed like that to the end of the service. Afterward we invited her to share our meal. There were twenty people or so. Daniel said grace, everybody sat down, and she suddenly started speaking a weird, terribly funny mixture of languages: Serbian, Polish, French, and Spanish. At first Daniel translated, managing somehow to conjure meaning out of incoherence. She had come from the village of Garabandal where the Virgin Mary and the Archangel Michael had appeared to them, and above them in the sky a great eye of the godhead had shone. At this point Daniel interrupted her and said that people were hungry, so they should first have their dinner and then she could tell us everything properly. She got very cross and waved her arms at him, but he said to her very strictly, as if talking to a child, "Sit down and eat your dinner! Our Savior also first fed people and instructed them afterward."

I immediately started trying to remember how it had been with the Savior, and actually I think it was the other way around. Anyway, everybody started eating and so did she. The food on the table was what our women had brought from home. We ate and drank and then Daniel said, "Tell us, sister, what you want to. Only not too quickly. I have to translate it."

Her story was that ten years ago or so, the Virgin Mary appeared in their village to four girls. She appeared over a period of several months and through the girls conveyed tidings to all humankind. There were three messages in all. In the first she called for repentance, in the second she warned that the chalice of patience was overflowing, and that pastors were particularly sinful. She predicted punishment in the absence of repentance. In the third there was something important about Russia, but I don't remember what exactly. The Virgin also told the girls ten secrets. They were on white sheets of some celestial material on which for now nothing could be seen, but with time the letters would appear and it would be possible to read them. The nun then produced from her rucksack some brown vestments exactly like the one she was wearing and said that anybody who died wearing this habit would never know the eternal fire. The Virgin Mary had promised. She then invited us to buy them at a modest price.

At this point Daniel stopped translating and started speaking to her very rapidly in Polish. She replied in some Slavonic language and they appeared to be arguing. It ended when she shouted, "The sun is dancing! The sun is dancing!" and departed. I think he had simply told her to get out. The congregation were perplexed. They had never before seen Daniel so annoyed. He sat unspeaking, looking at the table. The women cleared away the dishes and washed everything up but still he did not speak. They all went away without having received any explanation. Only brother Elijah stayed behind, fussing about as always with his tape recorder, and two students from Mexico who had asked to stay the night.

I made coffee for Daniel. He drank a little and said very quietly, "What an unpleasant episode. I should have explained my point of view, but I couldn't. I have to admit, Hilda, that it is always very difficult to decide what you can say openly and what you should keep to yourself. When I was young I believed people should be told everything and that, as a pastor, I had a duty to share all my knowledge. Over the years I came to see that was a mistake. A person may know only what they are capable of assimilating. I have been thinking about this for half my life, and especially since I have been in Israel, but there are few people I can confide in. Really only you. You see, it is a terrible thing to disturb someone's equilibrium. If a person has become accustomed to thinking in a particular way, even a slight digression from that can prove painful. Not everybody is open to new ideas, to making their understanding more precise and supplementing it, to change. I have to admit that I am changing. Today my views on many matters have diverged from those generally accepted in the Catholic world, and I am not the only person in that situation.

"You see, the birth of the One whom the Christian world knows as Jesus Christ happened just 200 kilometers from here, in the town of Beit Lechem. His parents were from Nazareth, a village only two days' journey from here. We venerate Him as our Savior, Master, and the Son of God. We venerate his holy parents. However, the combination of the words 'God' and 'Mother' to give the concept 'Mother of God,' which is so widespread in Eastern Christianity as the title of Miriam, the mother of Jesus, is completely unthinkable in Hebrew to the Jewish mind. Yoledet El, 'she who gave birth to God,' would cause the outraged ears of a devout Jew to fall off! Yet half the Christian world venerates Miriam as none other than the Mother of God. The first Christians would have considered that expression sacrilegious. The cult of the Mother of God appeared in Christianity at a very late stage. It was only introduced in the sixth century. God, the Creator of all that exists, the Maker of the world and all that lives in it, was not born of woman. The concept of 'The Son of Man' appeared long before the nativity of Christ and had an entirely different meaning.

"The legend of the birth of Jesus from Mary and the Holy Spirit is an echo of Greek mythology. Beneath that is the earth of a powerful paganism, the world of the great orgy, the world of worship of the powers of fertility, of

Mother Earth. In the popular mind, the goddesses of antiquity are invisibly present, the cult of the Earth, of fertility, of abundance. Every time I encounter this, it drives me to distraction.

"All this has been taken over into Christianity. It is a complete nightmare! To cap it all, two dogmas are constantly confused, the later one about the divinely assisted conception of the Virgin Mary by her parents Joachim and Anne, and the dogma of the sperm-free conception of Jesus.

"I so love the Annunciation. It is a sweet picture. Miriam sitting with a lily, beside her the Archangel Gabriel, and a white dove above the head of the Virgin. How many innocent souls are convinced that Mary conceived from that bird! For me it is no different from Zeus as golden rain or a mighty eagle. The divinity of Jesus is a mystery, and the moment when he assumed that nature is also a mystery. Where did they get that idea of mysterious impregnation? What do we know about that?

"There is an ancient midrash, Vayikra Rabbah, which was written down in the third century, but the oral legend always predates the written version. I believe this midrash was written down after the Gospels, when the topic was beginning to excite everybody's interest. Be that as it may, there are words in it which touched the depths of my soul, and which seemed to me more true than all the dogmas of the Church. Those words were, 'For conception three elements are required: a man, a woman, and the Holy Spirit.' The word 'ruach' is right there and there is no way you can translate it other than as 'the Holy Spirit.' Accordingly, it participates in every conception and, what is more, it continues to watch over the woman and the fruit of her womb after conception. Animals walk on four legs and the embryo of an animal is more secure than the embryo in the belly of a woman who walks on two legs, whose infant is at risk of abortion. God is obliged to hold every child in place until the very moment of birth, and for the baby not to be afraid in the darkness of its mother's womb, God puts a light there. This speaks of something Jews knew before the birth of the Virgin Mary or of Jesus, that every woman conceives with the participation of God. I would even say to you that for the Jews, all great people have been born with the participation of God. The clear intervention of God was evident when Isaac was born to Abraham and Sarah, who were already too old for childbirth, as the coming to them of angels testifies. That is what the ancient Jewish manuscript says, simpleheartedly and naïvely perhaps, but I feel the truth behind these words. Poetic truth, yes, but truth nevertheless.

"What did the evangelists think about the sperm-free conception? Nothing in particular! That is, nothing fundamentally different from the views to be found in the Jewish tradition, like the midrash I have paraphrased for you. In Matthew the word 'betrothed' was applied to Joseph later, after this problem began to be discussed. That is a later insertion when everybody suddenly started taking an interest in the intimate details of Mary and Joseph's marriage and what really happened. Mark says not a word on this subject, and neither does John. You find it only in Luke. St. Paul makes no mention of any immaculate conception either. He says 'of the seed of David' and one who became 'the Son of God through the Holy Spirit.' Paul doesn't even make any mention of Miriam! He speaks of the resurrection. Death and resurrection!

"Do you know, Hilda, what this tells us? To a twisted mind sexual life is inevitably associated with sin. For the Jews, however, conception is not associated with anything of the sort! Sin is associated with people's bad behavior, while conception is a blessing from God. All these legends about the Immaculate Conception were born in sordid minds which saw the marital union of man and woman as sinful. The Jews never had that attitude toward sexual life. It is sanctified by marriage, and the commandment to be fruitful and multiply confirms that. Personally I cannot accept the dogma of the Virgin Mary's Immaculate Conception as it is currently presented by the Church. I greatly admire Miriam, quite irrespective of how she conceived. She was a holy woman, and a suffering woman, but we really do not have to turn her into the progenitor of the world. She is not Isis or Astarte, she is not Kali or any of the other fertility goddesses worshipped by the ancient world. Let them read their rosaries, pray to her as the Immaculate Virgin, call her the Mother of God, the Queen of the World if they want to. Miriam is so mild she will put up with the lot of it. She will even put up with those shrines stuffed with golden crowns, rings, crosses, and embroidered cloths which she is offered as a gift by simple hearts.

"I probably should not have kicked that nun out, Hilda, but when she started offering to sell a brown frock which could save you from hellfire, I could take it no longer. If she turns up again and asks for shelter, let her in. Only not when I am here.

"Perhaps now you understand why I did not say in front of everybody what I have said to you. I do not want to intrude upon ideas which have formed deep in the hearts of each of my parishioners. I do not want to entice anybody to follow me. Let each person find their way to God by the path revealed to them. We gather together here to learn to love, to pray together in the presence of the Lord, not to engage in theological disputation. I am telling you all this, Hilda, because it seems to me that you want to know it."

Mum, I have never felt happier than at that moment. When I am with Daniel I always feel that what is superfluous and unnecessary is being broken off me in lumps, and the more needless stuff falls away, the easier I breathe.

Then we closed the church up. We hurried Brother Elijah on his way because he was still recording with his tape recorder. He is constantly writing down everything Daniel says. He considers that all his sermons must be preserved. Daniel laughs at him and says his focus is on eternity, and making sure all our follies are recorded for posterity.

I realize, Mother, that this cannot impress you as powerfully as it does me. I need to think long now. There are some things I want to argue with him about, only I don't know how to. What he said was convincing, even inspired, but can it really be the case that millions of people have been in error for so many centuries? If we are to be completely logical, we will have to say that people value their illusions far more than the truth. Daniel seems to be suggesting that truth itself is a complex construct which exists in a minor, simplified form for some and in a far more complex and richer form for others. What do you think? Do let me know soon. I might even telephone you, although calls to Germany are expensive and we have money problems again this month. I'll write to you another time about how they have arisen.

Lots of love,
Hilda

14. 1973, Haifa
LETTER FROM HILDA TO HER MOTHER

Dear Mother,

I have been happy for the whole of this past year because our work has been going very well. We have managed to restore everything, even building a small old people's home in the grounds of the new community center. We have found the money for a nurse to work there and the doctor comes every week. The children's program is going well now, and donations have come in from Germany, so we have put in the boiler and replaced the pump with a more powerful one. Suddenly, though, we got a letter from the city council informing us that we are illegally occupying the site of the Church of Elijah by the Spring, which they say belongs to the city. That is, after we have restored it, twice (the second time was after the fire). There was a church here before, however, so either the earlier church had also been erected illegally or someone is playing games. Daniel immediately went to their office and was told that we could only have the land on lease. They want an enormous sum which is completely beyond our means. Daniel is calm, although they said that if we don't pay the rent within a month they will send in a bulldozer and knock everything down. I cried for two nights, but Daniel seemed unperturbed.

Yesterday he called me in and asked me if I would like him to tell me another Jewish parable. He told me about some Reb Zusya who had to pay a debt by the morning and did not have the money. His disciples were in a panic as to how to get it, but the rebbe was calm. He took a sheet of paper and wrote down 25 ways in which the money might arrive, and on another he wrote a twenty-sixth. The next morning the money arrived from somewhere. The disciples read through the list of 25 ways but did not find the means by which the money had actually come. Then Reb Zusya unfolded the other piece of paper on which was written, "God does not need the advice of Reb Zusya."

I laughed of course, but two days before the council's deadline, a group of American Protestants came to visit us who have a great liking for Israel, and their pastor wrote us a check for $5,000. That will pay the rent for a year!

In my heart I had already said good-bye to our young orchard and grieved for the people for whom we are responsible and would now have to turn out on to the street. Then everything turned out as it has.

Lots of love, Mama. Write and tell me about everybody, as neither Axel nor Michael have written a word.

Hilda

15. 1972, Haifa

LETTER FROM KASIA COHEN, PARISHIONER OF THE CHURCH OF ELIJAH AT THE SPRING, TO HER HUSBAND, ETHAN, IN THE UNITED STATES

Dear Ethan,

I've been meaning to write to you for a month about something very bad which has happened here. I have been so worried that I couldn't write. It was just so unwise of us to not all go together. We should have gone together. We could have gotten by somehow. If you didn't manage to earn enough for us to buy an apartment, we could have carried on living in our little . . . Anyway,

now Dina is pregnant. I am horrified. She is 15, what a foolish girl! It is
already five months and I've only just noticed. To tell the truth, it was not
even me, it was our landlady Shifra who noticed. She hinted, but even then
I did not get it straight away. It was only in the evening the penny dropped.
It's true. Dina is not saying who got her pregnant. Either she is pretending
nothing has happened or she really does not see she has ruined her life. I
can't even say she has been behaving especially badly. She's a girl like any
other, going to school, not staying out late, coming home at the right time.
What was I missing? I have been in a complete panic all month. You are not
here. I don't want to tell my friends, especially Melba. Even before this she
was always telling me how badly I am bringing up my daughter.

Last week I went to see Daniel. He made time for me and I told him
everything I knew. "What should I do?" I asked. "I'm even afraid to tell my
husband about it."

Daniel said, "That's all right. He is not half as stupid as you. He'll be
upset for five minutes and then pleased that a human being is being born.
You are still so young, and you will have a grandson! How I envy you. For my
whole life when I look at babies I feel so jealous of those who have brought
them into the world. Those little hands and fingers, their little ears. You
should be pleased, you silly woman! Tell Hilda to collect all that the baby
will need. She has an exchange scheme where mothers swap children's
things, cots, prams . . . Is Dina pleased?" I told him she just seems vacant, as
if nothing has happened, and won't tell me who the father is.

"Well, she is embarrassed," he says. "It's probably some little kid as young
as she is herself. Take her out of school or the other children will be unkind
to her and we can do without that. She will have the baby, leave it in your lap,
and go back to school. She is a clever girl. She mustn't see this as a misfortune. It is a great happiness. Do you want everything to go by the timetable?
From all I know about women, those who are unable to have babies see it as
a real misfortune. I congratulate you, Kasia. Tell Dina she should come to
Mass. Everybody here likes her, they will not be unkind. Go away, go away!
I'm very busy today. You can see how many books I have to read."

I came home, and Dina had a little boy with cauliflower ears visiting.
Rudi Bruk, who looks to be about twelve. He's half a head shorter than her
but the cleverest boy in her class. I arrived and he immediately headed for
the door.

"Well," I asked, "where are you running off to?"

"I promised to be home by 9:00, and it's already 10:30. My mum will be

worried." At that I burst out laughing, through my tears. "Well why didn't you
go home earlier," I asked, "so as not to be late?"

"Because Dina was frightened of being on her own. I was waiting for
you." I really wanted to kick him, but he has such a slender neck and Dina
was staring at me wide-eyed, like a wild cat. I thought, Lord, don't tell me she
is in love with him.

Ethan, my dear, now I've told you everything. Everything would have
been different if we had gone to the States together, but because of my greed
this has happened. I thought we couldn't live here without an apartment and
you might not be able to make enough. Now you will come with money, we
will buy a three-room apartment, and it will still be too small for us. I kiss you,
my dear. I miss you very much. I was wrong not to come with you. I can't wait
to see you. There are only four months left. By the time you get here, we will
have a grandson. For some reason I think it will be a boy. He could have
been ours.

Dina does not want to write to you. She is ashamed and scared. She
respects you far more than me, and does not want you to see her belly. Oy,
do you know the thought I had? We could have had the baby here and moved
to another town and told everybody it was mine. You and I could have
adopted him, but in view of the fact you have not been here for a full year,
our friends would all think I had been on the razzle! Which version do you
prefer? Both are worst!

I kiss you again,
Kasia

16. 1973, Haifa
LETTER FROM DANIEL STEIN TO EMMANUEL LEROUX IN TOULOUSE

Dear Brother Emmanuel,
You may remember we met briefly in Toulouse at the conference of our
Order in 1969. If my memory does not deceive me, you said that when you
entered the Order, you continued to work as a brain surgeon in a children's
neurological clinic. I have a woman in my congregation whose 15-year-old
daughter has given birth to a baby with hydrocephalus. The child is now six
months old and the doctors observing it here say there is an operation which
could halt the progress of the illness. They say it is not available in Israel but
that there are specialists in France. I remembered you and decided to ask

whether you might be able to find out where in France such an operation might be performed, and perhaps organize a consultation for the baby.

The girl who is the mother of this unfortunate child is herself still a child and is deeply traumatized. I will be grateful for any information you can give me in this matter. I would also like to know how much such an operation might cost. The family of the sick boy is in dire circumstances, so we shall need to busy ourselves with raising the money.

With love,

Brother D. Stein

17. 1973, *Toulouse*

LETTER FROM EMMANUEL LEROUX TO DANIEL STEIN

Dear Brother,

Your letter has found its way into the right hands because it is at our clinic that the method of performing this operation was devised. It is a fairly complex operation performed on very young children. The results are good but much depends on the stage the illness has reached. There can be cases where we are no longer able to help. Please send the results of the child's tests and then we will be able to decide whether it would make sense for him to come. We will discuss financial matters later, when it is clear whether surgical intervention is possible. Our clinic attracts charitable donations and that might significantly reduce the family's expenses. Here in Toulouse we will at least accommodate them in our charitable center or with our parishioners, which will avoid the expense of a hotel.

With love,

Brother Emmanuel

18. 1972, *Haifa*

BULLETIN BOARD IN THE CHURCH OF ELIJAH BY THE SPRING

THANK YOU TO EVERYONE WHO BROUGHT MONEY FOR SHIMON COHEN'S OPERATION.

WE HAVE ALREADY COLLECTED $4,865. WE NEED ANOTHER $1,135 BUT CAN ALREADY SEND THE LITTLE BOY TO FRANCE FOR THE OPERATION. THANK YOU EVERYBODY!

HILDA

19. 1973, Toulouse
LETTER FROM KASIA COHEN TO ETHAN COHEN

Dear Ethan,

As soon as we arrived, little bighead was examined by two doctors, one a pediatrician and the other a surgeon. They examined him for one and a half hours. He did not cry and behaved well. The pediatrician said that mentally the child was perfectly fine, and that all the observable limitations of mobility are caused by the pressure of fluid in his head. They arranged one more examination, praised all the X-rays we had brought, and said the Israeli doctors were on par with French doctors.

Dina has delighted and amazed me. You remember we only knew about the trip in March and came here in July, but believe it or not, in the meantime she has learned to speak French. She sat with her nose in a textbook and I was secretly annoyed that she was just wasting time. Incredibly, she understands everything and can speak the language.

Little bighead was taken to the department. At first he was a bit naughty but Dina had brought a toy for him and we avoided any crying, although he was pouting a bit. He is such a sweet, clever little fellow. By comparison with other children here, ours is really not too ill. The day after the X-ray, the professor said that in his opinion the prognosis was favorable. My dear Ethan, there is a baby in the next cubicle in such a state it breaks your heart to see him. His little head is twice the size of ours, his whole face seems pushed down to his chin, and there is a great hernia in the skull as big as a largish apple. His mother sits there with him, poor woman. It's so terribly sad.

Dina is clearly feeling happier. Our little man is one of the very healthiest. Dina has met several of the mothers. Imagine, they give them psychological counseling. I will go myself later, but for the moment I feel more like looking around the city.

They have put us in a small room in the monastery guesthouse. This is a big community and the people are very welcoming. I didn't expect such warmth and goodwill from French people. They had always struck me as haughty and self-important. In the next room is a girl from Brazil called Aurora with that very sick baby I described. She is here with her twin brother, whose name is Stephan. Aurora's husband abandoned her when he saw the baby was ill but her brother has greatly taken to him. There's so much sorrow here, but also a lot that is heartening.

Dina is behaving very well. She seems to be less upset and has perked up. At least there is not a hint of the depression she was suffering from. They will perform the operation very soon, early next week. The professor said he does not like to second guess the future but thinks that he will be able to send us home two weeks after that. He hopes the operation will stop the process.

I shall phone you immediately after they have done it. Although we are living here without having to pay, we are spending a lot of money. Food is quite expensive, and Dina really wanted some sandals so I bought them for her. On Sunday we went to Mass. There were two Polish women there, very sweet people. We made friends immediately. Brother Emmanuel was celebrating the Mass, the monk who arranged this trip. After the service, he came over and asked whether there was anything we need.

I wanted to tell you, dear Ethan, that I have always slightly envied Jews having such a closeknit community and such strong family support—not including your family, of course—but this time I have found there is the same family feeling among Christians, and when we are all together we are like brothers and sisters.

I felt this most acutely when I was queueing for communion and we were all united in spirit and members of one family. How splendid that was!

I kiss you and hope (I don't want to say too much) that everything will be fine.

Your Kasia

Dina says she will write to you separately.

20. 1976, Rio de Janeiro
LETTER FROM DINA TO DANIEL STEIN

Dear Brother Daniel,

Mama has probably told you that Stephan and I registered our civil marriage while we were still in France, and now Stephan is insistent that we should get married in church. He says we need to put right the mistakes of our youth and that we should have a second child in accordance with all the rules, that is, after a church marriage. If we are to be married, then who would do it better than you? Please tell us when it would be convenient for you to come to Brazil, after the beginning of September, and we will immediately send tickets for you and Hilda. I very much hope you will not delay, because

236 / LUDMILA ULITSKAYA

otherwise the bride will not be able to find a dress to fit her. Our second child is due in January. The Brazilians are wonderful people but a marriage not sanctified by the Church strikes them as questionable. They also take a dim view of giving birth before the wedding.

I do not know whether Mother told you that my husband's family is very rich. They manufacture fashionable footwear which is famous throughout Latin America. Steve's parents want to arrange a huge wedding and say I can invite anybody I want from Israel. I would like to invite Hilda. She was so kind to me when I was going through a very difficult time. Apart from my parents, two of my schoolfriends and my father's brother and his children are planning to come to the wedding. Father is terribly pleased because this is the first time his respectable Jewish family will be joining our family in a Christian celebration. However, a second uncle, Leo, will hear nothing of it. Grandmother, too, is making her mind up. Let's hope that, when she has thought about it a bit more, she will forgive my mother her Polish origins and my father his unwise marriage.

Dear Brother Daniel, I am only now beginning to realize that my life is working out thanks to you. You brought my parents around when little big-head was born and father was going to walk out of the house. You arranged for the operation in Toulouse where I met Stephan and Aurora, and together with them suffered the death of little Nicky and then that dreadful complication of little bighead. He survived the infection by a miracle, and after going through all that we became quite inseparable. I gained not only a dear friend and sister but also a husband, the best in the world. Do you remember coming to me before the birth when I was practically suicidal, idiot that I was, and told me I would be happy? You told me everything would be fine if I could learn to live by the rules which everyone knows but which each person has to discover afresh with their own heart if those laws are not to become mere words.

I cannot say that I understood at the time what you meant, but I do now.

Little bighead, thank God, is fit as a fiddle. They have yet to correct his squint, but Brother Emmanuel says that operation should be done a bit later. Our little boy is physically rather less developed, both in size and in the movements he can make, than other children his age, but he is far ahead of them in mental development. Please do not think that I am just a typical mother exaggerating her child's progress. He is not yet four but can already read fluently, remembers everything he has read, almost by heart, and the whole family thinks he is wonderful, especially Stephan and Aurora.

I know for a fact that none of this would have come about if you had not prayed for me.

Dear Brother Daniel, Brazil is a Catholic country and Steve's parents are devout Catholics, but how different their Catholicism is from ours! It seems to me that they differ from us more even than devout Jews differ from Israeli Christians.

I really want to talk to you about this, because there are some questions I am afraid even to raise. Come and see us because, after all, I, too, am your spiritual daughter even though I live in Brazil.

Love from

Dina

21. 1978, Zichron Yaakov
LETTER FROM OLGA REZNIK TO DANIEL STEIN

Greatly respected Father Daniel,

This letter comes to you from a woman from Odessa whom you do not know. My name is Olga Isaakovna Reznik. I have been living in Zichron Yaakov for five years with the family of my son David, his Russian wife, Vera, and their children. In Israel everything was well with us until David began to have heart trouble and it was decided he needed a heart operation. During the operation, he died and was resuscitated. Vera is a very good wife and mother, and relations between her and her mother-in-law could not be better. God sent me Vera. She is more than a daughter.

While David was having his operation Vera closed the door and prayed. She prayed so fervently that I could feel it in my head. It was like a strong wind blowing. It was 3 o'clock, and later they said that it was at 3 o'clock that his heart stopped and the doctors started to resuscitate him. I believe, I am certain, it was not the doctors who managed to do that. She prayed to Jesus Christ and the Mother of God whom I have never before been much bothered about, but I know that day Christ saved my son through Vera's prayers. I know that and now I want to be baptized, because I believe in Him, no matter what the Jews say or think. I asked Vera to take me to a priest. She promised, but then refused. That is, it was not Vera who refused but the Orthodox priest she goes to. He said he does not baptize Jews. Then I asked her to find me a Jewish priest, because I heard that such do exist. She told me about you but said you are a Catholic priest. It is absolutely all the same to me, although it would be better to have an Orthodox one in order to be the same as Vera, but where is one to be found? So I'm asking you, greatly respected Father Daniel, to come to us and baptize me. I have been unable to leave the house for two years already because I have a bad leg.

I very much hope you will not refuse my request, because I am old and am so grateful to Him for doing that and there is nothing else I have to give other than being baptized.

David is angry with me and says I have gone crazy, but my heart tells me I need to do this. David leaves for work at 7:30 in the morning and gets back no earlier than 6:00, so please come when it suits you but during working hours so that he does not know what I am up to. I am 81 years old, almost blind, and cannot read any Gospels, but Vera reads to me, and there is nothing there saying there is any difference between Catholics and Orthodox. I look forward to your visit. Let me know when you are coming and I will cook something good.

Till we meet,
Olga Isaakovna Reznik

22. March 1989, Berkeley
LETTER FROM EWA MANUKYAN TO ESTHER GANTMAN

Dear Esther,
They say that statistically Americans undergo a major change in their lives every seven years, either of their job, their apartment, or their marriage partner. The first two have happened to me simultaneously, changing the place where I live and losing my job. I am looking for work. I have sent my résumé to various places and there is one job I would very much like. It is a splendid park with a small research center and soil science laboratory.

I used to think nowhere could beat Boston and Cape Cod, but California is better, or at least, certainly not worse. We have rented a wonderful house with a view of San Francisco Bay. I can't tear myself away from the window. If I don't find a job I shall just sit and look out the window. Things could be worse. On top of his day job, Grisha has received an offer to be a consultant to some firm and is pleased. In material terms everything is simply brilliant.

Alex is very happy and has finally decided to go to film school in Los Angeles. He has even abandoned his Greeks and now is inseparable from his camera. He is making some film of his own in which the main heroes are dogs and their owners. As a result, we almost constantly have three dogs and their young owners jumping around in our house. One is a very funny Chinese boy and the second is a stunningly handsome Mexican. They are all very sweet, but it is a purely male alliance in which the sole female is a bitch called Gilda. I have almost gotten used to the all-male scenery although I haven't given up hope that some sex-bomb girl will appear and turn Alex's head. He is 18; at his age Grisha had ploughed his way through half the girls in his class.

Grisha and Alex are still very sweet on each other, and I am grateful to you for putting a halt to my psychosis. It has to be said that seeing a psychotherapist is helping me regain my mental composure, too, but if all these friendships with boys came to an end and he found himself—I was going to say a "nice" girl, but then thought just any girl—my suspicions would dissolve like a bad dream.

Writing a letter is far more important than talking on the telephone. It is quite a different matter. I told you briefly how I found Rita during my last trip to Israel. She is now visited almost every day by a new friend she met at the hospital. She is a dismal Englishwoman called Agnessa, a nurse, without a hint of charm, a small mouth, and large teeth. She has lured mother into some Christian sect, which baffles me utterly. Agnessa has a good effect on her though. They talk together about religion and I find that weird. I remember only too well how furious she was when I started going to church in Warsaw. Agnessa is not Catholic but some kind of Protestant, and that seems to have clicked with my mother. At the same time I can't stop worrying. As you know, I am a religious person and formally a Catholic, but the disorder of my life gets in the way of my everyday practice. I pray only once in a blue moon, and as for reciting the rosary, well, no thanks. The fact that my Rita has suddenly started reading the Gospel puts me in a curious position. If I really am a Christian I should be glad that my godless Communist mother has been converted, but instead I am puzzled and even rather cross. It's as if I want to keep her off my turf. At least she hasn't converted to Catholicism. I would find that completely intolerable.

On the other hand, I can see that my mother is a wholly religious type. Her faith in Communism was stronger than mine in the Lord Jesus Christ. I understand that both those things are quite alien to you, but you do remember her when she was young. You are the only person with any recollection of my mythical father. Can you explain it? It's enough to send me straight to the psychoanalyst to try to make sense of an incomprehensible situation.

I have not yet had a chance to meet anybody here, but one of the advantages of working in a university is that there is a social life of sorts, concerts, receptions, and we are constantly receiving invitations. There is a very pleasant family, also from the university, living in the house next door. He is a professor of theology from Russia and his wife is an American, a historian who writes about the workers' movement. We are even getting on Russian terms with them and drop in on each other for a glass of tea. They have a lovely 15-year-old daughter and I am pinning my hopes on her. Perhaps she will take a shine to Alex.

Oh, yes. When I was in Jerusalem I visited Yosef, the restorer. They had buried Leya's mother, Praskovia Ivanovna, only the day before. I think I told you about her. She was the old lady in a shawl who made the sign of the Cross over the food on the Sabbath. Apparently she was a priest's wife, a simple woman from a Russian village who had immigrated with her daughter to Israel and was very homesick. When she died they naturally wanted to give her an Orthodox funeral. They went to the local Orthodox Church but the priest there was a Greek and refused to conduct her funeral service because, although Greeks are Orthodox, they are some different variety. Then Yosef and Leya went to Jerusalem. They wanted to bury her at the Moscow Patriarchate, but they said they didn't know her and would need to see a certificate of baptism. You can imagine, the old lady was christened 80 years ago in Torzhok. Next they went to Ein Karem, where there is an Orthodox monastery and cemetery, but there they demanded so much money, there was no question they could not find it. Land is very expensive in Israel. Five days passed without them finding anywhere to bury her. In the end they appealed to a Catholic priest who is a monk at the Carmelite monastery and he buried her in the Arab cemetery in Haifa. There is an Arab Catholic Church there where he had already buried many stray Christians, but then they stopped. The cemetery was small and they were concerned that soon they would have nowhere to bury their own people. Yosef and Leya took the coffin to Haifa but the cemetery watchman came out and would not let them pass. Yosef says he was in desperation. There was nowhere else to turn. Then this priest got on his knees before the watchman and said that if they wanted, they could throw his body in the sea to the fish, but they should bury this old lady. He let the car through, they quickly dug a grave, and the priest conducted a funeral service. Yosef said later that the funeral service in the Orthodox Church is one of the best of all services, but what he saw that day was a real celebration before the Lord. The whole point is that this Catholic priest is a Jew from Poland. I wondered, Esther, whether it was him you were talking about, the interpreter who helped the Jews to escape from the ghetto in Emsk. I wouldn't be surprised. Israel proved such a small world and everybody is either related or neighbors.

Oh, yes. Yosef got your book and said the miniatures were remarkable but he is working on a large commission at the moment and will not be able to start very soon. I said there was no hurry, the book would wait.

My table is right by the window. When I look out I forget everything. If I can get that job at the park, it will be just wonderful. Grisha says I would do better to stay at home, but I am completely unaccustomed to living without a job. Of course, it would be ideal if it wasn't fulltime, but I'll have to take what I can get. Full-time jobs are easier to find.

I'm looking forward greatly to seeing you again. I hope you won't put it off and will visit us soon. Remember it's best to come here during your hottest months. We don't get really hot here. We will drive to the ocean. The scenery is marvelous and the town is very pleasant, too. As for the vegetation, there is nothing to compare with it in Boston. Real great forests with paths and streams. It's a paradise.

All my love, dear Esther. Grisha says to say hello and invite you to come and stay.

See you soon,
Your Ewa

23. 1989, Berkeley

LETTER FROM EWA MANUKYAN TO ESTHER GANTMAN

Dear Esther,

I cried all night and couldn't get a moment's sleep. Grisha is not here. He has flown off to a conference in Germany. Alex went off with friends for two days to San Diego to visit some boys who are also making a film on their own. Before he left he wrote me a letter. I am sending you a photocopy. I can't bring myself to paraphrase it. I felt a sense of release but at the same time a new burden of responsibility. I am terribly saddened and really don't know what to do.

Now it seems to me that yesterday when nothing had been said, things were easier. There was still hope. Alex is a very good boy. I don't want him to be unhappy, but I do not want my son to be gay.

I may just have to adapt.
Lots of love,
Ewa

24. 1989, Berkeley
LETTER FROM ALEX TO EWA MANUKYAN

Mum! I haven't been feeling right recently so I have decided to tell you a truth which you already suspect. I know you will be disappointed in me: I have chosen a path in life which simply doesn't fit with your outlook. I know, though, that honesty is one of your main principles in life, and so in my situation the most difficult thing would be to lie to you. You always taught me to question myself and answer honestly, in every sphere of life. I remember when you left my father you told me you had fallen in love with another man and Ray had disappointed you. I was very upset by your bluntness at that time but now I understand that it was right.

You may protest that what I am talking about now is not honesty but falling into sin, but I have never felt more honest than now when I make this admission to you and, even more than that, to myself.

How many nights I have spent turning in my bed sleeplessly, trying to answer the question of who I am and what I want. All sorts of ideas came to me. For example, what a gap there is between what we think about ourselves, what other people think about us, and who we actually are. How great it is when these three dimensions more or less coincide, and how painful existence is when they don't.

I kept thinking how important it was to discover this truth about myself. When the question of my sexuality first arose, I very much wanted to be the same as everybody else, I wanted to believe that everything was in order in me! I was "straight," arousing suspicion in nobody, including myself. The whole problem is that, quite simply, I have no real sexual experience. I am altogether without sin in that respect! Gradually, though, the realization came from inside me that I was lying. The time came when I could not lie to myself any longer, and it had simply been a trap.

There is a Greek word, "skandal," whose primary meaning is "a piece of wood." This wood then became a trap for animals or enemies. Two thousand years later, in the Gospels, the word was always translated as "temptation." Is it any wonder I have found Greek so interesting?

Every morning when I woke up I had to put myself together bit by bit, and I dragged this unresolved question around with me, afraid that every-body could see it. From morning to evening I monitored every word I spoke, every gesture, every behavioral reaction. I wanted to dissolve, to disappear, I wanted other people not to notice me at all.

In the evenings, I put off the hour when I would have to go to bed and find myself alone with my demons. I sat at the computer, listened to music, and read. Do you remember how many books I read as an adoles-cent? The whole of world literature is full of love. Taking a break from my books I saw you and Grisha bound by such vital passion. I was so attracted to Grisha. Now I can recognize the nature of my feelings, but then I did not understand.

In the end, I had to admit defeat. I surrendered. Whether that was good or bad, I am what I am. Now I have to tell you. For a long time I did not have the courage because this concerns not only you, but all those people I love and respect and who, to put it mildly, disapprove of homosexuals.

Having come out as gay, I am transformed into a strange, marginal per-son and feel I am depriving myself of a fully valid place in the world. The majority of people hate gays, considering them, at best, renegades and, at worst, perverts.

This has all made me feel immensely unhappy.

I was very lucky to meet Enrique. He was born into a different culture. Although his family are Catholics, their Indian roots remain and there is no escaping that. They had a different view of sexuality, distinct from what is generally accepted in our world. In many Indian tribes there was no prohi-bition of homosexual relations. Enrique is far more educated in this respect than I am, and he showed me scholarly articles which describe even institu-tionalized homosexuality. In certain tribes, young men with warrior status were completely forbidden to have sexual contact with women and allowed only boys as sexual partners.

Please understand me correctly. I am not making any value judgments. It is simply a social situation which reflects an aspect of human nature. If you like, it is evidence that homosexual relations have not always been con-demned by society.

Enrique freed me from the terrible burden of feeling guilt toward the whole world and gave me a sense of confidence that our relations are a pri-vate affair. Our love is nobody's business but our own, and needs neither the approval nor the disapproval of society. In order for me to feel happy, however, for some reason I need you to stop pretending you don't know I am gay, to acknowledge the fact and accept it.

That will be honest and, in the end, it will be good.

I know that presenting you with this truth, I am making you confront a purely Christian conflict. In the eyes of your Church I am a sinner, and that hurts you. In consolation, I can only say to you that I hope God is more merciful toward a sinner whose sin is "the wrong kind of love" than toward those whose sin is outright hatred.

In spite of everything, I'm very glad that I have finally written this letter, which I couldn't bring myself to write for such a long time. I have nevertheless gone away to give you time to collect your thoughts and accept this admission. I love you very much, Mum, and love Grisha and all your friends who I find always so cheerful and noisy.

Your son,
Alex

25. 1989, Jerusalem
LETTER FROM YOSEF FELDMAN TO ESTHER GANTMAN

Dear Mrs. Gantman,

I have started work on your book. I was already familiar with most of the text. It is one of the versions of the Haggadah. The theme you are asking me about is fairly unusual. It is a depiction of a naked woman, whose upper part is sticking out of bushes. The hands braiding her plaits belong to the Lord God. This midrash is most probably medieval but appears for the first time in the sayings of Reb Simeon ben Manassia. I did not know that myself, but yesterday a friend visited who works in the manuscript department of the Museum of Jerusalem. The text is as follows:

"From the sayings of Reb Simeon ben Manassia:

With motherly care the Lord with his own hands braids Eve's hair into plaits before showing her for the first time to Adam."

My friend advises you not to sell this book unless you really have to. It is not particularly valuable because it is not of great antiquity but, as he says, it is exceptionally well composed. If you like, I can send it for valuation and you will obtain the relevant information, but valuation is itself fairly expensive.

I shall work on your book next week and hope to have everything finished by the end of the month.

Yours sincerely,

Yosef Feldman

26. 1959–83, Boston
FROM ISAAK GANTMAN'S NOTES

I never thought I could succumb to the passion for collecting anything at all. It always seemed to me rather base. Love for the item collected proceeds from the vanity of the collector. At a certain point, however, viewing the shelf with my latest acquisitions, and also the pile of invoices which I had kept separate, I realized that I have gradually become a collector. I buy books which I have no intention of reading, and some which I simply could not read. The 18th-century Persian book was bought solely for the sake of its delightful miniatures.

Having established that, I spent the whole of Sunday conducting a survey and compiled something along the lines of a catalogue. Art albums, which I have been buying ever since I had any money to speak of, do not count. I have included only miniatures. My collection comprises 86 books with miniatures, not so much rare as extremely beautiful. I looked through them systematically for the first time, one after the other, and saw that, without realizing it, I invariably only bought books with Biblical subjects. It struck me that my predilection went back to the impression made on me by the first such book I saw in the Vienna National Library when I was studying in the faculty of medicine. I loved going into the rare books section, and in those days valuable books were issued to readers right there in the reading room. I held in my hands the renowned *Book of Being* from the sixth century, and some of its miniatures were engraved in my memory for life. Of those, the most beautiful was Eliezer, the trusted slave of Abraham, meeting Rebecca by the well. Rebecca is depicted twice, once as she is walking with a bowl, and a second time as she is watering Eliezer's camels. In the distance the town of Nakhor is painted in a highly stylized manner, and the servant has not yet fulfilled his mission of finding a bride for Isaac but the matter is already in hand. Rebecca's countenance, as is customary in miniatures, is very finely drawn and resembles my wife, Esther, as I have only just realized. The long neck, the delicate hands, the slender waist, the small breasts without the fatty deposits which always cause so much trouble on the operating table—everything that to this day I still find attractive in a woman. Such is the way a man's preferences are formed, from a beautifully painted picture seen in his youth.

I once more looked attentively through the books I had bought and confirmed that the women in these highly diverse tales, where there are any, all have large eyes and long necks. They were the only type my attention lingered on. Neither amazons nor vamps have ever attracted me. It is amusing that I should have discovered this when I'm in my seventies.

Another question which belatedly occurred to me is why Jewish books have these miniatures with depictions of people at all. We know that representing the human form was forbidden, so what are we to make of the world-renowned Persian miniatures? After all, Islam also prohibits representation of the human form. I shall write a letter to the indispensable Neuhaus on this matter. Our correspondence is fairly discreet but has not broken off, although in the last three years we have only exchanged greetings during the holidays.

27. 1972, Jerusalem

LETTER FROM PROFESSOR NEUHAUS TO PROFESSOR GANTMAN

Dear Isaak,

I was very glad to receive your letter, primarily because you have not immersed yourself wholly in medicine but still allow yourself to look at other matters and have, moreover, chosen a good matter to look at. The question you asked is one I have been asked hundreds of times, and some twenty years ago I wrote a brief summary on the topic, in which I continue to take an interest. I am sending you an extract on the matter of interest to you, the prohibition of images. I hope you will find the answer to your question there. Only recently I was reminded of you in connection with a heart operation I face but which has been postponed for the time being.

Greetings to your wife.

Yours,

Neuhaus

EXCERPT FROM THE SUMMARY

Anybody who has decided to study the history of Jewish graphic art, whether in a professional capacity or simply out of curiosity, very soon discovers that a huge number of questions arise in relation to this topic which ultimately lead to one principal question: how can Jewish graphic art exist at all if there has been a prohibition of many forms of representation since ancient times, and what kind of prohibition is it?

Even some 100 years ago it was considered beyond dispute that there never had been and never could have been Jewish graphic art, precisely because of the clear prohibition in the Torah of representations of the real: "Thou shalt not make unto thee any graven image, or any likeness of any thing that is in heaven above, or that is in the earth beneath, or that is in the water under the earth." (Exodus, 20:4). The same thing, but in more detail, is repeated in Deuteronomy, 4:16-17: "Lest ye corrupt yourselves, and make you a graven image, the similitude of any figure, the likeness of male or female, the likeness of any beast that is on the earth, the likeness of any winged fowl that flieth in the air, the likeness of any thing that creepeth on the ground, the likeness of any fish that is in the waters beneath the earth."

In reality this is all less clearcut than it seems at first sight. In both cases, immediately after these words there follows, "Thou shalt not bow down thyself to them, nor serve them" (Exodus, 20:5); and in the second case, "And lest thou lift up thine eyes unto heaven, and when thou seest the sun, and the moon, and the stars, even all the host of heaven, shouldest be driven to worship them and serve them, which the Lord thy God hath divided unto all nations under the whole heaven." (Deuteronomy, 4:19).

Here we need to make a short digression. The immense vitality of Judaism, the great faith of a small people, lost among hundreds of other tribes of the Middle East, of Judaism which has given birth to two of the greatest world religions, is founded on two principles. One of these is restrictive. The behavior of a Jew is strictly regulated, and it often seems to modern man that the minute and, at first sight, inexplicable prohibitions governing social and personal behavior are comical and absurd. There are an intimidating number of laws and prohibitions, restrictions and prescriptions for every eventuality in life, from birth to death: how to eat, how to drink, how to pray, how to bring up children, how to give daughters in marriage, how sons are to marry . . . but at least everything is decided in advance, everything is written down, codified, every conceivable unforeseeable eventuality is accounted for. A husband must not dare to touch his wife while she is menstruating, may not sit on a chair on which she has sat, or touch objects which she has held in her hands. But what if, oh, horror, a woman's period should come unexpectedly and the husband discovers this when he has already embarked upon fulfilling his conjugal obligations? No cause for concern. Even for this eventuality there is a precise instruction on how to behave. Such is the Talmud, a comprehensive set of laws for good, correct behavior.

So then, what is the second principle I mentioned? It is the principle of complete and totally unfettered freedom of thought. The Jews were given a sacred text on which they have been working for centuries. This work is an obligatory part of the upbringing of a Jewish male. Admittedly, now women too have begun studying the Torah, but it is as yet unclear whether that is good for them or not altogether a good thing. In this area, Jews were afforded a fantastic freedom unheard of in any other religion. There is effectively a total absence of prohibitions on intellectual investigation. Everything is open to discussion and there is no dogma.

The concept of heresy, if not wholly absent, is nevertheless very diluted and blurred. The *Jewish Encyclopaedia* says of this, "the definition of heresy in Judaism is complicated by the absence of officially formulated dogmas or a central body with recognized authority in religious matters."

So, while there is no restriction of thought, there are restrictions on behavior. There are a lot of these, exemplified above, but they are compressed into the golden rule of ethics ascribed to Hillel, a Jewish philosopher of the first century: "Do not do unto your neighbor that which you would not wish him to do unto you."

Now let us return to the topic of our discussion—the prohibition of artistic representation. After the destruction of the Second Temple communities acquired very great independence, effectively now having autonomy to decide many important questions, with the result that the prohibition of representation was treated differently in different communities. Some considered it a categorical injunction and, in accordance with that belief, followed it literally. For them only inorganic ornamentation could be used for decorating objects of Judaica, synagogal or domestic. Others, however interpreted, it less literally, as a prohibition of worshipping what was depicted. This interpretation saw no prohibition of artistic appreciation. This is why we find images of animals and human figures on the frescoes of the synagogue in Dura-Europos in present-day Syria, on the mosaic floors of the synagogue of Beit Alpha in the Jezreel Valley, and a marvelous image of King David playing the harp in a sixth-century synagogue in Gaza.

Halacha unambiguously forbids the creation of an object depicting anything if the intention is to worship it, but unambiguously permits and even encourages artistic activity for ornamentation. The prohibition on worshipping anything material applies, however, not only to art. One contemporary Rav said, "That is called an idol which a person considers to be such, and if somebody sets up a brick and worships it, the brick becomes an idol and may not be used for any purpose. If a beautiful statue adorns a city, it will be a welcome guest." That is sound common sense.

The problem of resemblance did not trouble Jewish artists. Resemblance was not an end in itself. Moreover, it was customary to slightly alter something in the human figure, to depict it with some deformation or distortion so that it became, as it were, not exactly human. The distortion might be barely detectable, for example, an incorrectly formed ear, or it could be obvious, as in the famous Bird's Head Haggadah created in the fourteenth century in Germany, so called because the people in it have birds' heads.

A further characteristic of Jewish art is a system of symbols which has remained virtually unchanged over 2,000 years, despite the absence of iconographic and semantic canons. The ancient symbolism develops, as can be observed by researching art objects. Both in Jewish frescoes and in mosaics, in book miniatures, and in the ornamentation of objects of Judaica, any representation, be it a bird, person, or plant, is not a direct representation but a symbol, which is accordingly by no means obliged to correspond to reality.

28. *March 1990, Berkeley*
LETTER FROM EWA MANUKYAN TO ESTHER GANTMAN

My dear Esther,

Everything is just awful. I knew this was going to happen! I knew everything would turn out just like this. You shouldn't marry a man 10 years younger than yourself. It was bound to happen sooner or later. Grisha is having an affair with some assistant in the department. I have an animal intuition. I noticed her the first time I saw her at some banquet. Even then the bitch was circling Grisha very brazenly. I found her behavior so disagreeable that I was immediately on the alert, and some time later Grisha told me he had two more hours of lectures at Stanford University and would be going there on Fridays. As you weren't there beside me, there was nobody to tell me not to do something foolish. I rang that damned university and asked whether I could register for his course. They confirmed that they had no such professor on their permanent or visiting staff. Then I was guilty of a second act of folly: I demanded an explanation and he made no great attempt to deny it. He admitted it straight away, but added that I am his wife, he has no intention of divorcing me because he loves me, and whether I choose to accept the situation or not is up to me. Now I am sitting and wondering what to do. I have found out that Alex knew about Grisha's girlfriend because he met them in the town in some dive, and altogether it strikes me that Alex's sympathies are far more on Grisha's side than mine. I regard it as treachery on his part. It is male solidarity. I am terribly hurt. Now when I so need Grisha's support after all I have been through after Alex's confession . . . do you know what he said when I showed him Alex's letter? "Leave the boy alone. I've known that for ages."

What I most want to do right now is get on a plane and come and weep on your shoulder, but having just been taken on by this laboratory it would be the height of stupidity to give up the job. I am only too aware of how many foolish mistakes I have made, but alas I am one of those women who have to say what is on their mind and wreck everything, rather than keeping stumm and sitting out a crisis.

Another utterly amazing piece of news which I forgot because of all this stress. I don't want to write about it and am sending you a photocopy of my mother's letter. The letter had enclosures, a certificate of admission, exactly as if into the Communist Party, and a certificate of baptism. If I were in a normal state of mind I would react to this news much more sharply, but at present I can only shrug and say, "God Almighty, is this a joke?"

With love,
Your idiotic Ewa

29. January 1990, Haifa

Correspondence from Rita Kowacz to Ewa Manukyan

(Photocopies sent by Ewa Manukyan to Esther Gantman)

Dear Ewa

The moment has come for me to inform you about the most important event in my life. Last Christmas after thinking about it at great length and undertaking the necessary preparation I was baptized. This will come as a surprise to you of course but for me it has been prepared by the whole course of my life. It is not something random but predictable and I am happy that I have not died before I could be christened. There were so many times I might have died during the war in prison in the camp and even in recent years after all my heart attacks and strokes. This whole year past I have been urging Father John and Agnessa to hurry up. I was afraid of dying too soon but they just smiled and said that now I did not need to worry either about my life or about my death. Complete calm has come down upon me. In our Church the Anglican Church there is not a whiff of that exaltation which so repelled me in Catholicism, the exaltation which I always found unacceptable for myself and unacceptable in you.

Now the only thing I want is for you to meet my wonderful friends and pass on to you the precious things I have received at the end of my life.

You know that I knew Christ since I was a child. In Poland there was nowhere he was absent from he is everywhere. In Israel which has rejected him it is very difficult to believe you can meet him but I have been fortunate. Thanks to Agnessa the doors of the only Christianity acceptable to me have opened.

Dear Ewa I know much has been wrong in our relations and that I have wronged you. I need to explain to you why everything happened as it did in order to help you sort yourself out.

I think the best thing would be for you to come here for Easter. We could celebrate this first Easter in my life together as a sign of our complete reconciliation.

Now when all I do is read the Bible and the New Testament all the time I could help you to find the right path in life.

I have a very convenient folding wheelchair which can fit in a car and together we can go to the Easter service. I want to be with Christ until the end of my life and we will finally be able to say to each other "The Lord is among us!"

Your mother

Margarita

30. 1990, Haifa

RITA KOWACZ'S DECLARATION

My declaration

I, Rita Kowacz (Dwojre Brin), was born into a Jewish family. Since I was four I have believed in God. I do not know how I came to have knowledge of Jesus. Before 1939 school lessons began with a prayer and I also prayed although I was not christened. The works of famous writers and poets were full of Jesus. Although I never studied the catechism I knew a lot about Jesus. When I was young Renan's *The Life of Jesus* made a great impression on me. Polish Catholicism alarmed me by its aggressiveness and repelled me by its anti-Semitism. My path to Christ was not through miracles. What attracted me was the profound dignity of the Anglican Church as I saw it from being together with my Anglican friends, and the day came when I felt Jesus within me. I believe in him because he is the Truth. In my life I have many times erred in respect of what is the truth and took social justice to be the truth, the equality of all people, and other things which have let me down badly. Now I know that Christ is the Only Truth and that He was crucified for that. I believe that Christ is the Father and Lord.

Why do I want to be christened? Because the moment has come and the Lord has come through people, Agnessa Widow, John Chapman, Marion Selley and many others and I have realized that the love of Jesus binds people to each other with a special love. There is also a further reason why I want to be Christian. I am old and want to surrender myself entirely to His will.

I have thought a great deal about my sins. My greatest sin which has always tormented me is that I did not perform my duty to the full when I found myself under the occupation. Later, in Czarna Puszcza, I did not take part in partisan operations because I was in the last months of pregnancy, then I gave birth and had a six-year-old son on my hands. When I managed to send my children to Russia and joined the army some of my friends reproached me for not remaining with the children, but I do not consider that a sin because fighting Fascism seemed to me then to be my main mission. Subsequently when I found myself in the Soviet camp I collaborated with organs of the NKVD and some of the people I knew also condemned me for that.

Here too I do not feel I sinned because everything I did I did not out of self-interest but for the good of the cause. I sinned in that I did not respect my parents but to tell you the truth they were petty traders concerned only about having enough to eat here on earth and really did not deserve respect. I was unkind to them but they too were unkind to me. I think I wronged them somewhat.

Other than that I am not aware of any sins.

Rita Kowacz

CERTIFICATE OF BAPTISM
Go ye therefore, and teach all nations, baptizing them in the name

of the Father, and of the Son, and of the Holy Ghost.

    Matthew, 28:19

    This is to certify that Margarita Kowacz was baptized in the name of the Father and of the Son and of the Holy Ghost on the thirteenth day of January in the Year of our Lord 1990.

    Vicar (signature): Father D. Chapman

31. 1990, Haifa

FROM A LETTER FROM RITA KOWACZ TO AGNESSA WIDOW IN JERUSALEM

    I thank you for the beautiful Bible you have given me. Unfortunately it is too heavy for my hands. The table is too narrow and when I put it down it is difficult to read. It is easier for me to hold a thin book.

    Is there an edition which consists of separate booklets? I would like to have the Gospels and the Acts of the Apostles in that form. Of course cassettes would be ideal but to tell you the truth I would prefer them in Polish. I cannot say that I understand spoken English well. This is made worse by the fact that my hearing is getting worse and my sight is also not getting any better but you know dear Agnessa I have never before in my life felt such a renewal of life as now. I really have been born again!

    There is one question which is troubling me. God gives me so much and I cannot do anything now other than thank him with all my heart and all of you my true family. I would also like to participate in the life of the Church but my pension is very small. The trouble is that I refused to accept money from Germany. I did not take the compensation they paid out after the war to prisoners of the ghetto and even less did I want to have a pension from them. No money can compensate for the lives of the people they killed. The Germans pay money to those who by a miracle survived but that miracle was by the hand of the Lord and not of the German government. I disapprove of people who take that money it is blood money. As a result from my modest pension I have 200 shekels a month for my personal needs. It is not a lot but I spend money on the little silly things I need sometimes on books and all I can donate is five shekels a week which makes 20 a month. I very much regret it but I really can't afford more. Of course I could get money from Ewa but in the first place I do not want anything from her and in the second place it would not even be my donation but hers.

32. 1970, Haifa
LETTER FROM DANIEL STEIN TO HIS NIECE, RUTH

Dear Ruth,

I'm not just writing to you for no reason but because of a conversation I had yesterday with your parents. It was your mother's birthday and I went to wish her many happy returns. Almost the only thing they talked about was you. You were absolutely the focus of attention. Even not so much you as your departure to the theater school. There was a great deal of noise because two extreme views on the acting profession came into collision. Your father, as you can imagine, was badmouthing actors because they don't do anything useful and went so far as to say that your mother, looking after poultry on a farm, had done more for mankind than the actor Gregory Peck. I don't know why he so disapproves of Gregory Peck. Milka threw up her hands, chuckled, and announced that she would be very glad to change places with Gregory Peck. Then Milka's friend Zosia chimed in to say that all through her youth she had dreams of being an actress. Before the war she had been invited to join a theater company but her father had not allowed it, and you, Ruth, would have a great acting career because in your school play you had acted the part of Esther better than any of the others. Zosia's husband, Ruvim, told us what a bad end his cousin had come to, who once had happened to be in a film and then spent the rest of her life trying to be in another and not succeeding, as a result of which she lost her mind and drowned herself. Then people told a number of other instructive stories and I also offered my tuppence' worth telling them about a man I met in Kraków called Karol Wojtyła who was an actor and playwright in his younger years before becoming a monk and making a great career for himself. He is now a bishop in Poland. Ruvim said in some irritation that if Karol Wojtyła had been a good actor he would not have had to become a monk because that was no less mad than what his cousin had done.

I thought that a little provocative but said nothing. I claimed my own justification was that at least I had never had any artistic gifts but at this there was an even greater uproar. They decided that actually I had great acting ability because I had spent so much time in the service of the Germans and had played an uncongenial role so well that it saved my own life and the lives of many others. Suddenly everybody made peace and your artistic destiny ceased to seem so hopeless because it will give you an opportunity of resolving life's problems not headlong but in some devious artistic way. Ultimately, it was a good party.

For myself, I am very glad that you passed your exam and are learning a profession. Write when you start, I will be glad to hear your news. Your last letter made me very happy. France is a beautiful country and it is great good fortune that you will live there for some years, learn to speak French perfectly, see the life of Europe, and return home with new experiences. I am particularly glad that you will speak French fluently. I know quite a few different languages, but have to admit I speak all of them badly. I cannot read Shakespeare in English, Molière in French, or Tolstoy in Russian. I'm sure that each new language expands a person's mind and his world. It is like another eye and another ear. A new profession also expands a person, even the profession of a cobbler, as I know from my own life. Work hard, my child, do not be lazy. Be an actress. When I see a large poster by the bus station with your sweet, funny little face on it, I shall be very happy! Let's have an actress in our family, too!

Love from
Daniel

33. 1981, *Kfar Saba*
Letter from Teresa to Valentina Ferdinandovna

Dear Valentina Ferdinandovna,

A rare opportunity has arisen to send you a letter which will not be opened and pried into. It will be brought to you by a woman you know following a very complicated route. She will tell you all about it.

Gradually we are beginning to get used to the colossal change in our life which has occurred and to our new circumstances. The most extraordinary thing is that the temptations have almost left me. It has become easier for me to pray, and my awakenings in the night which were previously such torment now pour out into warm prayer. Sometimes, when Efim hears I have got out of bed, he joins me, and this shared prayer gives both of us great solace. I will not conceal from you that from the very first step, we have encountered major problems here for which we were ill-prepared.

We began our life in Israel with a deception. On our arrival Efim, filling in the immigration form, wrote in the box for faith, "Atheist." After some hesitation, I followed his example. In the papers we are recorded as a married couple and I did not want to create additional difficulties for him and concealed my faith, not for my own benefit but for his. We were settled in an ulpan, a language school with a hostel, to study the language and adapt. Actually, we could have avoided that because Efim knows Hebrew well, but his knowledge is book learning and not the language people speak. It is not so easy to understand the spoken language. For my part, I am entirely innocent of knowledge. I do not know a single word. We live in Kfar Saba in a tiny flat, two rooms, luckily, so each of us has their own cell and, after my communal neighbors, I feel happy here.

Every free day we take the bus completely at random, and sometimes go on trips with tour guides, some of them even free. It is very difficult to get to a church service. Sunday here is a working day so I have only been to the evening service in Jaffa twice. Of course, on our very first trip to Jerusalem we visited the Church of the Holy Sepulchre and climbed the Mount of Olives. I have to admit that at the gate of the Church of Mary Magdalene I felt very upset. It belongs to the Russian Orthodox Church Abroad. As members of the Russian Orthodox Church, admission is denied us. That is, we can go in and look around, of course, but there is no liturgical communion between these two churches. Everywhere there is division and strife, even here, especially here. My heart is not yet reconciled to the loss, but my path to the Catholics is now also closed. Efim told me to leave the solution to the Lord. In our peculiar situation we really have no choice.

Our visit to Moscow as we were leaving was a real turning point. Marvelous Father Mikhail, with whom Efim had long been in contact, in part advising him on bibliographical matters, gave us great comfort and strength. He is an ecclesiastical writer and his books are published abroad. It was precisely in connection with this that Efim gave him advice. There is a very large theological library in Vilnius, all in German, which was left intact and they did not even make an inventory. Efim drew from it much of the information for Father Mikhail's works on biblical theology. Incidentally, Father Mikhail spoke of you with great warmth. He rates your translations and articles very highly. He also gave us a number of addresses which he told us to learn by heart. He warned that address and notebooks, and also old letters, diaries, and manuscripts, in short anything in handwriting on paper is often confiscated at the border, so that all the most important things have to be committed to memory. Naturally, this was no difficulty for Efim. We thus gained a number of leads to believers of goodwill for whom Father Mikhail is a great authority. Efim said that he had never enjoyed talking to anybody more and regretted that their meetings had only ever been sporadic.

Everything is turning out exactly as Father Mikhail had warned, starting with the Orthodox brethren whose reception of Efim was far from friendly. The Russian Orthodox Church owns many churches in Israel, several monasteries, and accordingly lands. The Russian Church Abroad also has its representation, and indeed many Christian denominations have their own churches, monasteries, and, in a word, property in the Holy Land.

Efim went to the Moscow Patriarchate with a letter from his abbot to a certain highly placed cleric but it turned out that he had been recalled, so then he went to see his replacement. He perused the letter, was very unforthcoming, and said there were no vacancies and that priests were appointed from Moscow. I might add the detail everybody knows, which is, of course, that appointments require the blessing of the KGB! Efim was no use to him, although he told him to leave his application in the office.

Quite differently, one of the contacts Father Mikhail had recommended responded to our postcard immediately, phoned and invited us to visit. This was Father Daniel Stein, a Catholic priest from Haifa, but we have not had time to visit him so far. Next week I am planning to visit Mother Ioanna, also on Father Mikhail's recommendation. I think you knew her at one time.

Dear Valentina Ferdinandovna, I cannot tell you what a strange state of suspension I am living in at present, like a speck of dust in a sunbeam. What a joy it is that fate has presented me with Efim as my life's companion. He continues to reveal unexpected, touching characteristics. He helped me so much in the last years in Vilnius when all that unpleasantness began and impressed me as a strong, purposeful man. Now his weakness in the face of the world and his helplessness have been revealed to me. He is completely at a loss when confronted with dishonesty and insolence. He is pained by avarice and cynicism, and we have found that in some practical senses I am the stronger.

I gladly serve him in every way possible. He shows great tact, does not allow me to wash his underwear, and when I was cleaning the windows, he stayed close by because he was afraid I might fall from the second floor. Our relations are pure and nothing darkens them.

Efim is at present in a state of complete uncertainty as regards work. His only hope is to find a job with a certain religious publishing house in Europe, again through the good offices of Father Mikhail.

I fear I shall not have another opportunity of sending you such a complete letter any time soon. All that is sent through the post has necessarily to be very reserved. Write, I beg you! Write, in spite of the poverty of my letters. May the Lord be with you.

Your sister,

Teresa

34. 1980, Jerusalem

LETTER FROM MOTHER IOANNA TO FATHER MIKHAIL IN TISHKINO

Father,

Whom did you send me? A beautiful woman with curly hair and her head uncovered turned up and said she came from you. She gave her name as Teresa. She says that the telephone number and address of Ir. Al. which you gave them has now changed and they can't contact her. She asked me for her new address and telephone number. Can you imagine, she said to me, "I know you have links with that publishing house!" Why did you tell her that, Father? Please remember, you must never say a word more than is necessary to anybody here: everybody spies on everybody else, and slip-ups are not forgiven. What if she had said that in the presence of somebody else? I did not give her the address, but decided to ask you about her first. I showed her the convent, took her around everywhere, and went down to the cemetery. In the church she prayed, crossing herself from left to right! Why have you sent me this Catholic? You know, we should help everybody but we have many of our own people in need. It is said, first you give to children and only after that to the dogs.

The Lord be with you.

Mother Ioanna

35. 1981

LETTER FROM TERESA TO VALENTINA FERDINANDOVNA

Dear Valentina Ferdinandovna,

You are the only thread left which binds me to home. Perhaps it's foolish to say that. Where is home in my situation? For me, a half-Pole, half-Lithuanian, home is anywhere they speak Russian.

Our situation remains unclear. Efim has not lost hope of finding a job he can put his heart into. You know what I mean. He was offered retraining classes: the choice was between computer programming and plumbing. In desperation he went to the mission of the Russian Orthodox Church Abroad and was received very courteously. He talked to the head of the mission, a pleasant-looking archimandrite who was a considerable improvement on the official who received him at the Moscow Patriarchate, but they, too, had no vacancies. All he could offer was for him to transfer to their jurisdiction with the right to participate in their service. That was it.

For the time being we are being paid welfare benefits. I'm finding learning the language very hard going and envy Efim his flair.

One of my neighbors suggested I should work as a cleaner, not officially but privately. It seems a good offer but I'm not ready to accept it yet. At least my vocabulary has increased by one word, "nikayon." Cleaning.

It is particularly upsetting that Efim was relying on help from his abbot. He wrote him a letter but so far has had no reply. What he misses most is being cut off from libraries, because for his peace of mind he needs to be sitting somewhere he is surrounded by books.

The only good thing in spiritual terms is our acquaintance with Father Daniel, which also came with your kind help and on the recommendation of Father Mikhail. Unfortunately we have not yet managed to make contact with the publishing house: the nun we went to see on his recommendation was very unhelpful and said that she couldn't give us the address at present but might do so later.

Father Daniel, on the other hand, is an exceptional man. Unfortunately he lives quite far away and it takes three hours and two changes of bus to get there, but we have visited him several times already. He has a small Catholic community in Haifa and gives help to anybody in difficulty. Believe it or not, he speaks excellent Polish and even knows Lithuanian. The first time I went on my own, without Efim. He received me as if I was a member of his family. I have to say he bears little resemblance to any monks I had dealings with before: he emanates a kind of Franciscan joy, although he doesn't look like St. Francis at all, except that he had a cat in his lap which he stroked affectionately behind its ear. His outward appearance is very modest. He is short, with small round eyes, and a mouth with prominent lips like a baby. He doesn't go around in a soutane but in crumpled trousers and a baggy sweater and looks more like a gardener or a market trader than a priest. No matter what I said to him he responded, "Oh, you poor dear, oh, my dear . . ." At the end he asked for Efim to come and see him as there was something he wanted to talk to him about. I told Efim and he agreed, only we don't know when he'll be able to, because he is very busy. Daniel is a man of exceptionally broad views, but Efim is a bit prejudiced against Catholics and will not agree to take communion there if he can possibly avoid it.

Efim is suffering greatly and that has a bad effect on me indirectly. My cruel nocturnal attacks have begun again. I talked to Father Daniel about this. He heard me out very attentively and said that before making any reply he would need to talk to Efim.

Everything he said seemed strange, coming from a monk. He said the monastic path is not for everyone by any means, and possibly only for very few; that he has been burdened by his vows for many years and knows the weight of them. He thought that my expulsion from the convent might possibly serve to redirect me to a different but no less blessed path. What should I make of that?

Efim is busy. For now he is unable to go to Haifa with me, and I am impatient for him to have an opportunity to do so. He has been taken on part-time at the local library cataloguing a small archive and he sits there in raptures. I can't see him as a computer programmer, let alone a plumber. I have less difficulty seeing myself as a cleaner. I am not afraid of any job, but you will agree that I really had no need to emigrate in order to mop floors. I could have done that equally well in my homeland. I feel very down. The only thing that gladdens me is the sun. In Vilnius it is damp and cold at present but here at least the sun shines, and as a result light enters your soul. But my nights are a trial.

I ask your prayers, dear Valentina Ferdinandovna.

Your former Sister,

Teresa

36. April 1982, Jerusalem

LETTER FROM MOTHER IOANNA TO FATHER MIKHAIL IN TISHKINO

Father,

Your letter gave me strength and the power of your prayer is something I have long been aware of, since the time Mother Euphrosinia was alive and our elder was still with us. I can say that before your prayers, my child, misfortune has retreated. In the hospital here they took not an X-ray but some other new-fangled photograph and said they had found not cancer but a common garden-variety hernia. It will need an operation, but there is no particular urgency. That is all I was hoping for, that I would not have to go under the knife but just be left to die in peace.

They took me back to Jerusalem, to the Church Mission, in another connection: a visit from the top management. My fate is extraordinary. They rooted out nearly all the descendants of the boyards but for some unknown reason relented with me. Perhaps it was because for two centuries some of the men in my family have gone to serve in the Army, others into the Church, and that in both spheres they attained high rank, so that the people running the Church secretly respect me. Or perhaps sending me from an impoverished nunnery on the periphery to the Holy Land reveals that my illustrious forebears are watching over me. Or am I wrong, Misha?

A little monk, young Fyodor, comes to me claiming your recommendation. Assuredly, he emigrated from Russia some time ago, lived five years at St. Panteleimon Monastery on Mount Athos, then left it and came here. To be safe, I questioned him closely and understood that he really was one of yours and had been with you in Tishkino and knew your close circle and family.

He told me that he left the monastery on Athos of his own volition and complained about his superiors, but I stopped listening. It is because he is young. He is a deacon, loves the service and understands it, so I sent him to the abbot and he allowed him to assist in the service. He has a pleasant voice, but weak. He has a long way to go before he will compare with a real deep bass who can boom out from the pulpit. He does, however, conduct the service competently and meaningfully, Misha my friend, and in these times that is a considerable recommendation. He has a pleasant appearance and looks young, although it seems he is almost forty. Of course, I remember our elder, Father Seraphim, at the same age, before his first imprisonment. He was a country priest but even then his true spiritual stature was evident. This thought came into my head and I was taken aback yet again by how little the years matter. He at 30 was wise and radiant, while others even at 90 lack substance and are lightweight and capable only of making a loud noise.

I have to admit, Father, for me you are still that little Misha who was passed from hand to hand in our catacomb while the service was being conducted. How angelically your mother, Elena, sang, may God rest her soul! Age is not on my side except that it resigns me to my illnesses, and what sort of an illness is a hernia anyway? It brings neither death nor even suffering. It is mere nonsense and bother. How good it is to be thoroughly ill before dying, to be purified and prepared. Otherwise, we may be taken in an instant, without repentance, without absolution of our sins.

You no doubt have all the necessary information about Teresa, whom you sent to me. At first I didn't take to her, but having now learned more about her circumstances I feel great pity for her. I have not questioned her but it seems to me that she is muddled. Do you see, my friend, even advancing age is not putting me to rights: just as when I was young I was headstrong, so I remain into old age. I always decided for myself whom to love, whom to hate, and now in my dotage I have yet to acquire an even-tempered, benign attitude toward all. To this day I love my own choice and defend it.

I have finished those two icons, the meeting of Mary and Elizabeth and the small John the Baptist. It is all very much ours, local, what we see from our window here. Father Nicodemus gave me his blessing to paint them. I ask you, Father, to bless my painting of a big icon. I have long wanted to paint the Akathist. I have a certain audacious idea, a little artistic. How prettily I imagine it, not quite according to the canon. Will you give me your blessing?

When I was young, Misha, I was very vain and remain so to this day. You wrote that my icons gladden you, that they open windows to the heavenly world, as Father Pavel Florensky said. I am so glad and happy.

Spring is only just beginning, a wonderful time. The apple trees and acacias are blooming and I delight in one branch which peeps in my window. I am on the ground floor now. Because of my frailty I have been moved down from the second, nearer to the earth, which is fine. My little window looks out at the cemetery, and soon from the cemetery I will look at my little window. The last two monastic graves are a mother and daughter. A year ago a crazy Arab stabbed them right in their cell. The two dear graves are side by side. It is a domestic, family scene. The mother was as thick as two planks but had a good heart. Her daughter was brighter but less sincere. I have asked for a place to be reserved beside them for me.

I kiss you, Misha, my dear godson. I remember you always and do not you forget me in your prayers. You are blessed by God.

Give my love to Ninochka and the little ones.

Mother Ioanna

37. *June 1982, Tishkino Village*
LETTER FROM FATHER MIKHAIL TO MOTHER IOANNA

Dear Mother Ioanna,

Your letter awoke childhood memories from long ago, for I, too, remember resting in your arms, and in those of Marfinka and Maya Kuzminichna, and how the elder spoiled me. It was given to us to witness amazing times and amazing people. I do not weary of giving thanks for all of you, living and departed, into communion with whom the Church brought me from such an early age. In this respect you are richer even than I. How many truly saintly people you knew and what great spiritual accomplishments attended your generation. The present persecutions bear no comparison with those which fell to your lot. Two weeks ago I went after Easter to Zagorsk and walked toward Marfinka's house. There is a new building there now, a five-story block. My heart sank, for the elder was buried in the cellar of that little house. In those times all this was frightening and amazing, both the fact that he hid from those searching for him for eight years, and that nobody denounced him, and that he celebrated the liturgy in secret in the cellar, and that the people gathered with him in the night as in times long ago, his disciples, mostly old ladies, but they also brought their children with them.

From the age of seven I assisted at his services and never since have I had the feeling of such perfect mindfulness as by the side of Father Seraphim. Of course, all those priests who did not accept the Soviet regime, who went at that time against the will of the weakened Church, proved spiritually stronger than those who accepted the regime, and they were personally saints, but now when so many years have passed, and after Father Seraphim's will in which he commanded his spiritual children to rejoin the Church and cease that small schism, only now do I begin to understand how difficult that decision was for him. In that will was his repentance before the Church. All of us who remember him well understand the difference between the authority of the state, the authority of the Church, and the authority of our Lord Jesus Christ, in which alone we place our faith and in which we seek our refuge.

I have allowed my thoughts to wander and have not said what I meant to: before Marfinka's house was demolished, they reburied our father and again in secret. His remains were transferred to the Alexandrovsky Cemetery, next to the cathedral, where Father S. was the abbot, whom you knew well.

The cemetery has long been closed, and it was in one of the sacred graves they placed him, and Father S. conducted the funeral service in the night. He, too, was one of the righteous, a radiant man.

Thank you for Teresa. She is a restive soul, suffering, as you have seen for yourself. As regards your headstrong intuition, I trust it. Efim, her life's companion, is a very gifted man, but has yet to find his right place. Possibly a publishing house of religious literature would be a good job for him. I, for my part, have written them a letter of recommendation, but I do not know how much weight my word carries.

Your news of Fyodor Krivtsov surprised me greatly. I knew Fyodor ten years or so ago. He is an original person, a seeker after truth. When we came together he had already been a Buddhist but had not found truth with the Buddha. He converted to Orthodoxy fervently and passionately, aspiring to be a monk. I saw him often for two years, and he even moved in with us in Tishkino, but then seduced a girl here and fled. He vanished. I heard he was living as a novice in one of the monasteries in Mordovia, almost as a hermit, so your advice that he had arrived from Mount Athos is complete news to me. We did not become close, you know, I always am a little nervous of people who are too fervent in their faith, and he burned with the fire of the neophyte. I also remember that he was from a Communist Party family. His father was even supposedly some petty Party boss. His parents broke off relations with him and the two sides cursed each other. I had no idea he had made it all the way to Mount Athos. It would be very interesting to contact him again. Please send him my good wishes.

I have one other pleasant piece of news, but it is at the same time a little worrying. Nina is expecting a child. She is in the sixth month and her blood pressure is consistently very high. She has been in the hospital for two weeks. The doctors told her to abort the child, considering that the pregnancy puts her life in danger. She refused and now we are entirely trusting in the Lord. She lies in bed almost never getting up. The girls are behaving with great concern, even selflessly, although they are really quite little. Aunt Pasha is still living with us, doing a lot in the way of housekeeping, but she is already very aged and of course it is hard for her. Those are our circumstances, dear Mother.

I will stop writing. It is past one already and I have to get up at 4:30. My perpetual disorganization—I have no time to do anything. I keep meaning to write you a long and detailed letter, but time, time . . . I don't have enough. I send you my love. I send my blessing for the work you have told me about.

I look forward to receiving photographs, and I am sending you photographs of Katya and Vera.

Your loving
Mikhail

38. *January 1983, Jerusalem*
LETTER FROM FYODOR KRIVTSOV TO FATHER MIKHAIL IN TISHKINO

Dear Father Mikhail,

I am very glad that Mother has given me your address and told me to write to tell you what I have been up to all this time. It's a long story, of course, but I will try to keep it short. How many years have passed since I left Moscow? I went first to Mordovia and was a novice there for two years, then went to Valaam Monastery in the North, and from there God helped me make my way to Mount Athos itself. In Thessaloniki I was given a *diamontirion*, a permit for Athos. There was a Russian consulate there. They supported me. They were instructed not to obstruct me. There are few Russians on Mount Athos now, mainly Bulgarians, Serbs, and Romanians. Greeks, needless to say. There is a lot of Russian territory there, but little in the way of a Russian population. It made no difference to me then, Russians or Greeks. I did not understand, then began to understand that politics is one thing but spiritual works are another, and politics has nothing to do with us.

At the very beginning I found myself in the Karulya hermitage, on the slope of the mountain with the *arsanas* dock below. People walked with mules along the path up and down, dragging sacks uphill with food and greens. The fishermen sometimes leave fish. I went to Elder Paisius. He asked what I had come for. I said I wanted to live on Mount Athos. He said, "Are you a tourist?" "No, it's just my visa is a tourist visa," I told him honestly. He said to me, "We don't have tourists here, and people do not live here, they save their souls. Are you a monk?" Of course, I was only a novice, not a monk. Perhaps the reason I went all the way to Mount Athos was because I could not make up my mind, but I said nothing, and he said to me, "If somebody has even one percent of doubt, if something is holding them in the world, that percentage will be decisive." Then he added, "You may stay."

So I stayed. My work was demanding but very simple. I made incense. The resin of the Cedar of Lebanon is imported to Greece, only not from

Lebanon but from Ethiopia. It is brought to Athos and boiled. It is hard work milling this resin. It is not a manual mill but a kind of little cement mixer. Then you add the aromatics, the holy water or anfo oil, and mix everything into a dough. You add a little magnesium, like flour. Then with a rolling pin you roll out the dough into a thick pancake and with a two-handled knife cut it into squares. When the squares have dried the incense is ready. Making it damages your health. We wore breathing masks and gloves. We delivered it to the Panteleimon Monastery. I served three years like that, living not in the monastery but in a cell. There are a lot of cells around the monastery, some hewn out of the mountain, some built of stone. One had been abandoned since the last century and I was allowed to move in there, but rarely allowed to see the elder. I saw him mostly at the services. Occasionally, though, he would call me, tell me something or give me a present. I went to him twice and asked to become a monk, but he kept saying, "One percent!"

My last two years I was serving the elder. He had an *omologion* for the cell, a kind of lease. The cell belongs to the monastery and the elder is allowed to live there. When he dies he passes it on to someone else, usually his disciple. It is the elder himself who decides who is to live there after him, and mine told me, "You will not live here." He registered the name of a monk from Novocherkassk in the *omologion*. That's when I left.

On Athos the lady in charge is none other than the Mother of God. Whoever she accepts lives there, and anyone she does not accept leaves. She put up with me for five years. Nobody is ever expelled from Athos. Anybody who takes to the life can live there.

And there were all sorts living there! I should mention the Greek zealots, fanatics. They have proliferated new synods. There are "old-stylers" who live by the old calendar and do not accept the new-style calendar. Sometimes fights break out between them. From one cell to another they send each other anathemas, and the Mother of God puts up with them. Me, however, she did not accept.

I can only say, it did not work out. I miss Athos to this day. For the present I am in Jerusalem but can make no sense of the place. Everything is so mixed up!

Father, how happy I was with you in Tishkino. Whatever you said I accepted, but here it is impossible to understand. So many churches, so many denominations, but where is true Orthodoxy? I am indescribably disturbed at present. The Russians have just as many schisms as the Greeks.

I attend a variety of places, but go mainly to the Greeks. On Athos I didn't completely master Greek but I can understand and read it. I move from one place to another. My soul is in turmoil and cannot find its home but I cannot go back to Russia. I shall stay here, in the Holy Land. Perhaps I shall find some quiet monastic house, an elder. Joseph the Hesychast was on Mount Athos. He died only quite recently, in 1957. Perhaps here is where I shall find someone to attach myself to. I shall soon be over 40 years old but still have no decisiveness. I cannot cut myself off from the world. This year I had the idea of marrying a Greek woman, a good woman, a widow in Saloniki, but as things turned out I nearly came to a bad end.

Father Mikhail, I remember the advice you gave me. "Do not become a monk, do not go from one monastery to another. Work for the Church in accordance with your gifts." Alas, my pride turned my head. I thought, How come you became a priest and all I am good for is to sweep the church courtyard? But if I had then, as you advised, married Vera Stepashina everything would have worked out. How is Vera? I imagine she is married and has a dozen children. This letter has so disturbed my soul. I have recalled my life in Tishkino, my brother coming from Nalchik and getting drunk, and having to be taken to the hospital to have his stomach pumped. My respects to Mother Nina. I will write again, with your blessing.

With brotherly love from the slave of God.

Fyodor Krivtsov.

That is the name I have taken now. I did not become a hermit and am no longer a novice. I am still seeking the truth. Here in the Holy Land there are so many holy places of every description, but still I cannot find The Truth.

39. 1982, Kfar Saba
LETTER FROM TERESA TO VALENTINA FERDINANDOVNA

Dear Valentina,

How pleasant it is for me, although a little awkward, to address you by your Christian name, but this familiar form, of course, accords with a special intimacy which I have never enjoyed with anybody before. Your last letter I have learned almost by heart, so important and exact do the thoughts you expressed seem to me. Especially your bitterly true words about fidelity and the impossibility of human loyalty. I know the Gospels almost by heart, but never had it occurred to me that even St. Peter renounced Christ three times, and that this signals the impossibility of an ordinary person remaining loyal. But after all, if you look from the height on which our Savior is situated, perhaps the difference is not so great between the fear which prompted Peter to renounce him and the envy which provoked Judas into betraying him. It is a bitter thought.

I told Efim about your letter, and he took it very seriously. He gave me a whole lecture. You probably know all this, but I will briefly paraphrase what he said. It seemed very important to me. Jews have a prayer called "Kol Nidrei", which frees them from vows and oaths which a person has given to God. Once a year the service is held on the most important Jewish festival, the Day of Atonement. It is on this day that repentance and the absolution of sins are accomplished. After the prayer has been recited three times, all these vows are annulled. It embodies a very profound insight into human nature and a gracious attitude toward human weakness. I would go so far as to say that this Kol Nidrei embodies the grace of God.

Efim told me many very interesting historical details. For example, the Kol Nidrei prayer was seen for many centuries as grounds for considering Jews untrustworthy, since people who could so easily repudiate their vows could hardly be reliable partners in business. I thought, however, about the great wisdom and understanding of human psychology of the teachers who introduced this prayer into their religion. Efim is so erudite that any question you ask provides the topic for an absorbing lecture. I think lecturing is his true vocation. The trivial work he is doing at present is completely unsuited to his abilities and his inclinations.

We are both very dissatisfied with our strange situation. My intention of finding a congenial nunnery has evaporated. No place in the world would accept me. I can readily picture myself as Efim's assistant, but so far he, too, has been unable to find a proper, worthwhile application for his talents. My nocturnal alarms are affecting him, too, and increasingly we spend the night in a shared vigil.

Last week I was again in Haifa visiting Brother Daniel. There is an amazingly joyful spirit around him. It seems to me that there really is something of the first years of Christianity in his community.

I have got so carried away that I have forgotten to thank you for sending me your new translation. I have to admit that so far I have read only your Introduction, and it is very meaningful. Your thoughts about the fragility of the word, its mortality, its mutability are very profound. Lately I have been increasingly reading not the Synoptics but St. John and, as always, the Acts and Psalms.

Please pass on thanks from Efim and me to Father Mikhail. Our meeting with him before we emigrated was very helpful. His strict godmother, the nun Ioanna, who at first received me with great suspicion, has now relented and gave me the address of the publishing house. Efim has been in touch with Ir. Al. and they are currently discussing how he might be useful to them. Needless to say, I am quite certain they will be making a big mistake if they do not offer him a job, but how can you explain to people what is in their own best interest?

Were you acquainted with this Mother Ioanna before, in Russia? She has been living here for many years in a convent on a special basis because she paints icons. I don't know much about icon painting, but there is something quite enchanting about it as an occupation. She has a little table or easel, I don't know what it is called, pots with ground-up paints, and everything is so pleasing. She has almost finished one icon of Peter on the Waters. It took my breath away when I saw it. It really seems to be about me. The water is engulfing me but I cannot see the Master's hand. My move to Orthodoxy was so rapid, and partly involuntary, but now I am gradually understanding it and see its immense warmth, through iconography also.

Efim says there are great riches to be found in the Orthodox service, but I do not find it easy to access. In the Moscow Mission we are not welcomed, the Church Abroad are friendlier, but it is up to Efim to decide about that. And also Him above. I have to make the bitter admission that I do not feel I belong anywhere. I am neither a Catholic nor an Orthodox. I am in some ill-defined place which is completely unfamiliar.

My love to you, dear Valentina. I ask to be remembered in your prayers. Always thinking of you,

Teresa

40. 1982, Haifa

CONVERSATION BETWEEN DANIEL AND EFIM DOVITAS

DANIEL: How do they say it in Russian, we are to some degree compatriots: *zemeltsy*? *zemlyaki*?

EFIM: *Zemlyaki*. Yes, Lithuania and Poland are close. Do you miss Poland?

DANIEL: I love Poland, but I do not miss it. How about you?

EFIM: What I miss most here is Orthodoxy. I do not find it here, but this is where I belong.

DANIEL: You are a Jew. What is Orthodoxy to you?

EFIM: I have spent ten years in the Church. I love Orthodoxy. I am a priest. It is the Church that does not want me.

DANIEL: Here there are a score of Orthodox churches and an equal number of Catholic. There are a hundred Protestant. You can choose. It's a big bazaar.

EFIM: I did not know what awaited me here. Real Orthodoxy is what I am seeking!

DANIEL: Look, authentic *what* are you seeking? Why are you not looking for Christ? He is here, in this land! Why should we seek him in church doctrines which appeared one thousand years after His death? Look for Him here! Look for Him in the Gospels.

EFIM: That is true, but I have found Him deep within Orthodoxy, in the church service which I so love. I meet Him in the liturgy.

DANIEL: You are right. You are right. Forgive my presumption. This is probably my Achilles heel. The trouble is that I have spent half my life among people seeking the Lord in books and rituals which they themselves thought up. In fact, you can meet Him anywhere, in Orthodoxy, in the liturgy, on a river bank, in a hospital, or in a cowshed. The closest place to find Him, though, is in your soul.

EFIM: Yes, yes, Father Daniel, of course. Spiritual life is simply a search for the Lord in the depths of one's soul.

DANIEL: Oh dear, oh dear! Spiritual life is the very thing that makes me nervous. This spiritual life is what, in my experience, more often than not becomes an end in itself, as an exercise. How many small people I have met with big spiritual lives, and almost always it transpires that for them spiritual life is no more than digging around in themselves at a very superficial level. And everybody is looking for a spiritual mentor!

EFIM: Yes, that really is a problem. No matter whether spiritual life is superficial or profound, a father confessor is essential. Since I left Vilnius I have lacked a confessor to talk to, and I feel that loss. A confessor is indispensable.

DANIEL: Fine, fine . . . Forgive me, my premise is always that we need only one Master, so tell me, what is a father confessor?

EFIM: What? Someone who guides the spiritual life, so that what you mentioned doesn't come about: digging around in yourself, introspection.

DANIEL: Are you sure you can tell where spiritual life ends and practical life begins?

EFIM: No.

DANIEL: Good, then tell me what is troubling you more than anything else? What is your greatest concern?

EFIM: Teresa.

DANIEL: Your wife?

EFIM: We have a spiritual union.

DANIEL: I have always thought that any marriage is a spiritual union.

EFIM: We live as brother and sister.

DANIEL: Together? You live together as brother and sister? What are you, saints?

EFIM: No. Only our temptations are like those of the saints. For years Teresa has been suffering from terrible visitations, but I cannot talk to you about that. For the past year I have felt this dreadful presence myself.

DANIEL: Enough, enough! Don't tell me anything about it! I am not a father confessor! My brother always says I am an ordinary social worker, only unpaid. So, you are married, you live in the same apartment, and you do not sleep in the same bed?

EFIM: We decided on that from the outset. Teresa was expelled from a convent. She was in despair. I, meanwhile, could not be taken on by a monastery or ordained because I was not married. That was the quandary we faced. We got married so I could get ordained.

DANIEL: Then you have a fictitious marriage! What do you need such complications for? Go and sleep with your wife! How old are you?

EFIM: Forty-one.

DANIEL: And Teresa?

EFIM: Forty-one.

DANIEL: Well, get a move on! Women pass the age of childbearing when they get older. Go and have children and you won't have any spiritual problems.

EFIM: I do not understand. You, a monk, are saying such things to me?

DANIEL: Well, what of the fact that I'm a monk? It's my affair that I'm a monk. Life was given to me, and I vowed to give mine. That's all. But you are a Jew, and the Jews have never known monasticism. Even in the Essenes' community there were married people, they were not all unmarried. The Syrians and Greeks dreamed up monasticism. They invented all sorts of things which have no relevance to us. Go to your wife. You need a father confessor? You need somebody to take decisions for you? Right. I'll do it! Go and sleep with your wife . . .

41. 1983, Kfar Saba

LETTER FROM TERESA TO VALENTINA FERDINANDOVNA

Dear Valentina,

Your letters give me great succor and the last one, where you write about your trip to Lithuania, to Pater S., filled me with sadness. How much I have lost, but what a lot I have gained! I cannot say that my present life is worse or better than my past life, but the changes are so profound that there is no comparing them. At last a number of like thinkers have appeared around us among the parishioners of Brother Daniel. Of course it is not what we were used to at home. Here everything is far more diverse, including the people. They come from different countries and towns, and even speak Russian in different ways.

Efim is still lonely, but when there are the two of us, loneliness is not so hard. We are both suffering from the disorder in the Church. We are not fully satisfied with what we have now. Efim goes to the Russian Church Abroad. His relations with the 'red' Church have not worked out at all. Sometimes we visit the Catholics, the highly individual parish of Father Daniel who celebrates the Catholic Mass in Hebrew. I have made some progress in Hebrew now, I can talk a little. There is, however, no one I can talk to about the most important and private things. It is only with you that I can discuss my personal life.

Dear Valentina, you were married for 20 years and took vows after the death of your husband. That is the best thing a widow can do. We have a different experience, but you will understand me better than anybody else because you know both states: that of a married woman and that of a nun. Although, of course, covert monasticism, monasticism in the world, has its peculiarities, many who have been chastened by experience consider it the more difficult path. Your life seems to me an example of womanly service: getting married, being a faithful wife, giving birth to a child, becoming a widow, and taking vows.

Your translations too of the Gospel texts into modern Russian, revealing new meanings and nuances, which you undertake solely at the command of your heart, is not this true monastic service? As regards to myself, I see nothing in my time in the convent beyond a feat of discipline. The spiritual growth which is the whole purpose of monasticism did not occur. I venture even to think that my spiritual life has become richer since I left, and the sufferings associated with that have been a separate school of learning.

There are some intimate matters, dear Valentina, which I would proba- bly never be able to talk about aloud, but for some reason putting them in writing is simpler. My marriage to Efim, which we intended to be spiritual, has not remained so and has gained new meaning. Of course, we could never have taken this decision independently. We are both excessively shy people for such an audacious decision, but we were helped by Brother Daniel. No one could suspect him of being shy! He fought in the war, worked among the Germans, and performed acts of heroism.

Our marital life, blessed by Daniel, is blighted by one obstacle. Perhaps it is the fear and revulsion at physical relations between man and woman which has developed since my childhood that is the cause, but my gate is firmly barred and our intimacy is incomplete. That depresses me greatly, be- cause these are the most critical years, and if we cannot fulfil the main func- tion of marriage and have a child, would it not have been better for us to have remained in our previous state?

Efim comforts me, he is endlessly tender, does not let me out of his arms, and all my sufferings of many years associated with visits of the Enemy have departed.

At times I am downcast by thoughts about my renegacy. I have violated my vows and only the thought of a posterity which could justify that violation gives me strength.

As always, I ask for your prayers, but perhaps you will also be able to give me some practical advice. My poor husband, who beats against my impenetrable, in every sense, virginity, implores me not to be upset and tells me that he is entirely happy, but I am afraid he is saying that only out of com- passion. I beg forgiveness for burdening you with my tormenting problems. I wanted to write to you long ago but it is very difficult, and there is no other person in the world to whom I could turn about this.

Your loving
Teresa

42. 1983, Moscow
LETTER FROM VALENTINA FERDINANDOVNA TO TERESA

My dear girl,
We have been so close to each other these last years that the feeling arises of a complete and rich friendship and not only of a correspondence.

Your last letter greatly disturbed me. Your trust in my diversified experience of life, dear Teresa, is entirely misplaced. My marriage to Arkady Aristarkhovich was not happy, and I fear that the main experience I derived from my matrimonial state was that of enduring. My parents did not like Arkady and did not give me their blessing, but I insisted, and my difficult marriage I subsequently associated with that circumstance. I was passionately in love, blind and deaf to everything. He really was a brilliant man, much older than me, which I found particularly attractive. Already in our first year, when I was pregnant with Kirill, Arkady acquired a mistress, and that shocked me to the core. We lived 20 years together and I was compelled to live in accordance with his ideas about marriage. He had complete sexual freedom, something which I never contemplated. The most bitter thing in my life was that Kirill, as he grew up, inclined to his father's logic and scolded me for my mute subservience. There was a suggestion of disregard, if not of contempt.

The last year of Arkady Aristarkhovich's life, when he was seriously ill, his girlfriend came into our house constantly and literally tore the bedpan out of my hands, and that, too, I had to accept meekly. Even at the funeral, by the coffin, this Marianna Nikolaevna stood next to me dressed in deep mourning. I am writing all this so that you should understand, Teresa, that my marriage was very difficult, agonizing, although I preserved it to the very end and never gave Arkady Aristarkhovich a divorce. I did not allow our family to fall apart. For many years that was what he asked me for.

My parents are long dead, and it would seem a matter of no account that I married without their blessing. Now, however, I can say that only in monasticism have I found my vocation. My voluntary nocturnal labors, little different from slavery (you know how hard I find them), give great satisfaction. They are the only thing that I do for the Lord, and this is the one thing that gives me joy.

Life with my son's family is not easy, but in quite a different way from life with Arkady. Our apartment has long been too small. When the granddaughters were born, I moved into a small room, but now that they have married and are themselves having children, even this small room has become a luxury. Kirill is completely remote from me and I was never close to his wife.

I am writing this so that you should understand from my experience how important it is to follow your destiny. Perhaps if I had not disobeyed my parents, had not flung myself into the agonizing complications of family life, I would have gone into a convent when I was young and my life would have been more blessed.

I am saying all this so that you should ask whether there is some sign in your strange situation, and ask what it might be. Do you really not have near by any experienced guide who could help you resolve this agonizing situation? Spiritual and material things are very closely intertwined in our life, they do not exist separately.

I wondered for a long time how I could help you and finally talked to an old friend. She is a gynecologist and I told her, without of course naming names, about your problem from a medical point of view. She said the following: what is happening to you is not such an unusual disorder, it is called vaginismus, and it usually affects women who have experienced some sexual trauma in childhood or youth. There can be another explanation, a thickening of the hymen, which needs to be removed surgically. Another, very rare, cause of this disorder is a tumor. In all her 40 years of practice she has met only one case of that. She listened to me very attentively but said that from this distance she cannot help. When she heard that you live abroad she assured me that you need a good sexologist. Here that is an unusual profession, but abroad there are unquestionably such services.

She said that it would do no harm at all events to take an anti-spasmodic (something along the lines of No-spa) and a gentle sedative. You just need to find out what these drugs are called in your dispensaries.

Sweet Teresa, I retrace my steps back to the most important thing: no matter how your life has turned out, you must not despair. Of course the fact that you have broken your vows initially almost shocked me, but then I recognized that your attempt to live a secular life may not signify capitulation but a new and fruitful period. May God grant that your life works out and may he send you posterity, which will be the meaning and justification of everything.

Have courage, Teresa. I send you my most ardent prayers.

Yours,

Valentina

43. 1984, Haifa

LETTER FROM HILDA TO HER MOTHER

Dear Mother,

Now then, why have you still not come to visit us? Last week Daniel took a German group to Sinai and I went, too. The whole time I was thinking what a pity it was that you were not with us. From the very outset it was a complete delight, a real holiday! Everything went so well. First with the minibus, because it didn't break down. Usually something fails on the journey. Daniel did not get lost even once. Everywhere we came across people who knew him, and we were not delayed at the border when our documents were being checked. Even the customs officers were obliging!

And Daniel really is the best guide to Israel in the world. How admirably he showed us everything and explained it to us! He talked for four days and we looked to the right and the left. It was a very powerful experience, as if in those four days I experienced all of history, from the creation of the world to this night. Our country is very small (I forgot to tell you that last month I received Israeli citizenship, which is why I now say "our"). But can you picture how everything is squeezed into this strip of land from Sinai to Kinneret? The well beside which Abraham received the mysterious strangers; Jacob's well; the place where Jacob wrestled all night with his unseen adversary; the well into which Joseph's brothers threw him, and then pulled him out and sold him to merchants; and the burning bush out of which a voice spoke to Moses.

And then there was Sinai itself, which we went up at night and then watched the dawn and descended the mountain by the very path Moses came down with the tablets; and there is so much more which everybody knows from Scripture but when you read it, it seems abstract history, legends, myths, and when you get into a minibus and travel around all these places in a matter of hours, you realize it is not history but geography. This happened here, that happened there, and everything becomes true. Do you know where that feeling comes from? Because there are actual witnesses here, mountains, wadis, caves. Daniel showed us the cave where young David hid with his reed pipe from crazed King Saul. Saul came in and squatted down to relieve himself. David crept up and cut off the corner of his cloak and then showed him. See, you were defenseless, I could have killed you but I did not, so I am not your enemy. And this cave is a witness, and the plants and the animals which to this day live there just as they did then are also witnesses. At every such place we prayed, and everything was filled with such profound meaning that there is no describing it. In fact, everything that occurs here is very difficult to convey in words. They are inadequate and very approximate.

If you had stood next to me when Daniel was celebrating the Mass almost at the top of Mount Sinai! The sun was rising and what I wanted most was to die right then, because if I live a long time everything will be eroded, washed away, sullied by all sorts of rubbish, but at that moment there was such clarity and union with the world that it is difficult to describe. At all events, it had nothing to do with faith, because faith presupposes the existence of something which cannot be seen, and you make an effort to give that unseen and unfelt thing pride of place, and you repudiate seen things in favor of unseen things. But here there is an end to all faith because no effort is needed. You just stand and are happy and filled to the brim not with faith but with certainty. Forgive me, for God's sake, for this torrent of words, but I am writing to you in order not to burst. Perhaps I won't even send this letter. I'll reread it in the morning before deciding!

Mama, this year I will come and spend my holiday with you, but next year you really must promise to come here. Give me your word! I know, I have guessed long ago why you do not want to come. But do you know, half the Germans who were in the group are the children of those who fought in the war, children of SS men and all that, and you and I are not the only descendants of people for whom it is difficult to pray. Mama, I know perfectly well that you do not like Jews and are ashamed of it and still cannot like them. Please come. It will not be I or Daniel but the land here itself that will tell you more than you knew before, both about love and about history, and we will drive around Kinneret with you and then go up to Tsfat and you will see down below how small the Sea of Galilee is, like an elongated drop of water, and around it are the villages—Kfar Nahum, that is, Capernaum, Magdala, Cana, Gergesa—and you will take in at one glance all the Bible's history. It would be good if you could come in the spring when everything is green, covered in wild flowers, poppies, wild irises, and wild mustard.

But now I must not forget the most amazing thing about our trip. Believe it or not, we were already returning home and had passed the turn to Zikhron Yaakov, which is not far from Haifa at all. Daniel suddenly braked, turned the bus, and, without saying a word, took us to that town. Pretty cottages, some five-story blocks in which repatriates live. Daniel stopped at a small round plaza beside a café and said, "The perfect time for a cup of coffee! I'll just leave you for half an hour."

Off he went, somehow vanishing between the identical cottages. We sat and waited for him. Half an hour later he hadn't come back. He likes to say that he and I are very punctual people, but I in a German way and he in a Jewish way. To my question as to what the difference is, he replies, "A German comes on time, and a Jew when necessary!"

Anyway, he came back not half an hour but an hour later looking very pleased with himself. The whole way home he said nothing, although by this time he had lost his voice anyway and could only whisper. We reached Haifa, took everybody back to their lodgings, and returned to the community house. I put the kettle on and Daniel sat down and told me. "Listen, Hilda. What a day it's been. It must be five years ago that I received a letter from an old Jewish woman saying she wanted to be baptized. Her son had had an operation and his heart had stopped. The old lady was convinced that Jesus had saved her son because her Russian daughter-in-law, Vera, had prayed so fervently she had practically blown the roof off. I went to see her again. There was a whole district full of Russian Jews. They were all spying on each other, and the moment anything wasn't quite right they were writing denunciations. Well, not all of them, of course, but there are people like that. In this sense, whether they are Soviet or Polish all Communists are the same. They keep a close watch to make sure nobody else is getting more than them. Anyway, daughter-in-law Vera, because all the neighbors knew she was Christian, had a certain amount of trouble. The old lady, although she believed, was scared to death of the neighbors. 'Can you baptize me so that not a living soul should know?'

"She was a tiny little old woman, barely larger than a cat, but glowing. She was bent double and could barely move her legs, but she had cooked something for me, pies and the like.

"I looked at her and asked, 'Well, why have you taken it into your head to get christened, Olga Isaakovna?' 'Sonny,' she said, 'I'm alive and I'm so grateful, so grateful to Christ. I had a dream about him and he said, "Come, come to me!" He called me, and it was such fun, like when I was a girl! Perhaps I've gone back to my childhood. But when he said "Come to me," what else could he have meant? I decided it could only mean being christened. But in secret! Otherwise the neighbors will all spread it around and my son will lose his job.'

"The old lady was very frail, but so light and joyful! A cheery old lady like that would be loved by any god: baking pies, loving her daughter-in-law.

"I said, 'Fine, I will baptize you. Meanwhile, prepare yourself, read the Gospels with your daughter-in-law, rejoice and thank God, and before you die I will christen you. Not now, because you may change your mind and start being upset at being unfaithful to Abraham!'

"I left my telephone number and said that if she became seriously ill her daughter-in-law should phone me and I would come.

"I forgot all about the old lady until we were driving past that turn to

Zikhron Yaakov. As we went past, it was as if someone cuffed the back of my head. I had forgotten the old lady!

"While you were drinking coffee I went to see them. The daughter-in-law is tall, broad, and as soon as she opened the door, she threw up her great arms in the air and said, 'We've been trying to phone you at the monastery for three days and they said you were away. I'm so glad they got through to you. Olga Isaakovna is not at all well.'

"I didn't bother to tell them it was an angel from heaven who'd told me about their phone calls when he thumped me on the head at the turn. Olga Isaakovna was fully conscious but barely breathing. Her little eyes were shining. She saw me and said very weakly, 'You're keeping me back. I have waited for you such a long time.' The daughter-in-law was radiant. At the back stood an enormous bearded husband, David, and two sons who were also big lads. I had nothing with me, not even a crucifix. The daughter-in-law took a little cross from her neck and that was it. That was how I baptized Olga Isaakovna.

"Olga, the new Christian, died that very night. After being christened she fell asleep and died in her sleep. They phoned me in the morning and I thought, that's a worker who came to the vineyard in the last hour."

Daniel was thinking of the parable of the workers in the vineyard, where those who were hired first and worked from early morning till evening were paid exactly the same as the latecomers who had worked for only one hour.

Mama! Please stay well, look after your health. I want you and me to walk this land and not just look at it out of a car window. Please come to Israel! Life here is so buoyant.

Love to everybody,
Hilda

44. 1984

REPORT TO THE LATIN JERUSALEM PATRIARCHATE

To Monsignor Rafail Ashkuri, Secretary to the Patriarch
From Eldar Halil (Brother Elijah)

I bring to your attention the fact that on the 16th ult. Brother D., in the course of a sightseeing excursion to Sinai with a group of theology students from Germany, on the way, by the spring in Tabgha, celebrated Mass in the open air in which he was guilty of distortions, instead of the "Symbol of

Faith" reciting unauthorized prayers in Hebrew. What these were I could not discover, but in subsequent conversation at dinner, which Brother Daniel himself cooked for the group, he conducted a discussion which I did not understand since they were speaking in German. However, the assistant of Brother Daniel told me that he indicated that he did not accept the dogma of the Holy Trinity and justified his position by saying that Christ himself never spoke of the Trinity and it had been thought up by the Greeks. I asked Hilda, his assistant, for the text of the service he had conducted, calling it a Mass, and she has promised to give me that text. I will send it to you as soon as I receive it from her.

I enclose also a recording of a discussion which Father Daniel conducted in the parish house shortly before the service where the Trinity was also spoken of.

As my father's house in Haifa is being repaired, I request a grant to carry out the repairs.

Brother Elijah

45. 1984

TO THE ABBOT OF THE STELLA MARIS MONASTERY FROM THE SECRETARY OF THE PATRIARCH OF JERUSALEM

Reverend Father,
I request that you invite Brother Daniel Stein, a monk at your monastery, to visit me for a talk.

Monsignor Rafail Ashkuri, Secretary of the Latin Patriarch of Jerusalem

TO THE PROVINCIAL OF THE CARMELITE ORDER FROM THE PATRIARCH OF JERUSALEM

Your Grace,
I request that you review the case of a member of your Order, Brother Daniel Stein. According to information in my possession, he is guilty of gross violations in the order of conducting the Mass. He turned down my request to appear for a talk, which I consider a breach of ecclesiastical discipline. However, bearing in mind the fact that Brother Daniel Stein belongs to your Order, I request that you conduct an investigation and appropriate conversation.

Patriarch of Jerusalem

46. *1984*

TO THE HOLY CONGREGATION ON OUESTIONS OF THE DOCTRINE OF THE FAITH

TO PREFECT CARDINAL ROCKHAUS FROM THE GENERAL OF THE ORDER OF BAREFOOT CARMELITES, FATHER LAURENIS

Your Holiness,

I am regretfully obliged to inform you that within the Order entrusted to me, a certain doctrinal disagreement has occurred associated with the activities of one of our monks, Father Daniel Stein, and I have received intelligence from the Provincial of the Order in respect of sermons of the above priest which in certain matters deviate from the Church's dogma and traditions. Among the members of our Order there are few priests working with a congregation, and Brother Daniel Stein has a parish in the city of Haifa. Thanks to his active participation a church was restored through the efforts of his parishioners where he has performed his pastoral service for 15 years.

Under the State Law of Israel, missionary activity among Jews is forbidden; nevertheless we have on more than one occasion received warnings from the Ministry of Religions that, according to information in their possession, D. Stein performs the baptism of Jews.

Back in 1980 I had a talk with him on this matter and he asserted that he had performed individual baptisms of children whose Jewish parents profess the Catholic faith and did not have the right to refuse baptism to such people. Two other cases he told me about concerned people on their deathbeds and he could not refuse to carry out his pastoral and Christian duty. In one of these cases concerning the christening of a woman from Russia, who had been asking him for this for many years, he said that he had promised to carry out her request only if she was close to death. He did so on the eve of her death. You will agree that in such a situation I cannot hold infringement of the law against him. However, a hortatory talk was conducted.

At the end of last year I received from the Provincial of the Order a new message in respect of the preaching of Father Daniel Stein. At the same time I received an official letter from the Patriarch of Jerusalem in respect of the activity of Father Daniel Stein. This time the issue was more complex since it concerned non-acknowledgement by Stein of the primacy of the See of Rome in the Catholic world and his expression of the absurd idea that primacy should be with the Church in Jerusalem. Moreover, he had in mind not the Patriarchate of Jerusalem but the Church of St. James, the brother of the Lord, which ceased to exist early in the second century.

Affirming this idea, Father Daniel Stein celebrates Masses in Hebrew. Since the Second Vatican Council official permission has been given for services in local churches to be conducted in local languages, this can evince neither condemnation nor prohibition on my part. His thoughts on polycultural Christianity also seem to me questionable, but I would prefer that you discuss these issues with Father Stein yourself.

In the course of our conversation, basing myself on confidential information received, I asked whether he omitted the Symbol of Faith when celebrating the Mass. He admitted that in recent years he had not considered it possible to recite a text some of whose postulates he does not accept. On this occasion the matter in question was one of the fundamental dogmas of the Holy Church, the Trinity. His views appear to me so heretical that I will not venture even to paraphrase them, and this is one further argument in favor of your meeting him.

Instances of divergence of the views of Father Daniel Stein from the traditions generally accepted within the Holy Church are so numerous that I have temporarily banned him from celebrating Mass and leave a final decision to your Eminence.

Those charged with administration of the Order are prepared to send Father Daniel Stein to Rome for discussions at any time deemed acceptable by your Eminence.

Wholly devoted to you in Christ,
Father Laurenis
General of the Order of Barefoot Carmelites,

47. 1984, Haifa
FROM A CONVERSATION BETWEEN DANIEL AND HILDA

"Listen carefully and try not to interrupt! You know I was not expecting anything good to come of my trip to Rome and was ready for anything. Actually, the worst had already happened. My superiors had forbidden me to conduct services, although only temporarily, but I had had little hope of having the ban lifted. The more so since the Prefect of the Congregation on Matters of the Doctrine of the Faith, to which I was summoned, is extremely conservative. This prefect and the present Pope are a kind of balancing act who hold each other back from extremes, if I can put it that way. But the Pope is capable of emotional impulses, and I greatly admire that in him, while the Prefect is dry, emotionless, rational, and highly educated. He has a dozen degrees, speaks a dozen languages, and is very strict—at least that is how he seemed to me, and how he looked, too. He was slightly too rosy for an official, but that is in passing.

"I flew to Rome three days before the visit. It was not the first time I had been there. I know it fairly well, and do not like the city despite its charm. This time, too, as I walked around it my soul said no and no again to the city. I am a rural person and the grandeur of Rome repels me. It always has. It is some kind of madness that everybody wants to live in cities, and Rome is the city par excellence. It is redolent of the cruelty and grandeur of empire. Even the last historical Rome, the Rome of Mussolini, expresses the same thing— the power of force over the weak individual. In the Vatican you feel that even more strongly.

"I spent the whole day before the audience walking through the Rome of the catacombs. That is quite a different matter, a small, secret, hidden world trying not to be noticed by the urban power and create some kind of independent existence. Nobody ever manages that, although it is a very touching desire. Great faith, simplicity, and boldness are to be found in that reluctance to acknowledge grandeur and power. I came out of the catacombs completely calm and stopped worrying about my meeting the next day.

"I suddenly realized I was going to profess my faith and was prepared to say everything I think, concealing and keeping quiet about nothing. After that, come what may. Of course, I knew my judge was not like Pontius Pilate because he would never ask the rhetorical question, 'What is Truth?' He already knows for a fact exactly what it is.

"I had seen the Prefect before, the first time at a meeting with priests from Eastern Europe, and another couple of times, but not so close. He is tall. I'm sure you know, Hilda, that of all tall people you are the only one who does not disconcert me. Very tall and very short people belong to different species. Enough. Altogether, I feel more at home with people who are not tall, present company excepted, of course.

"He immediately told me he had read about me, knew about my past in the war and considered that priests like me who had experienced the war were particularly valuable to the Church. At that I thought that probably no sense would come out of our conversation. I did not bother to talk about the real meaning of all experiences of war. I thought he did not know how war brutalizes, distorts, and destroys a person, but he is a very subtle conversationalist, and immediately detected my reaction, changing the subject:

"'You conduct services in Hebrew?'"

"I explained the peculiarities of the Christians in my community to him, for whom Hebrew is often the only common language. Among my parishioners there is a couple, she is Dutch and he Spanish, who talk Hebrew between themselves. There are not a few such people.

"I used to conduct the service in Polish, but now a new generation has grown up and hardly any of the children of Polish Catholics speak it. Hebrew is their mother tongue. In addition, there are baptized Jews who have immigrated from other countries.

"He asked about translations and I told him that a number of translations already exist. Some we have done ourselves, but the Psalms, for example, we take from Jewish sources.

"I was well aware that he had a denunciation which no doubt informed him that I do not recite the Creed. What else was written there, I could only guess.

"The Prefect suddenly took a step in my direction and said that Christianity is multicultural, that the kernel, the heart should be common to all, but the shell can be different for different peoples. A Latin American is quite unlike a Pole or an Irishman.

"I was terribly pleased. I had never imagined I would find an ally in him. I told him about my meeting with á certain African bishop who told me bitterly that he had studied in Greece, served in Rome, assimilated the European form of Christianity, but could not require his African parishioners to become Europeans.

"'Our traditions are more ancient, and the African Church is extremely old, and my people dance and sing in church like King David, and when I am told this is impious, I can only reply, We are not Greeks or Irishmen!' That is what he told me, and I replied that I, too, could not see why Africans should have their service in Greek or Latin in order to understand what a rabbi from Nazareth had said!

"'Nevertheless, our Savior was not only a rabbi from Nazareth!' the Prefect commented.

"'Yes, not only that. For me, as for the Apostle Paul, he is the second Adam, our Lord, the Redeemer, the Savior! Everything you believe I also believe, but in all the Gospels he is called "Rabbi." That is what he is called by his disciples, and by the people. Do not take that "Rabbi" away from me because that, too, is Christ! I want to ask him about things that matter to me in Hebrew, in his own language!'

"You see, Hilda, I thought, yes he is right. Priests who have been through the war are a bit different. For example, I am not afraid to say what I think. If he prevents me from conducting services, I will celebrate alone in a cave. Here, in Rome, there existed a great Jewish church in the caves.

"I said, 'I cannot recite the Creed because it is full of Greek concepts. These are Greek words, Greek poetry, metaphors which are alien to me. I do not understand what the Greeks say about the Trinity! An equilateral triangle, one Greek explained to me, has all its sides equal, and if "filioque" is not used correctly the triangle will not be equilateral. Call me what you like, a Nestorian, a heretic, but until the fourth century nobody spoke of the Trinity. There is not a single word about it in the Gospels! It was thought up by the Greeks because they are interested in philosophical structures and not the One God, and that is because they were polytheists! I suppose we should be grateful they did not set up three gods, but only three persons! What persons? What is a "person"?'

"He frowned and said, 'St. Augustine wrote for us . . .'

"I interrupted. 'I very much like midrashes, parables, and there is one parable about Augustine which I like far more than all his fifteen volumes about the Holy Trinity. According to legend, when Augustine was walking by the seashore, contemplating the mystery of the Holy Trinity, he saw a boy who had dug a hole in the sand and was filling it with water which he was scooping with a shell from the sea. St. Augustine asked him why he was doing that. The boy replied, "I want to bail all the sea into this hole!" Augustine smiled and said that was impossible, to which the boy replied, "Well, why are you trying to bail all the inexhaustible mystery of the Lord with your intellect?" The boy immediately disappeared, but that did not stop Augustine from writing all those fifteen volumes.'

"You know Hilda, I do try to keep my mouth shut, but that got me going! How can they go on sounding off about this? With all this clever chatter they cast doubt on the ineffability of the Creator. They already know there are three persons. The structure of electricity is something nobody knows, but the structure of God is something that they know! The Jews also have speculators of this kind, the Kabbalah goes in for it, but that is of no interest to me. The Lord says, 'Take up your cross and follow me!' and man replies, 'Yes!' That I understand.

"'Prefect, you have just said that the nucleus, the kernel must be common to all, and this kernel of our faith is Christ himself. He is the necessary and sufficient factor. I see in him the Son of God, our Savior and our Master, but I do not want to see in him one side of a theological triangle. If anybody wants a triangle, let them worship a triangle. We do not know that much about him, but nobody doubts that he was a Jewish teacher. Allow us to keep him as a teacher!'

"You know, Hilda, I was of course talking too loudly, but I could see he was smiling. He said, 'How many parishioners do you have?' 'Fifty or sixty. Maybe one hundred . . .' He nodded. He realized he had not beaten me, but he also knew that few people were listening to me. We talked for another hour or so, and it was an interesting conversation. He was a profound and highly educated man. All in all, we parted on good terms.

"Hilda, I left the Congregation, I went to St. Peter's Cathedral, got down on my knees, and said to him in Hebrew, 'Rejoice, Peter. We are back! It has been a long time, but here we are again!'

"It seems to me I had the right to say that. Our little church is Jewish and Christian. That is so, Hilda, is it not?

"I went from Peter and sat on the steps in the sun and saw Father Stanisław, the Pope's secretary, coming straight toward me. The last time, three years ago, when I wanted an audience with the Pope, he did not grant me access. Perhaps it's unfair to say that, it's just how it felt. Now, however, he suddenly came over to me and said, 'His Holiness was talking about you recently. Wait here. I'll come back out in a minute.' I sat. It's a strange story. Fifteen minutes later Father Stanisław came running back and invited me to supper the day after tomorrow.

"For two days I walked around Rome. I like walking, as you know. Rome is a big city. I walked and thought about what I should say to the Pope that nobody else would say to him, and which I might never have another opportunity to say. I must not forget any of the important things. I felt I was back at school and about to take an exam.

"It didn't stop raining. Drizzle at times, heavier rain at other times, and then there was a really torrential downpour. My clothing was soaked and I could feel drops of water running down my back. I was walking along a broad deserted street with walls to left and right, wet trees, it was getting dark. In the distance I could see the skeleton of the Colosseum, and nothing else. Well, fine, I would walk to the Colosseum and get a bus there, I decided. I had just come right up to a telephone kiosk. The door opened a little and a wet girl shouted to me in English, 'Father, come in here with us!'

"I peeped into the kiosk. There were two of them in there, very young hippies, a boy and a girl, festooned with necklaces and bracelets of seashells and colored stones. They were such sweet children. They were having supper. There was a large bottle of water in the corner and in their hands they had a split baguette and some tomatoes. I squeezed in. There was room for three.

"They were from Birmingham. The girl looked very much like you, and so did the boy. They asked where I had come from and I said I was from Israel. They were terribly pleased and immediately asked if they could come and visit me. I invited them to do so. They are hitchhiking, but when I said it wasn't possible to hitchhike to Israel because they would have to cross the sea, they laughed at me. What was wrong with going through the Balkans, Bulgaria, Turkey, and Syria?

"So look out, my dear. They'll be here soon. The girl's name was Patricia, and the boy's . . . now I've forgotten.

"We ate their bread and tomatoes, talked about this and that, I left them in the telephone kiosk and went to the bus. The monastery hostel where I was staying was damp and cold and my clothes did not dry overnight, so I went to see Karol very well washed but also very damp.

"I was met by Stanisław on the same stairs where we had seen each other before and he invited me to the papal chambers, next to the cathedral. A door opened and he took me along a corridor to a room. I waited there. I looked and saw bookshelves, a library. A long table. It was fairly gloomy. A door opened to one side and the Pope emerged. He was dressed simply in a white soutane, soft slippers on his feet, leather, with holes. I saw they were from Kraków. His stockings were white and thick. He embraced me, and poked me fairly hard in the stomach.

"'Hey, you're getting fat! Are they feeding you well?'

"'Not badly. Come and see us, Holy Father, we will treat you to some Middle Eastern food!'

"'Brother Daniel,' he said, 'we have known each other for more than forty years and all that time ago we were already on familiar terms and you called me by a different name.'

"'Of course, Lolek, we all had different names.'

"'Yes, Dieter,' he smiled, and it was like a permission to return to the past, an invitation to a frank conversation. Hilda, I was so glad for him. I liked him even more. When a man rises so high he usually loses a lot, but Lolek has lost nothing.

"That is how it was, Hilda. What are you gaping at? I have known the Pope since 1945. He's from Kraków, for heaven's sake! I was a novice there, then I studied there. We served in the same diocese. We were friends. We traveled to give sermons. He didn't like traveling at that time, so sometimes I stood in for him. That's how things were.

"The secretary was with us, standing alongside, but it was as if he wasn't there. We went to the chapel, a small chapel with benches with cushions for kneeling on."

"Velvet cushions?" Hilda could not help asking.

"Yes, velvet, and with crests. A lot of doors. A server entered one and brought out the icon of the Mother of God of Kazan. We knelt and prayed silently. Then the Pope got up and took me to the dining room.

"A long table, for twelve people or so, three settings. I thought there would be a supper of one hundred people, but there was nobody.

"He went on to say that he had been wanting to talk to me for a long time, that he knew how difficult the situation of a Catholic priest and monk was in the Holy Land in our days. At that I got a little irate. 'In Israel,' I said.

"He is a clever man and immediately saw what I was getting at. The Vatican State does not recognize the existence of the State of Israel! He guided the conversation very carefully but not disingenuously.

"'Of course,' I said, 'the position of a Christian has never been easy, and the position of a Jew is also far from easy, as Peter testifies. But how about being a Jewish Christian in Israel in the twentieth century? That really is something. There are such people, however, and it gladdens me because it is not so important how many people there are in the Jewish Church—ten, one hundred, or one thousand—but that they exist, and that testifies to the fact that Jews have accepted Christ. This is the Church in Israel, but the Vatican does not recognize Israel.'

"'Daniel, I know. We have our Christians there, and we are in some sense hostages. Politics has to be carefully balanced in order not to irritate the Arabs, or the Muslims, or our brother Christians. There are no theological reasons, but there are political reasons. You understand that better than I do.' He seemed to be waiting for me to sympathize, but I could not. 'I would not like to be in your position,' I said. 'Where there is politics, there is disgrace.'

"'Wait. Wait a little. Even so, we are moving very quickly. People cannot keep up with us. Their ideas change slowly.'

"'But if you don't have time to change them, your successor may not wish to.' I said everything that was on my mind. At that. the server brought the meal. It was not Italian, but Polish: a dish of zakuski—cheese, Kraków sausage. Matka Boska! I hadn't seen sausage like that since I left Poland. Also a bottle of water and a decanter of wine. They brought soup, then bigos. I couldn't tell whether it was in my honor or whether the Pontiff retains old habits.

"'Daniel, when you were serving your rural parish in Poland, did they bring you the food like this?' he asked and laughed.

"Actually, they did, Hilda. After the war, times were very hard in Poland and old ladies really did bring me cakes and pies, and sour cream. Oh, my Poland, my Poland!

"I had been saving up what I had to tell him for so many years, and then between the soup and the bigos I could not find how to begin. He himself made it clear that he was prepared to listen to me. He said, 'You know, Daniel, it is very difficult to turn this great ship. There is a habit of thinking in a particular manner, both about Jews and about many other things. You have to change the direction without capsizing the ship.'

"'Your ship threw the Jews overboard, that's the problem,' I said. He was sitting almost opposite me, slightly to one side. He has large hands and the papal signet ring is large and on his head was the white papal skullcap, like a yarmulke, and he was listening attentively. Then I told him everything I had been thinking these last years, the things which keep me awake at night.

"'The Church expelled the Jews. That's what I think. But what I think is not important. What does matter is what St. Paul thought. For him the "one, holy, Catholic, and apostolic Church" was a Church of Jews and non-Jews. He never imagined a Church without Jews. It, the Church of circumcision, had the right to decide who belonged to that catholicity. Paul came to Jerusalem not just to pay his respects to the Apostles Peter, James, and John. He was sent by an affiliated Church, the Church of the Gentiles. He came to the mother Church, to that early Christianity, to Judeo-Christianity, because he saw it as the source of all being. Later, in the fourth century, after Constantine, the daughter Church usurped the place of the mother Church. It was no longer Jerusalem which was the ancestral mother of the Churches, and catholicity no longer meant unity, all-inclusiveness, global reach, but merely loyalty to Rome. The Greco-Roman world turned away from its source, from the primal Christianity which had inherited Judaism's attitude toward orthopraxis, that is, to the observance of the commandments, to dignified behavior. To be a Christian now meant principally to acknowledge doctrine emanating from the Center. From that moment, the Church was no

290 / LUDMILA ULITSKAYA

longer an eternal union with the God of the Jews, renewed in Jesus Christ as a union with the God of all peoples, following Christ, and thereby confirmation of loyalty to the first covenant of Moses. The Christian peoples were by no means the New Israel, they were the Extended Israel. Altogether we, the circumcised and the uncircumcised, became the New Israel not by rejecting the old one but by extending it to include the whole world. What was at issue was not doctrine but purely a way of life.

"'In the Gospels we find a very Jewish question: 'Rabbi, what shall I do to inherit eternal life?' The Master does not tell the questioner to believe this or that. He tells him to go and do this and that. Act in accordance with the commandments of Moses. But, he says, he is already doing that. He has no intention of breaking the commandments. Then the Master says, in that case everything is fine, but if you want to be perfect, give away all your property and follow me. That is Christianity—giving everything to the Lord, not a tithe, not a half, but everything! But first learn to give away, like a Jew, a tenth. Moses taught how a man should do his duty to the Lord, and Jesus how to do it not from a sense of duty but of love.

"'Why is Rome the mother Church? Rome is a sister! I am not against Rome, but I am not under Rome! What does "the New Israel" mean? Is it supposed to abolish the old one?

"'Paul understood that the Gentiles were a wild branch which had been grafted on to the natural olive tree. Israel opened up to receive new peoples. This was not a New Israel separate from the old one but an Extended Israel. Paul could never have imagined that there would be a Church without the Jews.'

"At this point he stopped me and said, 'Forgive me, I was wrong. I am happy to say that.'

"Hilda, he said that because he is a very great man, greater than one can imagine!

"He said, 'Yes, I was wrong and I want to put this mistake right. You are correct in talking of an Extended Israel!'

"But by now I could not stop. After all, I did not know whether I would ever see him again and I had to tell him everything.

"'For the Jews, as for the Christians, it is man, not God, who stands at the center. Nobody has ever seen God. You have to see God in man. In Christ the man, you need to see God. The Greeks put Truth at the center, the principle of Truth, and for the sake of that principle you can destroy a man. I have no need of a truth which destroys a man. More than that, anyone who destroys a man destroys God also. The Church bears a guilt toward the Jews!

In the city of Emsk we were shot down in a square between two churches, one Catholic, and one Orthodox! The Church drove out and cursed the Jews and has paid for that by all its subsequent divisions and schisms. These divisions cover the Church in shame right up to this day. Where is the catholicity? Where is its all-embracing nature?'

"'I know, Daniel. I know this,' he said.

"'It's not enough for me that you know it,' I said.

"'Don't be too hasty, don't be too hasty. It is an enormous ship!' That is what he said.

"The server came in and brought kissel."

"What did he bring?" Hilda asked.

"Kissel. It's a dessert, made from cherries. Like German Grütze. Yes, Hilda, I have remembered—the boy's name is Jonathan."

"What boy?" Hilda asked in surprise.

"That couple of hippies in the telephone box. The girl was Patricia, and the boy was Jonathan. He had a harelip which had been sewn up fairly neatly. You will recognize them."

48.

FROM THE BIOGRAPHY OF POPE JOHN PAUL II

1981, 13 May: in St. Peter's Square a Turkish terrorist, Ali Ağca, makes an attempt on the Pontiff's life, seriously wounding him.

1986, 13 April: for the first time since the era of the apostles a Roman pope visits a synagogue (in Rome) and greets Jews, calling them "our beloved brothers and, we may say, our elder brothers."

1986, 27 October: on the initiative of John Paul II a meeting takes place in the city of Assisi of representatives of 47 different Christian churches and 13 representatives of non-Christian religions and they pray together.

1992, 12 July: Pope John Paul II announces to believers his imminent hospitalization in connection with an operation to remove a tumor in his intestine.

1993, 30 December: Diplomatic relations are established between the Vatican State and the State of Israel.

1994, 29 April: John Paul II slips getting out of the shower and breaks his hip. Independent specialists consider that it is from this time that he begins to suffer from Parkinson's disease.

2000, 12 March: in the course of a Sunday Mass in St. Peter's Cathedral the Pope asks forgiveness and acknowledges the Church's guilt for its sins: persecution of the Jews, church schisms, and religious wars, crusades and justification of wars on the basis of theological dogmas, contempt for minorities and the poor, justification of slavery. He performs a ritual of repentance (mea culpa) for the sins of the sons of the Church.

2000, 20 March: beginning of the Pope's visit to Israel, in the course of which he prays at the Wailing Wall in Jerusalem.

2001, 4 May: in Athens the Pope asks forgiveness on behalf of the Church for the destruction of Constantinople.

2001, 6 May: in Damascus the Pontiff, for the first time in the existence of the Church, visits a mosque.

2004, 29 June: Bartholomew I, Ecumenical Patriarch of Constantinople, pays an official visit to the Vatican.

49. 1984, Haifa
FROM HILDA'S DIARY

Met Daniel at Lod Airport. He flew in from the Vatican. Met the Pope. He told me all about it. I feel as if I am standing next to the burning bush. It is scary.

50. 1996, Galilee, Nof a-Galil
FROM A CONVERSATION BETWEEN EWA MANUKYAN AND AVIGDOR STEIN

CASSETTE 4

On 18 March 1984, Daniel was sixty. It coincided with Purim. We decided to give him a family birthday party. The weather couldn't have been better, very warm and everything was already green. My Milka, as you know, survived the Warsaw ghetto, and any woman who has experienced such hunger is a little obsessed with food. When she cooks for a celebration she multiplies everything by ten. If there are gtwenty guests she cooks for two hundred. Well, on this occasion she cooked as if for a large wedding. At Purim it is traditional to have all kinds of sweets, so for two days Milka was cooking all manner of honey, nut, and poppyseed buns. Her elder son-in-law Adin brought a car trunk–full of meat and started cooking shashlyk first thing in the morning, heating coals, marinating something. Daniel, of course, had no idea of the scale of the celebration. Our grandchildren, at that time we had three boys and two girls, also made themselves useful rehearsing a play. Our large house, four rooms and two terraces, was as crowded with children and food as a beehive. Everything was buzzing, sizzling, and clattering. I was awarded the role of Haman, and in the morning my whole face was painted and I had bushy red eyebrows stuck on.

Children very much love Purim because they can stuff themselves with sweets and yell themselves hoarse. The producer was Moshe, our second son-in-law. He stuck a hessian wig on top of his skullcap, donned some kind of sack, and pulled red rubber garden gloves on to his hands to represent an executioner.

The entire family made a present for Daniel. On the seat of an old chair we moulded a whole life out of plasticine. Everybody lent a hand, Ruth, of course, more than anyone else. In the middle stands Daniel with a staff surrounded by three sheep. Our family is around him. Ruth modeled the figures very recognizably and Aaron, her elder son whom we have nicknamed Bezalel, draws wonderfully and has become an artist. So then, in the middle is Daniel and around him a great procession of little people, Jews in prayer shawls, Arabs in keffiyehs, Ethiopians, Germans in dreadful peaked caps, even with little swastikas on their arms, and a lot of mules and dogs. When everyone had been put in their place, Milka said, "Look, will you, we've forgotten Hilda," so Aaron also sculpted Hilda, very lifelike and taller than anyone else.

Daniel had promised to come at about seven but was very late. Milka was incensed that the food would get cold, but still there was no Daniel.

He appeared only at ten o'clock when it was already completely dark, but the children had hung lanterns and lit torches all through the garden. You should have seen how they welcomed him, with a clamor of rattles, shrieks, and beating drums. Then he was taken to the table and there in the middle stood our present, covered with a silk tablecloth. Daniel removed it and was so pleased and laughed and then for the rest of the evening kept coming back to look at it and finding amusing new details. A toy David, our grandson, was sitting on Shloma's back and had a cat on his head. Milka had a spoon and saucepan and there was a chicken in the saucepan. It was all so tiny that Daniel had to put his glasses on.

My grandchildren adored him and hung from him like a tree. At night when Milka had cleared everything away, Daniel, despite her vehement protests, helped her wash the dishes. When we were alone he told me he was being summoned to Rome by the Prefect of the Congregation for Matters of Doctrine of the Faith.

"The Inquisition? The Vicar of Loyola on Earth?" I joked, but Daniel did not go along with my joke. He looked at me in surprise and commented, "No, Loyola was the first general of the Order of Jesuits, but never headed the Inquisition. I hope they will not burn me at the stake, but some kind of unpleasantness is sure to follow."

I had never seen him so distraught before. I wanted to find some way of giving him strength and said, "Don't be upset. At worst we will find you a job in our moshav. Admittedly we don't have any sheep so you won't be a shepherd anymore, but we'll make you a gardener."

"No, I don't think I will go. I won't go and that's that."

About three weeks later he came to see us and I asked whether he was still refusing to go to Rome. "I shall have to go, but I have put it off as much as I could, until the autumn. I don't need a quarrel, I need understanding." He sighed.

He went to Rome in late autumn and returned very pleased. "Well, I asked, they didn't burn you at the stake then?" "No. Quite the contrary. I was in Rome and saw old friends. Poles. I drank mead, and was treated to Kraków sausage." "So what?" I said. "Why did you have to go so far. There are lots of Poles in Israel. You could even have found a few among your parishioners!" "That's true, but it's still pleasant to meet a friend from your old life."

"Daniel, half the world are your friends." He just laughed. "Yes, half the world. Not the first half, though, only the second." It was much later that Hilda told me which friend it was he had met.

8 June 2006, Moscow
LETTER FROM LUDMILA ULITSKAYA TO ELENA KOSTIOUKOVITCH

Dear Lyalya,

I got food poisoning from eating something ridiculous. I've been ill for a day and a half and experienced a whole gamut of emotions: first puzzlement— after all, I eat absolutely anything and never suffer any consequences—then irritation at myself—why on earth do I eat absolutely anything, after all, the tomato juice which I unreflectingly chucked into the dinner had been standing on the buffet for who knows how many days. I remember exactly that I bought it last week to make a Bloody Mary which one of my guests likes. Then I stopped blaming myself because I really felt very ill. I couldn't take any pills because I was vomiting every half hour from the bottom of my stomach. You can imagine that today my throat, flank, and stomach muscles are still hurting.

Then I remembered all my friends and relatives who had suffered long and painfully—and patiently!—before dying and thought yet again that the supplication for "a peaceful Christian death, painless and blameless" is the most important of all requests addressed to the Lord God. In the meanwhile I was endlessly drinking lemon tea, then soda water, then just water because I no longer had the strength even to plug in the electric kettle. As soon as I stopped drinking, the spasms of nausea became completely unbearable. All the unpleasantness was happening exclusively in the upper half of the organism.

Then Andrey came in and wanted to call an ambulance straight away. For some reason I knew that was not the right thing to do. Then, Lyalya, here is what occurred to me. Because by this time I had indubitably puked out all the tomato juice, I realized that I was expelling all the nightmare I have been gulping down these last months of reading, the painful reading of all those books about the destruction of the Jews during the Second World War, all the tomes of medieval history, the history of the Crusades and the earlier history of the Church councils, the fathers of the Church from St. Augustine to St. John Chrysostomos, all the anti-Semitic opuses written by highly enlightened and terribly holy men. I puked out all the Jewish and non-Jewish encyclopedias I have read over the last few months, the whole Jewish Question which had poisoned me more powerfully than any tomato juice.

Lyalya, I hate the Jewish Question! It is the most disgusting question in the history of our civilization. It should be abolished as a fiction, as nonexistent. Why do all humanitarian, cultural, and philosophical problems—to say nothing about purely religious problems—constantly dance around the Jews? God has laughed at his chosen people far more than at any of the others! He knew perfectly well that a person cannot love God more than himself. That is something only a very few chosen people can do. Daniel was one of them, and there are a few others. For these people the Jewish Question does not exist. It should be abolished!

At 4:30 this morning I stopped puking and at 2 o'clock this afternoon I more or less got up and sat down to finish the book.

I am sending you Part Three. Not much more to go.

Love,

Lyusya

PART FOUR

1. 1984, Kfar Saba

LETTER FROM TERESA TO VALENTINA FERDINANDOVNA

Dear, sweet Valentina,

It seems like unbelievable good fortune! When we had quite lost hope that Efim could become a serving priest, everything suddenly changed as if someone had waved a magic wand. Amazing as it may seem, it is Daniel who has got everything moving. He was received at the Ministry of Religious Affairs by the Minister herself, a woman, can you believe it? I do not know why the meeting took place, or even whether he was summoned by the Ministry or chose to go there himself, but what was being discussed was the existence of Christian churches in Israel. The lady minister said, We know that you love Israel and we need the kind of Christian Church which will not quietly engage in subversive games against us. Daniel said he loves this land, conducts sightseeing excursions through it, and is also helping to build it, although the minister might not agree with that. This lady is fairly young and, as Daniel said, very perspicacious and even witty. She commented that the further Christian building progresses, the more it resembles the Tower of Babel. "We Israelis would like to build our little orchard in the shade of that great tower but at a considerable distance from it, so that when it falls down, it does not bury our modest borders under its rubble."

Daniel said that Christianity builds relations between man and God, and the aggressiveness of modern civilization shows itself quite independently of denominations, while any dialogue between man and God leads to the restraining of aggression and to peacemaking.

She laughed and said that Israeli society completely disproves his point of view because there is not a country in the world where there is so much religious tension. Daniel said he had no answer to that. Then she asked whether he could recommend priests who love Israel as he does himself, or at least do not hate it like the majority of priests she knows. She wanted priests capable of peacemaking and not of fanning interreligious conflicts. At this, Daniel named Efim! I do not know how the mechanism works, but shortly afterward Efim received an invitation to visit the Russian Ecclesiastical Mission and went to the Church of the Trinity. He supposed he would be received by an archimandrite, but was met instead by someone who introduced himself as Nikolai Ivanovich and who proceeded to interview him.

Nikolai Ivanovich is a kind of personnel officer, and one may suppose that finally the letter from the abbot in Vilnius has had an effect. Efim is now awaiting appointment to a parish.

A week ago we went on a magical trip to the Dead Sea and spent two days in a guesthouse in one of the oldest kibbutzes. They have a marvelous botanical garden, old houses built by the first settlers, and one new building where they rent rooms to visitors. Everything is very clean and pretty, and there are rare plants and even a baobab tree. The whole kibbutz is situated on a hill. In one direction there is a view of the Dead Sea, and in good weather when there is no haze you can see Jordan. In the other direction there is a ravine at the bottom of which a river flows in the spring before drying up. In this rocky ravine there are a lot of caves and we were shown one in which, according to legend, the young David hid from King Saul who was persecuting him.

It was after this journey, which in some sense could be called our honeymoon, that our marriage was consummated. I know I have to thank you for your advice, and another doctor here to whom we had to go for consultations, but most of all God who united us by his great mercy. Efim and I are very happy and full of hope. Of course we are no longer young, but our prayers for the granting of offspring are now supported by the requisite actions.

One more substantial and also pleasant piece of information: the publishing house has proposed that Efim should edit *Readings on Reading*, a series of domestic lectures by Father Mikhail which you are very familiar with. The fee is modest, but I am almost certain that they will appreciate Efim and continue to give him work in the future. I hope that he will ultimately succeed in publishing his *Reflections on the Liturgy* there.

I think Father Mikhail already knows about this favorable development, but if not, please give him the glad tidings. The book should come off the presses at the end of this or the beginning of next year.

I will let you know the moment our news ripens.

With love,

Teresa

1984, Be'er Sheva

FROM A LETTER FROM TERESA TO VALENTINA FERDINANDOVNA

. . . hot and stuffy, oppressive and dehydrating. The wind is from the Negev Desert. I know now for a fact that hell is fiery and not icy. A hot, inebriating wind which blows away your brains and all your thoughts, your heart and all your emotions, and you wait for night when it will not be so hot, but your expectations are disappointed. The Hamsin blows and turns you into a cliff which feels nothing or a pile of rocks or a handful of sand. You pour water into yourself every five minutes, because without it you would be like a withered plant within hours. People do not sweat properly here because as soon as sweat is secreted on the surface of your skin it evaporates and the water you drank is already gone. I am hardly able to eat. Sometimes at night time I gnaw an apple or salt biscuit with sweet tea.

Efim laughs and says that salt herring with sweet tea is a favorite Jewish treat. We have been here for two months and until now I haven't been able to write because I could not get up and put pen to paper. I have become so thin that my clothes dangle from me as if I were a clothes hanger. I think I have lost about 10 kilograms. Efim has also lost weight, but he copes with the heat far better than I do.

The little church is wonderful, small, built of stone, and no services have been held in it for a long time because after the last priest, a Greek monk, died the few parishioners dispersed. How amazed Efim was when he discovered several Jews from Russia among his new parishioners, including a couple who lecture at the local university. Two large Bedouin families also came, several Greeks, and a Japanese man married to a Russian-Israeli woman.

The Japanese converted to Orthodoxy from Lutheranism. Not even the D—l knows what is going on in his head, but Efim very entertainingly relayed their discussion of ethics as seen from the viewpoint of a Shintoist Japanese and a modern Christian. When he was young, the Japanese was a Shintoist, but converted to Lutheranism back in Japan. He came to Israel 20 years ago with a Protestant tourist group, met an Orthodox monk in the Old Town whom he took as his teacher, and followed him into an Orthodox monastery near Jerusalem, where he lived for three years. This Shintoist Zionist decided to settle here temporarily but is now a permanent resident.

He is an architect and currently works for a large firm. He has married a young Russian girl who was studying at the University here where he was a teacher. He is a great zealot of Orthodoxy and he and Efim found they had much common ground. Another parishioner, the only one who knows the service properly and sings well, which means he acts not just as regent but as the entire choir, is a Leningrad doctor, Andrey Yosifovich. He has a large family of four or five children. Efim brought him to see me and he gave me some homoeopathic medicines which seem to help a little.

So that is our handful of Orthodox worshippers, all of them people with problems, both moral and material. Our own situation has not improved either, in fact it has become worse. Efim is no longer receiving benefits, and only receives irregular payments from the Patriarchate, which doesn't pay salaries but unpredictably gives money "for expenses." Everything is in the hands of Nikolai Ivanovich whom I have already mentioned, not of the archimandrite as you might expect. Nikolai Ivanovich's job in the patriarchate is as a driver!

From time to time I feel so nauseated, and this kind of heat will continue for at least three months. How am I going to live through it? It will be hot afterward too, but not to such an intolerable degree.

Yesterday I had a strange and very unpleasant dream. It was as if my belly opened like a flower, the petals separated, and out flew a dragon. It was a very handsome dragon with colorful silky wings shot with a green and pink sheen. It flew up into the sky and somersaulted beautifully and I realized it was not simply flying but writing something in the air with its long body. Then I noticed I had a string in my hand which was guiding it and it was actually me who was doing the writing by directing its flight. What I was writing, however, I could not tell but I knew it was something important and if I tried hard enough I would understand. It was frightening. I told Efim about the dream. He was surprised and anxious because he has come to see all my dreams and visions as temptations or mental illness. He said he had dreamed something similar but had been so confused he decided not to tell me about it. Now he told me he dreamed his belly split into quarters and a large colorful bubble came out, like a soap bubble but more solid. It, too, broke away from him and floated up into the sky. It's the same dream don't you think?

1984, Be'er Sheva
FROM A LETTER FROM TERESA TO VALENTINA FERDINANDOVNA

Andrey Yosifovich came, examined me again and asked when I had my last period. I could not remember. I have been feeling so ill all this time and have become so thin that I had somehow managed to forget. It was certainly two months ago or more. Andrey Yosifovich told me to go and see a gynecologist. Valechka, I have never been to a gynecologist in my life! A few months ago on your recommendation, Efim and I went to a sexologist, but I could not allow him to give me a medical examination. I felt I would prefer to die. The sexologist did not insist and said that this negative reaction was natural given my anomaly. He gave us a set of exercises which we performed and the problem resolved itself, but the idea of going to a gynecologist for an examination simply horrified me

I told Andrey Yosifovich about this and then he said he thought I was pregnant. I wept with fear for 24 hours and then went to see the doctor. Dear Valentina, it has been confirmed. The doctor, fortunately, was a woman. Hearing that I am 42 and that this is my first pregnancy, she wrote me a letter to a specialist clinic where I will be given some unusual genetic analysis and something else which I did not understand.

When I told Efim about it he said nothing for two days, then told me he felt exactly like Zacharias. He felt an inner need to be silent because he was afraid that if he spoke he might frighten the miracle away. I understand him.

I ask for your prayers, dear Valentina Ferdinandovna. Do not be worried if you do not get any letters from me for a time.

2. February, 1985, Be'er Sheva
TELEGRAM FROM EFIM DOVITAS TO VALENTINA FERDINANDOVNA

MARVELOUS BOY BORN WEIGHT 2350 HEIGHT 46 CM EFIM

3. March 1985, Be'er Sheva
LETTER FROM TERESA TO VALENTINA FERDINANDOVNA

Dear Valentina,
The baby and I have left hospital. He is tiny and very pretty. We are completely happy. We have called him Itzhak. What else could we have called a

304 / LUDMILA ULITSKAYA

child given to us at such a late age and under such circumstances? We feel
what has happened is a miracle from God. The little boy is not quite right,
he has Down's syndrome, as we were warned in the middle of pregnancy.
Because of that they offered to give us a termination but we refused without
hesitation. Now he is with us, our baby boy. He is very calm, very sweet, with
little oriental eyes. He looks Japanese. He is not good at sucking, but I have
a lot of milk and I am constantly expressing it because he can't suck at the
breast yet. I feed him with my milk but from a bottle.

It is an amazing feeling having three of us. Efim decided to have him circumcised before the christening. He invited a rabbi he knows who brought
a specialist with a stone knife, as in ancient times. I was terribly afraid, but
everything went well without complications, and when the little wound
healed the baby was christened in our church. Daniel christened him. After
all, our son was born with his blessing! Daniel came to us with a pile of presents, and even brought a pram. He held Itzhak in his arms all the time, cud-
dling him, and I have never seen an elderly person melt like that at the sight
of a baby. Perhaps it was because our little boy really is terribly sweet. That
same day they christened Andrey Yosifovich's daughter too. She is their fifth
child and was born three days after ours. We invited Andrey Yosifovich to
be his godfather. By comparison with our little boy his daughter is simply
huge, a veritable Brünnhilde, but her parents are also very large.

The weather is beautiful now, the short spring is not over and the heat
has not yet begun. One of my new friends has invited me to move for the
summer and stay with her near Tel Aviv. It is not so hot by the sea, but we
decided not to be separated when there is no great necessity. Efim borrowed
some money from the bank and bought an air conditioner. It uses a lot of
electricity but we will manage somehow. The main thing for us is not to be
parted. Itzhak is entitled to a separate benefit, and that will help us to pay off
the air conditioner. We enjoy every minute. The baby has given new meaning
to our lives. It is just over a month since he was born and we can't imagine
how we managed to live without him. I will write.

Love from
Teresa.

Oh, I forgot to tell you that Mother Ioanna has painted an icon for little
Itzhak, "Akeidah," the sacrifice of Isaac. A baby is lying on the altar, Abraham is
standing with a knife in his hands, and the quiet smiling face of a ram with curving spiral horns is peeping out of the bushes. When I look at this icon it brings

tears to my eyes. Can you imagine, Mother Ioanna came to the christening with this icon, in her monastery's car, and, incidentally, left some money in an envelope, the exact cost of the air conditioner. I keep going on about miracles.

PS. I forgot to say that Father Mikhail's book has been published, under a pseudonym of course, and Efim has been sent reviews of it. The best is from a Russian émigré newspaper. The worst is also from the Russian émigré community. Efim made a photocopy which I will put in the envelope. I hope it reaches you. There have been no comments about it from Russia. I suspect the book simply has not made it there.

4. 1985

FROM THE NEWSPAPER *RUSSKII PUT'*, PARIS-NEW YORK
Readings on Reading, Andrey Belov, Munster: Poisk Publishers

The author's premise is that the Bible is first and foremost a work for literary historians, like *The Divine Comedy* or *The Lay of the Host of Igor*. Accordingly he awards pride of place in Bible study to human knowledge—philology, history, and archaeology. This aggregate of sciences Belov calls "Biblical criticism" and this approach defines his reading of the Bible. Moreover, he considers it permissible to advocate a curious view which is profoundly at variance with the position of the Church. According to Orthodox doctrine, the Bible is the Word of God. That is, it is the only book in the world whose author is God Himself. The role of the person who wrote down the text, whether a prophet or an apostle, was merely to register in human language the divine revelation communicated by the Holy Spirit. Andrey Belov, however, has his own ideas about this.

In Orthodoxy there is a definite intellectual discipline whose basis is that Holy Scripture may be interpreted only in accordance with the sacred tradition of the Church and in agreement with the opinion of the Holy Fathers. The Nineteenth Rule of the Sixth Ecumenical Assembly reads: "Primates of churches should . . . teach all the clergy and people the words of piety, selecting from Divine Scripture the understanding and discourse of truth and not transgressing the already established boundaries and customs of the God-bearing Fathers; and if the word of the Scriptures shall be examined, then not otherwise than that it be expounded as it was expounded by the luminaries and teachers of the Church in their writings . . . in order not to depart from what is meet."

This is not "narrowness," not "despotism," but acknowledgment of the divinely inspired nature of Holy Scripture. Accordingly, all researches which are not sanctioned by the Church are without foundation and harmful.

Andrey Belov, the author of this questionable book, proceeds from different premises. For exegesis of biblical texts he adduces, alongside such Holy Fathers as St. John Chrysostomos and Grigoriy Nissky, the teachings of such heretics condemned by the Church as Feodor Mopsuetsky, Pelagius, and even modern freethinking philosophers of the like of Archpriest Sergey Bulgakov, Nikolai Berdyaev, and Vladimir Soloviov whose authority can in no wise be ranked alongside the authority of the Fathers of the Church. Belov goes even further, drawing on the arguments of Catholic and Protestant theologians and sometimes even of natural scientists—physicists, biologists, and such like.

Books of this kind are harmful and damaging for the Orthodox mind and can be welcomed only by people profoundly hostile to true Orthodoxy. Any person who puts his trust in the ideas expounded by Andrey Belov will fall into the embrace of anti-Christianity, which is worse even than "pure" atheism.

Archimandrite Constantine (Antiminsov)

5. 1985, Jerusalem

LETTER FROM MOTHER IOANNA TO FATHER MIKHAIL IN TISHKINO

Dear Mishenka,

I have been sent your book *Readings on Reading*. The title seems ill-chosen. I have started reading but it is a slow business. I have to use a magnifying glass because my eyes are now quite hopeless. It is interesting to read. It reminds me of our elder, and how well he said, "To whom wisdom is not given let him not speak words of wisdom, but read in simplicity; but whoever has been given understanding, let him discourse on reading." The Bible is a book of unbounded profundity, but each person draws from it in accordance with his faculties. The elder, although in old age he became very mild and deprecated his ego as much as is possible, in his younger years was an educated man with particular opinions and judgments. I remember him from the Religio-Philosophical Society, and he was excellent in conversation and debating with the greatest minds of our time.

Your book deepens and extends understanding of the Bible. It is audacious and in part impertinent. I am surrounded in the main by people with little education, meek, mainly with a monastic vocation, and monasticism in our times is in prayer, it seems to me, and not in teaching. There are no teachers now in the sense that was understood by the medieval Church. Those were learned theologians, interpreters, and translators, but today's are in the main conservators. If the present Russian regime has not completely crushed Orthodoxy, then that is to the credit not of learned theologians but of obscure old women and loyal priests who have professed Christ even unto death. As if we do not know that an army of them has perished in this battle.

Perhaps the times are changing and we should now be thinking not only of preservation but also of more profound understanding. Your critical thoughts about the patriarchs, the examination of their deeds from the standpoint of modern morality, stirred me greatly. Your thinking about the evolution of the idea of God in history—where did you get that from, is it something you have discovered yourself?—seems to me in part seductive and in part engrossing.

You also write, or rather provide a quotation to the effect that, in the last days there will begin an "unprecedented abuse—of matter by man." Where this comes from is not indicated in the book. The thought, however, is in itself extremely profound: all those robots, machines for supporting human life when a person is already dead, artificial organs, and almost conception in test tubes,—are so difficult to take in and evaluate from a Christian viewpoint. Moreover, my head is no longer as clear as it was when I was young. It seemed to me also that the book's bibliography is not very well compiled, or is that my eyesight? Reading it with a magnifying glass is torture.

It is a very substantial book. I'm quite amazed that in your village you manage to maintain such a high level, although we have long understood that we should stay where we have been placed and all that is needed will come of its own accord.

Heartfelt greetings to your family. I will not send the icon. I just cannot work anymore. May God bless you.

With love,

Ioanna.

6. *April, 1985*

FROM A NOTE FROM EFIM DOVITAS TO NIKOLAI IVANOVICH LAIKO

Dear Nikolai Ivanovich,

In compliance with our agreement I have to inform you that since the New

Year I have performed four rites of baptism: I have christened my newborn son, Isaac; the newborn daughter of the local doctor, Andrey Yosifovich Rubin; the cousin of our parishioner, Raisa Semyonovna Rapaport, at the age of 47 years; and a young Japanese student at the local university (Yahiro Sumato).

The congregation is increasing not only as the result of newly baptized infants and adults, but also with the appearance of new immigrant families, the Lukovich family from Belorussia and a young couple from Leningrad whose name is Kazhdan. The wife is Jewish and the husband is as yet unbaptized but inclined to adopt Christianity. These additions gladden me and give grounds to hope that the Be'er Sheva community will grow and strengthen.

There are of course difficulties and, mindful of our talk, I would like to ask you to find resources for mending the roof. Our district does not have a great deal of rain, indeed, on the contrary, annual rainfall is below the average for the country as a whole, but a single downpour can spoil a modest fresco. Andrey Rubin, the best qualified of our parishioners, assesses the work at around 5,000 shekels. We also need to repair the porch. We have partly mended it through the efforts of parishioners, but one of the supports needs to be replaced and that is something we cannot do with our own hands.

I enclose an account of our expenditure. I have taken 1,200 shekels from the amount sent, for my personal needs. If you were able to find a way of paying me even the most minimal salary that would ease our situation, the more so since the addition to our family entails extra expenditure and has temporarily deprived my wife of the opportunity of working.

We invite His Beatitude to visit our weekly service, which usually takes place on Sundays at 18:30 hours.

Father Efim (Dovitas)

7. 1 April 1985

DOCUMENT 107-M

MARKED "SECRET"

MINISTRY OF RELIGIOUS AFFAIRS

In accordance with our agreement I am sending the quarterly report with a list of citizens of the State of Israel who have accepted baptism in the period 1/01–25/03/1985 in the churches of the ROC.

1. Anishchenko, Petr Akimovich, b. 1930, Church of the Trinity, Jerusalem
2. Lvovskaya, Natalia Aaronovna, b. 1949, Ein Karem, Gorny Convent

3. Rukhadze, Georgiy Noevich, b. 1958, Monastery of the Holy Cross in Jerusalem

4. Rubina, Eva, b. 1985, parents Rubin, Andrey Yosifovich and Rubina, Elena Antonovna (maiden name Kondakova), Church of St. John the Warrior, Be'er Sheva

5. Rapoport, Raisa Semyonovna, b. 1938, Church of St. John the Warrior, Be'er Sheva

6. Dovitas, Isaak, b. 1985, Church of St. John the Warrior, Be'er Sheva

Total baptized, 11 persons, of whom citizens of Israel (listed above), 6 persons.

Kindly be advised that my superiors await your response in respect of category TT individuals. We hope to receive the relevant notification no later than 15/04 of the current year.

N. Laiko

DOCUMENT 11/345-E

MARKED "TOP SECRET"

FOR N. I. LAIKO

23-34-98/124510 IYR UKL-11

Ir. Al. - Kadomtseva, Irina Alexeyevna, French citizen, Poisk Publishers; Author - Mikhail Kuleshov, pseudonym Andrey Belov.

Informant: Ef. D.

8. 1984, Hebron

FROM A LETTER FROM GERSHON SHIMES TO HIS MOTHER, ZINAIDA SHIMES

. . . details. I was called up for the "miluim," a six-week retraining period for reservists. Deborah was left alone with the children, but our team is very solid and I knew she would be looked after. Deborah is a person who cannot bear having to ask for anything. Everything she can do for herself she invariably does. She needed to sort out our bank loan so she put the children in the car and drove to Jerusalem. We have a bus which takes about one hour to Jerusalem, the No. 160. It is armored and has security, but she decided to take the car. It wasn't even particularly urgent, the forms could perfectly well have waited, it was about some insignificant penalty. The children were in the back seat, the baby sleeping in a basket, the boys on either side holding it. On the way back, right next to our house, at the crossroads as she was about to turn in, 30 meters from the checkpoint, the car was fired on. Deborah heard the glass breaking behind her, put her foot on the accelerator, and within five minutes was home. She drove into the yard, looked at the backseat, and saw Binyomin sitting in blood, silent, his eyes open wide. The blood was not his, it was the blood of Arik. The bullet hit him in the neck. Either it was a sniper, or ordained by fate. Deborah believes this was the revenge of the Arab workers I drove out when the house was being built. I haven't been able to write to you for two months. Deborah is pregnant. She is silent and will not say a word. Her parents came from Brooklyn. Now they have left. That is our news. Our boy was buried in the old Jewish cemetery where Yishai, the father of King David, is buried and his great-grandmother Ruth. At that time nobody had heard of any Arabs. Then for seven centuries the Arabs owned these lands, profaned and fouled everything. One hundred and eighty years ago, Jews bought them out, and again the Arabs slaughtered everybody. That was in 1929, and now the cemetery has been partly restored. An artist from Moscow we know, whose newborn baby died, buried him in the cemetery ten years ago, without permission from any authorities, of course. Deborah decided to bury our little boy in this ancient place. There is a view from there over the whole of Judea. Our Arieh's funeral was attended by all of Jewish Hebron. Everybody loved him, he was always smiling, and the first word he said was "lovely." Deborah tries to speak Hebrew to the children, but in spite of that it's mostly English.

Soon after this terrible event, our local Rabbi Eliyahu, with whom we are great friends, invited us to move not far from the cemetery. We sold our new house and on the site of the old Jewish quarter of Admot Yishai we set up our caravan. Seven mobile homes, seven families. I do not want to restore an old house, I want to build a new one, I already have experience of that. We will leave here only to go to that land. Do not be afraid, Mama. I hope we will live a long time and have new children here, but I will never leave this place, no matter what anyone says. I don't give a damn that the graves of our forefathers are here. If Adam and Chava are buried here, Avraham and Sarah, Itzhak and Yakov, fine, but what holds Deborah and me here is the grave of our son. You will have to agree that the graves of children are a different matter from the graves of ancestors from thousands of years ago.

The Well of Avraham really is next to our house, though. I send you our last photograph of Arieh and the view from our mobile home over land which we will never leave.

INSCRIPTION ON PHOTOGRAPH: This is our little house. We planted the orchard behind it ourselves. Deborah is standing with her back to you and you cannot see her enormous belly.

9. *1984, Moscow*
LETTER FROM ZINAIDA SHIMES TO HER SON GERSHON

My dearest son,

We have been weeping for the past week over the photograph of Arik whom we were never able to see. You know what losses we have endured. Your elder brother died when he was 10 as a result of a terrible mistake by the doctors. I lost a beloved husband before he was even 50. The history of our family is terrible. We have been killed young and old, men and women. Almost nobody has died of old age in their own bed. What has happened to you, though, is unimaginable. Knowing how you hate wordiness, I will not describe to you all our thoughts and feelings about it, but simply tell you that Svetlana and I have decided to come to Israel. It will not be tomorrow, because although it is already two months since Svetlana left Sergey and is living at home with Anya, it will take some time to formalize the divorce. I also need time to complete my work, to get my class through to their school-leaving exams, and sort out my pension. What a panic there will be at school when I announce I am retiring! I carry all the literature teaching in the older classes because the second teacher is very weak. I cannot imagine how this ridiculous Tamara Nikolayevna is supposed to teach nineteenth-century Russian literature. She's completely uneducated. For your part, find out what documents we need here, and yourself sort out whatever is needed in Israel.

I keep wondering what my departed Misha would say in this situation, and I feel that he would approve of our decision. Even though you and your father were constantly arguing and quarrelling, and you left home before you were even 18, your father always loved you most of all. It seems to me that what he liked about you were precisely those characteristics which he did not possess himself.

What you called cowardice was actually his boundless love for his family, for all of us. He was prepared to put up with anything in order to preserve the life of his children. When Vitya died of straightforward appendicitis, Misha told me—he allowed himself to say this just once in his life!—what a dreadful curse lay on our family. His grandfather had buried his son, and now he was doing the same. Who could have imagined that it would happen to a third generation?

1984, Moscow
LETTER FROM ZINAIDA TO GERSHON SHIMES

Dear Grisha,

My congratulations to you and Deborah on the birth of your son! How I am longing to see your children, such a large family, and you at its head! Of course I could never have imagined, and neither could your father, that you would choose this way of life. I am happy to the bottom of my heart. I can just imagine how difficult it is to raise so many children at one time. When I was young all our friends had one or two children, and two was regarded as almost heroic. I suppose the only family with many children was that of Rustam our yard keeper, who was a Tartar. You must remember him. His son Akhmed was in your class at primary school and Raya studied together with Svetlana. I can't even remember how many other children they had. Only now, when I'm an old lady, do I realize what joy and riches it is to have many children. Svetlana has divorced Sergey but unfortunately he has refused outright to give permission for Anya to emigrate. When Svetlana tried to tell him the child would get a much better education and have far better prospects, he said absolutely definitely that he would never give permission and she could just forget it. Svetlana is in a very bad mood, saying nothing and crying, and it is depressing to talk to her. I do not think I have the moral right to emigrate without her. She is a helpless sort of person and for all her splendid spiritual qualities has difficulty coping with life's everyday problems. I went to Leningrad for three days for Alexander Alexandrovich's 70th birthday and when I came back found a radiator in the house that had burst just after I left. When I got back three days later, there were still puddles of water around the place. Now I shall have to do something to the floors. The parquet has all buckled. It's very expensive to replace and we will probably just have to cover it with linoleum. If she had at least mopped up the water straight away and not waited for me to come back. She just cried. So do you think I could emigrate and leave someone as helpless as that behind?

Anyway, Grisha, it will have to wait for now. I can't apply without her. In any case, I hope that when Sergey has new children—he has married a colleague—he will nevertheless give permission for Anya to leave.

Please send more photographs. It is the joy of my life to look at those wonderful children's faces. They are all so good looking!

Don't be angry that I can't just decide to come on my own. Of course, I realize that my place is with my grandchildren, and I could help Deborah and teach the children Russian and literature. I could teach them to read Pushkin and Tolstoy. That is what I am really good at! It greatly saddens me that your little children do not speak Russian. If you only knew what a clever and talented niece you have. She even writes poetry!

I kiss you, dear Grisha. I greatly look forward to your letters. Since you emigrated, the mailbox has a big place in my life, which in other families would be occupied by a pet cat or dog.

Mama

10. 1985, *Hebron*
LETTER FROM GERSHON TO ZINAIDA SHIMES

INSCRIPTION ON A PHOTOGRAPH:

Mama! Our little family celebration. This year for the first time we had a harvest from the beds beside the house. It is a little vegetable garden which the children put such a lot of time into. In addition to our own children there are the two sons of Rab Eliyahu and the big girl is our neighbor's daughter.

11. 1987, *Moscow*
LETTER FROM ZINAIDA TO GERSHON SHIMES

Dear Grisha,

My congratulations to you and Deborah on the birth of your son! How I long to see your little children. Your family is growing and that is a great joy. I find it hard to picture you in the role of patriarch!

Thank Deborah for the photographs. What wonderful children! You are such a lovely couple! Svetlana immediately noticed that all the boys have inherited their mother's red hair while your daughter looks like you. There is a Russian belief that if a girl resembles her father, it will bring her happiness. Anya took the photographs of her cousins to school. She is very proud of them. Anya is a good girl, top of her class. Svetlana and I have hired an English teacher for her, Lyubov Sergeyevna. You may

314 / Ludmila Ulitskaya

remember her. She worked with me at the school in the 1970s but then changed jobs.

I give private lessons, too, so we get by entirely satisfactorily in material terms. I very much love my profession, but have to admit that cramming is not as satisfying as teaching in a school, although of course I get good results. Last year I had eight private pupils and they all passed literature with top marks and went to the university. How it saddens me that your little children do not know Russian!

A few days ago we heard on the radio about disturbances in Hebron, and I am just trembling with fear for your life. Tell me, dear Grisha, can you really not move to a less dangerous area? If you were on your own I could understand it, but a family which has been through such a tragedy, can you really stay in such a perilous location? You said yourself that the German Jews who refused to leave Germany when Hitler came to power were crazy. I remember very well that you said they had been seduced by German culture, made the wrong choice, and paid for it with their lives and those of their children. Why should you, seeing such deadly danger, stubbornly persist in clinging to such a place?

I know you have your own convictions and arguments, but sometimes our circumstances are more powerful than our arguments, and sometimes life forces us to compromise. Do not be angry with me for saying this but understand me correctly. I am so worried for you and your children.

All my love,
Mama

12. 1987, Hebron
Letter from Gershon to Zinaida Shimes

Dear Mama!

Have you still not understood that we are talking about our life and not about where we choose to live? Jewish life can only be lived on the soil of Israel. It is not a matter of reuniting families but of restoring our destiny and history in its highest sense. You have no idea why we are here!

Twenty years ago Rabbi Shlomo Goren, a general in the Israel Defence Forces, entered the Cave of Makhpelah, took in a scroll of the Torah, and a Jew prayed there for the first time in 700 years. Since 1226, Jews and Christians had been forbidden to enter this holy place. Rab Shlomo Goren drove into Hebron in a jeep with only his driver, ahead of the whole army, and since that time Jews have been returning here. I will not leave.

We live here and will continue to live here, and I request that I should hear no more of these pathetic words because I am losing the last remnants of my sentimental attitude toward my close relatives. Your bleating about Svetlana and her problems with her former husband is simply ridiculous. My opinion is that you should come here so that your granddaughter can live in this land. Under Jewish law a child born to a Jewish mother is Jewish. For the opportunity to move here I spent five years in the labor camps. By remaining in Russia you deny yourself a future.

I find what you say about teaching my children Russian absurd. They have two languages, Hebrew and English. Deborah thinks they need to learn English and I do not object, but all the children will receive a religious upbringing and are already doing so. Rabbi Eliyahu teaches them, and in our settlement there are five times as many children as grown-ups. They were all born near the graves of their forefathers and are unlikely to have any need of the language of Pushkin and Tolstoy, as you put it. When my sons undergo their bar mitzvah at the age of thirteen, they will read the Torah in Hebrew, and believe me, the elder is already making great progress in his studies. This generation of children must be able equally well to read the Torah and to hold a rifle. We have called our younger son Yehuda.

If you want me to reply to your letters, please do not write nonsense, and give me less advice. That's what your daughter Svetlana is there for.

Your son

Gershon

13. 1989, Moscow

LETTER FROM ZINAIDA TO GERSHON SHIMES

Dear Grisha,

I do not know whether my news will gladden or distress you. Svetlana is getting married again. On the one hand I am very glad for her, on the other I realize that this will again change all our plans. You will, I am sure, remember her fiancé. He is her classmate Slava Kazakov. He was in love with her from Grade 6 but she paid no attention to him at all. Imagine, they had a school reunion party, met again, and this new relationship flared up. He has already moved in with us. Svetlana is simply blooming. He is exceptionally caring and attentive. Incidentally, he is very nice to Anya. You must know how difficult it is to get by at present. I have to stand in queues from morning till dinner-time if I want to buy any food at all. After dinner there is nothing in the shops. It is just as well that where Svetlana works they occasionally give them food as payment in kind. Also, Slava's sister works as a manager in a department store and has good links with the food shops, so Slava, too, brings bags home once a week with meat, cheese, and buckwheat. To a large extent that frees me from having to run around in the mornings.

Anya has been admitted to ballet school and since September I have been taking her to the classes. She is very enthusiastic, dances all the time and likes listening to music. She has turned out very musical. You wrote that Shoshanah is also studying music. Quite certainly she has got that from her grandfather. Misha was very gifted and could quickly learn to play any musical instrument. He even learned to play the accordion. I am sending you a photograph of Anya, so that your children should know what their cousin in Moscow looks like.

Your Aunt Rimma, about whom you never ask, has been found to have breast cancer. She was taken to the hospital, operated on, and is now undergoing a course of chemotherapy. They say the medical services in Israel are very good and perform real miracles. If only we could send her there for treatment. You wrote that you have a friend in the settlement who is a surgeon. Perhaps you could ask him if he could help her in some way. She is ten years younger than me and was always such a healthy woman.

All my love, dear son,

Your Mama

PS Did Deborah receive the toys I mailed two months ago?

14. 1990, Hebron
LETTER FROM GERSHON TO ZINAIDA SHIMES

What is this stuff you are writing to me about, Mama? To tell the truth, I don't even want to hear! I remember that goat, Slava. He is highly suitable for my sister in that they are equally stupid. Ballet, accordions, special food deliveries, poor Rimma, who all her life was a complete bitch, and who when I was in prison was afraid even to telephone you. What kind of drivel is this? You are living on a different planet which is of no interest to me whatsoever. Live your life how ever you like.

Everything here is fine. Deborah will send you photographs of our second daughter, who was born two weeks ago.

Look after yourself,

Gershon

15. December 1987, Haifa
FROM HILDA'S DIARY

After the service Musa arrived. He wanted to talk to Daniel. Pale, gloomy. I have never seen him like that before. I suddenly realized it was just that he has grown old. His hair has become lighter as it went gray and his face has darkened, not from the sun but from age. Even his mouth, which was always so striking, has faded and sagged. My heart suddenly sank. We have both grown older and have strangled our poor love. When the people had gone, Musa and Daniel sat down in our little room. I made tea. Musa declined. I wanted to leave, but Daniel told me to stay. I did not know why. It seemed to me that Musa wanted to talk to him alone. Anyway, I sat down. Musa took an Arab newspaper out of his pocket and pushed it over to Daniel. He looked at it and said, "You read it. I don't read Arabic fluently."

Musa read excerpts from Arafat's speech: "Oh, heroic sons of Gaza! Oh, proud sons of the West Bank! Oh, courageous sons of Galilee! Oh, stoical sons of the Negev! The flame of revolution raised against the occupying Zionists will not be extinguished until our land has been liberated from the ravenous occupying forces. If anybody takes it into his mind to stop the Intifada before it achieves its ultimate aim, I shall fire a dozen bullets into his chest."

He put the newspaper down and said things could not be worse. Daniel's face had also fallen. Musa shook his head and covered his eyes with his hand. "We need to leave. My uncle is in California now. Perhaps he can find me a job or give me one," Musa said. "You are an Israeli." "I am an Arab. There's no getting around that." "You are a Christian." "I am a bag of flesh and bones, and I have four children."

"Pray and work," Daniel said quietly. "My Muslim brothers pray five times a day," Musa shouted. "They perform namaz five times a day! There's no way I can out-pray them! And we are praying to the same One God!" "Don't yell, Musa, try rather to see it from His point of view: the Jews are praying to Him to destroy the Arabs, the Arabs are asking Him to destroy the Jews. What is He supposed to do?"

Musa laughed. "Yes, He should never have got involved with such a bunch of idiots!" "He has no other peoples, only such as these. I cannot tell you to stay here, Musa. Over the past years half my parishioners have left Israel. I am thinking myself that although God never suffers defeats, what is happening today is a real victory for mutual hatred."

Musa left. I saw him to the door. He stroked my head and said, "I wish we could have a second life."

Daniel's car was being repaired and he asked me to drive him to brother Roman, the abbot of the Arab church where he was allowed to conduct services in the early 1960s. I was amazed. He and Roman had quarrelled and since Roman changed the lock on the cemetery gates, Daniel had not wanted to talk to him. I took him to Roman's apartment. I saw them embrace in the doorway. I saw how pleased Roman was. Daniel knew that when the patriarchate tried to take away the Church of Elijah by the Spring, Roman had gone to the Patriarch himself and told him that not one of the Arab Christian communities in Haifa would agree to occupy it. The Patriarch just shrugged and said, "Come now, come now, it is a misunderstanding. Let us leave everything as it is." Daniel did not go to thank Roman for his intervention, but I know he was very pleased. Now they were meeting again for the first time after all these years.

I drove home thinking that if there was to be another bloodbath, like in 1929, I would go back to Germany. I would not choose to live in the midst of bloodshed. Admittedly Daniel says that people can get used to all manner of vile things: captivity, camps, prison, but ought we to? Probably Musa is right. He needs to go away so that his children do not have to learn to live like that.

But what about me?

16. 1988, Haifa
FROM HILDA'S DIARY

I never thought I would be in this cemetery again. Yesterday we buried Musa, his brother, father, wife, and some other relatives. It was overcast and raining. What a dreadful place this Israel is. There is a war here inside every person which has neither rules nor boundaries nor sense nor justification. Nor the hope that it will ever end. Musa had just turned 50. He had applied to leave to work in America and had bought the tickets. His uncle had sent a photograph of the house and garden in which he and his family were to live. Musa was hired as a gardener by one of the richest people in the world, who now will have to make do with another gardener.

The coffin was sealed. I saw neither his face nor his hands. I have no photograph of him. I have no family, children, relatives, not even a native language. I haven't known for a long time which is my first language, Hebrew or German. We were lovers for almost 20 years, then it ended. Not because I stopped loving him, but because my own heart told me that was enough. He understood. These last years we met only in church, when we stood side by side and both knew there was nobody closer to us in the world. The tenderness was still there but we had buried our desires very deeply. I shall remember him as I saw him that last time, three weeks ago or so, with his darkened face, gray hair, prematurely aged, and with the gold tooth which glinted when he smiled.

He hadn't offered to see me home, and that was right. Turning, I waved to him, and he looked after me, and I went away with a light heart because I felt that now I had a different life, without the madness of love against which we had both struggled so ingloriously and not won but simply grown deadly tired and surrendered. I felt empty and free inside and I thought, thank God, a little more space has been freed in my heart. Let it be filled not by human love, selfish and hungry, but by another love which knows no selfishness. I felt, too, that my ego was much diminished. Daniel remained for the wake but I left. A nauseating smell of roast chicken rose mercilessly from the tables.

This morning Daniel and I went to a cheap supermarket to buy disposable plates, incontinence pads for the old people, and various other things, and when we had shoved it all into the car and were about to move off he unexpectedly said, "It is very important that your ego is declining, taking up less space, and then more space is left in your heart for God. On the whole it's right that a person takes up less space with the years. Of course, I'm not talking about myself, because with the years I keep putting on weight."

When we had unloaded everything and arranged it on the shelves in the store, Daniel said, "Do you really think you could leave? It is tantamount to deserting the battlefield at the critical moment." "Do you really think right now is the critical moment?" I asked rather irritably, because the thought of leaving was stirring in my heart. "My dear girl, that is what a Christian has to choose, to always be at the critical moment, in the very heart of life, to experience pain and joy simultaneously. I love you very much. Have I really never told you that?"

At that moment I experienced what it was that he was talking about: a piercing pain in my heart, and a joy as strong as pain.

17. 1991, Berkeley
LETTER FROM EWA MANUKYAN TO ESTHER GANTMAN

Dear Esther,

Now that you have gone, I am missing you even more. I wanted to talk to you about everything, but was embarrassed. In any case, you already know it all. My whole life I have been longing for a mother, both when I had none and when she reappeared. I never found contentment. It seems to me that my life has evolved in such a complicated way because I never had a mother beside me. You have become my mother more than Rita. Only with you have I formed a link which sustains me and makes me stronger and wiser.

Shortly after you left, Enrique moved into our house. You have seen him, one of those two friends Alex has been spending all his time with for the past year. Alex asked whether I would feel better if he and Enrique rented an apartment in town or lived at home. I said, at home. Now they come down together to breakfast, happy and handsome. It's as if I have two sons. I smile and make coffee. Admittedly, only on Saturdays and Sundays—on working days I am out of the house before anybody else. Enrique is a great boy. He is helpful and friendly and there is absolutely no aggression in him. Although he is five years older than Alex they look the same age. They have the same physique and love exchanging clothes. Four years ago he left Mexico. He had problems with his parents. He mentioned it in passing and with a subtext which suggested he was praising me for being so tolerant. Enrique is finishing a design course and has already been invited to join some well-known firm. Alex is completely committed to sociology, but his interest is exclusively in the homosexual aspect.

Grisha gets on marvelously with them. Just as before, the house is full of openhearted laughter every time I come back from work and they are in the front room. I smile and ask if I may join them. I am exactly how my son and my husband want me to be: kindly and tolerant. Terribly tolerant. I allow everybody everything: my son to sleep with a boy, my husband to sleep with a girl. I am magnanimity itself. Everybody thinks I am wonderful. Grisha is attentive and gentle as never before. I do not say a word about Liza and he is very grateful. His embraces are as ardent as ever, and when I stopped going to university events he was simply delighted by my tact. I had ceded my place by his side at social events to Liza. There are still two university couples whom, as in the past, Grisha and I visit together.

We have an ambiguous and unarticulated but entirely consensual relationship. It seems only a matter of time before the three of us go out visiting together. Grisha would like nothing better, although he tries not to let on. I don't, however, think that my tolerance will stretch that far. I can finally bring myself to tell you honestly that I have this terrible fear that he will leave me. I have consented to any form of relationship just as long as he stays with me. You may no longer respect me.

Anyway, that's quite enough about that. We have talked about it plenty. Here's some news! I was talking to Rita on the phone. She has a new and grandiose plan. Next year will be the fiftieth anniversary of the day she escaped from the Emsk ghetto. (Incidentally, two and a half months after that day I shall be 50!) They have decided to arrange a reunion in Emsk of those who are still alive, and my mother, imagine it, is also planning to go. It's an insane idea but something she is perfectly capable of doing. In a wheelchair, by three modes of transport—from Haifa to Odessa by ship, from there by plane to Minsk, and from Minsk by train to Emsk. I was terribly cross at first and thought she should have the decency just to stay where she is! Then I suddenly realized this was another demonstration of her idiotically heroic character. She refuses to be daunted by any difficulties, least of all by her own disability. She is telling me that I have to come and collect her in Haifa and accompany her throughout the journey.

And yes, I do want to! I realize I want to see all this with my own eyes. It will be more powerful than a session on a psychoanalyst's couch, not a Freudian peeping into the parental bed at the moment of your conception, but coming into living contact with the past of my family and people. Forgive the histrionics. Do tell me whether you have been invited to the reunion. Are you going? For some reason just the thought that you will be there makes the journey infinitely important to me.

Do you know what my life is like? It's like living in a minefield. I avoid danger zones, don't think about this, don't talk about that, don't mention something else. In fact, I try to think as little as possible! It's only with you that I can talk without fear of disrupting the unstable equilibrium of my idiotic life.

Love,

Ewa

18. December 1991, Haifa
LETTER FROM RITA KOWACZ TO PAWEŁ KOCIŃSKI

Dear Paweł,

You and I have lived our entire lives side by side we had the same ideals the same goals the same friends but as it happened the Lord has been revealed to me at the end of my days and now I want just one thing to share my joy with all my friends. When a person takes one step toward God God immediately takes two toward them. Only one small gesture is needed to acknowledge that man can do nothing without God. When I think how much energy and strength and what heroism we showed for the purposes not of God but of man I feel great sorrow. I am not asking you to come to Haifa knowing how difficult it is for you to leave poor Mirka but I would like to suggest a little trip to Belorussia. The thing is I have had a letter from an old geezer I was with in the ghetto and from which we escaped together. Anyway they are organizing a reunion of all those who survived and that Jewish priest is coming who helped us to get arms for the escape. It will be interesting to take a look at him. I invite you to come to Emsk where we will meet no doubt for the last time.

Ewa will take me but my English friend Agnessa may come with me too. Not to Łódź or Warsaw of course I shan't go from there but you could if you wanted to. You are after all still on your feet.

Moreover Paweł I will not conceal that I very much want to share with you what I have gained. I regret that my encounter has occurred so late but while a person is alive it is never too late. I pray fervently that our meeting should take place mine with you and yours with the Lord. May God bless you and your dearest.

Your old friend Margarita (Rita) Kowacz

19. January 1992, Jerusalem
LETTER FROM EWA MANUKYAN TO ESTHER GANTMAN

Dear Esther,

I didn't even have time to phone you from home, it was all so urgent. I had a call on the morning of 5 January from Haifa to be told that Rita had died during the night. Grisha immediately took me to the airport. By a completely monstrous route, with two changes and an eight-hour wait in Frankfurt, I got to Haifa and my mother's funeral took place the next day. Many things today surprised, touched, and even shocked me. It is night now, I am full of impressions and cannot sleep, and then there is the time change. So I have decided to write to you. My mother looked beautiful. At the end of her life she had earned that! The tense, suspicious expression so typical of her all through her life had changed to one of serenity and profound contentment.

Shortly before she died, she had had her hair cut. She had gray hair and a dense fringe at the front instead of that schoolmarmish bun she walked around with all her life. It sounds ridiculous, but it suited her very well.

The funeral service was conducted with great ceremony. The coffined body was taken to the Anglican Mission in Jerusalem, a place whose existence I had never suspected. Before the service, in a very austere hall in the Mission, a Jew wearing a skullcap and prayer shawl came in, a perfectly ordinary-looking Jew, and recited Jewish funeral prayers over the closed coffin. I was sitting on a bench with Agnessa next to me. I was going to ask what was going on but then thought better of it. Let everything take its course. Next a vicar came and conducted the funeral service.

We went out into the garden and I saw how beautiful it was. Lemon trees were in bloom as they are in Sicily at this time of year. Several fruit trees were bare, and one had pomegranates but not a single leaf. The whole orchard was green and there were shrubs which looked like juniper, cypresses, and palms. The sun was bright and cold and everything was very still and dazzling.

"Now we shall drive to the cemetery," Agnessa said and took me to the railings. Beyond them I saw an intricately eroded cliff of stratified rock.

"We think this is the actual Golgotha, the place of a skull. Don't you think it looks like it?" Agnessa smiled, revealing her long English teeth. I didn't understand but then she explained, "It is an alternative Golgotha. You see, at the end of the last century they dug up a water cistern here and came upon the remains of an ancient garden. This garden is new, planted not long ago at all. When they found the cistern they suddenly saw Golgotha, too, although it had never been hiding. This cliff has always been there but nobody paid it any attention until they found a grave in a cave. It seems very likely that it is the grave which Joseph of Arimathea prepared for himself and his relatives." As she spoke I saw that the rock face really did look like a human skull, with empty cave eye sockets and a sunken nose.

She took me down a side path to a small door set into the cliff. A window had been knocked through above it. Right beside the entrance lay a long stone with a rut hewn in it which looked like a rail. Slightly farther away was a round stone.

"This stone is from a different place, it is slightly smaller in size than the one which sealed the entrance to the cave. That one has disappeared in the course of 2,000 years. If the round stone sealing the entrance is placed on this stone rail, it is easy to move, it simply rolls. That was still difficult for the women. They called the gardener to help them. Go in and take a look."

I went in as if in a dream. I have after all been to the official Church of the Sepulchre, and on more than one occasion. There I walked into a commotion in an enormous space where one church jostles another and everything is fenced off and chaotic, and there are crowds of old women in black and tourists and servers. The church above the sepulchre has a queue to get into the cave, the tourists are snapping away with their cameras, the tour guides are rattling on in every language, and the whole thing said nothing to my soul.

Here, however, there was nobody and I was suddenly certain that when I went in I would see the abandoned grave clothes. The cave was divided into two crypts, and in the farther one was a stone couch. Goose pimples ran up my arms and I felt that recurrent chill of mine.

Agnessa was standing outside. She smiled. "It does look very much like it, doesn't it?" It did. Beneath a great fig tree two women in long skirts were sitting on a bench with their large hands folded in their laps. One took a piece of pitta bread out of her bag, broke it, and held out half to her neighbor who made the sign of the cross over her mouth and took a bite.

Four men carried my mother's coffin to the bus and we drove to the Anglican cemetery. There were no flowers. I had had no time to buy any and the other mourners, fellow Anglicans, put whited stones at the head of the grave as is the Jewish custom.

After the funeral the vicar came over. Like Agnessa he had long teeth and pale eyes. I thought they were brother and sister but then realized they were husband and wife. He shook hands and gave me two forms. On one were written the words and music of a prayer, a stave with clusters of black notes. The second was a certificate about the holding of the funeral service.

Rita always kept documents and papers in perfect order, so now she can rest in peace. Esther, dear, something I never hoped for occurred. I was completely reconciled with her. Later I will have plenty of time to repent and feel guilty and hard-hearted, but today I am completely at peace with her.

I will fly home the day after tomorrow. All my love. Good night. It is already dawn here.

Yours,

Ewa

20. *November 1991, Jerusalem*

LETTER FROM RUVIM LAKHISH TO DANIEL STEIN

Dear Daniel,

I came a couple of times to see you at the monastery but they didn't call you. The second time I left a note for you with my telephone number but you did not phone. Your monks are so surly that I am not convinced they passed the note on to you. Do you know that I have an extensive correspondence with those who survived in Czarna Puszcza? There are quite a few still around of those who emerged from the ghetto on 11 August 1942 and lived to see the liberation, but with every year that passes there are fewer and fewer. When I met David, who now lives in Ashkelon, we thought it would be a good idea to arrange a commemoration of the 50th anniversary of the day you pulled that off. I correspond with Berl Kalmanovich in New York, Yakov Svirsky in Ohio, and a couple of other lads who were partisans.

There are very few Jews in Belorussia. I have heard there is nobody at all in Emsk, but the bones of our parents are there and of all our families. You know I have two sisters and nieces buried there. I will organize everything. You will understand that you are the main figure for us. You will sit at the head of the table and we will drink and recall all that happened.

Now, to business. Who have you met, who are you still in touch with of those who were partisans? Send me their addresses. David and I talked things over and decided people could bring their children, to show them the way we lived then. I think I shall go in advance this year to see whether there is at least a commemorative headstone. You were not from our locality and do not know what a grand Jewish cemetery there was in Emsk before the war. There were monuments of marble and granite. Has it survived? I doubt it. What the Germans did not wreck the Soviet regime will have destroyed. We will need to have a collection and erect a joint monument for all. Anyway, give me a call or write.

On behalf of the Association of Former Citizens of Emsk,

Ruvim Lakhish

21. 1984, Jerusalem
LETTER FROM FYODOR KRIVTSOV TO FATHER MIKHAIL IN TISHKINO

Dear Father Mikhail,

I came to give my good wishes to Mother Ioanna on her name day and she gave me a letter from you. I was delighted. She told me to write a reply.

The Lord has brought me to the kind of place I prayed for. I have found a real elder. He lives in a cave like the Syrians did. What he eats I do not know. There is a spring for water but many a young person wouldn't have the strength to crawl up the hill to it. He goes up there with a gourd, God knows how. He washes, fills the gourd with water, and heads back down the mountain like a lizard. There is no grass there, no goutwort, or anything else, only rocks. Whether a raven brings him food or an angel feeds him I do not know. He has been living in this cave since time immemorial, a Greek told me, about 100 years. I believe it. Or are they wrong? He reads while it's light and when it's dark he prays. He has no bed. There is a rock shaped like a couch and he sleeps on that. For a long time he would not allow me near or speak to me. One time I brought him a flat-bread and he would not come out. I left it by the entrance to his cave. The next day I came and it wasn't there. Had it been eaten by wild animals? He is called Abun, but that is a word which means "Father" and nobody knows his real name. Beside his cave is a small landing, a stone like a table, and he places a book on that and kneels before the book. He reads Greek. When I climb up the cliff to him, my spirit soars and this trying, inhospitable place seems to me a paradise. Father Mikhail, if he accepts me, if he allows me to live somewhere nearby, I will leave this place 100 percent because as Elder Paisiy said on Athos, one percent holds me in the world and here truly there is no percent at all. I want to stay here forever, near Abun. I have visited Mother Ioanna, now I will go to the cliff and, if he accepts me, I will remain there.

With brotherly love,

Fyodor, Slave of God

22. 1988, Jerusalem
LETTER FROM MOTHER IOANNA TO FATHER MIKHAIL IN TISHKINO

Dear Father Mikhail,

Greetings on this holy day! You probably thought it was time to include me in the bead-roll but here I am, still alive. I was entirely ready to die, had received extreme unction, taken communion, but my new lay Sister Nadya took me to the hospital. They put me on a table, cut me with knives and took out a tumor, a very large one, but benign. I will admit to you that I felt very well after the operation. Light, and my belly was empty. It was so good.

Before, I felt a great heaviness all the time. Well, I thought, everything is in God's hands, including the doctors, but Nadya is from a new generation, a girl with higher education and a secular upbringing. Now she has such authority over me, she is insisting I must have my cataracts removed. Next week I shall be taken to Hadassah, a hospital here, to the eye department. First one eye, then the other.

I have on my tripod the unfinished "Akathist," with a sheet draped over it. Nadya says, "There, the Lord wants you to finish it, Mother." For three years I have seen only a window, but what is beyond the window I cannot see. I do not know, really. By the time you receive this letter I shall either have my sight back or will remain in darkness to the end.

My dear son, I sent you my blessing, but now I am sending it once more. At my age you have to expect the end at any moment. We had Mother Vissarioniya who completely lost her wits. For two years she was able to walk at least, but completely demented. That I really can do without! I value the light of reason more highly than the light outside the window. As Pushkin wrote, "God, do not let me lose my mind, far better beg or prisoner be, far better toil or hunger see." But that's nonsense, too. Toil is good and a joy in itself.

If the operation succeeds I shall write to you myself, because this, as you can see, has been written by someone else's hand. Nadya's. The Lord be with you. My blessing to Nina and to Yekaterina, Vera and Anastasia.

Ioanna

23. *1988*

LETTER FROM MOTHER IOANNA TO FATHER MIKHAIL IN TISHKINO

My dear friend Mishenka,

I am writing this myself! The scribble is barely legible for my hand has forgotten how to write, but my eyes can see and they say that later they will make spectacles and everything will really be fine. The doctor was Russian, a cheerful man. He praised my cataract and said it came away like a sweet wrapper. He has promised to do the second operation in two months' time.

On Sunday I went into the church and everything was shining! So much light! Everything seemed to be golden, the iconostasis, the windows. Oh, dear, how sad it was living without the sun!

How glad I am, my son, that you have an addition to your family. I know men want sons and are not too pleased when they get daughters. Well, your patience has been rewarded, you have a boy in your home. Thanks be to God! You didn't write what name you have given him. Did you forget? Or do you want me to guess? Is it really Seraphim? In the past children were often named in honor of St. Seraphim of Sarov, but now that seems to be out of fashion. I have no time to write, the bell is ringing to call me to the liturgy.

The Lord be with you,

Ioanna

24. 1 August 1992, Jerusalem

LETTER FROM MOTHER IOANNA TO FATHER MIKHAIL IN TISHKINO

Congratulations, Mikhail. I received both your letter and the *Church Herald*. Twenty-five years in the priesthood is not to be sneezed at! Send me a photograph of how you were feted. Did His Holiness really come to you in Tishkino himself? Oh, fear and trembling! As they say, accept praise and calumny with equanimity! Misha, how everything has changed! Who would have thought it! The accursed regime has ended and you are having church awards pinned to your breast! We have read here that the new government is fraternizing with the Church, but I am mistrustful. I have never in my life had any love of authorities. But do not listen to me, I am an old woman. Now it is time for me to boast: I, too, have been feted. Who remembered I do not know, I myself had forgotten, but I, too, have had a round anniversary. I am 90 years old. And what did I start remembering? My birthdays, as I recall them. I remember particularly well when I was nine.

That year we didn't go to our estate at Gridnevo for the summer because mother had had a difficult time giving birth to my brother, Volodya. She had an operation which she barely survived, and was ill, and our departure was constantly postponed. We went after my Angel Day on 11 July. I remember all the guests. There were not many because everybody had left town, and I was afraid there would not be many presents. We were not spoiled, but that year Mama gave me a French doll with eyes which closed, with locks of hair and wearing a sailor's costume, with leather boots with a button. We were enjoying the last years of happiness before the war began. Papa was an admiral. You probably did not know that. There, I'm giving way to singing an old woman's songs, there's no one to stop me.

Apart from sending greetings, what I wanted to write to you about is your pal Fyodor Krivtsov. He finally found himself an elder and disappeared. There are lucky people like that who are constantly looking for someone to give themselves to. He found some kind of desert dweller, and to this day there are any number of them here of every description: some who fast, some who live up a pillar, healers and miracle workers. Hordes of charlatans and lunatics. A saint is a quiet being, unnoticeable, who sleeps beneath the stairs and dresses inconspicuously. You have to have keen eyes to spot one. But enough. Fyodor came yesterday. In Jerusalem we've seen it all before. When I had just arrived here I walked through the Old Town and saw lepers, and people possessed, and dressed in every conceivable way. But Fyodor came and surprised me. He was in a filthy shirt, thin as a rake, his eyes blazing with a mad ardor. He looked above everybody's heads, his beard down to his belt, his head covered in sores. At least he was wearing a skullcap.

His elder has gone to his rest! Fyodor needed a priest for the funeral rites. I know our Kirill. There's no way he will drag himself up a mountain, he is stout and gets out of breath. The second, Nicodemus, is sprightly, wiry, and might make it, but he is not here, he's on Mount Sinai.

I told him to go to the Greeks, they have plenty of priests, but he shook his head. No, the elder was at loggerheads with the Greeks. I told him to go to the Syrians, the Copts. Again he shook his head, they had already refused. At that I thought of Brother Daniel.

There is, I said, a Carmelite monk who never refuses anyone, only he probably won't suit you. Off poor Fyodor went. Yes, in parting he said that his elder, Abun, was the Bishop of the True Church of Christ, its Patriarch. Is that a large Church, I asked? It used to have three members, Abun, the one before Abun, his teacher, and Fyodor, but now there is only Fyodor left. The rest of us, it seems, are not true. Have you heard of that Church, Misha? I sent him with my blessing to Daniel in Haifa. He will not refuse, I'm sure. He would as lief conduct the rites for a vagabond as for a patriarch. He is one of our inconspicuous people and has lived all his life somewhere under the stairs. I'm talking too much.

The Lord be with you, my dear friend Mishenka.

25. 1992, Jerusalem

TELEGRAM FROM NADEZHDA KRIVOSHEINA TO FATHER MIKHAIL IN TISHKINO

ON 2 AUGUST MOTHER IOANNA SUMAROKOVA DIED IN THE 91ST YEAR OF HER AGE. NADEZHDA KRIVOSHEINA.

26. January 1992, Jerusalem

LETTER FROM RUVIM LAKHISH TO ALL PARTICIPANTS

Dear . . . . ,

The Organizing Committee of the Reunion of Inhabitants of the Emsk Ghetto wishes to report:

1. The Reunion will take place on 9 August this year in the town of Emsk. Agreement has been reached with the town council. In view of the fact that the two hotels in the town (Sunrise and October) can accommodate no more than 60 guests and as of now our list of participants has 82 names (may they all continue in good health!), the council is putting the hostel of the Technical Teacher Training College at our disposal, which can accommodate up to 120.

2. Representatives of international Jewish organizations and of the governments of Russia, Belorussia, Poland, and Germany have been invited to participate in the Reunion. A number have already replied. It is confirmed that German journalists with film crews will attend. Permission to film has not yet been received, but I have already written to the relevant organizations.

3. In reply to an enquiry addressed to the Emsk town council regarding the erection of a memorial to Jews who died in the ghetto, I have been informed that there is already a monument in the town to Soviet soldiers who died during the liberation of Belorussia and that they have no need of another one. It would seem, however, that a monument could be erected in the old Jewish cemetery, which has apparently survived. The money we have collected will be used for that purpose.

4. The municipal authorities will accord us a speech by the current chairman of the town council and an amateur concert.

5. I shall pass on information from time to time in respect of tickets,

visas, and transportation but everybody is welcome to write to me with any questions.

Ruvim Lakhish

27. *4 August 1992, Haifa*
FROM HILDA'S DIARY

We left at four in the morning and after driving for two hours on an empty road rapidly reached the turning for Qumran. The whole journey Daniel was telling me about some new fragment of the Dead Sea scrolls which has just been published. Apparently the archaeologist who discovered this marvel told him about it himself. In Cave No. 4 they discovered a new manuscript from, one hesitates to say it out loud, the first century BC in which the author, writing in the first person, calls himself the Messiah and states that he has endured suffering and sorrow but now has been raised above the angels and is seated on the heavenly throne and closer than all the angels to the Almighty. From the text, one might imagine that it is a letter from the next world for fellow thinkers left behind.

"It occurs to me," Daniel said, "that today we shall see one of those who has been raised higher than the angels." I laughed, but then realized he was not joking at all. He told me entirely seriously that he had long ago heard of this elder and all kinds of miracles he performed before suddenly stopping.

At this point we saw a tall figure on the road. At first I thought it was a Bedouin. He was wound around in rags, but then I saw a skullcap on his head. So this was Fyodor. We parked the car and got out. He bowed. Daniel held out his hand to him but he shied away.

"Are you a priest?" he asked.

Daniel said to him, "Have no doubt about that, Brother, for more than 30 years. Do you not believe me?"

He opened his briefcase and took out his monk's scapular.

"Now do you believe me? I also have a cross, though not as large as yours," he said smiling. Fyodor did not smile back. He was wearing an extremely large wooden pectoral cross.

We walked through the gates of the park, turned left through the old cemetery, and began climbing the mountain. We left the famous Qumran caves behind us to our right and walked for quite a long time to the end of the path. Fyodor told us we would now need to keep close behind him, put our feet were he did, and hold on with our hands to the ledges he would cling to.

It was nothing short of rock climbing. Some rocks crumbled beneath our feet while others were firm. He knew them all and it was clear he often climbed up here. We dragged ourselves to a small flat area situated not on the summit but slightly to one side and in the shade, at least in the morning. During the day everything here was a sun trap. There was a narrow crevice into the cave. Daniel could barely squeeze through. I wanted to look in but Fyodor would not allow it. I saw only that an oil lamp was burning in there.

Daniel and Fyodor agreed on how they would conduct the funeral service, who would recite what. Fyodor asked Daniel to conduct the liturgy over the dead body as if over the relics of a saint. Daniel nodded. He put on his cross and prayed. He went into the cave with Fyodor behind him. There was no room for me so I stood outside. If chanting was needed I would join in, if it was something I knew.

The view was barren but it took your breath away. The Dead Sea gleamed below like mercury. Jordan was invisible behind the haze. How could anyone have lived here in isolation for so many years? Eighty, according to Fyodor, but that was impossible. Fyodor asked Daniel to conduct the service in Arabic. He had celebrated it together with Brother Roman many times but had asked me to bring the text. I passed it to him in the cave and looked in. On the bare rock lay a mummy wrapped from head to foot in a white sheet. A lamp was burning on the rock and Daniel was kneeling before the rock because it was impossible to stand up, even for him. Fyodor was to one side bent double. I could only have crawled in on all fours. Daniel told me to read the Gospel according to Matthew. I stood outside and began quietly.

I suddenly felt a chill the like of which I have never before experienced. It was almost noon, the heat was 40 degrees, but my teeth were chattering. I suddenly felt so ill, and I could tell that Daniel, too, was unwell. I had a water bottle with me and wanted to pass it to him, but Fyodor would not turn around. I took a mouthful, in that kind of temperature you need to keep drinking. I tried again to pass Daniel the bottle but Fyodor would not take it. There on the ledge the sun was beating down as if a fire were blazing nearby, but the sense of chill really did not pass.

I began reading again, finished Matthew and started on Mark. From the cave I heard Arab prayers and Church Slavonic reading. I read as if unconscious, but in fact I was fully conscious only in some abominable state. Something happened to time. It no longer extended but was rolled into a ball and hung immobile around me. Then it was all over. First Fyodor emerged and then Daniel behind him. I noticed there was a pile of rocks by the entrance to the cave and Fyodor began heaping them up until the cave became a tomb. Daniel and I were going to help but he shook his head. We waited for him to block it then made our way down. It was even more difficult going down than climbing up. I didn't remember the way well and would never have found it by myself.

We went back to the car and Daniel invited Fyodor to come with us but he said he had to go back. As we drove away we saw him running full pelt toward the hill. We drove some 40 kilometers in silence before I finally asked, "What was that all about?"

Daniel said, "I don't know, but the cave was seething with snakes. Or did I imagine it?"

28. July 1992, Berkeley
LETTER FROM EWA MANUKYAN TO ESTHER GANTMAN

Dear Esther,

Amazingly enough everything works out splendidly. I fly to Boston on Friday evening, we can spend Saturday together and I will help you pack. On Sunday morning we fly to Frankfurt and change for Minsk. We have a three-hour wait for the flight, but that is not only the most straightforward but the only option. There are two planes from Frankfurt to Minsk each week, and any other route would involve two transfers.

In Minsk we spend the night in a hotel, and in the morning go by special bus to Emsk. I swear no geographical point on earth has evoked so much emotion as this godforsaken town of Emsk. Unfortunately, Paweł Kociński will not be able to come. His wife is very ill and he has not been able to leave her alone for the last two years. Rita always condemned him for his predilection for the female sex. It seems he really did have endless romances on the side, but now when Mirka is so ill he is behaving impeccably. It is a pity I shan't be able to introduce you. Please do not worry and think that you will be the oldest person at the reunion. The organizers have sent me a list and there are some grounds to think you will be one of the younger ones. One Jew was born in 1899. Work it out!

Lots of love. I won't write to you again. See you soon.

29. *September 1992, Haifa*

WALL NEWSPAPER IN THE PARISH HOUSE

RUVIM LAKHISH'S REPORT ON THE TRIP

The trip to Emsk on 9 August 1992 was made by 44 survivors who nowadays live in nine different countries. In 1942, precisely 50 years ago, they escaped from the Emsk ghetto. Of the 300 who escaped at that time, 124 survived until the end of the war. Many have since died.

Nevertheless, 44 survivors came to Emsk to mark this event and we all give thanks to the Lord that he saved our lives and grieve for those who died in dreadful agony at the hands of the Fascists. Among us was the man to whom we owe our lives. He organized the escape at the risk of his own life. That is our brother, Daniel Stein, who is now a priest of the Roman Catholic Church.

We arrived in Emsk at noon on 9 August and immediately walked around the town. The castle is still half ruined, as it was when we were moved there at the end of 1941. Local townspeople came out, but there are very few left who remember those events. Young people, we found, know nothing about what happened here 50 years ago.

One meeting did touch us very deeply. Among the visitors was Esther Gantman from America. Before the war she worked in Emsk as a dentist and, after the escape, in a partisan unit helping her husband, Isaak, perform surgery. Isaak has died, may he rest in peace. An old man, a local Belorussian, came over to Esther and asked whether she remembered him. It turned out that since before the war he has been wearing teeth which she made for him. Three of his front teeth had been knocked out in a fight, and she made such good replacements that, although all his other teeth have since fallen out, he still has those three.

Everybody was very sad. Some had their parents and relatives killed here, all lost friends and neighbors. The inhabitants of the ghetto were shot not in the castle but in a ravine two kilometers from the town. We went there. Workers were already erecting the stone we had brought. It is not a satisfactory site, being overgrown with weeds. We did not, however, feel we could erect a memorial in Emsk Castle because, in the first place, there are none of our people buried there, and in the second place the authorities may need the castle in the future and throw our stone out. At least nobody is going to build over a ravine.

In the evening our main hero, Daniel Stein, arrived. He flew via Moscow and arrived by train. German journalists and film crews arrived, too. They swarmed around Daniel and his assistant, a German woman, and sat till late evening in the foyer of the hotel asking him questions.

The following day, 10 August, a public meeting was organized in Lenin Square at which Rymkevich, the chairman of the town council, and a partisan hero Savva Nikolaichik made speeches.

From Rymkevich's speech we derived the same pleasure as we used to from reading Soviet newspapers. It was an antidote to any possible nostalgia for socialism, although there was among our number Leib Rafalsky from Tel Aviv who no longer loves Stalin but still loves Lenin and Karl Marx. Then Savva spoke. I remember him from Czarna Puszcza. He was the head of a brigade further to the west but our people were in contact with him. He is a very good man. He later fought at the front and lost an arm, but at that time he had both arms. More to the point, he had a good head on his shoulders.

Then I spoke, Ruvim Lakhish, a citizen of Israel, and thanked the town council and local people for having preserved half the Jewish cemetery and having built a very fine sports stadium on the other half. When the speeches were over, we laid flowers at the monument to the Heroic Liberators of Belorussia and the Town of Emsk from the German Fascist Usurpers.

There was then an amateur concert in the square in which a group of schoolchildren performed Belorussian folk songs and dances, and the musicians from the Minsk Philharmonia performed arias from the operas of Verdi. Some actors read poetry by Pushkin and Lermontov, and the war poets Konstantin Simonov and Mikhail Isakovsky. A folk music troupe from the House of Culture performed folk songs, also very well.

One of our members, Noel Shatz, sang "Lomir ale ineynem" and "Tum balalaika," and everybody joined in.

In the local restaurant, which is called Waves, tables were set and everybody was very touched because there are no potatoes growing in Israel or Canada as delicious as those which grow in Belorussia.

The next day was the main event, the erecting of the memorial. There was an unveiling. The names of those who died was read out loud, more than 500 people. That was also a major task, compiling that list, making sure nobody had been forgotten

I said a few words and a local woman, Elizaveta Kutikova, spoke. Throughout the war she sheltered Raya Ravikovich and her little daughter Vera and saved both their lives. Vera is a grandmother now herself. They met like family. Raya died last year in Israel. Everybody cried of course. In the Yad Vashem Museum to the memory of the slain in Jerusalem, trees have been planted in honor of righteous people who saved Jews. Each one has a tree, but in Yad Vashem there is no tree in honor of Elizaveta. Raya, of course, is to blame for that. She did send Elizaveta money, but she was not given the honor she deserved. How that happened I do not know, but here was one more righteous person. Of course, when we get home we will put that right and invite Elizaveta over, and plant the tree, welcome her as she deserves and show her everything. Everybody who saved Jews during the war is respected as a righteous person, but she had been forgotten.

Rymkevich this time sent a deputy in his stead, a pretty woman, and she, too, spoke. At the end our Rabbi Chaim Zusmanovich came forward. He is the son of Berl Zusmanovich who also escaped from the ghetto but did not live to see this day, having died in 1985. Chaim was born in Israel in 1952. First he gave a speech and then he read the Kaddish.

There was one more event, a service at the Catholic Church, but I did not attend it. That is one place I would not go.

How can I describe the feeling of sorrow and gratitude. Six million people were killed—what a tragedy. The European Jewry who spoke Yiddish no longer exist. Our children speak Hebrew, other Jews speak English or Russian or all sorts of different languages. Of the 5,000 Jews who lived in Emsk before the war, only one Jewish woman remains. I will not speak on her behalf, she will tell her own story.

Our gratitude is to fate, or God, or I don't know how best to put it, that we 44 are still alive and have had many children and grandchildren. I calculate that the posterity of those who survived Emsk, who came out from the ghetto, is more than 400 souls. There is one other person to whom we are all grateful: Daniel Stein. Our thanks to him for leading us forth, like Moses.

August 1992

SPEECH BY RAV CHAIM ZUSMANOVICH

Do you know that today is the day of deepest mourning for Jews, the ninth of Av? Our day of grief has inexplicably fallen on the ninth of Av. This is the day we broke out of the ghetto and a day when hundreds of our relatives and friends died here. It is a day of fasting and on this day we eat and drink nothing and do not put on leather footwear. The fasting begins on the evening of the eighth of Av, a few minutes before the setting of the sun, and ends after the appearance of stars in the sky in the evening of the ninth.

Originally the fast of the ninth of Av was associated with the "sin of the scouts," when Moses had brought the Jews to the borders of the Promised Land. They were afraid to enter it immediately and asked Moses to send scouts so that they could come back and describe what kind of country lay before them. Although this request in itself revealed a doubting by the people of the Word of God, Moses nevertheless agreed to send people to reconnoiter. The scouts who returned 40 days later reported that "the cities are walled, and very great" and populated with giants against whom the Jews were "as grasshoppers." Two of the scouts said that the Promised Land was beautiful, but they were not believed. All night from the eighth to the ninth of Av the Jews wept, saying that God had brought them to this land to destroy them and that they would rather die in the wilderness. Then God was angered and said that this time the Jews' tears had been wasted, but now they would have many causes for lamentation on this night. Such would be their punishment for the sin of unbelief.

The first punishment was that the generation which came out of Egypt was not destined to enter the Holy Land. For forty years they wandered in the wilderness, one year for every day spent by the scouts, and they died in the wilderness as they had asked to in their moment of cowardice. Only their children were able to enter the Promised Land.

The second punishment, for the Jews having been frightened of the people inhabiting Canaan and refusing to go into Israel at the time ordained by God, was that now they faced years of terrible wars for that land although, if they had obeyed the Lord, they would miraculously have been granted it without effort.

Even after entering the Promised Land the Jews continued to sin. They still did not believe in the One Being. They needed images and idols, material things.

The prophet Jeremiah, a witness of the destruction of the First Temple, said that people had made even the Temple itself into an object of worship. People thought it was the Temple that protected them and not God, and that the Temple would redeem any crime they might commit. It was for this reason that the Temple was destroyed as God removed that temptation.

God expects faith from the Jews, and until the Jews repent of their sin of unbelief, this punishment will be with them, and they will have ever new cause for lamentation on this day.

Here is a list of the sorrowful events which have occurred over the centuries on the ninth of Av:

On 9 Av in 2449 from the Creation of the World (1313 BCE) the Almighty passed judgment that the generation coming out of Egypt was doomed to wander in the wilderness for 40 years and to die without seeing the land of Israel.

On 9 Av in 3338 from the Creation of the world (422 BCE) the Babylonian King Nebuchadnezzar destroyed and burned the First Temple built by Solomon in the 10th century BC.

On 9 Av in 3828 from the Creation of the World (68 BCE) the Roman warlord (subsequently Emperor) Titus Vespasian destroyed the Second Temple, built in the 4th century BC.

On 9 Av in 135 CE the last bastion of the Jewish rebels fell and the leader of the rebellion, Shimon bar Kokhba, was killed. According to the Roman historian Cassius Dionus, in the battles of that war, 580,000 Jews perished, and 50 fortified cities and 985 settlements were destroyed. Almost all of Judaea was turned into a scorched wilderness.

On 9 Av a few years after the defeat of bar Kokhba, the Roman ruler Turnus Rufus ploughed over the territory of the Temple and its surroundings. The prophecy was fulfilled that, "Therefore shall Zion for your sake be ploughed as a field, and Jerusalem shall become heaps, and the mountain of the house as the high places of the forest." The occupiers forbade Jews to live in Jerusalem. Anybody violating the ban faced the death penalty. Jerusalem became a pagan city under the name of Aelia Capitolina.

On 9 Av in 1095 Pope Urban II announced the start of the first crusade, as a result of which the warriors of Jesus killed tens of thousands of Jews and destroyed numerous Jewish communities.

On 9 Av in 1290 mass expulsion of Jews from England began, and on 9 Av 1306 the same began in France.

On 9 Av in 1348 European Jews were accused of organizing one of the most widespread epidemics of plague (the Black Death) in history. This accusation led to a brutal wave of pogroms and killings.

On 9 Av in 1492 King Ferdinand II of Aragon and Queen Isabella I of Castille published a decree expelling the Jews from Spain.

On 9 Av in 1555 areas where the Jews of Rome lived were enclosed by walls and turned into a ghetto, and two years later, also on 9 Av, Jews from the rest of Italy were moved into the ghetto.

On 9 Av in 1648 there was a massacre of tens, perhaps hundreds, of thousands of Jews in Poland, Ukraine, and Bessarabia organized by Bogdan Khmelnitsky and his accomplices.

On 9 Av in 1882 pogroms of Jewish communities began in Russia within the boundaries of the Pale of Settlement.

On 9 Av in 1914 the First World War began.

On 9 Av in 1942 deportation of the Jews from the Warsaw ghetto began, and on the same day the death camp in Treblinka began operating; and that same day 500 of our nearest and dearest were shot in Emsk; But on that day 300 people were led forth from the ghetto and saved.

9 Av is the saddest day of the Jewish calendar but, despite that, Jews believe that it will one day become our greatest festival. When all Jews repent of their sins and turn to God, on that day the Messiah will be born.

INTERVIEW WITH LEJA SZPILMAN

"Tell me, please, Leja Pejsachowna, how has it come about that you are now the only Jewish woman living in Emsk?"

"After the war several dozen Jews left. They were all penniless. They had nothing left, no houses, no property. Some of it had been burned and some confiscated. We had Jews living not only in the town, many lived on farmsteads or small farms. Almost all of those were killed. My brother and his family were shot in 1942. The town Jews were mainly in the ghetto, but I did not go into the ghetto. Before the revolution, we had a servant called Nastya, and her daughter Sima was like me. We were very friendly from when we were children. When the war began, the Germans immediately came and Nastya took me to stay with her in the countryside. I was eleven. Nastya cut my hair off and told me to wear a headscarf, to keep my head covered, because my hair was so Jewish, but if it was close cropped it wasn't obvious. At that time many children had their hair cropped because of lice. We didn't have paraffin to rub on."

"How is it that you are today the only Jewish woman?"

"I'm telling you, at first there were several dozen. Mama's cousin came back and wanted to take me away, but I did not want to leave Nastya and Sima. I was crazy, afraid of everybody. I don't think I was entirely right in the head. Perhaps I'm still not.

"That's what my daughter says, 'Mama has a screw loose.' Then Nastya's son Tolya came back from the front, an invalid, of course. I married him but he soon died. I brought my daughter up. In 1970 she emigrated to America. Everybody went off to different places, some west, some east, some north, some south. At first a lot emigrated from Belorussia to Russia. One, an engineer, went to a construction site in Norilsk. People went to Israel and America, too, of course. My daughter went to study in Minsk, met a Jewish boy, they decided to emigrate together, but Sima and I live here. My daughter keeps inviting us to come and see her but what for? We have everything here, our house, our vegetable garden. Sima never got married, she is a spinster. Nastya we buried long ago. My graves are here, all of them, Mama, Papa, my eight brothers and sisters, grandmothers, grandfathers, all murdered on the same day. That's how I come to be on my own now."

"Leja Pejsachowna, why do you not want to emigrate and stay with your daughter?"

"There's no way I will do that. How could I emigrate to that America of theirs, what use is it to me? If Lilia likes it let her live there, but I don't like anything about it. Last time she brought me a suit, but I've never once worn it. It's got such a collar and it's green! And such soft shoes that your feet slip around in them. Well, I'm just saying that, I'm joking of course. Here are all my graves, I go there every day, tidy them, keep them clean. We have our own house, and Nastya re-registered it to the two of us. Sima has attacks, how could I leave?"

"Leja Pejsachowna, have you ever been to visit your daughter in America? What town does she live in?"

"I have never been there. It's too far to travel. If it was nearer I would go but judge for yourself, I have never in my life been even to Minsk. I've never traveled further than Grodno, and to go to America you have to change so many times! It's so difficult with luggage. No, don't ask me, nothing would make me go. If she misses me she can come and visit me herself. Her town is called, like our places here, Ostin, the place of bones. It's in Texas."

"Leja Pejsachowna, you go to the graves but do you know who is buried where? After all, we've been told 500 people were shot here."

"What, do you think I go to the ravine? Not for anything! No, you don't understand. I don't go anywhere near there. I only go to the old Jewish cemetery, to the part that's still there. Of course, many of the graves have been broken, but I clean the paths, and keep clean the railings where they have them, pull out the weeds. You see, our town was not backward. We had a lot of scholars and rabbis. There was a yeshiva here. My grandfather's brother was educated, too. Those are the graves I tend. I don't remember much of the Jewish language, very little now, but I know all the letters, I can make out the names and I know who lies where. The numbers, of course, I can't translate, what year it is by our reckoning."

"Do you have any trouble with your compatriots?"

"How could I? They're all my people here, some in the ground, some walking around in the street. They treat me well, although I am Jewish. They never say anything bad, you know. Of course I'm glad our people have come but none of my friends or relatives among them. All the people I know are here. The dead and the living. Come home with me, I'll introduce you to Sima. She is more than a sister to me."

"How do you get by in material terms?"

"Very well. We have two pensions, a vegetable garden, chickens, and so much clothing that we can't wear it out fast enough. That whole part of our street wears our clothes. We had a goat before, but don't keep one now."

"We were told that here in Belorussia many of the local inhabitants collaborated with the Germans during the war, betraying Jews. What you think of that?"

"People vary. Some helped against the Jews, of course, but others didn't. They don't like them, the Jews. Us, that is. But Nastya saved me. She had a sister Nyura, and she kept coming to her all through the war and saying, 'I'll denounce you, I'll denounce your Yid.' Nastya just said to her, 'Go and do it, go on! They'll kill me and Sima, and arrest you at the same time. And I'll tell them your husband joined the Red Army.' She would give Nyura some food or some clothing and away she would go. Life was always hard for people in Belorussia, especially during the war.

"People who betrayed a Jew were given 20 German Marks and clothing taken from the person. Our neighbor Mikhei betrayed the taylor Nuchman to get a good sheepskin jacket. They looked for Poles as well, but less.

"I wish more people were good and that there were no wars, that's what I have to say to you. Good-bye."

DANIEL STEIN'S ACCOUNT OF THE CHURCH SERVICE IN EMSK

No church service was planned. All the former captives of the ghetto were Jews to whom Christianity is entirely alien. First there was a memorial service, the Kaddish was celebrated beside the stone we erected at the place where our brothers and sisters are buried. Then we went all together into the town. I wanted to show my Christian brothers from Germany the Catholic Church. A stone wall surrounded it but the gate was open. We went in. The church was a building site, covered in scaffolding, and the courtyard was strewn with building materials. Perestroika was going on here, too. Women were sitting on stone slabs and they said they were waiting for the priest because the service was to take place at 5:00 pm. I wanted to go in and perhaps assist, but the verger came out to me and said there would be no service. The priest had phoned to say he was ill and could not come.

I told him the last time I was in the church was during the war. I had survived and become a Catholic priest and would like to conduct the service. He unlocked the church and we all went in. Inside, the church was also covered in scaffolding, but it was possible to have a service in a side chapel. I put on the stole. I began the Mass with the reading for the day from the Prophet Nahum. I must quote this text, because you couldn't have found more appropriate words for that day:

"Behold upon the mountains the feet of him that bringeth good tidings, that publisheth peace! O Judah, keep thy solemn feasts, perform thy vows; for the wicked shall no more pass through thee; he is utterly cut off. For the Lord bringeth again the excellency of Jacob, as the excellency of Israel: for the emptiers have emptied them out, and marred their vine branches. Woe to the bloody city! It is all full of lies and robbery; the prey departeth not; The noise of a whip, and the noise of the rattling of the wheels, and of the prancing horses, and of the jumping chariots. The horseman lifteth up both the bright sword and the glittering spear: and there is a multitude of slain, and a great number of carcases; and there is none end of their corpses; they stumble upon their corpses."

I finished the Mass and then preached a sermon. Hilda recorded it on a tape recorder. Here it is:

"Brothers and sisters! Fifty years ago I sat for a long time here in a pew during confession and was afraid that the priest would recognize me as a non-Catholic. Circumstances developed in a way which meant that I had to flee the town, but later I returned and nuns took me in. They hid me for fifteen months. A few days after they admitted me, I was baptized.

"Today I would like to thank the Lord for three things: for the saving of those people who came at that time out of the ghetto, and for saving me also, for the fifty years of my Christian faith and the thirty years of my work in the country where Jesus was born and performed his service, in Galilee, for he was a Galilean and spoke the Hebrew language. Today we once more have a Jewish Church in Israel.

"I did not specially choose the texts for today's reading. If you were listening carefully, it was a description of what occurred here in August 1942.

"Today we have come from the land of Israel to remember the dead. Their blood, shed here, served the arising of new life, as it is said in the reading: 'For the Lord bringeth again the excellency of Jacob, as the excellency of Israel.'

"Here, between two churches, in November 1941, before I came to Emsk, fifteen hundred Jews were murdered. Their blood is here. In August 1942 not far from this place in a ravine a further five hundred Jews were shot, old men and children who had not the strength to flee the ghetto.

"Here, too, was shed the blood of our brothers, Poles and Belorussians, Russians and Germans. In my heart I always pray by name for those who were kind to me personally, the Poles Walewicz, the German Reinhold, and the Belorussians Harkevich and Lebeda.

"I would like to thank all of you, because the nuns who hid me were also members of your community. The Lord will reward you for what you did for me and my fellow citizens."

Then Hilda sang in a delicate voice the words of the Patriarch Jacob which he spoke in Beit El, "Surely the Lord is in this place and I did not know it." Then there was the concluding prayer:

"Fortified by your food, O Lord, we ask that your servants our brothers and sisters who left the world in agony in this town, freed of all guilt, should rise together with all of us to eternal life. Amen."

Then we came out of the church and an old lady who was weeping bitterly came over to me. I remember old Belorussian ladies like this very well, wearing a headscarf, felt boots even in the middle of summer, with a staff and a sack. She pressed a large green apple on me and said "Father, accept our poisoned apple . . ."

She put the apple in my hand, knelt down, and said, "Ask your God to forgive us and no longer be angry with us. For those innocent Jews who were killed he has sent his wormwood star upon us."

At first I did not understand, but a German journalist explained that among the people, the accident at the Chernobyl nuclear power station was being linked to an apocalyptic utterance about a wormwood star which would fall to earth and poison it.

"Don't cry, grandmother," I said. "God does not bear grudges against his children."

She reached for my hand holding the apple. It is the custom in Orthodoxy for the people to kiss the priest's hand. I offered her the apple to kiss and she went away as she had come, very tearful.

No, I really cannot accept the idea that God punishes peoples. Neither the Jews, the Belorussians, or any others. It is impossible.

ALL PHOTOGRAPHS TAKEN BY HILDA ENGEL

Captions

1. This is what Emsk Castle looks like 50 years after the ghetto was housed within its walls. On the right are the two buses in which we came from Minsk.

2. The memorial stone erected by those who escaped from the ghetto in memory of those who were unable to leave.

3. A group of reunion participants.

4. The meeting in Emsk town square. Speech by Mayor Rymkevich.

5. Amateur performance. Children's choir, dance company, folk music band.

6. Kaddish. In the center is Rabbi Chaim Zusmanovich.

7. Leja Szpilman, the only Jewish person in the city of Emsk, with her adopted sister Serafima Lapina.

8. The square where mass extermination of the Jews took place in November 1941 (1,500 people, and there is no list of the names). To the right, the Catholic Church behind wooden scaffolding; to the left, the Russian Orthodox Church.

9. Ruvim Lakhish, organizer of the reunion.

10. Brother Daniel and Ewa Manukyan, born in winter 1942 in Czarna Puszcza. Her mother, Rita Kowacz, escaped from the ghetto with others on 10 August, but a few months later left with her children to fight the Fascists in the Armia Ludowa.

11. Esther Gantman, widow of Isaak Gantman, the doctor who operated on all who lived in the forests and on the partisans. She, too, was a doctor and assisted her husband during operations.

12. Other young people, born after the war to those who escaped from the ghetto. Their children and grandchildren. (These photographs have been provided by reunion participants.)

30. *August 1992*

FROM A CONVERSATION ON THE FLIGHT FROM FRANKFURT TO BOSTON BETWEEN EWA MANUKYAN AND ESTHER GANTMAN

"Ewa. Isn't it extraordinary, Daniel had no knowledge of my existence. He did not know my mother or even that there was a pregnant woman among those who escaped from the ghetto. I told him everything I knew, and added what I did not know but had been told by Naphtali, a cheery old man from Israel who helped my mother and remembers my brother Witek. He was amazed I had survived, as you were when you heard the tale.

"While I was telling Daniel my story, he said nothing, but from time to time put his hand on my head, stroked my hair, and sighed, 'My dear daughter . . .' It was very important to him that I had adopted Catholicism. I told him that since I was young I have only glanced into the church and lit candles, but do not take communion. I told him I was at loggerheads with my mother throughout my life and was only fully reconciled after her death. He asked whether my father was alive and I said he was one of those who refused to leave the ghetto. He was an electrician and believed he would survive because of his profession. Daniel remembered him immediately. Bauch! I tried questioning him, but he said only that he had seen my father several times, the last time being the morning he, Daniel, was arrested. Daniel supposed Bauch had been shot along with all the others. I had a moment of meaningless grief, hearing about the death of a father who to all intents and purposes never existed for me.

"When I had seen you to the hotel, I went to the Catholic Church with him. He conducted the service very quickly and passionately, partly in Polish, partly in Hebrew and, I thought, very beautifully. Then he was surrounded and tugged at by people for a long time, but held me by the hand like a child and did not let go. Afterward we sat in the church on the very pew where he sat fifty years earlier and he asked me why my eyes were so sad. I would hardly have burdened him with such frank admissions if he hadn't asked. I told him how tormenting I found the situation with Alex. I cannot accept his sexual choice. Daniel was at a loss, then said something amazing, 'My child, I really cannot understand this! Women are so beautiful, so attractive. It is quite incomprehensible to me how anyone can turn away from this beauty and take a man instead of a woman. Poor boy!'

"That is what he said. Not one of the psychologists ever said anything like that. They tried to conduct an analysis, to deduce something and in some way link Alex's sexuality with my family life, with some kind of problems of my own. Daniel said that, like me, he was quietly horrified when faced with this vice, and he had encountered homosexuals on more than one occasion. He said it would be better if Alex lived away from home, not involving me in his mutual relations because I should protect myself. In just the same way he asked about and was upset when he heard of my difficulties with Grisha. He closed his eyes and was silent for a long time. He said we never know what further trials may be ahead of us, illness and problems, and it would be good if I could learn to rejoice in things not associated with my family and my relationships with other people. It would be better if I directed my attention elsewhere, to trees, the sea, all the beauty that surrounds us, and then all the destroyed connections would be restored and I would be able to go to church and receive help from the Source which is always waiting for us.

"I should think less about my emotions and altogether less about myself, and be prepared for serious trials. He would like me to come some time to see him in Israel. He promised to show me all the things he knows and loves. He said I should write to him, but he would either not reply at all or only very briefly. He said he would always pray for me and told me that I should also pray, imagining that I held in my hands all the people I love and was lifting them up to the Lord. That would do it.

"I told him I had lost my faith when I was a teenager and now have no idea whether I am a Catholic. He gave me such a friendly smile, passed his hand over my hair, and said, 'My child, do you really think God only loves Catholics? Do what your heart bids you, be compassionate, and the Lord will not abandon you. And pray.'

"When I got back to the hotel I immediately tried, and filled my hands with all those whom I love and those who are loved by those I love, and Rita, of course. I gathered them all up and said, 'Lord do not forget my people.' What do you think Esther?"

31. August 1992, Berkeley

LETTER FROM EWA MANUKYAN TO ESTHER GANTMAN

Esther, my dear, a week has passed. Grisha is still in intensive care in a coma. The lunatic who drove out into the oncoming lane was killed instantly, along with his wife and mother-in-law who were sitting in the backseat. It is a pure fluke that Grisha is still alive. In a headlong collision like that nobody survives, not even with airbags. I waited a whole hour at the airport, then took a taxi and went home. Alex was there. Grisha was going to come to collect him and go to the airport together, but rang to say he was short of time and would drive straight there. I thank the Lord he did not take Alex with him because the passenger seat next to the driver is the most dangerous. But that was only afterward. The first thought which came into my head was that while I was in Belorussia he had not been living at home. Now that is of no consequence.

The doctors' prognosis couldn't have been worse, but then yesterday I was told that Grisha was a little better. They had removed his spleen and operated on his lungs, because the ribs had torn the pulmonary tissue, but all the other traumas were not dangerous. The main operation was on his spine, and they could not say whether mobility would be restored. At present his legs are paralysed. I keep remembering what Daniel said about my being prepared for serious trials. I am not prepared for them.

They don't let me in to see Grisha, so I haven't seen him since I came back, or rather, since I left.

I am living like a robot. Only now do I realize how dear he is to me. I even thought I would prefer it if he left me completely and went to live with his vixen, just as long as he lived. I have not phoned you yet because I'm afraid of blubbing down the line. When I write it's quite another matter. I feel as if our trip was three years ago, but only one week has passed.

All the time I have this strange thought, not so much a thought as a feeling, that something of this kind was fated to happen, and that it was my obsession with my inner travails which did not let me avert it. Mother told me one time about her grandmother who was a complete witch and knew everything in advance. She once tore up my grandfather's train ticket and thereby saved his life, because the train crashed and a lot of people died. Another time before a scarlet fever epidemic began she took her three children and went to stay in the country with a relative. In their street in Warsaw half the children died of scarlet fever. What nonsense I am writing to you. Forgive me, please.

With love,
Ewa

32. *August 1992, Redford, England*

LETTER FROM BEATA SEMYONOVICH TO MARIA WALEWICZ

Dear Marysia,

I cannot tell you how sad I was that you refused to go to Emsk. I really do not understand. If I, the wife of a deceased Nazi collaborator, decided to undertake the journey why did you not want to? I got home two days ago and am still walking around sorting out my impressions. The town has not forgotten our family. Father's grammar school stands in the same place, our house has been remodeled and has a history museum in it now. Can you imagine, I found a portrait of father and uncle and our family photograph taken five years before the war. You are in a short dress and I am already a young woman. There is also a photograph of grandfather Adam in the museum. There are almost no Poles left in the town. First the Germans shot them, then the Russians arrived and dealt with the rest. In the whole town only Sabina Rzewska remains of the people we knew.

My most important meeting was with Dieter Stein. I got on very well with him in those years. He ate at our table and helped me a great deal with Ivan. When Ivan got drunk, he had a way of pacifying him, but when it turned out that he was a Jew and a partisan, I thought his helpfulness had not been out of kindness but only because of the need to conceal who he really was. I was the first to say, when Ivan brought him home, that he was a Jew. It was only when I saw how he sat in the saddle that I was persuaded he was a real Pole. Now everything is the other way round. Dieter is a hero and for everybody Ivan is a war criminal. They were looking for him and if they had found him, they would have put him on trial. He died at just the right moment. After his death there were several trials in England of Belorussians who worked for the Germans during the war, and one was sent to prison.

But enough of me. Who was I for him? The wife of a nightmarish boss, and the sister of the girl he couldn't keep his eyes off. He came, old, gray, dressed not like a monk but in secular clothes, in a sweater. He was always in the middle of a crowd of people. The same day I went to the church where uncle officiated. It was being repaired, there was scaffolding everywhere, everything was under dustcloths, but Mass was being celebrated in a side chapel. I couldn't believe my eyes, could it really be Dieter? I had already heard a rumor that he had become a priest, but to see it with my own eyes was something else. He is a Carmelite. Brother Daniel!

He began giving a sermon, saying that he was in this church 50 years ago and, imagine, our name is among those he prays for. People were crowding around him, women were like flies around a honeypot, but I found a moment when he was alone, went over, and asked, "Do you recognize me?" "Beata, Beata, you're alive! What a joy! " He rushed to kiss me as if I were his sister. Of course I began crying, and so did he. "All my life," he said, "I have been praying for you as souls of the departed but you are alive." I said, "And do you pray for Marysia?" "Of course." He nodded. "For Marysia, too. It was a long time ago, and I loved her very much."

"She is alive, too," I said. "She lay one night in a pit under the corpses and climbed out in the morning. I myself thought for many years that she had been killed but she's alive, alive!" "Jesus, Maria," he whispered. "How is that possible? Where is she now?" I said, "The same place as you. She is a nun." "Where?" he asked.

It was just like a film. I said again, "The same place as you, in Israel, in Jerusalem, with the White Sisters of Zion." "At Ein Karem? In the House of Pierre Ratisbonnne?" he asked. "Yes," I replied. "She is there." "Don't go away, Beata, don't go away," he said. "It is like the resurrection of the dead that you and Marysia are still alive. We shall be reunited with our parents and those we love just as we have met today." Tears flowed down his cheeks.

Can you believe it, Marysia, he hasn't changed at all. He still has that same childlike face and childlike heart. I had a wicked thought that if you had married back then, you would have been such a happy couple, but just at that moment he said, "See how it was fated for Marysia and me to be joined together in the Lord?"

My dear little sister, I felt so happy in my heart, although I felt a bit hurt on your behalf. I think he will come to see you soon. For you, though, it is less momentous. You have known for a long time that he survived and became a monk, and if you had wanted you could easily have found him. For him, though, this is nothing less than a miracle. For 50 years he has been praying for you as one of the departed, and has discovered that you are alive. Now we know everything is possible in our world, to be lost and to be found.

Then I went to see Daniel off. He left that day.

I also met Sabina. Do you remember the daughter of the agronomist who was in the same class as I was? She is one of the few Poles who have survived here. She told me how hard life was after the war. Many people who found relatives went back to Poland. Others were sent to Siberia. They always regarded Poles as nationalists. It's perfectly true, we are nationalists. Ivan always respected Poles. He considered that we, unlike the Belorussians, were a strong people. Admittedly, he respected the Germans even more, but we shouldn't talk about him, only pray. Maria, he was bad and cruel and a drunk, but he loved me. Perhaps in everybody's else's eyes he was a sinner, but I sinned against him. I married without love and never did learn to love him. I can truthfully say I was never unfaithful, but the real truth is that all through my life I loved a certain Czesław. It was fated not to be.

At first I was upset that you did not come to Emsk. I pictured us wandering through our childhood haunts, but now I think everything is for the best.

I have found the path to your door and perhaps next year I will visit you again. We will sit on your hill beside the grille where there is such a lovely view.

When all is said and done, I am glad I went to Emsk. It brought about something like a reconciliation. For many years I looked into the past and alongside me stood hapless Ivan with all his war crimes. Is that what they were? I can't say for sure, but his presence beside me was always burdensome. Now I feel free. I have been recognized, and most probably remembered, as the daughter of Walewicz rather than as the wife of Semyonovich. And of course, there is Daniel. It is he most of all who heals me and shows that out of this dreadful experience one can emerge joyful and pure.

I look forward to your letter. Think when it would be best for me to come. Perhaps in the spring after Easter? Or, indeed, for Easter.

Your sister,

Beata

33. *September 1992, Tel Aviv*
LETTER FROM NAPHTALI LEJZEROWICZ TO ESTHER GANTMAN

My dear and respected Esther,

This letter is from Naphtali, if you remember such a person. For my part I remember very well also your husband, Isaak, who lopped my leg off in the forest, and just as well he did because gangrene had already set in and he saved me from death. The only anesthetic was a tumblerful of spirits and a wooden stick I chewed to bits before I lost consciousness from the pain. And you, respected and sweet Esther, handed your husband the tools, and he cut the bone with an ordinary hacksaw but sculpted such a marvelous stump that I have worn out many artificial legs but the stump has never once given me any trouble. It is as good as new. God gave Isaak, may he rest in peace, the hands of a craftsman, and you, too! Just a little about myself. With my one leg I made it to Israel in 1951, and before that was sent all over the place, to Italy, Greece, and Cyprus to camps for prisoners of war, then camps for displaced persons, then just camps. In 1951 I got home, met our lads, and found a place in the military industry, I can tell you as a secret.

I worked in a design office. They had great respect for me there, although I had no proper education. I married a Hungarian Jewess. She was a beautiful woman but had G-d knows what kind of personality. I had three children with her, two sons and a good daughter. One son is like me, he works, I'll tell you in secret, in electronics in America. The second is in banking, but in Israel. My daughter, incidentally, is also a doctor. My wife died nine years ago, and at first I wondered whether I should get married again, then I stopped wondering and decided I was fine on my own.

I have a decent pension as a war veteran, an invalid, and so on, and a good apartment. My daughter comes once a week, and I don't need more. I will say frankly that first I had women courting me, one, two, three, but then I asked myself what I needed that for. I had a nurse from Holon and she came to me in that connection, even while Zhuzha was still alive. So I had no need of anything.

Dear and respected Esther, I like you so much that I immediately decided to get married. I will soon be 80, it is true, but as much as we have left we could live life together. Think about it carefully, but not for too long. However you look at it, we don't have much time left to think about things, although my grandfather died at the age of 103. What else can I say about my faults? I am a bit hard of hearing. That's all. You would suit me very well. I will tell you truthfully, I like you very much. We have a shared past, you were also in Puszcza at that time. If you like, you could just come to visit first. I will meet you at the airport with a taxi.

Write to me at the address on the envelope.

I await your positive reply,

Naphtali Lejzerowicz.

Oh, I forgot to say also that I have five grandchildren and a great-granddaughter.

34. 1994, Be'er Sheva

LETTER FROM TERESA TO VALENTINA FERDINANDOVNA

Dear Valentina,

This will be the last letter, I think, before you leave. Phone so that we can meet you at the airport. Our whole family is preparing for your arrival. I think Sosik is fully aware that we are looking forward to you and is excited, too. He is an exceptionally sensitive creature with unerring reactions. You only have to be able to decipher them. Both Efim and I read all his impulses like an open book. He plays marbles for hours at a time. He has favorite ones and unfavorite ones and he endows them with different qualities. When something disturbs him or he is not pleased, he brings a yellowy-pink pebble which is misshapen and puts it very delicately in your hand. A black pebble with a white belt is a stone for something which has turned out well, and it is a particularly good sign when Sosik puts it in his mouth. Altogether his behavior reveals an amazing connection between the spiritual world and the world of nature. He is an ideal mediator between different forces and can pacify all around him. Literally a few days ago a young family looked in on us, parishioners of Efim, and they were having a terrible quarrel. Efim instructed them for one and a half hours but things only got worse. Then Sosik came and immediately reconciled them. He said some word or other. I need to warn you, dear Valentina, that what you will see is unusual. Our boy speaks but people cannot understand his language. He speaks the language of the angels. He utters some words we do not know over a withered flower and a few days later the flower revives. There is an amazing aura emanating from the child but he hardly says anything in human language, although he can say "Mama," "Papa," and "me."

He can walk but his movements are not very smooth. The doctors think he should do exercises but he doesn't like that. From the day he was born we decided to raise him without compulsion and not to force him to do anything he found difficult or did not want to do. For the same reason we do not take him to a special school for children with Down's syndrome, to be taught by pedagogues and psychologists. It is difficult for us to explain to the doctors that he is a higher being, and not disabled.

I am writing in so much detail to prepare you a little for meeting him. There is so much in this child that is enigmatic, mysterious, and hidden, not yet revealed, that Efim and I keep the knowledge to ourselves and do not share it with anyone. We can see from the reaction of many people that his special chosen status is evident not only to us. The sense of reverence which our boy evokes in us, his parents, is something you will of course be able to share.

Dear Valentina, I do not want to burden you with requests but, please, the only thing I would ask for is cassettes with children's songs. In Russia there were so many wonderful cartoons which we cannot get hold of here. We don't have a video player and Efim doesn't consider it appropriate to bring a television into the house, in which I fully agree with him, but it would be good to give Sosik the opportunity of hearing children's music and songs. It seems to me that he understands Russian far better than Hebrew. I have to admit that I communicate with him on an extra-lingual level which is difficult for me to define, but you will immediately feel it as soon as you meet him.

Efim has arranged with a nun we know, who lives in the Old Town, to find you a place in her convent for a few days so that you can live in that incomparable atmosphere.

Efim and I have devised a whole program of trips. One of them, to the Dead Sea, we will take as a family, together with Sosik. He very much likes bathing in the Dead Sea and the doctors say that salt has a beneficial effect on relaxed muscles.

I'm simply burning with impatience to see you as soon as possible, dear Valentina.

With love,

Teresa

35. 1994, Moscow

LETTER FROM VALENTINA FERDINANDOVNA TO TERESA AND EFIM

Dearest Teresa, Dear Efim,

I could not write a letter to you immediately because I was so overflowing with impressions. It is impossible to convey over the telephone even the hundredth part of my gratitude to you and to fate which gave me the good fortune this late in life to visit the Holy Land. Two weeks were a single drop of time and flew past like two minutes. Now I am going through my impressions and notes and trying to articulate what exactly it was that most impressed me, apart from seeing you in your home, which I will come to.

Perhaps the most amazing discovery for me was the enormous diversity of the Christian trends in Israel. Theoretically I, who all my life have been translating Christian literature for samizdat and only in recent years have seen my translations brought out by official publishing houses, on good paper and with my name as the translator, should have been well acquainted with the diversity of opinion which exists on any theological question. But it was truly during these two weeks that I saw for myself the diversity of Christians—Greeks, Copts, Ethiopians, Italians, and Latin Americans, messianic churches, Baptists, Adventists, and Pentecostals. The history of all the splits and schisms came to life. There are neither conquerors nor conquered, the Monophysite and the Aryan, the Pharisee and the Sadducee coexist in the same time and space.

I am full of joy and perplexity. What puzzles me most of all is the fact that all this fire-breathing diversity is situated in the heart of active and self-sufficient Judaism, which appears not to notice the immense Christian world. Furthermore, all this is embedded in the domain of Islam, for which Israel is also one of the centers of life and faith. These three worlds appear to exist in the same space but almost without intersecting.

I stood through the long liturgy which Efim conducted, and then drove to Haifa to Daniel, and his Mass had nothing in common with the service conducted by Father Efim. Incidentally, in the small room on the table I forgot two sheets with the text of the liturgy which Father Daniel conducted. It was a beautiful, joyous, and very meaningful service which all fitted into half an hour, and I did not find half the prayers which are recited at Mass. Even the Creed was missing!

What a lot of food for thought! Here in Moscow I have always been considered too emancipated. Many members of the Orthodox clergy have told me that I am infected with the "Latin heresy," and I have gone to great efforts to return the cultural dimension to the stagnant medium by the only means available to me, my new translations into Russian of the texts of the New Testament. In this I saw an opportunity of serving church unity. At least, that was my intention. My situation as you know is unusual. As a child I was baptized by a Russian grandmother into the Orthodox Church, I was brought up by a Lithuanian aunt, a Catholic, and so my whole life I have stood at this crossroads and, coming closer to the Dominicans who support my translation work, I am realizing the ecumenical idea. It is not I who chose this, but destiny ordained this place for me.

It always seemed to me that a certain narrowness of mind is characteristic of many in our country precisely because of the state ban on intellectual and spiritual exchange during the last 70 years of our history. In the Western world, however, this ban did not exist, so where does the total refusal to "mix" and the nonacceptance of each other come from? I would like to know what Efim thinks on this issue.

Now, about Itzhak. Sweet Teresa, dear Efim, at the risk of wounding you and incurring your displeasure, I have to say the following: your little boy is perfectly marvelous. He is touching and infinitely sweet, but your sense of anticipation and hope that he is, I can hardly bring myself to write the words, the One Who Is Promised, let us put it that way, seems to me a delusion of profound parental love.

If I am wrong and he really does possess the "second nature," again I cannot bring myself to repeat your words, then it will manifest itself independently of your involvement. It seems to me more correct from every point of view to give him the opportunity of going to the special school which you so categorically reject. You yourselves told me that children with this syndrome cannot under any circumstances be considered intellectually backward, that it is simply a special kind of person who develops in accordance with other laws, and they should converse and read and socialize. The fact that under the guidance of special instructors they can act in plays, make music, draw, and do other things to develop them is splendid and will do Sosik no harm at all. If he really is the one for whom you take him, these skills will not detract from the mission which he is to fulfil.

My dears, your heroic and even saintly life fills me with admiration. The path you have chosen is worthy of the most profound respect. Of course I understand that the path of each person is unique and each makes his own way to the truth. But why do so many people concerned exclusively with seeking truth move in completely opposite directions?

That is a matter to ponder.

My dears, I thank you once more for this trip. Next month I shall be 73 and I do not think I shall be able ever again to come see you. The more precious therefore was this meeting for me. I will always pray for you.

I ask for your prayers,

Valentina

36. 1995, Be'er Sheva

LETTER FROM EFIM DOVITAS TO VALENTINA FERDINANDOVNA

Dear Valentina Ferdinandovna,

We have received your letter and Teresa has asked me to reply. A matter which we will not discuss is the destiny of Itzhak. That is the province of a different department. All that is required of us is attention and the ability to hear the inner voice which comes into our hearts from above. Discerning spirits is a special gift, and Teresa possesses it to a high degree, that is undoubted. I make no mention of my own modest abilities.

The part of your letter that upset me was where you wrote so frivolously about the pluralism which is increasingly taking possession of the Church. What you believe to be modern and important and what you call mutual understanding is something entirely impossible. I do not doubt that this is linked to the unnaturalness of your position: I have in mind your simultaneous dwelling in the bosom of Orthodoxy and your collaboration over many years with Catholics. It must be some kind of a misunderstanding. I find it hard to imagine any bishop who could give his blessing to the work of an Orthodox person virtually within the Dominican Order.

My personal path went by way of the East. In my younger years I was enamored of Buddhism, and the freedom of Buddhism seemed to me a supreme achievement. I practiced a great deal and advanced quite far along that path. I was halted by the void. There is no God in Buddhism, and I found that God was more important to me than freedom. I did not want to be free from God, I longed for a personal God, and he was revealed to me in Orthodoxy. The principal and most fruitful path is that of Orthodoxy. I do not want simplified Christianity. Those of whom you speak, all those hosts of reformers and popularizers, are seekers not of God but of an easy path to God. You will get nowhere along an easy path. I find attempts to create bilingual gospels laughable, in particular the attempt to translate the service from Church Slavonic into Russian. What for? In order not to make the effort and not to learn the divine, if somewhat artificial but solemn, language specially carved for this purpose? This language also provides a link with a tradition which is realized at depths and which the modern Russian language cannot plumb.

We do not know the canons well enough, but it is precisely through them that the full profundity of Orthodoxy is revealed.

You talk of a diversity which delighted you! Valentina Ferdinandovna, do you really not understand that a sumptuous, immensely rich fabric is taken, a little snippet is cut out of it, and people say, look, this is entirely sufficient! It is for this reason that I broke completely with Father Daniel Stein. His search for a narrow, minimal Christianity is a deleterious path. In that scrap which he has defined for himself as "necessary and sufficient" is contained one thousandth, one millionth part of Christianity. I did not try to restrain you when you decided to go to his Mass. I thought you would yourself see this violation, this penury! But you brought into my home a paper with a few truncated texts which he considers to be a liturgy! I had never seen this text before and would not have taken it into my hands. Our break with him occurred before he had arrived at this minimalism or populism or whatever you want to call it. Now I have investigated this text. Daniel has no right to call himself a priest. It is only through a dereliction of duty on the part of the Church authorities that such a disgusting thing can be perpetrated.

Personally I feel grateful to him. He played an important role in the life of our family and helped the marriage of Teresa and myself to occur (it was also thanks to you, and I will always intone a prayer of gratitude for you), and the miracle of the birth of our son was accomplished with his blessing. However, Daniel's views seem to me totally reprehensible.

The Son of God came to the world through the flesh. In Hebrew, good news is "besora" and meat or flesh is "basar." The words are kindred. That is the greatest news, God in our flesh. Truly it is. In the flesh of my son Itzhak. This boy has joined us to God in a special way. My flesh has taken on the divine nature through him. I had my son circumcised not so that he should be a Judaean but so that he should become the Messiah.

A battle is raging in heaven and on earth, and the battle is ever more furious, and one must stand at the place where one has been put and not seek facility and comfort. Only in this way can we return to the sources of the Church, to its martyrs, to its heartland.

Of course, it is easier to talk to the reformers. They are prepared to accept anything you like, abortions, homosexual love, even the priesthood of women, and they are prepared to throw out anything you like, even the Holy Trinity!

Dear Valentina Ferdinandovna, our disagreements are so great that further communication does not appear to me to be possible. As a husband responsible to the Lord for my wife, I have forbidden Teresa any further communication with you, and I hope no further supplementary explanation will be required of me in this respect.

Sincerely yours,
Hiereus Efim Dovitas

37. 1995, Be'er Sheva

LETTER FROM EFIM DOVITAS TO THE LATIN PATRIARCH OF JERUSALEM
(Copy to the Abbot of the Carmelite Monastery of Stella Maris)

Your Excellency,

Pressing circumstances oblige me to address to you a letter the nature of which profoundly dismays me. However, my Christian duty has prompted me to write it since, as I am profoundly persuaded, the information contained therein requires close scrutiny on the part of those in charge of the Latin Patriarchate.

Coming to Israel in 1980, since 1984 I have served in a pastoral capacity within the Orthodox Church in Be'er Sheva. In the community which I lead the service is conducted in the Church Slavonic language, which is in accordance with the spirit of the Orthodox Church. The greater part of my parishioners are Russian or Russian speakers and only at Easter do we joyfully mark the festival with proclamations in many languages of Christian Churches.

Within the tradition of the Orthodox Church since ancient times, two variations of the liturgy have been accepted, that of Vasiliy the Great and of St. John Chrysostomos, to which we adhere.

As a specialist in the sphere of the liturgy, I am also well familiar with the structure of the Latin Mass in its generally accepted version. It is well known that in local churches certain variations in the service are permitted in respect of the sequence of the reading of psalms and hymns. However, in the churches both of the Eastern and Western rites there exists an immutable liturgical canon.

Some time ago there came into my hands by chance the text of a Mass which has been adopted for service in the Church of Elijah by the Spring on Mount Carmel, entrusted to your wardship. The text, compiled by the father superior of the Church of Elijah by the Spring, aroused in me such profound consternation that I have considered it my duty to forward it to Your Excellency for your information. In the depleted text the Symbol of Faith is absent, and this circumstance alone is cause for concern.

I cannot imagine that a service of this kind has been approved by the Holy See.

Efim Dovitas, Priest of the Russian Orthodox Church

38.

TEXT OF THE "SUPPER OF REMEMBRANCE" (LITURGY) OF THE JEWISH CHRISTIAN COMMUNITY OF HAIFA, COMPILED BY BROTHER DANIEL STEIN
(After the lighting of candles and pronouncing of the blessing)

DANIEL. The grace and peace of God our Father and the Lord Jesus Christ be with you.

CONGREGATION. Amen.

(Psalms 43 and 32, or Penitential Rite)

Readings—Psalms and canticles.

Sermon.

Bracha (Blessing)

DANIEL. Blessed be Yahweh, the God of Israel, maker of heaven and earth.

CONGREGATION. Blessed be Yahweh, the God of Israel, who alone works wonders (Psalm 72:18)

DANIEL. Blessed be Yahweh, the God of Israel, who created people in the image of Himself and created the heavens and the earth. (Genesis 1:27)

CONGREGATION. Blessed be Yahweh, the God of Israel, who alone works wonders. (Psalm 72:18)

DANIEL. Blessed be Yahweh, the God of Israel, who covenanted with Abraham and his descendants.

CONGREGATION. Blessed be . . .

DANIEL. Blessed be Yahweh, the God of Israel, gracious and merciful, liberating and redeeming, who delivered us from captivity in Egypt and has now assembled the sons of Israel 2,000 years after their dispersal.

CONGREGATIONn. Blessed be . . .

DANIEL. Blessed be Yahweh, the God of Israel, for the Torah which He gave us through Moshe, His servant, and through the prophets who came after Him.

CONGREGATION. Blessed be . . .

DANIEL. Blessed be Yahweh, the God of Israel, who in the fullness of time sent His only Son, Jesus of Nazareth, to be our Savior.

CONGREGATION. Blessed be . . .

DANIEL. Blessed be Yahweh, the God of Israel, who has found it meet to renew His covenant with us through His Son and to join all the peoples of the earth in sharing the inheritance of His children.

CONGREGATION. Blessed be . . .

DANIEL. Blessed be Yahweh, the God of Israel, Father of our Lord Jesus Christ, who by His great mercy gave us new life in the resurrection of Jesus from the dead.

CONGREGATION. Blessed be . . .

DANIEL. Blessed be Yahweh, the God of Israel, pouring down upon us his spirit for the forgiveness of sins and leading us along the path to our inheritance.

CONGREGATION. Blessed be . . .

DANIEL. Blessed be Yahweh, the God of Israel, faithful in His every word.

CONGREGATION. Blessed be Yahweh, the God of Israel, who alone works wonders. Blessed forever is His glorious name. May the whole world be filled with His glory! Amen! Amen! Amen.

DANIEL. The Lord be with you.

CONGREGATION. And with you.

DANIEL. Proclaim with me the greatness of Yahweh.

CONGREGATION. Let us acclaim His name together. (Psalm 34:3)

DANIEL. Let us give thanks to the Lord our God.

Trisagion.

Holy God, Holy and Mighty, Holy and Immortal, have mercy on us.

CONGREGATION. Holy, holy, holy Lord, God of power and might, heaven and earth are full of His glory. Hosanna in the highest. Blessed is he who comes in the name of Yahweh. Hosanna in the highest.

ALL. May the Lord hear our prayers and send us His holy spirit that we may become one in Jesus Christ, His Son, in the hour when we celebrate the feast of the covenant as we were commanded.

Remembrance

DANIEL. When the time came He took his place at the table, and the apostles with Him. Then He took bread, and when He had given thanks, He broke it and gave it to them, saying, "This is my body given for you; do this in remembrance of me." (Luke 22:14–19)

Blessed be the Lord our God, ruler of the world, who causes bread to come forth from the earth.

CONGREGATION. Amen.

(They receive the bread.)

DANIEL. He did the same with the cup after supper, and said, "This cup is the new covenant in my blood poured out for you. (Luke 22:20). Do this in remembrance of me. Blessed be the Lord our God, ruler of the world, creating the fruit of the vine."

CONGREGATION. Amen.

(They receive the wine.)

DANIEL. Each time you eat this bread and drink from this cup, remember the death of our Lord until He comes.

CONGREGATION. We proclaim His death and testify to His resurrection until He comes. Maranatha!

OR

DANIEL. Each time we eat this bread and drink from this cup, the Messiah is with us and we are with Him.

Praise

Psalm 23 (or another)

DANIEL. Sing a new song to Yahweh, for He has performed wonders.

CONGREGATION. His saving power is in His right hand and His holy arm. (Psalm 98:1)

DANIEL. Great is Yahweh and worthy of all praise, His greatness beyond all reckoning.

CONGREGATION. Each age will praise Your deeds to the next, proclaiming Your mighty works. (Psalms 145:4)

DANIEL. Yahweh is generous to all, His tenderness embraces all His creatures.

CONGREGATION. All look to you in hope and you feed them with the food of the season.

DANIEL. With generous hand, you satisfy the desires of every living creature. (Psalm 145:16)

CONGREGATION. Blessed is Yahweh, the God of Israel, ruler of the world, feeding all.

Hymn of thanksgiving.

DANIEL. Give thanks to Him and bless His name, for Yahweh is good.

CONGREGATION. His faithful love is everlasting, His constancy from age to age. (Psalm 100:5)

DANIEL. He remembers His covenant forever, the promise He laid down for a thousand generations, which He concluded with Abraham, the oath He swore to Isaac. He established it as a statute for Jacob, an everlasting covenant. (Psalms 105:8–10). You freed us from slavery through your great mercy and in the desert you did not leave us and gave us, Lord our God, manna about which neither we nor our fathers knew. We praise you for the bread with which you fill us and for your word which you have put in our hearts, we praise you Lord, Father of our Master, Jesus. You have blessed us through Him, through the Messiah, with all heavenly blessings.

Blessed be the Father who has made us able to share the lot of God's holy people and with them to inherit the light. Because that is what He has done. It is He who has rescued us from the ruling force of darkness and transferred us to the kingdom of the Son that He loves, and in Him we enjoy our freedom, the forgiveness of sin. (Col. 1:12–14)

CONGREGATION. (Canticle) Who speaks of the power of the Lord let him sing his praise to Him.

DANIEL. May the Lord our God have mercy on His people and his creation. Spread over us the tabernacle of your peace and let all your children live in peace. Look down upon the Christian community and direct us by your spirit and gather us from the four corners of the earth into the kingdom which you have prepared for your children. Lord, hear this prayer, and remember . . . (here are added particular prayers and names of people).

CONGREGATION. Hear our voice and save us.

DANIEL. Through Jesus we were named God's children and we all say together: Our Father . . . (standing, as witnessed by the Didache).

DANIEL. The peace of the Lord be with you all!

(Bow, greeting)

DANIEL. May God show kindness and bless us, and make His face shine on us.

CONGREGATION. Then the earth will acknowledge your ways, and all nations your power to save. (Psalm 67:1–2)

(Bow, greeting)

Blessing of Aaron (or Thessalonians 3:16 etc.)

39. *November 1990, Freiburg*
FINAL TALK BY BROTHER DANIEL STEIN TO SCHOOLCHILDREN

Since 1959 I have been living in Israel. It is a great joy to live in that country. It is the land of our Master, who walked the length and breadth of it. I, too, have walked almost all the length and breadth of it because it is not that large, our country. Even though there are modern cities and research centers, medical clinics and atomic energy in Israel, even tanks and planes—everything a modern state is expected to have—you can still walk through the countryside. In Central Europe you can no longer just go for a walk in the forest. Everything is fenced off, every scrap of land is spoken for, but in Israel there is still a lot of dry, empty, hilly land and there are deserted places where you can walk along a path and meet nobody. The scenery has not changed since the Master walked here. Perhaps that is what is so attractive about these places, especially in Galilee. Our land evokes love and it evokes hatred but it leaves nobody indifferent, not even those who do not acknowledge the existence of God the Creator. Since childhood I have been aware of the presence of a divine power which preserves our world, and when that feeling weakened I was given proof which confirmed that man is not alone in the world. We sometimes long for proof of the existence of God and it is something that even great philosophers have investigated. Not only St. Augustine, but also Kant.

In Israel there are places which testify to this themselves, for example, the banks of Kinneret, the Sea of Galilee as it is called in the New Testament. The harbor there is in the same place and there are the same reeds by the bank, the same rocks on the shore. This is the place from where the boat with the Master set off and the place where he proclaimed the Beatitudes, where five thousand people, almost half the population of this region, spread over the mountain where the miracle of the multiplication of the loaves took place. The very land here testifies. It is amazing that little Lake Kinneret in a remote province in the outer reaches of the ecumene should become known to the whole world. It was from this place that two millennia ago the news went out to the world that all people, the bad, the irrational, the wicked, the foolish, and also those who have no belief in the Redeemer at all, are forgiven because the best of all people, the true Son of God, took their sins upon himself. He said that today people are free from sin and confirmed that the Spirit of God can exist in a person if only that person so wishes.

I know several dozen people who have come to Israel for a week and stayed for the whole of their lives. There is a Japanese man who came on a tourist trip twenty years ago and never left. Today he conducts tourist trips for his compatriots. I know a Dutchman who, from the bottom of Lake Kinneret, salvaged exactly the kind of boat the Apostle Peter had. The Dutchman spent ten years restoring it, saved it from beetles and worms which attacked it, and to this day he lives on the bank of the lake next to this boat. I know several Germans who have been unable to leave our country because they have come to love it so much.

This is a land of living history which continues to be measured on a biblical scale. What is happening in it today could perfectly well be written in the Bible. The history of humanity is concentrated in this place. It is not chance that something explosive occurred here which changed the consciousness of the world, or at least of the European and Arab worlds. From here, from within a very small people, there emerged a great teacher, Yeshua. He spoke a language that a modern Israeli could understand. He lived in this culture, wore the same clothes, ate the same food, observed all the customs of the Jewish religion, which he practiced. His first disciples were in a sense Judaean Protestants. Christianity, a word that the first disciples of Jesus, his twelve apostles, never heard, began as reformed Judaism. Only a century later did it break its umbilical cord and go out into the world of Greece, Rome, and Asia Minor. The Jerusalem community of the followers of Yeshua, headed by the Apostle James, existed for several decades. It was this community which was the mother Church of all later Christian communities, and it

364 / Ludmila Ulitskaya

was in its language—Ancient Hebrew with an admixture of Aramaic—that the paschal meeting of the Master with his disciples took place which in the Christian world is known as the Last Supper.

On the Cross of Yeshua the inscription INRI—Iesus Nazarenus Rex Iudorum—was written in three languages, Ancient Hebrew, Greek, and Latin. For the first one hundred years, Christians celebrated their liturgy in Ancient Hebrew and today, in Israel, we are again conducting services in this ancient, original Christian language, the language the Master spoke.

When I came to Israel, it was important for me to understand what our Master believed. The more I immersed myself in study of that time, the more clearly I saw that Jesus was a real Judean who called in his sermons for observance of the ten commandments, but considered that mere observance was not enough, that love is the only response man can make to God, and that the most important thing in human behavior is not to do evil to another, to show sympathy and compassion. The Master called for an expansion of love. He did not hand down any new dogmas, and the novelty of his teaching is that he placed Love above the Law. The longer I live in the world the more obvious I find that truth.

Thank you for your patience and for listening to me so attentively.

I will be happy to answer any questions you may have.

ELKE RAUSCHE. What is your most terrible memory of the war years? And what is your most joyful?

DANIEL STEIN. In the course of many long years I have been guilty of a lot of wrong and foolish actions. There is one act I have been grieving over my whole life and it is also my most terrible memory. One time there came a phone call to the police station and we were informed that partisans had attacked two German soldiers inspecting a telephone line. One was killed but the other managed to escape. As he escaped, he noticed that people working in the fields were showing someone the direction in which he had run. After he returned to his unit they phoned and informed us about the incident. We were ordered to exact retribution from the village. That meant they would shoot one in every ten inhabitants and burn the village to the ground. Large forces were assembled, subdivisions of the German army and gendarmerie, some two hundred fifty soldiers and policemen. The village was surrounded, the houses were searched, everybody was driven out into the fields. Of two hundred people twenty were to be selected to be shot.

I went to Major Reinhold and said, "Herr Major, we are not on the frontline. You are in charge of this district, responsible for the life and death of

these people. Why kill the innocent? These are peasants who provide themselves and our army with provisions." Major Reinhold and I were on good
terms, so I could allow myself this sort of liberty. He replied, "Fine, then
find those who helped the partisans in the field. That will be enough."

I was in great difficulties. I went to the village elder and explained that
somebody had to die, and that if he could find two it might save the life of
twenty others. He needed to point someone out. The elder immediately understood the situation. He summoned the local fool, a mentally backward
lad of about seventeen, and the forester. This forester, a few weeks before the
incident, had betrayed a boy who had been shooting at Germans from his
house, which was some way outside the village. The police had found the
boy, found he had a rifle, and shot him. I was present at this event and had
to translate the order to execute him:

"In the name of the Great German Reich . . ."

Now this informer had himself become the victim. I remember thinking
at the time that justice had triumphed. The forester fell to his knees and
began imploring me, "Mein Herr, tell them I am not guilty. I am prepared
to show them where the partisans are hiding." The situation was appalling
both for him and for me. For him, because the country people had heard
what he was saying and would certainly take revenge on him. For me,
because I had to translate what he had said and there might be Silesians
among the German soldiers who had understood him. I took a risk. I needed
to be sure to use the word 'partisans' in my reply, and I told the police chief,
"He says he is not guilty and did not show the partisans which way the soldier
had run."

The police chief said, "Waste him."

At this the forester began begging the chief of police, promising to take
them all right now, if they wished, to the partisans' camp. I again translated
falsely. Then they were shot, the forester and the idiot. The forester's house
was burned down, but only one house, not the whole village. I later learned
that he had eleven children; and the idiot was completely innocent. To this
day that memory is a heavy burden on my heart. It is a terrible memory.

Yes . . ., a joyful memory? Forgive me, right now I can't think of any.
Perhaps those hours I spent with Marysia Walewicz. It was the first time I
had fallen in love and there was such a powerful sense of joy at the beauty
of a woman, a woman's charm. Yes, probably that.

CHRISTOPH ECKE. Do you like our town?

DANIEL STEIN. Freiburg I find very touching. The day I arrived here I noticed a stream which winds all round the town in a stone channel. I thought how much this modest stream beautifies it. I assumed it was one of the sights of the Middle Ages which have survived to our days, but then I came to the town square and was shown the new synagogue, built in place of the one destroyed during the war. I found that the stream originates as a fountain beside the synagogue, a fountain symbolizing the tears of those who mourn the Jewish people of your town who perished. Some two thousand of them were taken to France and died in a death camp there. I think this is the most beautiful memorial to the Shoah I have seen. The stream really is a very beautiful feature of Freiburg.

ANDREAS WIEGEL. Could we come to Israel in the holidays for you to show us your favorite places?

DANIEL STEIN. Yes, of course. I conduct tours all over Israel. Being a monk is not a profession. My profession nowadays is that of a tour guide. I will leave you my address. If you write in advance we will be able to show you around, but do be sure to write in advance, because sometimes a lot of tourists arrive at the same time and I don't much enjoy showing large groups around.

ELISABETH BAUCH. How do you get on with the Jews? I mean, what is their attitude toward you?

DANIEL STEIN. The Jews are my brothers. My own brother has a family and they long ago got used to the fact that they have a weird relative who is a Catholic priest. I have very close, warm relations with my three nieces and nephew. There are scholarly Jews and even rabbis with whom I have friendly and indeed profound relations. When I came to Israel I was welcomed as someone who had fought Fascism, even as a hero. Some have accepted the fact that I am a Christian while others find it bothersome, but I have no sense of hostility toward me personally. Of course, there are pages in the history of Christianity which one would like to tear out, which, alas, is not possible. If Jews fear and mistrust Christians there is a historical basis for that. After all, the Catholic Church often organized pogroms against the Jews.

FATIMA ADASHI. What is your attitude to unbelievers?

DANIEL STEIN. Dear Fatima, I have to admit that I have never in my life come across an unbeliever. Well, almost never. The majority of people, apart from those who completely and unconditionally accept the faith they have chosen or inherited from their parents, have their own ideas about a Supreme Power, a Mover of the world which we believers call the Creator. There are also people who deify some idea of their own, proclaim it God, serve and worship it. That idea can be anything at all. This type of person includes convinced Communists and Fascists. Sometimes it is a very modest idea, for example, about extraterrestrials or vegetarianism, but human beings are capable of deifying any idea. In the case of vegetarianism there is no danger to other people, but in the case of Fascism there certainly was.

Among my friends there was a doctor who, in theory, rejected the presence of God in the world, but he lived a life of such selfless service to the sick that his verbal non-recognition of God was of no significance. I have exactly the same attitude toward believers and unbelievers. The only difference is that I am particularly ashamed of Christians when they commit crimes.

THOMAS LÜTOW. Next time you come to Germany, which town will you go to? I would like to hear you again. It seems to me I have a lot of questions, but right now I can't think of a single one. Oh, I have a question! Have you not written a book about all your adventures?

DANIEL STEIN. I do not know when I will next come to Germany. I have a lot of work at home and it is always difficult to get away. It is good when a person has a lot of questions. When a question ripens inside someone, it begins to disturb them and the answer invariably appears in one way or another. I am not writing any books, I am a very bad writer. In addition, I speak so often that I really have no time for writing. I barely manage to reply to letters.

40. 1994, Haifa
FROM HILDA'S DIARY

A few days ago I was tidying up after the children's group, scraping off plasticine, washing dishes, and was sure I was alone in the house. I went into the room which we ceremoniously call "the Office" and saw Daniel sitting in the semidarkness on a chair in the corner with his eyes closed, his lips moving, and his fingers darting to and fro. He had knitting needles in his hands. He was knitting! Or did I imagine it? He didn't even hear me come in. Actually, his hearing is going, I've been noticing that for a long time. I went out again quietly, feeling a little sad. It was a bit comical, too, as if I had caught him doing something improper.

Yesterday we celebrated my 50th birthday. We decided for old times' sake to have a picnic next to the church. It was Sunday and after the service there were lots of people, almost the entire parish. We had visitors. Several

368 / L U D M I L A   U L I T S K A Y A

people from Jerusalem, Beba from Tiberias, Father Vsevolod, Friedman, Kopeishchikov, Nina and Syoma Ziegler, and a lot of children. Our favorite "little brother," Julien Sommier from Akko, came; our crazy "little sister" Sofia, who lives on top of a cupboard because her small apartment is crammed with all the homeless people she manages to attract; an American lady professor; a Russian lady writer; and a Hungarian beggar who has settled beside our church. There must have been 50 or 60 people. We put out tables.

The children sang "Happy Birthday," Father Vsevolod sang "Long Life" in Russian with his bass voice, then they all gave me presents, lots of foolish nonsense. Heaven knows where I'll put it all. The children's drawings were the best, both pretty and not taking up any space. Doctor Friedman gave me an amazing book about the art of the Cycladic Islands with its decorative marine beauties, dolphins, and shells. This is believed to be the art of lost Atlantis. It would be great to be an artist in my next life. Then Daniel came out with a big bundle, opened it, and took out a red sweater. It was the most unexpected present. He had knitted it himself! He unfolded it, laid it on the table, and said, "I thought I had forgotten how to knit, but my hands remember. I knitted all sorts of things with the nuns, they taught me how. They sold socks and sweaters in the market, during the war of course. They spun the wool themselves, but they didn't have such good wool. Enjoy wearing it. Red suits blondes." It is a big red sweater with a golf collar.

Later, when everyone had left, I went through the presents and found one I hadn't opened. It was a round Bedouin mirror in an embroidered cloth frame, one of those things they had in their tents attached to the walls. I looked into it. A wrinkled, red, sunburnt face looked back at me, and light-colored hair, far lighter than I used to have because it was half gray, and small, pale eyes in pink eyelids. Dry dark lips. It was me. At first I didn't recognize myself.

What would today have been like if 30 years ago I had stayed in Bavaria, in an outlying suburb of Munich, on the banks of Lake Starnberg?

June 2006, Moscow
LETTER FROM LUDMILA ULITSKAYA TO ELENA KOSTIOUKOVITCH

Dear Lyalya,

As I write, tears are streaming down my cheeks. I am not a real writer. Real writers do not cry. Those live people I saw beside the live Daniel were different people, mine are invented. Even Daniel is part invention. There never was a Hilda, instead there was a hard, authoritarian woman whose life is completely closed to me. There never was a Musa, a Teresa, or a Gershon. They are all phantasms. There were other people I did meet, but I have no right to make free with their real lives.

That marvelous German woman whose angelic image I have placed beside Daniel left her home in Germany and moved to a small Orthodox community in Lithuania. The abbot there is a Georgian, phenomenally musical, and sometimes sisters from Georgia come to visit him and organize such spiritually uplifting concerts that "Hilda," with her German musical sensitivity, is reduced to tears. But what on earth am I sobbing about?

I will not give her real name, but I can't deny myself the satisfaction, dear Lyalya, of telling you that she is one of heaven's angels, not a human being. Only recently she arrived back in Lithuania from Germany on a small tractor she had urged under its own steam for 500 kilometers along village tracks at a speed of 10 kilometers an hour, a thin, graying blonde woman with a rucksack on her back, mounted up on the driver's seat. Their community is poor and desperately needed a tractor. I could never have invented anything like that.

I am not a real writer and this book is not a novel but a collage. I snip out pieces of my own life and of the lives of other people and glue together "without glue" (pause . . .) "a living tale from fragments of days."

I am terribly tired. Sometimes I go into Andrey's room. From his window you can see a maelstrom of branches, and our diseased poplars, maples, and birches look much better from the sixth floor then from down below in the children's playground. I look at the foliage—the leaves are still fresh and green—and my eyes are healed.

I am sending you a fourth part, in fact a fifth part of the whole.

My love,

L.

PART FIVE

1. 1994, Israel

FROM NEWSPAPERS

The whole of Israel was shocked by the events of 25 February 1994, on the eve of the Jewish festival of Purim. Many details remain unclear. On the eve of the festival, agreement was reached between the sheikh of the Cave of Makhpelah and Hebron City Council to allow Jews to pray in the Hall of Abraham in the cave.

During the night-time prayers of the festival, a large number of Muslims assembled in the adjoining Hall of Itzhak. The Islamic and Jewish calendars coincided on this occasion, so that the eve of the festival of Purim was simultaneous with the celebration of Ramadan. People were praying in both halls.

A Jewish settler of American origin, Dr. Baruch Goldstein, burst into the Muslim Hall of Itzhak and fired an assault rifle into the crowd of worshippers, killing 29 and injuring about 150.

Goldstein was put to death on the spot by enraged Arabs. Beneath the carpet of the prayer hall, iron bars were found with which Goldstein was killed, and also a large quantity of firearms.

A commission set up by the government to investigate the incident published a report referring to evidence from the intelligence services of preparations for a pogrom of Jews in Hebron. The commission has information that the shooting by Goldstein in the Cave of Makhpelah was a premeditated prophylactic measure. Two settlers from the nearby district, Rabbi Eliyahu Plotkin and Gershon Shimes, were detained as suspects.

Today the report runs to many volumes and the commission does not expect to publish its conclusions in anything less than three months from now. Public opinion in Israel is divided over the crime, and Goldstein himself is viewed in radically different ways by different groups. For some he is a national hero who laid down his life to save the Jewish population of Hebron from a massacre in the making. For others he is a provocateur and maniac. The interrogation of people associated with Goldstein, his friends and fellow thinkers, Rabbi Eliyahu Plotkin and Gershon Shimes, are of considerable interest. So far, however, their statements remain unpublished.

2. 25 February 1994, Hebron

FROM THE RECORD OF THE INTERROGATION OF GERSHON SHIMES

"Did you drive Baruch Goldstein to the Cave of Makhpelah?"

"Yes."

"At what time?"

"At about five in the morning."

"Can you remember more precisely?"

"I remember precisely leaving home at 4:40. I looked at my watch."

"Who was in the car apart from you?"

"My son Binyomin. Then Baruch arrived."

"It didn't surprise you that he was wearing military uniform and carrying an assault rifle?"

"Yes, but he said he was going to the Miluim."

"When did you agree to give him a lift to Makhpelah?"

"He rang the day before, at around nine in the evening, and we made the arrangement."

"Did he tell you anything about his intentions?"

"No. We didn't talk about anything like that."

"Where did you separate when you arrived at the cave?"

"We went into the Hall of Abraham together. It was the eve of Purim and there were around ten people there. I did not see him leave."

"What occurred then?"

"About ten minutes later I heard a burst of rifle fire, then another. I realized immediately that the shooting was coming from the Hall of Itzhak. I ran there but there were security people at the entrance and they were not letting anybody in."

"Did you run there together with your son?"

"Yes. They did not let us through."

"What did you do after that?"

"My son and I left the hall and went to the car park, but everything was already cordoned off. We stood at the cordon and waited for it to be removed so we could leave."

"What happened in the square? What did you see?"

"They were carrying out the dead. There were a great many. Many wounded were taken to ambulances."

"Did you see anybody you knew in the crowd?"

"What do you mean? There were only Arabs there and our soldiers. Today is Ramadan for the Arabs and a lot of people had come to the Hall of Itzhak. There was nobody there I knew."

"Fine. You are to go now with the officer for identification."

"What identification?"

"Identification of the body of Baruch Goldstein."

25 February 1994, Hebron
FROM THE RECORD OF THE INTERROGATION OF BINYOMIN SHIMES

"Did you travel to Makhpelah with Baruch Goldstein in your father's car?"

"Yes."

"Did you know him well?"

"Of course. He is a doctor and he often came to see us. Sometimes when we were ill, sometimes just to visit. My parents were friends with him."

"At what time did you leave home?"

"About five in the morning."

"Can't you remember more precisely?"

"No. I wasn't even fully awake. My father said to go and I washed quickly."

"Who, apart from you, was in the car?"

"My father and Baruch."

"It didn't surprise you that Baruch was wearing military uniform and had an assault rifle?"

"I didn't notice it."

"What were you talking about on the way there?"

"I wasn't listening to them. Like, my father would pick him up on the way back."

"You can't remember more precisely? Where exactly? When?"

"Like, Baruch was going to go off somewhere on some business and then intended to come back to the Hall of Abraham. Something like that."

"Did he say that in the car?"

"I think so."

"So, you arrived at the cave together and went inside together?"

"Yes."

"Did Baruch say anything else about his intentions?"

"No. He talked about something with my father, but I was not listening. Nothing about intentions."

"Where did you separate when you got to the cave?"

"We went into the Hall of Abraham together. I did not see him go out."

"What happened next?"

"A short time afterwards, I heard a round of rifle fire, then another. I knew immediately that it was from the Hall of Itzhak. My father and I ran there, but everything was already sealed off. Then we went outside to the car park. They wouldn't let us go anywhere. An incredible number of soldiers arrived and about a thousand Arabs came running. From where we were standing we could see the dead being brought out. A huge amount of blood, and a great many wounded people."

"Did you see anybody you knew in the crowd?"

"No."

"Do you know that Baruch Goldstein went into the Hall of Itzhak and shot a great many people there?"

"Yes."

"Do you know that he was killed on the spot, in the Hall of Itzhak?"

"Yes."

"You will now have to go and identify the body of Baruch Goldstein."

3. March 1994, Kfar Shaul

PSYCHIATRIC HOSPITAL

FROM A CONVERSATION BETWEEN DEBORAH SHIMES AND DOCTOR FREIDIN

"We have talked to him, Deborah. He is very unwilling to communicate, and without a desire to communicate on his part, it will be difficult to help him out of this condition. I would like you to tell us about his behavior after all that happened."

"I have already been questioned."

"I'm not interested in your political views or the degree to which your husband was involved in what occurred. Why are you looking at me like that? I try to cure illnesses, not political views. From what moment did Binyomin's behavior strike you as abnormal?"

"Well, I don't know what should be considered normal or abnormal. When an adolescent boy is taken to identify the mutilated corpse of someone he saw almost every day, can that be regarded as normal? What right did they have to take him there? At the time he wasn't even sixteen."

"I would have objected myself if I had been asked, but I wasn't. So now we need to get the boy back on his feet. As I understand it, he was deeply shocked by that identification?"

"Yes, he was out of his mind. He went up to his room and did not want to see anybody. Not even his younger sister."

"Did that last for long, his unwillingness to communicate with anyone at all?"

"Long? It is still continuing! He does not want to talk either to me or to his father. He did not come down to dinner, even on Saturday. I took him food and drink to his room and did not once see him eat. When he became so thin that the skin on his face was stretched, I realized he was throwing the food down the toilet."

"Did his father try to talk to him?"

"At first he did try, one time he yelled at him, but then ceased all attempts to communicate. One time he suggested going to Baruch's grave. He was buried in Kiriyat Arba, in the Kahane Memorial Park, but Binyomin flatly refused."

"How does he get on with you?"

"He wouldn't reply to me either. He turned to the wall. He lay almost all the time facing the wall."

"Why did you not call a doctor to see him?"

"We simply didn't have the time. His father considered he was too impressionable and that it was something that would pass. I have seven children and each child has its problems. At precisely this time two younger ones were ill, and then my elder daughter was found to have gastritis. I was constantly taking one or the other to hospital."

"All this time Binyomin was not going to school?"

"No. He refused, and we did not insist. We thought it was better for him to miss a year than to exercise that much force."

"Did he express any suicidal intentions?"

"What intentions? He didn't talk to us at all."

"Did he talk to anybody? His brothers or friends?"

"He did not want to come out of the room when his friends came to visit."

"What happened on the day he tried to slit his veins?"

"I left home at seven in the morning and took the youngest to the kindergarten, the others to school, and then went shopping for food. When I came back, water was pouring through the ceiling. Our shower cabin is on the first floor and he had emptied the whole boiler. I rushed upstairs, he was sitting in the shower cabin with his veins slit, but there was not much blood. He was almost unconscious. More in shock, I would say, than having fainted. I picked him up. He made no attempt to resist. I immediately called the ambulance. That is all. But now I would like to take him home if I may."

"No, in his present state he needs further treatment."

"Will it take long?"

"I think at least six weeks, possibly more. Until we are sure his life is no longer in danger, we cannot discharge him."

4. Psychiatrist's conclusion

DIAGNOSIS: Severe prolonged reactive depression, protest behavior within the context of a youthful affective crisis. Suicide attempt.

ADDITIONALLY: In connection with the extremely negative attitude to treatment prescribed after the suicide attempt, the patient gives serious cause for concern in respect of the possibility of running away and new attempts at suicide. Requires constant observation. Inform staff.

5. Psychiatrist's conclusion

Anxious attitude. Contact extremely difficult. Taciturn. Negative outlook. Prefers not to respond to questions, only sometimes replying in monosyllables and without looking at the person he is talking to. Refuses to participate in psychological tests. Clearly in need of corrective psychological treatment. In the initial phase methods of non-verbal psychotherapy appropriate.

6. 1994, Kfar Shaul
FROM AN INTERNAL MEMORANDUM OF THE PSYCHIATRIC HOSPITAL

In connection with the escape on 12 April this year of Binyomin Shimes, a patient in Section 2, Doctor Michael Epshtein and orderlies Taisir Badran and Braha Yosef are reprimanded.

Head of Security Uzi Rafaeli has been dismissed by order of the Director of the clinic.

Eliezer Hanor
Principal Consultant

7. 1994, Kfar Shaul
NOTE FROM THE KFAR SHAUL PSYCHIATRIC HOSPITAL TO THE INVESTIGATIONS DEPARTMENT, MINISTRY OF POLICE

On 12 April this year a disturbed adolescent, Binyomin Shimes, age 16 years, escaped from Section 2. General characteristics: height 179 cm, red hair, blue eyes, elongated face, irregular teeth, brace on upper jaw, small scar on left upper arm. This adolescent is not dangerous to other people but may harm himself. Please issue a search warrant. Photograph attached.

Eliezer Hanor
Principal Consultant, Kfar Shaul Hospital

8. 1995
FROM HILDA'S DIARY

An odd young man came up the mountain to us some time ago. Very thin, looked a complete ragamuffin, but very handsome. Asked in English whether he could stay with us for a few days. Daniel was away at the time conducting tour groups, and in any case I don't usually ask his permission if somebody needs accommodation. I allowed the boy to stay in the community house. He was very disappointed because he wanted to stay here on the mountain but nevertheless went down with me. I asked his name. He said he had stolen nothing but did not want to give his name. I have had a lot of experience working with children and decided he was a teenage runaway who had fallen out with his parents because they would not pay for ice cream or a Walkman. "No problem, I shall call you Mr. Hyde."

He laughed and said he'd prefer to be Doctor Jekyll, and after that we were friends.

I took him to Daniel's little room in the community house and said he could stay there till the incumbent came back. As luck would have it, the pump had broken down and we were having to carry endless quantities of water to wash our old ladies. Mr. Hyde carried water from morning till night without a murmur. He read at nights or did not put the light out in his room. When Daniel arrived three days later, he very politely thanked me, drank a cup of tea with us, and left. Daniel frowned and said I should not have let him go. It was obvious he was in a bad way. Something had happened to the boy.

I was already cursing myself. Although he was well built and very strong, there was something defenseless and distracted about him. I had him on my mind for several days and then forgot about him.

He came back two weeks later, in tattered trainers, completely in rags and very dirty. In the morning I came to the community house and he was sitting in our little garden, either asleep with his eyes open or meditating. I called to him, "Mr. Hyde!"

"Can I stay here?" he asked again.

At that I wondered whether he was a drug addict. I have marvelous people in the city who work with young addicts. I have been in touch with them on more than one occasion when we have had trouble with children in the parish. I asked and he said, "No, of course not. I have no problems with drugs. I have a great aversion to life, without needing any drugs."

I made coffee, we sat there, talking quietly. I didn't ask him anything else. He was a likeable boy. I decided he was an American because he spoke American English very fluently.

Then Daniel arrived and Mr. Hyde immediately clammed up. He is slightly crazy of course. I said something he took the wrong way, and he suddenly stopped talking to me and fell silent. But he dug up the whole garden for us, evidently knowing how to work with trees. He's a very workmanlike lad.

A few more days passed and Daniel sat him in the car and took him off somewhere. I was terribly curious of course, but did not ask, thinking that Daniel would tell me himself. But for the time being he said nothing.

9. *1994*

Letter from Binyomin Shimes to his mother, Deborah

Dear Mama,

Forgive me for running away. I had no choice. Please do not look for me. I am fine. I'm not sure I will come back home. Father told me he left home when he was 16 because he decided to build a life on his own model. I am 16, too, but so far do not know what model I want to build my life on. Certainly not yours. It seems to me that you put too much pressure on me. Please do not worry, I will let you know where I am when I have sorted myself out.

I was not going to write to you but somebody advised me to be kind so that is what I have done.

Binyomin

10. *1994, Haifa*

Talk between Daniel and Hilda

Daniel. I took him to Rafail. It is quiet there. You can think and recuperate. I feel sorry for the boy. On the other hand, his parents . . . He said he wrote them a letter telling them not to worry. I'm quite sure they're beside themselves with worry.

He said he had run away from a psychiatric clinic. He is going through a crisis. What do you think?

Hilda. As you've taken him to Rafail, he is your responsibility.

Daniel. So what do you think, should I send him away from us? Is that what you think?

Hilda. I don't know. If he's found there, it will cause a lot of fuss.

Daniel. I suppose it will.

Hilda. But we couldn't put him out on the street.

Daniel. I don't know. Hilda, did you never run away from home when you were a child?

Hilda. I did one time. They found me toward evening and my stepfather gave me a right telling off. How about you?

Daniel. When I was about the age he is, I ran away from home with my whole family. The Germans were advancing.

HILDA. Let's take him away from Rafail and move him to some good family. Either to Adam or Josef.

DANIEL. We need to talk to them.

11. 1994

FROM A TELEPHONE CONVERSATION BETWEEN THE POLICE AND DEBORAH SHIMES

Is that the Shimes' apartment? Police station here. We have detained your boy. He won't make a statement. In fact we can't get a word out of him. We have no grounds for holding him apart from your statement. It's not for us to decide whether he should be put in a psychiatric hospital. We have called a psychiatrist and an official from the Ministry of Education, and please come yourselves as soon as possible.

12. 1995

BULLETIN BOARD IN THE PARISH HOUSE.

Hurray! We're going on holiday!

Everybody who can, bring your children and friends. We are going to Kinneret for two days!

The German Mission is allowing us to put up tents on their land!

We will be going swimming, so don't forget your bathing suits!

We are collecting money for communal meals, everybody give what you can!

Hilda, Zhanna, and Anastasia Nikolayevna will do the shopping.

Great children's games and fiendish competitions.

At sundown there will be a service, and then a shared meal round the campfire!

The next morning little Simeon and his father, Nikolai, will be baptized.

We will have fun and enjoy ourselves the whole day, and before leaving we will tidy up everything down to the last speck of dust!

Two buses will be at the parish house at 8 am.

Do not be more than 10 minutes late.

Or 15 at the outside!

Hilda

13. 1996, Galilee, Nof a-Galil
FROM A CONVERSATION BETWEEN AVIGDOR STEIN AND EWA
MANUKYAN

"To tell you the truth, I had never before been on one of their holiday
outings. In the first place, Milka had gone to see Ruth in America. Noami
brought me two grandchildren for the holidays. She was finishing her doc-
torate and wanted to sit down and work for three days. Fair enough. In the
second place, it was Daniel arranging the trip, and the whole of Israel said
he was an incomparable guide. My grandchildren would hear what their
great-uncle had to say. I was confident that he would not say anything bad,
and when he started waving his Cross about, we would go off to play football
or take a boat and go sailing. In any case, he always came to us for Passover
and nothing happened. He read the Haggadah better than anybody else in
our family. And besides, he was my elder brother. You know, Ewa, I really
take no interest in all this religious stuff. Of course, when I was young I was
interested in everything, but mainly because of Daniel. When I grew up I
found tractors far more interesting. I really did have some good ideas about
tractors. If only I had had the time and opportunity I would have designed
a small-wheeled tractor which would have been sold all over the world. I will
come back to that when I have more free time.

"So anyway, we got on the bus and went to Kinneret.

"We didn't take the short route, but drove by way of the Jezreel Valley
to Afula. There we picked up a woman called Irina and her three daughters
and went past Gilboa, past Mount Tabor, and on to Tiberias. What can I say?
It was as if I was traveling through these places for the first time because of
what Daniel told us about every village, every bush, every donkey we met on
the way. What a lecture he gave us about donkeys! I'm not joking. He knows
everything about the donkeys and she-donkeys of Israel. How he praised
them, especially the one which recognized the angel when its owner, Balaam,
failed to recognize it himself. How many stories there were about donkeys
which were lost, donkeys which were carrying valuables, to say nothing of
the she-donkey which bore Yeshua into Jerusalem. Altogether, the children's
ears were flapping, both the little ones and the older ones. It was a whole
treasury of stories. Wherever you looked there was an hour-long story. He
told them something about serpents, but I fell asleep at that point and missed
the most interesting part.

"We reached Tiberias but he said straight away that we would not stay for long. I have been there a few times but he took us to parts I had never seen before, and talked so interestingly about them, too.

"I have been living here for the whole of my life and do not know this land. Incidentally, he said he had doubts about the ruins of the synagogue there. He thinks it is a Roman temple of a later period, and argued his case like an architect. How does he know these things? My grandchildren were again all ears. Then we got to Tabgha. There is a river there, a swimming pool, a beautiful garden, all on the shores of Lake Kinneret, their Sea of Galilee. A German came and showed us where to put the tents and provided a few rooms for the old women. We went to the shore. There is a jetty there and Daniel turned and said this was the very place Peter and his brother set off in their boat to catch fish. Do you know, Ewa, I believed him. It is true, the fishermen were going out from there to fish.

"He organized everything so well. We sat on the grass, had something to drink, a snack, then they went to the shore on their own business. There is a Cross and they conducted a service on a stone table. I took the grandchildren down to the jetty and made little boats for them to sail. Then the Christians said their prayers and we all sat down at a big table in the orchard with bread, wine, and roast chicken and everyone was happy. All the people were smiling, and they love each other. That is a really special talent my brother had. What a great pedagogue he could have been. He could have taught history, or botany. In fact, he could have taught the Jewish tradition, too. He knew it all inside out.

"The next day a family from Russia came to have their child baptized in the Holy Land. That struck me as a sound idea. If they were going to baptize a child, it was better to do it here than there. In the old days, you know, you would be persecuted, you could lose your job for christening a child, but now there's no problem. You know, Ewa, when my grandsons were circumcised, they cried, especially Jacob, and my heart sank. Why cut them? It could all be done symbolically.

"In that sense, christening is better, it's completely painless. The baby was very happy, and I have to say that Daniel performed it very adroitly. I would have been afraid the baby might slip out of my arms.

"Then there was a big party but there was nothing particularly Christian about it. They even had a competition to see who could hit one pebble with another, and who could skip a stone across the water. Well, actually no one can rival me at that. I won hands down.

"You know, he looked after all of them, the grown-ups and the children, like a kindly old grandad and I thought that he really was very good at his job. We Jews don't need that so much, but for other people having such a good teacher and guide and counselor is splendid. It struck me then that Daniel was a man of God. He never did evil to anyone, only good. He never said a bad word about anybody and never needed anything for himself. Anything at all. If all Christians were like him, Jews would have a very favorable view of them. Ewa, I'm so sad that I never said anything like this to him. I didn't see him alive again.

"What are you wailing about, my girl? Of course, he should have lived many, many more years."

14. 1995, Hebron

POLICE RECORD OF QUESTIONING OF DEBORAH SHIMES AFTER THE SUICIDE OF BINYOMIN

"I understand your grief, but I must ask you to stop shouting. This is a formality, but we are required to take a statement. Do you think I'm enjoying having to question you? Please, stop shouting or you will have your baby."

"That's not your problem."

"Fine, fine, you're quite right it's not my problem. Tell me, who found Binyomin in the attic?"

"Sarra, our daughter."

"When?"

"This morning."

"What time?"

"At 6:30. I had made coffee and asked Sarra to take a cup to Binyomin."

"Please stop shouting. Please. We'll be finished in a minute. It's not going to take long. Tell me in more detail."

"Sarra went into his room. Usually he locked himself in but the door was open. He wasn't there. She put the cup on the table and went to the attic because he would sometimes sit up there."

"And?"

"She came and said Binyomin's feet were cold."

"Take some water. There."

"I didn't understand. About ten minutes passed before she said we ought to take him down because he was hanging and not saying anything. At that moment Gershon came in. He had been outside in the yard and ran upstairs. Binyomin was dead. He had done it during the night. It was too late already."

"Deborah, we know the boy was ill. Tell me, had he quarrelled with you or his father?"

"Yes. He wanted to leave and his father would not let him."

"He wanted to leave your house?"

"No, he wanted to emigrate to Russia to his grandmother. We were planning to send him to America to my parents and brothers, but he wanted to go to Russia. His father wouldn't let him. That is what they quarrelled about."

"When did this occur?"

"It was in the air all the time."

"Did his father beat him?"

"Leave me alone . . ."

"Deborah! Are you unwell? Shall I call a doctor?"

"Yes, get a doctor, get a doctor! My contractions have started."

15. 1995, *Hebron*

POLICE RECORD OF QUESTIONING OF GERSHON SHIMES AFTER THE SUICIDE OF BINYOMIN

"I understand your grief but this is a requirement. We have to question you."

"Go on then."

"Who discovered Binyomin in the attic?"

"My daughter Sarra."

"And . . . "

"I was in the courtyard, came into the house, she said we had to take Binyomin down because he didn't want to himself. I ran to the attic. He had hanged himself in the only place that was possible, attaching a rope to the rafters."

"Why did you take him down? He was dead, and the rule is that you should call the police."

"At that moment I was not thinking about police rules."

"There are items lying here—shorts, a silver chain with a charm in the form of the letter 'shin', and a woollen rosary. Are these his possessions?"

"Yes."

"Why was he holding a rosary?"

"That's something I would like to know. That's what I'm most interested in. In April, after the first suicide attempt, he ran away from the hospital and disappeared for a couple of months until the police caught him. He would not say where he had been. I think it was some Christian sect, and they had held him against his will."

"What makes you think that? Do you have any information?"

"No. He didn't say anything, but now I shall find everything out. He would be alive but for their interfering."

"Are you sure of that?"

"Absolutely sure. And it is the police who should be looking into this, not me."

"Have you made a statement to the police?"

"All this time I have been held in prison without being charged with anything. What opportunity have I had to make a statement?"

"Yes, I know that. You were being investigated in connection with the Baruch Goldstein case."

"Yes. I was being held for no reason whatsoever."

"Right now we have a different problem. Did you quarrel with your son?"

"Yes. Only I do not consider he was crazy. That is, he was crazy, but not in that sense of the word."

"I am not concerned with medical problems. Did you quarrel with him shortly before his suicide?"

"Yes. We had a big argument but he got what he wanted. I gave him permission to go to Russia to stay with his grandmother. I have nothing to hide, before that I boxed his ears."

"He has a fresh scratch on his lip. Was that a consequence of having his ears boxed?"

"Yes, I suppose so. I have nothing to hide. He is my son, and these are our relations, and they are no business of anyone else."

"Were no business, Gershon. Please now sign the statement. You must understand yourself that in a case like this, the police have to exclude the possibility of murder."

"What? How dare you say that to me, his father! Do you suspect me of killing my own son? Well I'll . . ."

"Stop. Don't start coming at me with your fists. I do not consider you a murderer, and I will be writing that to the appropriate authority."

"You bloody fuzz! (The following text is unprintable.) You're all the same everywhere! (Unprintable text). You'd do better to go looking for those who imprisoned the boy, who dunned this protest against his parents into his head! Your (unprintable text) police only think about keeping the Arabs happy! You don't give a thought to your own people, you don't protect your own citizens!

"You only protect your own backsides! You'd do better to search for those monsters who filled my boy's head with nonsense! You might as well not be here! You can all just (unprintable text). I'll find them myself! I'll take my own vengeance! . . . Your government . . . your Rabin . . ."

(The last section was in Russian. Translated by V. Tsypkin.)

16. *November 1995, Haifa*

FROM A LETTER FROM HILDA TO HER MOTHER

Dear Mama,

You must already have heard that Yitzhak Rabin has been assassinated. It is the only thing people are talking about, the newspapers, television, people in shops, and even the parishioners in church. Daniel, too, is very agitated. He was always convinced that only a joint Jewish-Arab state had a realistic chance of survival, and that the creation of two independent states is impossible because the borders are not territorial but in the recesses of people's minds. If you can heal people's minds there is a chance of survival. I look on all this as an outsider or, more exactly, from my own standpoint. I am not a Jew or a Palestinian. No matter how much I love Israel, in my heart I have immense sympathy for the Arabs, ordinary civilians whose situation becomes more difficult by the year. I am only freelancing here. I can return to Germany at any time and do there exactly what I am doing here: look after sick old people, work with unfortunate children, and distribute charitable aid.

I don't remember if I told you the psychiatrists here have introduced a new term, "Jerusalem syndrome." It is insanity on a religious basis. After the Baruch Goldstein saga the whole country is suffering an acute attack of this ailment. The right-wingers and settlers have become terribly hostile toward left-wingers. Some want peace at any price, others with equal passion thirst for victory over their enemies. The situation is desperately tense and over-heated.

I'm planning to take a holiday and Daniel and I have agreed that I will return to Germany for a couple of weeks in early December, so that I can be back home here for Christmas. Well, a few days before, in order to have time to prepare for the festival. I will call you as soon as I know my departure date.

17. 1 December 1995, Jerusalem
FROM THE NEWSPAPER *HADASHOT HA'EREV*

According to newspaper reports, on 22 June 1995, four months before the assassination of Yitzhak Rabin, an ancient death curse ceremony, the "Pulsa de-Nura," was performed in the old cemetery of Rosh Pina in Galilee. Twenty extreme right-wing activists, all bearded men over 40, none of them divorced or widowed, prayed under the guidance of a rabbi that the "angels of destruction" should kill "the sinner Yitzhak Rabin."

The ritual curse was recited at the grave of Shlomo Ben-Yosef, a member of the Betar ultra-nationalist movement. Ben-Yosef was hanged in Palestine in 1938 for attempting to destroy an Arab bus. Reports of the ceremony appeared in the newspapers even before the murder, but it was only after that tragic event that the public took an interest.

Our correspondent has met a number of people better informed about this event than most. He has managed to put a number of questions to Rabbi Meir Dayan who performed the ceremony. He told us that the Pulsa de-Nura is imposed in exceptional cases on individuals who represent a threat to the integrity of the Torah and can be used only against Jews.

Accordingly, myths that Jewish sages used the curse against Hitler are entirely without foundation. As far as he is aware, in the twentieth century the Pulsa de-Nura has been used only twice, against Trotsky and against Yitzhak Rabin.

As regards Yitzhak Rabin, there is at least a certain logic there. As regards Trotsky, the explanation given by the participants in the ritual appears totally absurd: they held that Trotsky had caused great harm to the whole Jewish people by replacing veneration of the Torah with veneration of an idol, which in his case was social revolution.

A present-day Jewish authority, Rabbi Eliayahu Luriye, the descendant of a great rabbi and kabbalist, has stated categorically and succinctly that if this ritual really was performed, then it was at the hands of semiliterate activists. While the public is still heatedly discussing whether the villainous murder of the Prime Minister was linked to this ancient curse or whether the two events were unconnected, reports have come in of a further nocturnal gathering at Rosh Pina Cemetery. Once again a group of bearded Jews dressed in black, and one dressed in white who performed the ceremony, gathered at the grave of Ben-Yosef.

The cemetery watchman, an involuntary witness of the secret assembly, reported it to his superiors but asked not to be named if the information became public. Although he was in the immediate vicinity of the ceremony, he also declined to reveal the name of the person cursed. The registration number of the minibus in which the nocturnal visitors to Rosh Pina departed was noted while it was in the car park. Our correspondent, Adik Shapiro, has with great ingenuity established that the vehicle is registered in Hebron and that its owner is the notorious extremist settler, implicated in the Baruch Goldstein case, Gershon Shimes.

The Kabbalists pictured this curse as a blow with a fiery spear threaded with rings of fire.

The question now is, who is next in line to be struck this "fiery blow"?

18. 1996, Haifa

FROM A CONVERSATION BETWEEN HILDA AND EWA MANUKYAN

"On the way back we stopped at Mount Tabor and Daniel conducted prayers there. Everybody was already tired and I thought it was unnecessary. He performed a short prayer service and at the end he said, 'Look at each other! See what ordinary faces we have, not all beautiful, not all young, some even quite indifferent. Then imagine the moment which will come when we shall all have faces radiant with God's beauty, such as the Lord intended. Look at little Simeon, we shall all be as innocent and beautiful as babes, and perhaps even more so.'

"Nikolai, the father of baby Simeon, who had also been christened that day, kept pestering Daniel the whole journey with theological questions, about the Fall and Original Sin. I didn't understand all of it, because they spoke in Russian some of the time. I only saw that Daniel was constantly trying to talk to him about the Holy Theophany, the Transfiguration, and was wreathed in smiles, while the other, a dreary individual, was only interested in Original Sin and hell. I know for a fact that Daniel does not believe in hell. He shrugs and says, 'Christ is risen? What room does that leave for hell? Don't create one for yourself, and there will be no hell.'

"That night, however, a dreadful evil befell us."

June 2006
LETTER FROM LUDMILA ULITSKAYA TO ELENA KOSTIOUKOVITCH

Dear Lyalya,

With God's help I am coming to the end of this story. It began in August 1992 when Daniel Rufeisen came to my home. I don't remember whether I told you about this. He was passing through Moscow on his way to Minsk. He sat in a chair, his sandaled feet barely reaching the floor. He was very friendly and very ordinary, but at the same time I could feel something happening. Either the roof had been removed or there was a fireball under the ceiling. I realized afterward that this was a man who lived in the presence of God, and that the presence was so powerful that other people could feel it, too.

We ate, drank, and talked. People asked him questions and he replied. Happily somebody turned on a dictaphone and I was able to replay the whole conversation afterward. Parts of it have been used in this book. Altogether I have used quite a lot of information taken from books written about him: *In the Lion's Den* by the American professor Nechama Tec, *Daniel Oswald Rufeisen, der Mann aus der Löwengrube* by Dieter Corbach, and some others. Everything that has been written about him seemed to me far less than he deserved. I tried myself to write about him, went to Israel after his death, met his brother and many of the people around him. As you know, that came to nothing.

In those years I bore many grudges, not just against the Church so much as against the Lord God himself. All the revelations I had so cherished seemed suddenly dull, grimy rags. Everything about Christianity seemed airless and nauseating.

You atheists have an easier time of it. You measure everything only against your own conscience. In your Catholic Italy the Church is always victorious. In the West the Church is deeply embedded in your culture, while in Russia it is deeply embedded in our lack of culture. How bizarre that cultured Italian atheists like Umberto Eco and a dozen or two others, and you, too, the epitome of Italian womanhood, disdain contemporary Catholicism while remaining fully aware that if it were to be taken away from your amazing culture, there would be nothing left. In Russia the Church's links with culture are much weaker; its links with primitive paganism are far stronger. At this point every anthropologist in the world will turn against me for deprecating the pagan world, but it would still be interesting, using that principle of subtraction, to see what would be left of Christianity in Russia if we took the paganism away.

Poor Christianity! It can be only poor. Any victorious Church, whether of the West or the East, totally rejects Christ. That is an inescapable fact. Would the Son of Man in his worn sandals and poor raiment accept into his circle that Byzantine pack of greedy and cynical hangers-on at court who today comprise the Church establishment? After all, even an honest Pharisee he viewed with suspicion! And what need do they have of him as they anathematize and excommunicate each other, denouncing erroneous professions of faith. Throughout his life, Daniel moved toward one simple idea: believe whatever you please, that is your private affair, but observe the ten commandments and behave with dignity. Incidentally, in order to do that you don't even need to be a Christian. You can believe in nothing, you can be a hopeless agnostic or a materialistic atheist. Daniel's choice, however, was Jesus and he believed that Jesus opens hearts and that people are freed by Him from hatred and malice.

During the Soviet period, the Church in Russia got out of the habit of being victorious. It found that being persecuted and humiliated suited it better. Now see what has happened. With the change of regime our Church has rolled over and started purring to the state. "Love us and we will love you. Let's thieve together and share the spoils!" The Church community has accepted that arrangement jubilantly. It filled me with revulsion. If only you knew what amazing Christians I met when I was young, men and women of a departed generation, people who returned from emigration and had never been infected by the Soviet corruption: Father Andrey Sergiyenko, Elena Vedernikova, Maria Mikhailovna Muravyova, Nina Bruni. Of the people who stayed in Russia there were all those old ladies who remained steadfast: another Maria Mikhailovna with the unaristocratic surname of Kukushkina, who looked after Alyosha and Petya when they were little while I was celebrating my love in Andrey's studio; our lift attendant Anastasia Vasilieva, who gave us her touching pictures of cockerels and dogs. And indeed, Father Alexander Men, Father Sergiy Zheludkov, Anatoliy Emmanuilovich Krasnov-Levitin, the Vedernikovs. For me those people were the Church.

I catch myself listing admirable priests of the present time, Fathers Alexander, Vladimir, Georgiy, Viktor (Mamontov). I can think of perhaps another 10 or so. Anyway, who says there have to be a lot of righteous people? Perhaps 36 are enough to save the world.

Daniel was a righteous man. In human terms he suffered defeat. After his death his congregation dispersed and now, just as before, there is no Church of St. James. In a sense, Jesus, too, suffered defeat. First he was not understood or accepted by his own people, then he was accepted by many other peoples but still not understood. If anyone wants to argue that he was understood, where is that new human being, that new history, those new relations between people?

None of my questions have been answered. I have had finally to abandon the cozy clichés I found useful in my life. Daniel just sat in that chair, radiant, and the questions went away. In particular, the Jewish Question went away, that unbridgeable gulf between Judaism and Christianity which Daniel managed to bridge with his own personality. While he was alive, within his life, everything was one. By the effort he made in living his life, that bleeding wound was healed. Not for long, only while he lived.

All these years I have been thinking a great deal about these matters, and coming to a better understanding of things which were closed to me before. Judgment is not always required. You don't need to have an opinion on every issue. The urge to pronounce judgment is misguided. Christianity inherited from Judaism a fraught relationship between man and God, of which the most vivid image is Jacob's wrestling all night with the angel. The God inherited from Judaism challenges man to fight. God toys with man like an indulgent father obliging his young son to test his strength, training his soul and, of course, smiling into his metaphysical beard.

Only I cannot understand where those 500 people fit in, the young and old who were shot in the night in Czarna Puszcza while 18-year old Daniel was hiding in the forest. And a few million others.

Whenever I am in Israel, I look around amazed, scandalized, joyful, indignant, admiring. My nose constantly tingles at that inimitable sweet-and-sour Jewish sensitivity to life. It is difficult to live there. The stew is too thick, the air too solid, passions too heated. There is too much pathos and shouting. It is, however, also impossible to turn your back on. This small provincial state, a Jewish village, a homemade state which remains to this day a microcosm of the world.

What does the Lord want? Obedience? Cooperation? Mutual destruction of the peoples? I have completely repudiated value judgments. I'm not up to them. In my heart I feel I lived an important lesson with Daniel, but when I try to define it, I recognize that what you believe doesn't matter in the slightest. All that matters is how you personally behave.

Pretty profound, eh? But Daniel has placed that right in my heart.

Lyalya, you have been a great help to me all this time. I do not know how I would have emerged from this undertaking without you. I would probably have resurfaced somehow, but the book would have been different. It is foolish to thank you, just as it is foolish to thank someone for their love.

By the time you finish these major books, they have torn out half your soul and leave you staggering about. At the same time, amazing things happen and characters who are partly fictitious do deeds it is impossible to imagine. The community of Daniel Rufeisen has dispersed. The community of Daniel Stein, the hero of my book, half-remembered, half-imagined, has also dispersed. The Church of Elijah by the Spring is in ruins; the community house is boarded up but will soon be back in use because it is a very fine house and its garden is beautiful. The old people's home has closed its doors. The pastor is gone and the sheep have strayed. The Church of St. James, the Jerusalem community of Jewish Christians, exists no more. And yet the light shines.

Lyalya, I am sending you the last episodes. I am mortally weary of all the letters and documents, reference books, and encyclopedias. You should see the mountains of them piled high in my study. The rest is text.

L.

19. December 1995, Jerusalem-Haifa

The engine didn't start the first time he turned the ignition key, or the second. Daniel took the key out and closed his eyes. He prayed that he should get back home while also thinking that tomorrow he really must go and see Ahmed the garage mechanic in the Lower Town. Somewhere deep in his consciousness the thought stirred that the car was eighteen years old and it was time to lay it to rest. He turned the key one more time and the engine started. Most likely it would not break down on the journey now. The main thing was not to let it stall. It was after eight in the evening on the seventeenth of December.

Neuhaus was going to die in a few days' time, perhaps even tonight. How magnanimous and wonderful it was of him to take his farewell of his friends like that. Daniel, too, had been honored. This morning the professor's son had phoned to say his father was very ill and wanted to say good-bye.

Daniel had got in the car and driven to Jerusalem. The son, in a crocheted skullcap and a black jacket shiny with age, took him to his father's study. "I need to warn you that some years ago my father was fitted with a pacemaker. They hesitated for a long time because his heart was worn out and it was very risky, but Father told them to do it anyway. That was nine years ago. Now the pacemaker has failed. He has constant fibrillation. During the night we phoned for an ambulance and Father asked how much time he had left. The doctors said very little, so he refused to go to intensive care. He has heart pains now. When they lessen a little he asks for someone to go in."

Daniel waited forty minutes in the study until the professor's wife, Gerda, called him through. She was a tiny woman, a doll who had been acknowledged the prettiest girl in Vienna in the late 1920s, before people knew that a woman can be beautiful only if she is over 1 meter 80 centimeters tall.

"Five minutes," she whispered, and Daniel nodded.

The old man was sitting on a chaise longue, his back supported by large white pillows, but his hair and he himself were even whiter.

"It is good you have come," the old man said, nodding. "Gerda told me you had been on television, but she couldn't remember what the broadcast was about."

"It was about the war. They were asking me about working as an interpreter for the Germans," Daniel said.

"Ah yes, I wanted to ask you: did you not have to go with them to the bathhouse?"

"I did just once. There was a lot of steam and they noticed nothing. It contracted so much from fear, they didn't see, but I was expecting to be exposed," Daniel admitted.

"Yes. I wanted to say good-bye to you. You see, I am leaving." A smile spread over his clever face with its big nose, and he closed his eyes. "I am going to see my Teacher, your God."

The professor's son was already standing at the door. Gerda, who had turned away to the window, was intently examining a large acacia. She saw Daniel downstairs, thanked him, and shook his hand.

It was said that when Neuhaus met his wife, a golden halo gleamed above her head and he knew she was destined for him. It was said that one time their children, a son and daughter, caught meningitis and almost died. Neuhaus negotiated with God to let them live. They survived, but had no children of their own. All their lives they worked with other people's, the son as headmaster of a school for retarded children, and the daughter teaching deaf and dumb children to speak. It was said that when Neuhaus had his heart operation, one of his rich friends vowed that if the patient survived, he

396 / L U D M I L A U L I T S K A Y A

would give away all his wealth to the poor, and Neuhaus bankrupted him. It was said that during one of his lectures, Neuhaus took off his skullcap, waved it over his head, and put it down on the table. "This is cloth! You see, it is cloth. It bears no relation to the problems of faith. If you have come to my lecture to learn faith, you have come to the wrong door. I can teach you to think. Not all of you, though!"

There were as many stories and parables told about him as about Rabban Yochanan ben Zakkai. It was a pity Hilda attended his classes for only two semesters. Something had prevented her. Yes, they had organized a kindergarten in the community and she wasn't able to drive to Jerusalem so often.

The engine was running sweetly and without laboring and Daniel passed Latrun. On the other side of the valley was Emmaus. It was probably at just this time, in the short twilight after the evening meal, that two travelers had come together there with a third. They spoke to him but did not recognize him. Now there is a small monastery there, vines and olives are grown, and the produce is labeled "Emmaus."

Darkness fell. Emmaus was left behind and he drove on toward Tel Aviv. He knew the road well. He would pass through Tel Aviv and ten kilometers before Haifa would turn off to the kibbutz of Beit Oren. This was a wonderful region, with the best mountain views in Israel. Already he could see Mount Carmel. Another twenty kilometers and he would be at the monastery. Evening prayers. Four hours of sleep. Would Neuhaus be alive when he woke in the morning or would he already have departed to "my Teacher, your God," as he put it? *What a splendid way to go, surrounded by family, friends, and pupils. What a wife he had been sent. Did I see that golden halo above Marysia's head? Of course I did. Not a halo, but the radiance of my own love directed toward her.*

Hilda shone with the same light of femininity and spiritual innocence. How many marvelous women there were in the world. Were none of them for him? There had been no Marysia prepared for him, no Hilda, no Gerda. Their hair braided in a plait or gathered in a bun, or in curls down to their shoulders; their necks, shoulders, fingers, breasts, and bellies. How good it would be to live with a woman, a wife, being one flesh like Professor Neuhaus and his Gerda. Even crazy Efim and Teresa consoled themselves one in the other. *And I with You, Lord. Glory be to You . . .*

The road was almost empty. It was a weekday evening and people had already come home from work. The strands and clusters of lights had been replaced by darkness transected by the probing needles of headlamps.

What infinite experience of death! There is no counting how many people have died or been killed in front of my eyes. I have dug graves, closed eyelids, collected parts of bodies which had been blown to bits, heard confessions, given the last rites, held hands, kissed the dying, comforted relatives, and conducted funeral service after funeral service after funeral service. Thousands of dead people.

Two deaths I have never forgotten, those two standing to the right and left of me. That great lean forester and the half-witted lad I sent to their deaths by firing squad in 1942. "These," I said, bearing false witness. Twenty healthy young peasant men were saved, a traitor was shot, and along with him the guiltless village idiot. What did I do? What was it that I did then? I made one more saint for the Lord.

And in all that time I have never known an easier farewell than with Neuhaus. Natural, like friends parting for a time who know they will meet again soon. Great Neuhaus! He laughed at the idea of salvation. First you need to practice here on earth, to learn to cope with local unpleasantnesses like mosquitoes, indigestion, the wrath of superiors, a querulous wife, naughty children, loud music played by neighbors. If you can manage that in this life, there is some hope you will manage it in the next.

Who have I been fighting all my life? What for? What against? I seem to have brought a lot of passion to it, a lot that was personal to me. Perhaps I am jealous beyond all reason. Perhaps I am too much a Jew. I know better than everybody else? No, no. Honestly, no! It is just that I could see clearly where You are and where You are not. Lord, have mercy. Lord, have mercy. Lord, have mercy.

The steady hum of the engine, the familiar murmur of prayers, the flash of oncoming lights responding to his headlights, and even the alternation of light and darkness combined wonderfully together. Everything had its rhythm in harmony with all the other sounds, noises, and movements, and even the beating of his own heart seemed to have its place in the overall orchestral score. It was probably the feeling jockeys have, hunters, and pilots who become welded into a single unit with a creation of a different nature.

He thought once more of Neuhaus. The whole world so beautifully in harmony and only his heart faltering, forgetful of the sacred order of systole and diastole, the unseen driver in the sinoatrial node having lost its sense of timing and the rhythmic wave no longer driving stimulation through the atrium to the ventricles. Something ceases to occur which has taken place for many years, minute by minute, deeply hidden from the person who carries the heart in their chest and gives never a thought to this beating which never ceases throughout a lifetime.

He had long passed Tel Aviv and took the sharp turn uphill toward Beit Oren. It was a narrow, one-track road and even though there were no oncoming vehicles, he lowered his speed. This slightly disrupted the even rhythm because the engine labored with lower notes. On a steep incline it strained and sneezed and all but stalled, but it did not stall, and the vehicle crawled on. The small mountain pass was very near and now revealed itself as a dark space with distant lights and a coastal rim with a double chain of streetlights. Then the road fell away, fairly flat but with many curves. Daniel held back, braking slightly, but suddenly felt the brake was not complying. He pressed it down to the floor, but the car continued to accelerate downhill.

The road twisted, he took the bend skilfully, and engaged first gear but the car was gathering speed and he was unable to control it at the next bend. Breaking through the barrier as if it were a twig, the vehicle flew 10 meters downward and crashed into the rocky slope. Flame branched upwards in two broad tongues, the car overturned slowly, found the only opening between two rocky outcrops, and hurtled downward, trailing a red veil behind it. A fiery track ran from where it hit the ground up to the roadway. The dry grass burst into flames and in an instant the fire reached the road. It could move only sideways, the road forming a barrier beyond which was a cliff on which no grass was growing. The fire spread in both directions beneath the roadway, a beautiful and terrible sight.

Hilda woke in the middle of the night as if the alarm had told her it was time to get up. She looked at her watch. It was 1:30. She was wide awake. She went outside and sat in a chair in the orchard. She had a strange sensation, a chill sense of anticipation as if something terrible and magnificent must be about to happen. Someone had left a box of matches out on the plastic table. She struck one, watched the cone of blue flame as it took light, and suddenly regretted not being a smoker. The match went out, almost burning her fingers. Her anxiety did not lessen, but nothing happened.

She went to the wall of the tiny garden and gasped. In the distance Carmel was in flames. A wedge of fire, crimson, bright and living, was running over the mountain from the crest downward. Hilda went back inside to phone the fire service. The number was engaged. Evidently somebody was already calling them, she decided, and guessed it must have been the fire which had wakened her. She lay back down on the narrow camp bed and fell asleep immediately.

20. December 1995, Haifa
CHURCH OF ELIJAH BY THE SPRING
FROM CORRESPONDENCE ADDRESSED TO BROTHER DANIEL STEIN

5 December 1995
TO FATHER DANIEL STEIN
FROM THE GENERAL OF THE ORDER OF BAREFOOT CARMELITES

In accordance with a decision of the General of the Order of Barefoot Carmelites, Member of the Order Priest Daniel Stein is hereby banned from further service. By 31 December of this year he is required to surrender all documentation relating to the renting and exploitation of the Church of Elijah by the Spring to a commission consisting of a representative of the Order of Carmelites, a representative of the Roman Curia, and a representative of the Jerusalem Patriarchate.
GENERAL OF THE ORDER OF BAREFOOT CARMELITES

This letter was delivered after the death of the addressee in a car crash on 17 December 1995.

21. 14 December 1995
ENVIRONS OF QUMRAN. CHURCH OF ELIJAH BY THE SPRING

Above a cave entrance blocked by stones, Fyodor carved a small cross and beneath it in Hebrew letters, but from left to right, the name ABUN, and beneath it a small 'ф' in Cyrillic script. He finally felt at ease. This sense of ease and a soaring feeling told him he had done everything properly. He bade farewell to the grave and climbed down the mountain.

He walked along the road. Several times cars stopped to offer him a lift and then he turned off and walked as far as possible through the hills. When a path came to an end or led off in the wrong direction, he returned to the road, moving northwards until he reached Jericho. He walked part of his way through the Jordan valley and at Jiftlik turned west toward Samaria, which he crossed unhurriedly until he reached the sea at Netanya. He took pleasure in the walking and slept at night wherever he found a place to lie down. Sometimes this was a pile of dry twigs, sometimes a bench in the children's playground of some nameless village. One time some men who'd had a bit to drink bought him a meal in a café, another time an Arab shopkeeper gave him pita bread. In the fields he could forage for grapes.

Fyodor had long been used to eating very little and was barely sensible of hunger. His black cassock was bleached by the sun, a rucksack containing three books and a bottle of water bounced up and down on his back. It also held a censer and a small supply of incense. His dry hands clutched a long woollen rosary.

From Netanya he walked toward Haifa, in the footsteps of crusaders and pilgrims.

He knew now the full extent of the deceit. The Jews had tricked the whole world by tossing it the bauble of Christianity but keeping back for themselves the great mystery and the true faith. There is no God in the world other than the Jewish God, and they would keep Him to themselves until the secret was taken from them by force. This little Jew who pretended to be a Christian knew the secret. Abun had said they had secret knowledge. They possessed God. God listened to them. For all that, what mattered most was not the secret knowledge they had gained but their theft. They had stolen our God, and tossed the world a bauble. Abun understood it all: they had let us have colored pictures, a fairy-tale Virgin, saints' calendars, and thousands of abstruse books, but God they had kept for themselves.

Fyodor stumbled and the strap of his sandal came away from the sole. He threw it aside and went on, wearing just one. A breeze was blowing from the sea but the shore, unlike the shore at Athos, was flat and inexpressive and the sea had not the same intoxicating smell of spirits that it had in Greece. He spent a night and half a day at the archeological remains at Caesarea, feeling suddenly lethargic in the morning. He lay in the shade of an ancient wall and dozed until noon. Then he walked on. On the third day he approached Haifa. Now it was no distance at all.

He climbed up to the Church of Elijah by the Spring in the evening. There was nobody there but the watchman, an Arab called Yusuf, a distant relative of Musa and like him also a gardener. Hilda had employed him eight years earlier. Yusuf was deaf and Daniel joked that Hilda had a special talent for finding help. She had a deaf watchman, a lame courier, and it would be best if Daniel washed the dishes himself because she would be sure to hire a dishwasher with one arm.

Fyodor lay down behind the arbor and fell asleep. When he woke it was already dark. He went to the church. He needed to examine the books in there to see if he could find the ones he needed, the ones with the secret. The church was locked so Fyodor went to a window, took off his cassock, folded it in quarters, and deftly pushed the glass out. In no hurry, he put the cassock back on, looked around, found a candle, and lit it. He immediately intuited the internal layout of the building and moved through to the extension, pushing the door. It opened. The desk and cupboard were locked.

He had a knife in his belt and the rigid sheath had been digging into his stomach all the way there. He grasped the sheath and pulled the knife out. It was an Arab knife with a black horn handle and a bronze insert between the horn and the blade. It was not a knife for slaughtering livestock. The book cupboard opened as soon as he touched it. Fyodor laid the books in neat piles and began leafing through them.

What an idiot I am, he chided himself as he read the spines. He recognized the Greek Typikon, the Slavonic Psalter, and several books in Polish, but everything else was in languages of which Fyodor had no knowledge: Hebrew, Latin, Italian. Even if the secret was writ large in them, there was no way he would be able to read it.

He set the books to one side and started on the desk. The middle drawer was double locked and the bolt did not yield. Fyodor picked at the faceplate with his knife, trying to remove it and with it the lock. He did not hear Yusuf come into the room. Yusuf had seen light in the window and decided that Hilda or Daniel must have come back unnoticed. Seeing the burglar, Yusuf cried out and seized him from behind. Fyodor twisted round. The knife was in his hand and before he could think, he had slashed the watchman's neck. Blood spurted everywhere. There was a strange gurgling.

Fyodor immediately saw that all was lost. Now he would be unable to coerce the Jews' secret out of Daniel. He had needed the knife not for murder but only for extracting the great secret. The lifeless watchman lying in an excessively large pool of blood had spoiled everything. Fyodor would now never learn that thrice accursed secret of the Jews. Ever. A great rage seized him. He threw the books aside and went out into the church itself and smashed everything that could be broken. The force of his madness was so great that he demolished the altar which had been put together from heavy stones by four strong lads. He trashed the benches and lecterns, wrecked the collection box at the entrance, and smashed his fist into Mother Ioanna's last icon which, in anticipation of the move to its ultimate home in Moscow, was hanging in accordance with her wishes in the Church of Elijah by the Spring.

Fyodor suddenly became placid and squatted down by the outer wall of the church. Nobody came that day because they were at Daniel's funeral service in the Arab church where he had once officiated. The service was conducted by Roman, with whom Daniel had once fallen out over plots in the cemetery.

The dreadful occurrence became known only the day after the funeral, early in the morning when Hilda came to the church. Fyodor was still sitting on his heels by the wall. Hilda called the police and the men in white coats. As a disciplined Westerner, she did not touch anything until the police arrived. "The Jerusalem syndrome," she thought. Yusuf was buried next to Daniel.

The only thing she did move was the icon, which she took to her car. It was a marvelous depiction of "Praise the Lord the Highest Heavens." On the icon the sprightly hand of Mother Ioanna had represented Adam with a beard and moustache and Eve with a long pigtail, hares, squirrels, birds, and serpents, and all of creation which had formed a long queue to embark on Noah's Ark and was now leaping and rejoicing and praising the Lord. The flowers and the leaves gleamed, palms and willows waved their branches. A child's train crawled along the earth and childish smoke spiraled joyfully from the funnel. A plane flew in the sky, leaving a slender white vapor trail behind it. The old lady had been a genius. She had envisaged all creation praising the Lord: rocks, plants, animals, and even the iron creations of man.

July 2006, Moscow

LETTER FROM LUDMILA ULITSKAYA TO ELENA KOSTIOUKOVITCH

Dear Lyalya,

I had a strange, wide-ranging, and protracted dream last night. It lasted for an immense time, longer than a night and, as often happens, I didn't manage to retain everything and bring it back to the light of day. A lot was left unrehearsed and unarticulated.

There was a system of rooms, not an enfilade but a far more complex pattern, with an internal logic which I simply could not crack. There were no people there, but many nonhuman beings, small, attractive, their nature indescribable, like hybrids of angels and animals. Each was the bearer of a word or idea or principle (I am already struggling for words). Among this host of beings and rooms I was looking for one in particular, the only one which could give the answer to my question. Alas, I could not formulate what my question was. I was afraid of missing the one being I so needed in the throng of all the other, similar beings. Two unfamiliar ones compelled me to wander from room to room in a fruitless search.

The rooms were sketchy but their purpose was clear. I gradually realized as I wondered about that they were not for eating, or meeting, or religious purposes. They were for study. Study of what? Study of everything. The world of knowledge. That sounds funny, like the name of a bookshop. In Russia we have shops called World of Footwear, World of Leather, even World of Doors.

We have become used to treating knowledge and the process of acquiring it as something not subject to moral law. Knowledge and morality are seen as coordinates of separate systems, but here this was not the case. These little bearers of knowledge of objects, ideas, and phenomena bore a moral charge. That's not quite right. Again I can't convey the thought perfectly. Not moral so much as creative. Creativity, though, correlates with positive morality.

Forgive me, my dear, for writing so opaquely. I cannot put it more clearly because I am myself groping here, falling back on intuition and a kind of internal navigator. To oversimplify disgracefully, the old-fashioned antithesis of science and religion is balderdash. In this place, in my dream, there is no doubt that science and religion grow from the same root.

Anyway, I was wandering through these halls looking for I don't know whom, but looking very conscientiously. I needed him at all costs. And he came, nuzzled me like a dog, and I immediately knew it was he! A small, compact, soft being suddenly expanded, unfolded, and turned into something vast so that that room and all the others vanished and he himself was larger than any of them. He held a whole world within himself, and I myself was within it. The essence of the world was victory, but in the present continuous tense. It would be better to say, "being victorious."

At this point I guessed what the question was which had been tormenting me so and why I was looking for this conquering angel. My dear Daniel seemed to have been vanquished, to the extent that in his specific mission ("reestablishment of the Church of St. James in the Holy Land") he had failed. There had been no such church when he arrived and now again there was no such church. It had lasted the few years he lived there, working as a priest, praising Yeshua in his own language, preaching christianity with a small *c*, a personal religion of the mercy and love of God and of one's neighbor, and not the religion of dogmas and authority, power and totalitarianism.

When he died it became evident that his living body had been the sole bridge between Judaism and Christianity. When he died the bridge was gone, something I experienced as a sad defeat.

In my dream, the creature which expanded into a whole world had a sword, and eyes, and a flame, but it also incorporated all of Daniel, not swallowed like Jonah in the whale, but embodied within the substance of that world. I very clearly detected Daniel's smile, even some semblance of his outward appearance, his little chin, the childlike upward glance, surprised and asking simple questions like, "How is it going, Lyusya?"

As soon as I understood that he had departed unvanquished, I woke up. It was already fairly late in the morning and I was separated from the previous evening not by eight hours of sleep but by the vast temporal expanse of this knowledge which had so undeservedly come to me and which I cannot precisely formulate. I now know something about the nature of victory and defeat which I didn't know before, about their relativeness, their temporary nature, their mutability, about our complete incompetence to decide such an elementary question as, "Who won?"

Then I dug through the notes from my last trip to Israel. I was taken around by my friends Lika Nutkevich and Seryozha Ruzer. We drove around the Sea of Galilee, through the kibbutz at HaOn where they breed ostriches. On both sides of the road, the poppies and bittercress, which Lika calls wild mustard, were in flower. We passed through Gergesa, the Arab Kursi. In Capernaum we found a monastery with a single monk. The priest comes to officiate every second Saturday. This is the place of the miraculous healing of the man with the palsy. Here, too, Jesus came after the feeding of the 5,000.

We stumbled on the Church of the Apostles. Something is being rebuilt and the jetty is being repaired. The workers were a Greek and a Yugoslav. That church was locked but a Greek monk came, opened it, and talked to us about life. He spoke Russian fairly fluently. They conduct the liturgy in Russian because many Russians come from Tiberias. He does not like Hebrew and other languages being used together in a single service, as is generally accepted now. He is sure the next generation will conduct services entirely in Hebrew because the children will grow up and forget Russian.

Lika and Seryozha and I exchanged glances. Here it was, the Church of St. James. Here, in Israel, Orthodox and Catholic Christians will talk to God in Hebrew. But will there be Jews among them? Is it really what Daniel envisaged? Perhaps it doesn't matter.

Then the monk said that Israel would do better to christianize the Arabs, because Christian Arabs are easier to deal with than Muslim Arabs. "They don't understand that," the monk said ruefully. Altogether the state gives Christians a hard time with visas, duration of stay, naturalization, and insurance. He said the Jews do not want peace, but admittedly the Arabs want it even less.

Then the conversation moved on to the selling of church lands, a complicated matter. I stopped listening because one person's head cannot take in as much as I have learned recently.

That's it.

Love from

Lyusya

ACKNOWLEDGMENTS

A part from characters that I invented, real participants, real eyewitnesses, the spiritual children and friends of the real Daniel, are alive to this day. Father Michael Aksenov-Meerson is a priest in New York; his wife, Olya Schnittke, teaches Russian literature at Georgetown University; the brilliant Henri Volokhonsky, who formerly worked in the limnological station at Kinneret, now lives in Tübingen and is said to be studying Jewish texts. There are others I cannot mention in order not to cause trouble. Some have become rabbis, some engineers, some have entered a monastery. My good wishes and love to all that remarkable circle of people.

I thank all my friends, near and far, who were present, supported and helped me from the very beginning of this work till the last day: my dear and much loved Elena Kostioukovitch, Alexander Borisov, Pavel Men, Sasha Hawiger, Sasha Bondaryov, Pawel Kozhets, Michael and Olga Aksenov-Meerson, Mikhail Gorelik, Hugh Baran, Alexey Yudin, Yura Freidin and Elena Smorgunova, Tanya Safarova, Judith Kornblatt, Natalia Trauberg, Mark Smirnov, Mikhail Alshybaya, Ilya Rybakov, and Daniela Shultz.

I am especially grateful to my Israeli friends Sergey Ruzer and Lika Nutkevich, Moshe Navon, Alik Chachko, Sandrik and Lyuba Kaminsky, Sasha Okun, Igor Kogan, and Marina Genkina who with great generosity shared with me everything I needed, accompanied and guided my wanderings throughout Israel.

I am grateful for extensive and extremely detailed interviews to Arieh Rufeisen, Elisheva Hemker, and other unnamed heroes of this story.

I am greatly indebted to Professor Nechama Tec of the University of Connecticut and Professor Dieter Corbach, whose materials were extremely important in the preparation and work on this book.

I thank Natalia Gorbanevskaya for her heroic emergency aid in preparing the text for the press.

I beg forgiveness of all those I will disappoint, those who will be irritated by my outspokenness, or who will totally reject me. I hope my work will lead nobody astray but serve only to encourage personal responsibility in matters of life and faith.

My excuse is my sincere wish to tell the truth as I understand it, and the craziness of that ambition.

—LUDMILA ULITSKAYA

ABOUT THE AUTHOR

LUDMILA ULITSKAYA was born in western Russia and worked as a scientist before becoming Repertory Director of the Hebrew Theater of Moscow. She is hailed as Russia's bestselling literary novelist and has written fourteen novels, three tales for children, and six plays. *Daniel Stein, Interpreter* won the Russian National Literary Prize and previous novels have received the Russian Booker Prize, the Penne Literary Prize, and the Medici Award. Ludmila Ulitskaya has just been awarded the 2011 Simone de Beauvoir Prize, an international human rights prize for women's freedom.

ABOUT THE TRANSLATOR

ARCH TAIT learned Russian at Trinity Hall, Cambridge and Moscow State University. From 1993 he was the UK editor of the Glas New Russian Writing translation series. His numerous other translations include Anna Politkovskaya's *Nothing But the Truth*, which was awarded the 2010 PEN Literature in Translation Award.